THE JOURNEY'S END

BOOK 3 IN THE FORGOTTEN FLOWERS TRILOGY

MICHAEL J. SULLIVAN

Publish Authority

Publish Authority
Newport Beach, CA and Roswell, GA USA

Copyright © 2021 by Michael J. Sullivan
ISBN: 978-1-954000-16-2 (paperback)
ISBN: 978-1-954000-17-9 (eBook)

The Library of Congress Cataloging-in-Publication Data is available.

Cover design lead: Raeghan Rebstock
Editor: Nancy Laning

www.PublishAuthority.com
Printed in the United States of America

DEDICATION

As our time on earth draws to an end, we will be fortunate to have our memories though they too have an expiration date. We will become less important to loved ones who will be consumed with the complexities of guiding lives yet to be lived, of dreams yet to be achieved. We will also be fortunate to have those willing to be both friends and companions and individuals who will see that our lives retain some semblance of dignity and respect. To those caregivers of the elderly who are victims of longevity and seemingly unimportant to all, I thank you from the bottom of my heart.

Oscar Wilde is credited with the following quote: "Life imitates Art far more than Art imitates Life." How appropriate for my current situation. As I was completing this third and final book of the "Forgotten Flowers" trilogy, my wife, Ginny, suffered a debilitating stroke. She is paralyzed on her right side and has great difficulty speaking. She is in a rehabilitation center receiving three hours of intensive physical, occupational, and speech therapy each day. I am living the life of Eddy Pinafore.

INTRODUCTION

It stole the past. It was stealing the present, and ultimately, it would steal the future. He hated it. He despised it. It was unlike any foe Eddy Pinafore had ever faced. Pinafore had fought determined enemies before. As a Navy Seal, he had seen the enemy. He had fought them and had spilled their blood before they could spill his. But this enemy was different. He couldn't see it. He couldn't hear. All he could do was deal with the tragic aftermath it spread. Never in his life had Eddy Pinafore felt so helpless, so utterly incapable of protecting his wife, Maddy, from this satanic enemy. The doctors had a name for it; dementia. It would take Eddy and Maddy on a painful journey that would end at Magnolia Gardens.

Theirs was not the only journey in this final part of the *Forgotten Flowers* trilogy. Tina Pinafore, Eddy and Maddy's daughter, had struggled for years as a single mother with a special needs child. Abandoned by the child's father and facing mounting medical expenses, Tina felt even God had forgotten her, that is, until a minor fender-bender brought a savior into her life.

1

THE ENEMY

E ddy stood silently before the antique maple door that led to the bedroom he had shared with his wife of many years. It was a simple process; he reasoned, opening a door and walking through like he had done countless times before. Just walk in and approach the prone figure lying peacefully asleep on the old-fashioned king-sized poster bed. Simple? Easy? Hardly! What had always been a pleasant moment in the afternoon had grown into an experience of anxiety that he could not mask or shield despite years of discipline and training. For as time had moved inexorably on, there was a change in the woman he had at first coveted and then deeply loved in their years as a couple united in matrimony. Yet, enter, he must!

Placing his one good hand on the old-fashioned glass doorknob, he turned it as stealthily and quickly as he could manage. With his physical limitations, he was not going to move to any location particularly quietly or speedily. Once inside the room, his eyes had to adjust after transitioning from the glare of the brightly lit hallway to the dimly lit bedroom. Squinting a bit, he was just able to make out the peacefully sleeping form of his beloved spouse. She could not have been more serene, lying on her side with a favorite multicolored comforter pulled past her neck. Growing ever so sensitive to declining temperatures, she wore a hand-knitted beanie on her head. Large as this accessory was, it failed to cover all of Maddy's now very gray locks completely.

Still not seeing clearly, Eddy awkwardly moved toward the bed and collided with the heavily formed metal nightstand immediately next to the bed. The resulting noise slightly disrupted Maddy, and she turned toward her anxious husband, though still in a state of slumber. Now seeing more clearly, Eddy gazed upon his wife. Her gaunt face seemed more wrinkled and aged as if to stand witness for every day of her seventy-five years on the planet. One protruding arm revealed long, slender fingers with knuckles demonstrating the telltale signs of advanced arthritis.

None of this was a deterrent to Eddy's affection for his wife. In his mind, she continued to be the beautiful and vivacious young woman that had captivated him decades prior. During that time, her auburn hair was bright and lavish to behold. Her large and lively hazel eyes revealed a soul filled with compassion and tenderness for those around her. Topping all these physical qualities, Maddy was an absolute wit. This was the characteristic that most endeared Maddy to Eddy, even if that wit was sometimes used at his expense.

Further, Maddy was an avid reader, devouring books and newspapers with a relish seldom seen in people. Obviously gifted with a superior intellect, a quality that served her well during her time as director of Magnolia Gardens, it was not what struck most people that came to know Maddy. What stood out in Maddy was her unending compassion for the plight of her fellow man. This characteristic made her so successful in her chosen field of endeavor and rewarded her with a long list of friends and admirers.

Gazing upon his wife, the flood of such memories was nothing if not bittersweet; those attributes that made Maddy the woman she was were slowly and permanently ebbing away. Evidence of the paradigm shift was everywhere. Once so very organized (another characteristic of her success), she seemed incapable of managing her life schedule, often missing appointments no matter how many prompts she created to assist her memory. Telephone conversations, her lifeline to her expansive list of friends and associates, became fewer in number and shorter in duration. Often, and regardless of the importance of the call, she was unable to recall even the most elemental aspects of the conversations. Even worse, Maddy's lifelong compassion for the suffering of others appeared to be vaporizing.

Eddy's attempts to point out these mental lapses were met with a variety of responses, ranging from a rather uncomfortable silence to outright hostility and anger. Unaccustomed to arguing with his spouse and sensitive to the source of the conflict, Eddy chose to avoid these confrontations as much as possible. He could see that any attempts he made to reach Maddy on this subject would be fruitless.

Moving directly next to the bed and careful to maintain his footing on the dainty and flowered throw rug beneath his feet, Eddy placed a loving hand on his sleeping wife. As he did so, she slowly escaped from her state of sleep. This gave him the opportunity for further thought, and he quickly concluded that this matter must be brought to the attention of their daughter— the sooner, the better for Maddy!

∼

AFTER LEAVING her attorney's office, Tina Pinafore had doubts about telling her father and mother about the meeting. After all, Matthew Adams had not exactly laid out a compelling strategy to force Trevor Barrington to support their daughter. In fact, his only strategy, if you could call it that, was a biblical reference to David and Goliath. Eddy and Maddy Pinafore had raised their daughter to believe in God. They provided her with a minimum of religious training by sending her to Catechism class at Saint Michael's, a local Catholic grammar school. Once a week classes over a few years was hardly fertile grounds to make a firm believer in the Word of God. Tina had never developed that ardent, deeply felt faith in the Scriptures commonly found in those steeped in their Christian faith. Regardless, Adams' biblical reference was all she had to tell them. Upon leaving her attorney's office, Tina was perplexed by the course of events, so much so that she was disinclined to inform her parents of the outcome. Also brooding beneath the surface was her frustration when the school bus dropped Missy off at the Recreation Center for the Handicapped, where Tina worked for the Executive Director, Edith Monroe. Little Missy's blue flowered dress had several grass stains on it, and the child's white and yellow tennis shoes were smeared with grassy dirt. She dared not think about Missy's answer when Tina asked her about her dress and shoes. *Didn't anyone at that school have a lick of sense about letting a small child wearing a leg brace run?* Tina thought to herself. With a sleeping child in the back seat, Tina would save her rant for her father.

~

EDDY HAD TAKEN advantage of his wife's afternoon nap to prepare dinner. It had been a Friday family tradition that he would make spaghetti with his family's deeply guarded secret sauce. Growing up, it had been Tina's favorite meal. It delighted Eddy and Maddy whenever Tina would bring her friends home from college for the weekend after bragging about her father's famous spaghetti. There they would discuss the burning political issues of the day over a large pot of home-made spaghetti, loaded with chunks of Italian sausage, a green salad, and loaves of garlic bread. Eddy and Maddy would joyfully watch as their passionate debates were interrupted with swallows of spaghetti, requests to pass the salad, and demonstrative waving of wine glasses, leaving plentiful stains on the white table cloth as if to emphasize their arguments. Turning his attention to the sauce, Eddy added a final sprin-kling of oregano, put the lid atilt on the pot, and turned the burner down to a low simmer. The kitchen and living room were soon filled with the aroma of Eddy's secret sauce.

There was a gentle rapping at the door. Eddy hastened his awkward gait lest it awaken Maddy from her nap. As he opened the door, he saw his daughter holding her sleeping child in her arms. Clutched in the child's arms were finger paintings from school. Tina managed to get one finger to her lips to signal she wanted to let Missy continue her sleep. Eddy nodded. His daughter's furrowed brow and pursed lips made Eddy feel ill at ease. Something was bothering her. Without saying a word, Tina went through the living room, and down the hallway, to the extra bedroom she and Missy used when-ever they stayed overnight with her parents. Once she had Missy on her bed and covered with a pink afghan knitted by her mother, she returned to the kitchen. Awaiting her was a glass of a Wendy Oaks Pinot Noir, her father's favorite to serve with spaghetti. Tina slowly twirled the glass, mindlessly watching the legs form on the inside of the glass. Noting her absent-minded stare, Eddy asked, "Your day didn't go so well, did it?"

"You wouldn't believe it!" Tina exclaimed, indicating a volcanic eruption of emotions was imminent. If her elevated voice didn't catch Eddy's attention, the slamming of her fist on the tabletop certainly did. She had been so self-absorbed in her own emotions that she had failed to notice her mother was not in the living room when she first entered. Tina quickly changed the direction of her tirade.

"Where's mom?" she asked, glancing at the empty spot on the living room couch.

Eddy looked at his daughter, thinking to himself, *Was this the moment to tell her?* He bit his lower lip contemplating whether or not to share with Tina her mother's current plight. Sensing his daughter's unhappiness, he blurted, "She's resting. Tell me what's bothering you."

Before he could ease himself of the burden that had been preying on his mind, the self-centered Tina announced in a rather defeatist tone, "My visit to that attorney was hardly uplifting. He seemed in awe of having to deal with Paris Barrington and his army of Wall Street attorneys. He even tried to be humorous by referring to himself as my David."

Tina stiffened herself against the kitchen counter and took a rather healthy sip of wine.

"Some obscure reference to David and Goliath, I guess," she shrugged.

The tone in her voice told Eddy she had totally missed the implicit power of the biblical reference. He tried again to introduce the subject of her mother, but once more, Tina's self-interests took precedence. After another sip of wine, she continued.

"Then, when the bus dropped Missy off at my work, I found out she had been running at school. The bus driver said they had been practicing for the Special Olympics being held next month. I can't believe the school would allow Missy to run. They know how I feel about that."

Eddy realized he would have to be more forceful if he was to get his daughter's attention.

"Tina, have a seat. There's something I need to talk to you about, and it's not about your attorney or Missy."

Oblivious to the urgency in her father's voice, Tina replied, "I'm just too wound up to sit, Dad."

Oh, you'll sit, and you'll listen! He thought.

"That wasn't a request, young lady! Set aside whatever is on your mind, sit down, and listen to me. It's your mother. She's not doing well."

If the stern rebuke from her father to sit down wasn't enough to get Tina's attention, the subject of her mother's health certainly did. As if numbed by her father's declaration, she pulled out a chair from the kitchen table and slowly sat down. *What did he mean not doing well,* she thought? Her mother seemed perfectly fine to her, some age issues, but nothing that warranted the urgency expressed by her father. She struggled to contain the panic she felt in her heart.

"Daddy, what do you mean not doing well?" she asked, hoping her premonition of impending bad news was wrong.

Eddy settled back in his chair, trying to compose his thoughts so that what he was about to tell his daughter was factual and not some emotional rant by a disconsolate husband. It tore at his heart to have to talk about Maddy's decline.

"For some time now, your mom's memory has been failing her. At first, it was small things, a hair appointment, or a missed meeting with her book club. Then it got worse. She once called me from outside your house. She didn't remember where she was or why she was there."

His words weighed so heavily that Eddy found himself taking deeper and deeper breaths of air. Tina now found herself defending her mother's behavior.

"Really, Daddy, after all, mom is in her mid-seventies. A little memory loss is to be expected."

Eddy knew what he was about to tell Tina would strike at her heart. Maddy's failing memory wasn't just with dates and appointments. He took his daughter's hand in his, as much to strengthen his resolve as to comfort her for the impending news.

"Honey, it's more than that," he said. He squeezed her hand as he said, "It's people. She's struggling to remember people."

"You mean like old friends? Honestly, Daddy, I run into people I went to school with all the time, and I can't remember their names. I just don't think this is that big of a deal."

If only it were old friends, he thought. His mind fought to think of an easy way to tell her, but there wasn't one.

"God, I wish it were that, honey."

Her face grimaced at his words. Her pulse rate began to rise. Tina had never heard such desperation coming from her father. He had always been a paragon of strength and determination. Growing up, he never allowed her to doubt her ability to succeed at anything she tried. He never allowed her to quit anything she had started. Eddy was the quintessential source of parental encouragement. In his own life, he had never allowed his status as a double amputee to stop him in pursuit of his dreams. The appearance of this most basic of human failings shocked Tina to her very core. She put her other hand over his. Like a child frightened by an unknown sense of fear, her eyes filled with tears. Her breathing became rapid. She starting crying, "Daddy, what's going on? Who is mom having trouble remembering?"

Eddy now wished he had told his daughter of her mother's condition long ago. What started as minor and occasional memory lapses had now progressed to repetitive short-term memory issues. Most alarmingly, her long-term memory began to have huge gaps. Oddly, Maddy could remember some past events, but other significant events seemed to have disappeared from her memory. His hand tightened its grip on hers. When he first recognized the signs, Eddy's spirit sank both physically and spiritually at the reality facing him. Maddy was the love of his life, a love that had helped him endure horrible injuries and years of lost time together. The thought of losing her was unbearable to the once superhuman Navy Seal. Maddy's years as the Executive Director at Magnolia Gardens and his own stint as Executive Director when he retired from the Navy had not fully prepared him for it. He had that same feeling again as he faced his daughter. The answer to Tina's question was simple, not long-winded or complicated, yet as painful as any injury he had ever endured. Through reddened eyes and tears that rolled down his own face, Eddy's lips uttered but a single word.

"Us."

Her head jerked from side to side as if to deny what she had just heard. Her defensive explanations for her mother's behavior seemed to crumble before her. But it was the word "us" that caused Tina Pinafore to think the impossible. Her heart screamed for her to run to her mother's bedside and say, "Mom, it's me, Tina. You remember me, don't you? Please say you remember me!" She sat silent, staring straight ahead until Eddy finally said, "Tina?"

Awoken from her frozen state of disbelief, Tina could only mutter, "I just can't believe it. Not mom, not her!"

Eddy knew exactly how his daughter felt. When he first began to notice the episodes of forgetfulness, like his daughter, he attributed them to aging. However, when forgetting began to encompass more than dates and appointments, Eddy feared the worst. He had seen this same scenario played out many times during his tenure as Executive Director at Magnolia Gardens. Soon dreams of his screaming, "Not my Maddy, not her!" became frequent nighttime occurrences. Morning stares into the bathroom mirror reflected the depth of emotional energy his dreams demanded. A splash of cold water could not revive his gaunt face or tired eyes. He began to recount several incidents to Tina of her mother's failing memory.

"We used to keep a small picture in a silver frame of you and Missy on the end table next to the couch. One day I noticed it was gone. When I asked Maddy about it, she said, 'We don't need pictures of strangers cluttering up the house.'"

In disbelief, Tina quickly turned to look at the end table. The picture her dad spoke of was there. Eddy recognized the sense of relief on his daughter's face.

"Later, I found it in the garage. When I put it back, your mom would smile at it like it was never gone in the first place. Another time I got a call from the pharmacy. They had called to say medication for Mr. Pinafore's high blood pressure was ready to pick up. Your mom told them there was no Mr. Pinafore. They were concerned about her state of mind."

It had been years since Tina had focused on anything but her own problems. The issues of a special needs child were always front and center. Years of denial of any parental responsibility from Missy's father ever preyed on her mind. If she needed something else to worry about, there was Missy's medical issue with her knee. Her father's emotional purging over her mother's mental failings had revealed a vulnerability in him Tina had never seen before. The impact on her was undeniable. She had never wanted for anything because of them. She had never had to ask for anything because they thought of it first. With an emerging reversal of focus, her parents' physical and emotional welfare took on new importance.

"We're going to take this one day at a time," Tina said. "First, let's get mom seen by a neurologist. Maybe we can even find some support group for families whose loved ones suffer from memory loss. I promise you, daddy, whatever else is going on in my life right now, you and mom will always come first." she reassured him.

Her father smiled then nodded. His throat clogged with emotion. The sound of Missy's awkward shuffle on the tile floor coming down the hallway came as much needed relief from the emotional conversation that had just taken place. Her curled hair was matted from her nap. She rubbed her eyes as she made her way into the kitchen and into her mother's arms. Tina swayed slowly side to side, speaking softly to her still drowsy child.

"So, my baby is finally awake."

A simple nod of her head was all the child could muster. She cuddled deeper into her mother's arms.

"Shall I wake up mom, dad? Otherwise, she'll sleep right through dinner time."

"You two do that. I'll start the pasta."

Eddy turned the knob to high after setting a pot of water on the stove. Even such mundane tasks as setting the table with silverware and glasses and folding the napkins gave Eddy a brief respite from the mental agony of the call he knew he would have to make. The hissing sound of boiling water spilling over the top of the pot told him he had ignored the pasta water. He quickly moved to the stove and lowered the heat. From a blue canister on the kitchen counter, he took out a handful of pasta, broke it in half, and then placed it in the simmering water. He added a pinch of salt and a drizzle of extra virgin olive oil. He gave the sauce one final stir, then turned off the flame under it. He had just taken the chilled tossed green salad from the refrigerator and set it on the table when Tina and her mother appeared. Maddy was holding Missy in her arms.

"Look, sweetie, Papa's made his famous spaghetti for dinner."

The tone of her voice and alertness in her eyes were certainly not indicative of someone with mental failings. Eddy had alerted his daughter to enjoy any moments of mental clarity.

"Here, mom, let me take Missy."

Tina took the child and placed her in a plastic riser strapped to a kitchen chair so Missy could be at table level. Eddy transferred the pasta from the colander to a large platter. Then he poured several large ladles of sauce over it. He minced up several leaves of fresh basil and sprinkled them over the pasta. He deftly carried the platter to the table along with a jar of grated Parmesan cheese. This Friday night's meal would be like those of old; no corrections of Missy's eating habits, no snide remarks to her father's questions, or shrugs of annoyance to her mother's inquiries. There was laughter about her father's latest sojourn on the golf course, encouragement about Tina's plans to finish her degree, and excitement about Missy's first Special Olympics competition. Through it all, Maddy was an active participant. Tina prayed her mother's alertness was more permanent than transitory. By dinner's end, reality took over. Maddy's concentration faded. She no longer participated in any conversation. Tina attempted to draw her mother back to the conversation. When Maddy failed to respond, Tina looked at her father. The sense of loss was unbearable. "Where is she," her eyes pleaded. Eddy leaned over and gently caressed the back of his wife's hand. Softly he answered his daughter's question, tapping his heart.

Seeing that it was after six, Tina knew she had to be going. Missy needed a bath before going to bed, and no doubt would be irritable when she had to be awakened after the car ride home. Tina fought the flood of tears from seeing the reality of her mother's decline. She desperately needed her own alone time.

"Daddy, let me help you with the dishes before I have to go," she said as she stood up from the kitchen table. Her offer was as much to break her concentration on her mother's situation as it was to help her father.

Eddy smiled at the offer. Little Missy was fidgety, trying to get out of her seat. Maddy sat silently, staring straight ahead at nothing in particular. *No, this was a good time for her to go*, he thought.

"That's not necessary, sweetheart. You get that precious little one home and in bed. I'll handle things here."

"At least I can help clear the table," she insisted.

Taking Missy's plate and hers from the table, Tina headed to the kitchen sink. Preoccupied with thinking about her mother, the small collection of silverware on the top plate slid off and on to the marble tile kitchen floor. The harsh crescendo of metal on tile startled Maddy. Tina had dropped to her knees to retrieve the fallen utensils. Maddy's head twitched slightly left then right, searching for the source of the noise. She called out to her husband.

"Eddy, what was that?"

"No worry, Maddy. Tina's helping me clear the table, and she dropped some silverware on the floor."

Tina got to her feet, hoping her father's explanation would return her mother to her prior state of tranquility. As she put the utensils and plates in the sink, Tina heard her mother ask, "Do I know her?"

Tina could not bear to turn around.

2

A DAUGHTER'S CHOICE

hortly before Christmas break of her second year at the University of South Carolina, Tina Pinafore told her mother and father that she was bringing her boyfriend home to meet them. Maddy had the front of the house adorned with Christmas decorations; icicle lights hung from the eaves, letters spelling "Merry Christmas" glowed on the lawn. A large evergreen wreath was centered on the front door. Its dozen silver bells rang out with every opening and closing. In the far corner of the living room stood an eight-foot-tall Douglas fir Christmas tree. They provided a majestic aura with strings of multicolored lights blinking randomly, reflecting through strands of silver and gold tinsel. Several Nativity Scenes were set out on the living room coffee table and smaller versions on each end table.

Tina was sitting at the kitchen table, helping her mother decorate a batch of Christmas cookies. She took this opportunity to break the news to her.

"Mom, I want you and Daddy to meet Trevor. He's really special. He's a grad student at Furman working on his MBA, but I don't want Daddy to stress over it. We're going to stop by

Saturday for a few minutes before we have dinner with his parents at the country club. So please don't make a big deal about this."

Maddy burst into laughter at the colossal lack of understanding her daughter displayed about her father.

"Oh sweetheart, he'll more than stress over it. He'll examine the boy's every word, every nuance, and opinion, to determine if he'll treat you to his expectations."

Eddy was sitting in his nearby favorite easy chair, intentionally eavesdropping in on the conversation between mother and daughter. *She's got that right,* he thought to himself, returning to the article on the sports page about his favorite football team, the Carolina Jaguars.

～

FAILING to heed her daughter's advice, Maddy had labored several hours preparing several exquisite appetizers with imported cheeses and crackers. She even prevailed upon Eddy to purchase a couple of bottles of expensive wine, one red, one white.

Tina's text, "We're on our way," was Maddy's signal to put out the display of appetizers and for Eddy to open the wine. Knowing his daughter's propensity to make rash judgments in affairs of the heart, Eddy mumbled, "I hope he's worth it."

"What?" Maddy asked, as her attention was focused on where to place the wine glasses.

"Nothing," replied Eddy. His hope for worthiness would soon be crushed.

At the sound of the doorbell, Maddy said, "Eddy, would you get that?"

Maddy had chosen to wear a particularly attractive cocktail dress with matching pearl necklace and earrings, at least Eddy thought so, and he reluctantly wore a blue blazer, white shirt, and red tie. When he opened the door, he hardly recognized his daughter. Before him stood a stunning blonde in six-inch heels, dressed in a form-fitting off-the-shoulder black satin dress with sufficient cleavage to turn heads. It made Eddy a bit uncomfortable.

"Sweetheart, you look absolutely gorgeous," he said, hugging her while taking a sideways glance at her boyfriend.

Wearing an expensive custom-made Armani suit, Trevor Barrington looked like a storefront mannequin. He had piercing blue eyes, a George Hamilton tan, and teeth so perfectly formed that they looked a bit unnatural. His brown hair was meticulously layered to the degree that it looked artificial to the eyes.

"You must be Trev," Eddy said, now turning his attention to Tina's companion.

"That would be Trevor, Sir. Trevor Barrington."

The smugness of the correction riled Eddy Pinafore's sense of social equality to the point that he thought the better of extending his hand and merely said, "Well, please come in."

"Maddy, the kids are here," Eddy announced as Tina and Trevor entered their home.

Maddy came to Eddy's side and echoed his sentiment over Tina's appearance.

"You look like a queen, honey, and you look like a king, Trev, isn't it?"

Annoyed at the overfamiliarity of strangers using his nickname, young Barrington stiffened his shoulders and was about to correct Maddy as to the proper pronunciation of his name when he saw the look in Tina's father's eyes. They were squinted and filled with the protective glare of one about to defend his loved one. Wisely, Barrington said nothing.

"He prefers to be called Trevor, Maddy," Eddy said, unwilling to hide the "Well, la-de-dah" feeling swelling inside him.

Displaying an incredible naiveness to the tension between

the two men, Maddy merrily continued, "Please, Trevor, you and Tina have some of the appetizers I made, and perhaps a glass of wine."

Having told her mother not to go to any great length over their visit, Tina was visibly annoyed.

"Mom. I told you we could only stay a few minutes. This is really unnecessary." Tina said.

Clearly, she was more concerned about being late for dinner with Trevor's parents than acknowledging her mother's efforts to make them feel welcomed.

"We really shouldn't," cautioned Trevor. "Mother and Father have ordered a very expensive meal for us at the country club."

Maddy sensed Tina's awkwardness at not partaking in her mother's hard work.

"Of course," Maddy acknowledged. "I should have known better. Can we sit for a while?"

Eddy was not so quick to forgive his daughter for her rudeness. His focused stare quickly told Tina she had crossed the line.

Grabbing a couple of napkins, Tina gathered several of the appetizers for her and Trevor. Glancing at his expensive gold Rolex watch, Barrington wisely conceded to giving Tina's family a few precious minutes of his time. He found the Christmas decorations gaudy, adding nothing to what he considered a cookie-cutter home. Everything was a bit plebeian for his tastes.

At least Tina took time to peruse the Christmas decorations her mom and dad had set up. "Mom, you and Dad have the house looking so Christmassy, what with all the decorations."

Two long brown faux leather couches faced each other with a wrought iron glass top coffee table in between. Tina and Trevor sat on one, Eddy and Maddy on the other. Once seated, Eddy tried one more time to "make nice" with the young man.

His brain told him to take his daughter into the kitchen and scold her with a "You've got to be kidding me. This is your choice for a boyfriend?" Recognizing that two stubborn minds were a recipe for disaster, Eddy thought the better. Trying his darnedest to be accommodating, Eddy asked, "So Trevor, you and Tina are meeting your parents at Beaufort Greens?" referring to the local country club.

"No, Sir. We'll be dining at Barrington Fairways. My grandfather founded it as a private golf course over eighty years ago."

His snobbery made Eddy want to vomit. *When had his daughter become so attracted to such superficiality?* He thought to himself as he fidgeted in his chair till Maddy finally asked, "Are you okay, honey? Is your leg bothering you?"

"No, I'm fine," he replied. Turning his attention back to the boy, Eddy asked, "It sounds like your family has a long history here in South Carolina," as he continued to make small talk.

"My family's bloodlines go back to the colonization of America," Barrington said with a sense of unbridled superiority.

"Oh, your ancestors were on the Mayflower?" asked Maddy.

"Oh, hardly. My ancestors financed the expedition to settle the colonies. My great great grandfather was the Duke of Essex and a very close friend to King George of England.

"It sounds like bloodlines are very important to your family, Trevor?" Eddy asked.

His stomach now churned at the thought his daughter was in love with this sanctimonious cardboard cut-out of a man.

Casually crossing his legs and leaning back into the softness of the couch, Trevor responded as if he had just been asked the stupidest question ever.

"Aren't they to everyone?" And thus, proceeded the family's introduction to the father of Tina's future child.

As much as Eddy despised him, Trevor Barrington was responsible for providing Eddy and Maddy with a most precious gift, their granddaughter. Melissa, or Missy as she was called, was indeed a special child. When Tina's pediatrician told her there was a high likelihood of developmental problems with the unborn child, the biological father, Trevor Barrington, showed his true colors. He ended the engagement and had nothing more to do with Tina or her family. Eddy Pinafore suspected from the moment that he was first introduced to the son of one of South Carolina's wealthiest families that Tina was making a mistake, but what child, no matter how old, listens to their parents when it comes to matters of the heart.

～

IN HIS BEDROOM, Eddy Pinafore awoke from a deep sleep after hearing the all too familiar uneven gait of a shoe sliding across the tile floor in the kitchen. He sat on the edge of the bed to clear his head, then arose and put on his gray bathrobe, careful not to wake his sleeping wife. Halfway across the living room that led to the kitchen, he called out softly, "Tina, is that you?"

A second voice called out not so softly and with obvious glee, "Papa! Papa!"

Eddy smiled to himself at the sound of his granddaughter's voice. Tina had called a couple of days prior to see if her folks could babysit Missy while she had an appointment with an attorney. His wife had forgotten to tell him. Forgetfulness had become habitual as of late.

"It's me, Daddy," Tina responded, then adding, "Missy's with me."

The hurried scraping of his granddaughter's shoe on the tile floor told Eddy his special one would soon be in his arms. Tina placed a plastic container on the table.

Tina was well aware of her father's fondness for sweets. As

she laid the freshly baked macadamia nut cookies on the oak table, she commented, "I made these for snacks later. Don't you eat them all, Daddy. They are her favorite," came a mild rebuke.

"There she is!" exclaimed Eddy, as he reached down with one arm to pick up his granddaughter, who had scurried to his side.

Little Missy was indeed special to Eddy Pinafore. Though not in looks, she bore a physical resemblance to her grandfather. She wore a metal brace on her left leg, the result of a knee joint that never fully developed. Her right arm extended only to her elbow. Intellectually, the girl labored with recognizing numbers, identifying primary colors, and matching shapes. Amazingly, her speech development was near normal, with the exception of a sudden stutter when excited. There had been problems during Tina's pregnancy. Early sonograms had indicated there might be physical and mental abnormalities. "Might" was the operative word for Tina. She refused the urging of her fiancé, Trevor Barrington, to get an abortion.

The ideological conflict over abortion was insurmountable. Tina and her family were prepared to accept any child as a gift from God. Trevor Barrington's family saw abortion as the only option to remove imperfection from their bloodline. Ultimately, the younger Barrington broke off their engagement, leaving Tina alone to deal with the consequences, if any, of keeping the child.

"Honey, I've told you not to run. You could fall and hurt yourself," Tina said. Her voice echoed authority, yet a loving concern.

Unwilling to accept or comprehend her mother's admonition, the child's stubbornness erupted into a dramatic reaction, complete with stuttering and broken sentences.

"Pa, Pa, I, I, want...want...run," she cried while clinging to her grandfather's neck.

"I know, sweetheart," Eddy responded, his tone determined

to calm the unsettled child. As he gently patted her back, he consoled her, "Someday you will."

Tina did not hesitate to display her frustration with her father's unwarranted enthusiasm. Simmering anger caused her brow to furrow. She spoke through clenched teeth. Though her given name was Mary, she preferred to go by her middle name, Tina. She thought it had more zing. Her response to her father certainly reflected that.

"Daddy, I've told you I don't want you or Mom to fill her head with false hope!"

She let the child's daypack slam to the floor as if to emphasize her point. *Why can't he just accept her limitations and let it go!* She thought.

Dad was no less frustrated with her response than she had been with his. He turned quickly to face his petulant child. *Accept limitations? Never!* Thought Eddy Pinafore. The VA doctors never allowed him to see his injuries as limitations, and he wasn't about to let his daughter set limits for his granddaughter.

"Do you really want to take away any hope she might have for a...."

Fortunately, Maddy appeared, having been awakened by the harsh words between her husband and daughter. As she clumsily tied her bathrobe, her eyes blinked several times to gain clear focus. Age had not affected her spirit. She still remained that sweet, kind, thoughtful person Eddy had fallen in love with decades ago. Her physical appearance was another matter. She walked with a stoop, the result of scoliosis. The back of her hands were lined with blue varicose veins, as were her ankles and calves. She had taken to wearing her long hair, now mostly gray, in a ponytail with an elastic band she could still manipulate. The child awkwardly swung her left leg out to take the three steps to her Nana's arms. Missy had never quite adjusted to the Osteo Align Aluminum frame of her knee brace.

Maddy picked her up and rained kisses and hugs upon her special one.

Eddy went to the kitchen cabinet to get Maddy her morning meds, as was his normal morning routine. He set them on the kitchen table in front of her.

"Coffee's on the way," he said, smiling.

The previous benefits of the ocular medicine her ophthalmologist had prescribed her had faded in recent years. Her macular degeneration had returned, necessitating that Eddy prepare her coffee for her. After pouring a cup of coffee, he grabbed her favorite creamer from the refrigerator and walked to the kitchen table. With a towel draped over his arm and the elegance of a professional waiter, he said, "Your coffee, my dear, with just a smidgen of creamer."

"You remembered!" she exclaimed with a smile, after tasting the French Vanilla flavored coffee.

Eddy struggled with the realization that memory loss was yet another problem he would have to face. With Maddy occupying Missy's attention, Eddy turned his thoughts to Tina. He steadied his nerves, lest he start another argument.

Trying to be less confrontational, Eddy asked, "What's the latest report from the orthopedic surgeon regarding her knee?"

Tina now felt terribly guilty about snapping at her father. For some reason, saying "I'm sorry" had always been difficult for her. Somehow, she saw it as a sign of weakness. It had cost her friends in school and a few relationships as an adult, still she was repentant. Her voice softened measurably as she stated, "He's recommending an operation on her patella. Apparently, it should have been done at an earlier age, but she could still benefit from it."

"It doesn't exactly sound optimistic," Eddy said as he sipped his coffee, wishing he had added some of his wife's creamer.

"I know, Daddy," a now completely contrite Tina sighed.

"Without the surgery, she'll have to wear that brace to stabilize her leg for life. Even with the surgery, there's no guarantee there won't be recurring problems. I just want her to look more normal. It's so unfair, Daddy."

Tears began to run down her cheek. Missy was fully engaged with Tina's mother's diddling and did not notice her mother crying. Her father could offer no consolation but a hug. The fraternal comfort of his arms eased her pain.

"Thanks, Daddy," she said.

Somewhat recovered from the agonizing decision facing her, Tina shifted her attention to the morning paper. It pained Eddy to hear his daughter refer to his granddaughter as looking more 'normal' without a leg brace. What did she think he looked like – a double amputee with a scarred face – some sort of grotesque creature people could not bear to witness? The urge to defend himself to his daughter seemed repugnant to him, but nonetheless, a feeling he felt compelled to address.

"Looking normal is no guarantee of happiness." The calmness in his voice more eloquently expressed his disappointment than any outburst of anger ever could.

Overcome with guilt for the second time in their brief conversation—Tina realized how hurtful her comment had appeared to her father. She had always been "Daddy's girl." She had vivid childhood memories of gleefully looking up her father's shirt sleeve when he would play a game he called, "Where's my arm?" Her idolization even went so far as to say at times, "I want a leg like yours, Daddy!" The instant realization of how deeply she must have hurt her father caused her tear ducts to respond accordingly. She rose from the table and went to the kitchen island where Eddy stood.

"Daddy, I'm so sorry. I never meant to hurt you!" she cried as tears of disappointment rolled down her cheeks. She hugged him with all her strength as if to emphasize her sincerity.

His one arm encircled her waist and pulled her close to him. His prosthetic arm cradled her head against his chest.

"I know, sweetheart. I know. Sometimes things just come out," he whispered.

His words were like an anesthetic against the self-inflicted pain of her ill-spoken remark.

With peace made, Tina returned to the kitchen table to contend with her mother's opinion about Missy's impending surgery. Tina often referred to her overprotective mother as a helicopter mom. At the moment, Maddy lived up to that title.

"Well, I think it's a shame you have to make that decision on your own," she said, unashamedly referring to Missy's missing biological father. Any chance this attorney will be of help?"

Tina said nothing. Her mother's inference had not gone unnoticed by Tina or her father. It touched a rather sensitive nerve in both of them, bringing back the most unpleasant of memories.

3

HOPE

The thought of the attorney's visit had caused Tina's grip on the steering wheel to tighten. Her stomach muscles followed suit until she thought she was going to vomit. She had no one to blame but herself. What was she thinking when she wrote that letter asking Trevor Barrington one last time to help with the medical expenses their daughter was facing? His response was more than she could take. Tina acted out of anger and revenge. Had she started an irreversible process? She pulled off the interstate into a nearby rest area. She hurriedly walked to the women's bathroom, where she splashed cold water on her face. Cupping her hands under the spigot, she took a quick sip. Staring into a cracked mirror, she saw eyes reflecting the fatalism of the task she was about to undertake. *What possible good will this do,* she thought. *He'd never been there before for his daughter. Why should she expect anything different this time?* She straightened up, adjusted her blouse, and headed back to her car. For Missy's sake, she'd try.

In her dreams, her attorney's office would have been on the tenth floor of a high-rise business building in downtown Charleston, where the law firms have five names as partners, and they charged four hundred dollars an hour. Perhaps then she would have had better luck going up against the New York City law firm the Barrington family kept on retainer. But working for the Recreation Center for the Handicapped did not earn her a six-figure income. With minimal medical insurance, the Law Office of Matthew Adams, Esquire, General Practice would have to suffice. Matthew Adams had not been Tina Pinafore's first choice. After her first, second, and third choices had turned down her plea for representation, she turned to Find-a-Lawyer.com. Picking from the top of the alphabetical listing of attorneys on the website hardly seemed solid criteria for making her selection. Oddly enough, it was the best choice Tina Pinafore could have possibly made. Adams' office was located a few blocks from city hall, occupying a street-level space once the home of Abe Shapiro's Bail Bonds. Had Tina done any research into Matthew Adams's background, she might have had more enthusiasm about her meeting. Matthew Adams' grandfather was Morris Dees, cofounder of the Southern Poverty Law Office and an icon in the civil rights struggle in the South. Matthew had followed in his grandfather's footsteps and attended the University of Alabama Law School, where he finished second in his class. Adams had turned down offers from several prestigious law firms, choosing instead to open his own office specializing in general practice. He had no desire to be a pettifogger but rather hoped to represent those who needed representation, not just those who could afford representation. He hadn't been disappointed.

～

"Sir, I mean, Law Office of Matthew Adams. How may I help you?" asked a surprised, heavily tattooed Hispanic female. She was sitting at a desk munching on a taco from a Taco Bell paper bag. With not a hint of embarrassment, she wiped her face with a brown napkin she had taken from the bag.

As if Tina needed something else to shake her confidence in her selection, she let the door close slowly behind her. The small receptionist area had enough room for a work table and a somewhat oversize desk. Efficient would be the descriptive word used by a real estate agent. There was the odor of freshly laid carpet and new paint. Obviously, some redecorating had been done. There were several prints hanging on the back wall, all of the legendary Alabama football coach, Paul "Bear" Bryant. The large tabletop had several textbooks scattered about, along with an opened spiral notebook.

Clutching her glasses in her hand, she desperately tried to hide her disappointment. She had purchased a new dress for appearance's sake and had her hair trimmed to look more professional. Had it all been for naught?

Tina replied, "Yes, my name is Tina Pinafore. I have an appointment with Mr. Adams."

Recognizing the awkwardness of the moment, the woman quickly responded, "I was expecting my brother, Ricardo, for lunch. Please come in and have a seat."

The woman could not have been more literal. There was only one chair next to a window ledge lined with very old issues of National Geographic. Tina took a seat, ignoring the cover of the closest National Geographic issue with naked women of Borneo on the cover. The receptionist picked up the telephone on her desk.

"A Mrs...." paused the receptionist, now looking at Tina.

"Ms.," She emphasized, "Ms. Tina Pinafore."

"A Ms. Pinafore is here to see you."

Within moments, a tall, not unattractive man in his late thirties, if she had to guess, appeared in the hallway—a pair of reading glasses nestled in his thick brown curly hair, more gray than brown. A stylish five-o'clock shadow gave him the appearance of added maturity. He wore a blue long-sleeved shirt unbuttoned at the collar, with a blue and red striped tie fashionably loosened around his neck. From the crumbs of broken taco shells on his shirt and docker pants, Tina surmised the secretary and he must have shared a twin pack from the Taco Bell across the street.

"Am I interrupting your lunch?" she asked, with more snobbery in her voice than needed.

Adams ignored the inference to his eating habits and calmly brushed the front of his shirt, eliminating any evidence of the super taco package he had just devoured.

"Not at all, Tina, please come with me," he responded, rather nonchalantly.

She had not expected the sudden familiarity of hearing her first name, but she had to admit there was a modicum of comfort in it. Tina followed him down a poorly lit hallway where a painter was finishing the gold letters on a frosted glass door reading, "Matthew Adams, Esquire."

"Excuse us, Gus," said Adams, as he stepped around the painter and opened the door to his office.

Tina's confidence could not have sunk any lower. No lushly carpeted floor, no richly decorated office furniture or those impressive bookshelves made of mahogany and full of law books. Instead, there were half-assembled metal shelves against two walls, stacks of cardboard boxes labeled "law books" spaced evenly around the perimeter walls, and a large oval conference table, which apparently doubled as both his desk and work area. The floor had the original white and black linoleum tiles. The table had all the earmarks of a Salvation Army purchase, old and outdated with a badly faded stain over the oak veneer top. There were several large plastic buckets filled with paint rollers, drop cloths, and brushes in one corner of the room.

"Please, have a seat, Tina, and excuse the appearance. Once

the decorator is done, you won't recognize the place," he said with a comical grin on his face.

"I would hope so," replied the somber Pinafore. "The decorator certainly has her hands full," Pinafore said with a hint of indignation in her voice.

Adams chuckled a genuine little laugh. "As a matter of fact, I do have my hands full. Now, tell me how I can help you."

Oddly, the one aspect that seemed to soothe Tina's waning confidence was the set of chairs around the oval oak conference table. The tenseness in her body seemed to ease as she settled into the thickly cushioned, soft ruby red leather chairs with wide armrests so your arm didn't continually slip off. The slightly tall chair allowed one to lean their head back when contemplation was needed. The sensitive spring-loaded chair automatically adjusted to one's natural body weight, giving one the illusion the chair was a personalized piece of furniture. Tina's comfort as she settled into the chair was almost sensuous in nature. Still, between her anger and underlying embarrassment, her words sounded staccato in delivery. Adams had a legal-size pad in front of him. He would soon realize what he really needed was a recording device. Momentarily, Tina stared out the office window, her mind recalling old and unpleasant memories. Suddenly her head turned to face Adams.

"My daughter has special needs, and she's facing an expensive operation. I don't have the best medical insurance."

She paused, realizing the harsh tone of her words. "Sorry, but some things are difficult to share. All I ever wanted from her father was some financial assistance. When I wrote him, this was his response," she said, as she took an envelope from her purse and placed it on the table in front of Adams. "Do you think you can help?"

Adams took the letter from its crumpled envelope. It was short, heartless, and arrogant. "I am not responsible for your imperfection. You won't get a penny of my family's money."

This was what stirred Adams' initial purpose to become a lawyer, a client, facing impossible odds and defeated before the battle even begins. He leaned forward, eager to hear more.

"Good," replied Adams. "Now, tell me about your family. Your mother, father, where you were raised. You know, the family background sort of thing."

Tina's defenses stiffened.

"Is all that really necessary?" she asked, still not completely trusting the man who was asking her to bare her soul.

Adams had seen this type of protective behavior before, and he understood perfectly. The vulnerability of opening up all of one's background to a complete stranger was not an easy thing for most people. Tina Pinafore epitomized that vulnerability. Adams rose from his chair and moved to the other side of the table to sit next to Tina. He didn't need a barrier between them. He needed trust. Slowly and compassionately, he began.

"Tina, there are two parts to your case that are equally important to me. The lack of faith in either one will cause me not to represent you—one, the facts, those neutral, emotionless deeds of who did what to whom. Of equal importance is you, the person, and those emotional experiences that made you what you are. You were molded by more than nature. You were nurtured and loved by people. I want to know about them. Tell me about that Tina Pinafore."

Completely taken off guard by his humanistic approach, the tension seemed to ebb from her body. Against her better judgment, an unexplained sense of comfort and trust took over.

"My parents are Eddy and Maddy Pinafore. Dad retired from the Navy, and Mom was a stay-at-home mom. I led a normal life growing up, played soccer and softball." With a smile on her face, she said, "Mom and Dad pretty much spoiled me. I got anything I wanted, within reason."

As the details came forth, Tina's sense of comfort increased.

"In high school, I got good grades but was something of a

wild child when it came to boys. Mom's advice was always to find someone like my father. If only I had listened to her, maybe...."

"Things would have turned out differently," replied Adams, finishing her sentence for her.

With a fatalistic shrug of her shoulders, she answered, "Maybe."

"Let me tell you something my grandfather used to tell me when I was growing up. Your future is to be. Your past is what it was; embrace both with equal passion." Continuing with his probe into her past, he asked, "Is Pinafore an Italian or Hispanic name?"

"Neither, it's English. Why do you ask?"

"I was wondering if you got your complexion from your father or your mother."

Her adoption was a subject her family had never talked about openly. Not that there was anything to be ashamed of, but explaining it to others only brought on unnecessary questions about details her mother and father had preferred to keep private. Tina sensed Adams was only interested in generalities.

"My birth father was Hispanic."

"So, you're adopted?" Adams asked.

"Actually, I'm twice adopted," she responded before realizing that answer would undoubtedly lead to more questions.

Adams was genuinely interested in this unusual revelation and could not contain his curiosity.

"Sorry if I'm prying, but that's the most unusual story I've ever heard. If you don't mind, could you tell me more?"

His sincerity moved Tina to go on, though with some reservation,

"According to my mom and dad, I was abandoned not long after I was born. My first parents, Daniel and Jane Kilgore, adopted me through Family Social Services. I don't remember a thing about them. They were killed in an auto accident when I was about three. Mom and dad, my godparents at the time, adopted me."

A huge sense of relief swept over Tina. This was only the second time in her life she had told anyone about the specifics of her background. The first time was Trevor Barrington's family. Their reaction had been quite different than her attorney's.

"Then you've been twice blessed by God, young lady," Adams opined.

The silence that followed suggested to Adams that she had not thought of her past that way. Her willingness to open up to Adams seemed natural, not fraught with anxiety.

"My dad had been injured in some kind of accident as a young man, the details of which were never shared with me. He had lost an arm and a leg, but that never stopped him from teaching me to play sports or volunteering to help coach my soccer and softball teams as a young girl. In high school, I was a bit of a wild child. I mean, I got good grades and all that stuff, but my choice of friends was questionable at best. In my sophomore year at USC, I met Trevor Barrington. He was a grad student at Furman. He was drop-dead movie gorgeous and flaunted his family money. He kind of swept me off my feet, and in no time..."

"You got pregnant," Adams said, finishing her sentence for her.

Her shoulders slumped, and she nodded. It was clear to Adams the pregnancy was a consequence, not an intention.

"How did your mom and dad take the news?"

For the first time, Tina's face brightened.

"They were great. It wasn't the way they had hoped my adult life would start, but they were so supportive."

"And your boyfriend's family?"

Her posture stiffened. Her attempts to restrain her anger at what had happened seven years ago failed miserably. She needed to stand up. Walking over to the office window that overlooked a city parking lot, the anger and pain of the past overwhelmed her. Tina's acrimonious words were sharp and pointed, her breathing deep and labored. As if speaking to no one, she started.

"Trevor flew us to their family estate in Darian, Connecticut. They were horrible, especially his mother. First came the questions about my family background. Who were the Pinafores? Where had they gone to college? How far back could we trace our heritage? I told her I was adopted and that my heritage started with Eddy and Maddy Pinafore, my parents. When she questioned my complexion, suggesting I might be of mixed blood, I lost it. What the hell does mixed blood have to do with anything if you're in love? I asked her. Trevor grabbed my arm to calm me down, but it was too late. I hollered my birth father was Hispanic, and my birth mother was white. Why did that matter a hill of beans? That's when his father stood up and said, 'End this relationship now, Trevor!'"

Her blood pressure slowly subsided. The angry flush on her face faded.

"Anyway, as you can guess, the silence was deadly. His mother finally broke the silence by asking if we would consider an abortion. I stood up, walked over to where she was sitting. I was pretty emotional with my answer. I yelled, 'That's out of the question. Don't you understand I have a living being inside me, your grandchild! And I walked out of the house."

Adams leaned back in his chair, folded his hands behind his neck, and mused, "I can't imagine things could get much worse."

"Oh, imagine! Three months later, I had an amniocentesis test done. The doctor told me that because of chromosomal deficiencies while developing in the uterus; there was a real possibility that the baby would be born with physical and mental problems. Trevor insisted on my getting an abortion—I refused. I clung to the word *possibility*. If my spat with his mother hadn't been enough, this news was the final straw for Trevor. I never heard from him again. All my letters to him were returned, marked, **Not at This Address**."

"What about your baby?" Adams asked.

Tina opened her purse lying on the table. She pulled out a small brown leather wallet. She flipped it open and handed it to Adams. A glow of maternal pride swept over her.

"Her name is Missy. Her left arm never developed beyond the elbow. Her right leg had a malformed patella. She has to walk with a brace. Intellectually, she is what the specialists refer to as mildly mentally retarded."

Adams returned the wallet to her. He reached across the table and pulled his laptop computer closer. He flipped it open and began typing into the search bar. In seconds, the picture appeared with the biography below it. He slid it over for Tina to see.

"So, this is your Goliath. Paris Barrington is a billionaire developer of resorts for the rich and famous with private estates in four different countries, a fleet of Wall Street attorneys to do his bidding, and number three on Forbes list of the wealthiest men in the world."

Sensing that Adams was attempting to let her down easily before telling her he would not be able to represent her; Tina queried, "Is that bad news?"

Adams closed the computer.

"Yes, I'm afraid it is," he said with a resounding sigh.

The disappointment at his words caused her stomach to cramp. She had really been taken with his sincerity and interest in her as a person. Then came the words she had not expected to hear.

"The good news is, I'm your David."

Fortunately for Tina Pinafore, there was another "David" in her future.

4

THE UNSUSPECTED HEART

Early spring in Charleston, South Carolina, was Ryan Callahan's favorite time of the year. He basked in the coolness of the early mornings and the mild temperatures throughout the day without that ungodly humidity. Even more, he enjoyed the temperate evenings where you only needed a light sweater or windbreaker to be comfortable. Ryan was barely three years old when his mother and father bought their first and last home. The fifty-ish style Craftsman painted a sea green color was in an older, well-established neighborhood on a raised corner lot. Though it did not meet either Samantha or Mike's personal taste, it fit well within Mike's income as a public servant serving on the Charleston PD.

Ryan had finished mowing the sloping front lawn and was tending to the hedge of shrub roses lining the driveway when his mother called out, "Are you getting thirsty?" The smell of freshly cut grass and the aroma of the rose blossoms had been something that his father relished, often sitting on the step of the porch and commenting, "This makes all the yard work worth it," while extending his arms and inhaling deeply.

"Sure, mom," Ryan answered, dropping the rose shears and

brushing off his jeans. He walked over to the steps of the porch to meet his mother, who had a cold iced tea in one hand and a chilled bottle of Samuel Adams pale ale in the other, which had been his father's favorite.

"You pick," Samantha said to her son, who, with a twinkle in his eye, held one finger against his cheek as if to mimic the difficult decision he had to make.

"Sam Adams," replied her smiling son.

Samantha sat down, placing her shoulder against the porch rail.

"You are your father's son," mocked Samantha, as she daintily sipped her tea.

"Yes, Ma'am," answered a proud son, as he took a deep swig of the chilled beverage in his hand.

"Do you still play your guitar?" she asked.

Holding his cold bottle of beer to his forehead, Ryan replied, "At times."

Samantha smiled to herself. Her husband had taught Ryan how to play the guitar when Ryan was in high school.

"Easy way to attract the girls," he had told his son.

Mike would have been so proud of him. Following graduation from high school, there was no doubt what direction Ryan Callahan would take, what with pictures of his dad in dress blues, and several pictures of his mom and dad at the annual Marine Corps Birthday Ball in the living room. When his graduation from boot camp at Camp Lejeune arrived, there had been a slight disagreement between mother and father. Mike had wanted to wear his dress blue uniform though he had long retired from the Marine Corps Reserves. Samantha insisted that their son should be the focus of attention and not the father on that day. Mother prevailed. Four years as a Military Policeman in the Marine Corps had taken a barely 6' tall, 160 lb high school senior and turned him into a 6' 3", 220 lb chiseled hunk of humanity with a poster board recruiting image.

The last year of his enlistment had been very difficult for Ryan. He had been able to secure thirty days' leave to go home for his father's funeral but then had to leave his mother to deal with all the post-funeral details. He had adored his dad. And like his dad, he was very protective of his mother. Being stationed at Camp Lejeune for his last year made it a lot easier to get home on a regular basis to see her. Following Mike's death, Samantha was able to get her old job back at Magnolia Gardens, working with the Director of Volunteer Services. Though financially stable from Mike's retirement as well as several life insurance policies, Samantha Callahan needed to feel a sense of service, and Magnolia Gardens provided just that.

Ryan rubbed the cold bottle of beer against his forehead. Even without the humidity, his body was reacting to the exertion required to get an ancient Toro lawn mower up and down the steep front lawn. Looking at his watch, he commented, "I'd better get back to work, mom. I've still got the back yard to do, and I'm starting a new assignment—night shift with the Drug Task Force."

"I don't understand! Why don't you stay with the Patrol Division? You said you liked the work, and you get to work days." There was more than just a trace of disapproval in her tone. Crossing her arms and staring up at the sky, Samantha could not help but feel history might repeat itself.

Ryan fully understood the source of his mother's fear. As if his decision to follow in his father's footsteps as a police officer hadn't caused her enough grief, his father had elected to go to the graveyard shift because the Department needed a seasoned training officer. Assigned to work with a rookie officer, Sergeant Mike Callahan had taken the lead in answering a domestic violence call. He had told the rookie with him to wait next to their patrol car. That decision cost him his life when a drugged-up boyfriend fired a shotgun through the home's front door.

Samantha was horrified by the possibility that she might receive another phone call in the dead of night informing her that she had lost her son just as she had her husband.

"I've got to get started, mom," Ryan stated, hoping to end the uncomfortable conversation with his mother.

He stood up and finished his beer.

"I'll put this in the recycling and then get started on the backyard."

Samantha gave him a half-smile. She knew she had gone a bit far with her comments, but after all, he was her only child. Like any child, there was a way to make things right. She went to the kitchen and began her quest for forgiveness. The old mower gave out a groaning hum as Ryan maneuvered it around the backyard, circling two peach trees and more single shrub roses in flower beds lined with river rock. The sputtering sound of the engine was an indication he was almost out of gas. Samantha checked the time on the oven, then looked out the kitchen window to a meticulously mowed back lawn, the place where a younger Ryan had caught the winning touchdown in some futuristic Super Bowl and hit the winning home run, a grand slam at that, for his favorite Atlanta Braves in the World Series. *Three minutes to go, plenty of time,* she thought, *to prepare his going away gift.* He had placed the mower back in the detached garage in the backyard and hung the blower in its spot on the rack along with several rakes and shovels. His father had obsessed with keeping a neat and organized garage, a habit inherited by his son

As he headed to the back porch, the smell of engine exhaust clogging his nostrils was quickly replaced by the aroma of freshly baked cookies, chocolate chip macadamia nut, if he had to guess. When he was deployed overseas, Samantha regularly sent her son care packages filled with her bakery creations. Ryan would write home that the guys in his squad devoured them like piranha after a fresh kill.

As he stood at the kitchen sink washing his hands and face, Samantha said, "Don't forget these," tapping the top of a large cookie tin filled with his favorite as she set the fresh delectable on the kitchen table.

"Dinner for two days," he chuckled, knowing his mother worried about his eating habits.

Samantha slowly shook her head.

"I pity the girl you fall for, young man. Sweets are the way to your heart."

Ryan smiled. Since no one could bake like his mother, the likelihood of that happening was slim to none. Having assured his mother he would be careful on the first night of his new assignment, Ryan hugged her, then climbed into his almost new black Dodge 2500 super cab pickup truck with chrome wheels and a five-point Hemi engine. Clearly, it was a grownup boy's pride and joy.

~

RYAN'S CHOICE of residence was far from that of his fellow officers, who, if single, opted for some upscale apartment or condo in the livelier part of town, or if married, some "Better Home and Gardens" stereotypical three-bedroom home in suburbia. He had saved much of his separation pay from the Marine Corps, and with the help of the GI Bill, he had purchased a quaint two-bedroom fixer-upper farm style home on three acres on a hill overlooking the outskirts of Charleston Bay. It had taken Ryan nearly three years, with the help of two of his best friends, Billy Epperson and Dutch Hendrickson, to transform the structure into what Epperson referred to as an "above average bachelor pad." Epperson's father had been an electrician. He completely replaced the old knob and tube wiring with modern Romex hidden within the existing walls. Installing new outlet boxes had been time-consuming but well within Billy's skill set. Epperson had insisted on the installation of the sixty-five-inch HD Visio TV with surround sound, solar panels to save on electricity, and an upscale alarm system. As the trio sat in the living room admiring their work, Epperson said in a self-congratulatory tone, "Now this is what I'm talkin' about!" he chimed, as he scanned the NFL and MLB packages Ryan had purchased. Ryan and Dutch tapped beer bottles at Billy's delight.

Dutch Hendrickson's father had been a general contractor. With help from his father's crew, Dutch and Ryan had been able to install a vaulted ceiling, a new green metal roof, and a wrap-around porch. With help from Samantha, whose advice Ryan grudgingly but wisely accepted, the crew transformed the two-bedroom, one-bath home into a three-bedroom, two-bath home with wood flooring throughout, complete with a kitchen with every modern convenience known to man. The living room and dining area were far too womanized, as Epperson called it, but secretly something Ryan liked.

'You'll thank me someday for this!" Samantha reminded her son when the final coat of paint to the outside of the home was completed. In his late twenties, and with no romantic interest on the horizon, Ryan could not appreciate how much those "womanized" features would appeal to someone else.

❧

IT WAS dark when Ryan arrived home from working at his mother's place. The motion sensor lights lit the way from the driveway to the front steps. As he stepped inside the front door, another of Epperson's inspirations was activated. The opening of the front door triggered a signal for the living room lights to go on. Ryan chuckled as he remembered telling Billy he didn't need this kind of thing. But with his arms occupied with fresh uniforms from the dry cleaners, the day's mail, and his mother's gift, he appreciated Billy's insistence. The fresh uniforms found their way to the back of the living room couch. The cookies went into the refrigerator, and the day's mail was tossed on the dining room table. With his new shift starting at ten p.m., Ryan had enough time to shower, shave, get into his uniform, and get to work in plenty of time. The Drug Task Force was an elite group within the Charleston Police Department. Its members were more than just partners. Their personal lives were as intricately involved as their professional lives. He had no way of knowing how transferring to the Drug Task Force would change his life forever.

5

THE NEW JOB

As he pulled into the city parking lot next to Police Headquarters, Ryan Callahan was anxious to start his new assignment with the Drug Task Force. This was one of the few operations in the Charleston PD that was staffed by the recruitment process. Unsolicited applications were simply not accepted. In five years on patrol, he had seen more than his share of the human carnage caused by those who distribute illegal drugs to the population of Charleston, South Carolina. He had never forgotten the look on that mother's face as she held the lifeless body of her thirteen-year-old son in the side alley next to their apartment building, OD'd on fentanyl. Her screams echoed off the building's brick walls and into the night. This was but one dream that haunted Ryan Callahan, much like soldiers suffering from PTSD. Add to that the countless deaths attributed to overdoses of cocaine, meth, and a host of other so-called recreational drugs, and Ryan Callahan had developed an intense loathing toward those who profited from such activities.

Once out of his truck, he was struck by the loudness of the droning sound emanating from the overhead neon lights illuminating the parking lot. He reached into the bed of his truck and lifted out a medium-sized black gym backpack loaded with two extra black jumpsuits, a field first aid kit, two Glock 9mm handguns with extra magazines, and several bottles of water. A dozen or so officers were stashing their gear in the back of their patrol cars. Ryan heard a voice call out, "When you want a real job-fighting crime, your old job is waiting for you." It was Ryan's old patrol partner, Don Evans, who had recently been promoted to Sergeant on the graveyard shift. Ryan smiled in acknowledgment of the compliment. Don Evans hated losing Ryan as a partner. He admired the kid's grit and his innate ability to read people. Mostly, he thought of Callahan as a younger brother.

Hey, Ryan. Hold up a sec," Evans called out.

Walking over to Callahan, he placed his hand on Ryan's' shoulder.

"Listen, you'll never by my ex-partner, understand? Be careful," he said.

The hug he gave Callahan was not symbolic. It tugged at Evans' heart to lose the kid.

"I know," replied Ryan, suddenly caught in the emotion of the moment.

Ryan crossed the street and headed up the marble steps to the double glass doors of the Police Department building. The Drug Task Force office was located in the back of the building, which allowed ready access to its tactical field van, yet was away from the brass's prying eyes. The sign over the door read, "Drug Task Force." Ryan hesitated a moment. Should he knock or just presume it was okay to enter? He chose the former, knocking several times on the frosted glass door. When the door opened, he was greeted by a giant of a man. Standing six feet five, 250 pounds, with a shiny bald black head, Willie Root smiled at Callahan. Ryan seemed transfixed by the brilliant gold tooth in the center of Root's grin. Callahan was not small by any means at 6' 3" and 220, but the height and girth of the man standing in front of him caused him to pause. Both stood silent for a time, evaluating the other. Finally, Ryan was able to utter a meek, "Callahan reporting for duty."

Root called out, "Hi. Red, It's the new guy."

A dozen or so officers turned around in their chairs to size up the newest member of their elite squad. Ryan was glad he had taken the extra effort to press his black utility jumpsuit and spit-shine his boots. Additionally, every man there looked fit and trim, so Ryan's extra time in the gym and daily four-mile runs eased some of his apprehensions. Then came the banter.

"That uniform won't stay pressed and creased for long!" laughed one officer.

Another hollered, "Same goes for that shine!"

Ryan maintained a stoic expression. He had taken and given his share of hazing while in the Marines. He could give back such banter later. Now was the time to accept his position in the pecking order—at the bottom. There were thirteen members of the Drug Task Force team, one lieutenant, two sergeants, and ten officers. Their home was a large rectangular room. Along one wall was a line of extra-wide lockers for each member. Along the other wall was a caged weapons armory extending 5" out from the wall with everything the team could possibly need: night vision goggles, radio headsets, tactical grenades, two Barrett M82 caliber sniper rifles, a row of AR-15s, and below that were rows of fully loaded magazines. There were four rows of tables twelve feet long, and uncomfortable-looking black metal chairs, and a single table at the front of the room.

From the front of the room, a deep baritone voice bellowed, "Callahan?"

"Yes, sir," responded the well trained former Marine. Ryan found himself feeling more like a new recruit at Paris Island than the seasoned officer he had become. His response reflected that feeling.

A few of the men snickered at Ryan's use of the term "sir" in addressing their boss, whom they affectionately called Red. The boss thought this would be a perfect teachable moment.

"That's right, you jerk-offs! Sir, do I need to take you on a five-mile hump to remind you of protocol?"

The rebuke resulted in instant silence. Outside of the Drug Task Force's situation room, Lieutenant William, "Red," Caruthers demanded and received a level of respect due his rank and years of service. More than a few people over the years had received Caruthers' rather stern rebuke for using his nickname, Red, in reference to him or assumed they could call him Red. Those were terms of endearment reserved for his men and his men only. He relished the reaction of people who saw him walking down the hallways of police headquarters. He was just over six foot three with a body trimmed to a svelte one hundred and ninety pounds thanks to his avocation of running marathons. The seven gold stripes on his left arm, reaching almost to his elbow, indicated twenty-eight years of service. He would chuckle to himself as he watched people trying to count them before he passed by them.

The resulting silence in the room caused Ryan to think he had brought unnecessary attention to himself. Caruthers let his words sink in before responding, "Look, Callahan, don't let these moks get to you. Inside this room, there is no sir. My name is Red. Root, you give him a rundown of our home away from home. I've got a meeting with the Chief and a DEA agent." With that, Red Caruthers, a camo notebook in hand, left, taking his two sergeants with him, leaving Willie Root to introduce Ryan to the rest of his teammates.

A man of few words, Root raised his hand and started pointing.

"That's Butch Hanson, A squad lead man," a hand raised. "Rich Reed, sniper, Mike Harrison, Barry Woodson, and Billy Edwards make up the rest of A squad, I'm B squad leader.

Ryan, you'll be B squad's sniper when needed. Russ Ortega, Al Hodgner, and Eddie Popkey are your team members."

With the introductions finished, each man came up to Callahan, extending a hand and a "Welcome to the team" greeting, including the customary law enforcement hug of comradery.

Ryan Callahan felt immediately at home. Turning to Root, Ryan asked casually, "Who was the old sniper?"

"That would be Eddie Popkey's brother, John."

Seeing that Ryan was not completely satisfied with a genealogical answer, Root continued, "He did his twenty and decided to open a weapons training school here in Charleston. You ever want to sharpen your shooting skills, go to John. There's none better."

Tapping the top of a locker, Root went on, "This locker is yours. Stow your gear here. Then it's all about waiting for Red to get back."

Having just returned from their quarterly range qualification that morning, most of the team returned to the business of cleaning their weapons. Cloth patches, ramrods, small cans of gun oil soon littered the tabletops. Roots had applied a thin coat of oil to the trigger assembly of his Glock 19, then laid it on the table. He closed his eyes and, in a matter of seconds, had the 19 reassembled.

"Impressive," Ryan said.

Root smiled, "Practice like you fight, fight like you practice."

∼

HAROLD McMURRAY, the Chief of Police for Charleston, had given specific instructions to his secretary that he was not to be disturbed, as he led Lieutenant Caruthers and Sergeants Parsons and McKnight into his private conference room. His predecessor, Clive Nelson, had previously decorated the conference room for the purpose of personal aggrandizement. The array of photographs with city dignitaries, celebrities, personal awards, and any newspaper clipping of positive note with his name in it covered two walls. All of that had been summarily removed when McMurray ascended to the job.

MacMurray was guided more by recognizing his men and functionality than appearance. Photographs of fallen officers and those who had received any sort of commendation were tastefully displayed on one wall. The opposite wall displayed historical pictures of the Charleston Police Force dating back to the 1800s. Depending on what he was using his conference room for, there were either rows of black padded chairs with a center aisle or three long oak conference tables formed into a U.

"Gentlemen, meet DEA senior agent Jerry Sloan. Agent Sloan, these three men ran my Drug Task Force Unit. There's none better, anywhere," McMurray added for emphasis, "Lieutenant Bill Caruthers, Sergeant Derek Olson, and Sergeant Marty Knight."

Caruthers answered for his men.

"Senior Agent Sloan."

Jerry Sloan hadn't lasted twenty-five years in the DEA without the ability to judge people. The lieutenant had that command presence that only exceptional leaders have, a presence that causes the men under him to be willing to meet any challenge, any foe. Sergeant Olson was about six-foot-two and no stranger to the gym. His extra-large jumpsuit could not hide bulging biceps, a broad chest, and thick legs. No doubt, he'd be the one leading the charge at Satan's door. The other sergeant was slight of build, probably a runner if Sloan had to guess. A narrow face with wire-rimmed glasses resting on his nose, he had an almost stoic demeanor, as if to say, "Show me!" *The cerebral one,* Sloan thought.

The three men simultaneously took seats on one side of a large white oak conference table on Caruthers cue. The chairs were nicely padded and on rollers, a luxury the three quietly enjoyed compared to the folding metal chairs in the Drug Task Force room. The chief sat opposite them. Sloan stood at the head of the table, a PowerPoint pen in his hand. A large-scale map of the east coast marking numerous shipping ports appeared on the wall with a single click. With another click of the pen, a map of the United States appeared next to it.

Interestingly to Knight, there were a dozen cities marked in red. A fan of geography, Knight quickly recognized the cities of Los Angles, San Francisco, Seattle, Denver, Aspen, Dallas, New Orleans, Miami, Charleston, Hilton Head, and Atlanta. Stepping to the side so as to not obscure the view of his attendees, Sloan began his presentation.

Using his laser pen, he pointed to the map of the United States. "Over the last two years, each of these cities has experienced an increase in deaths due to drug overdoses, specifically, cocaine and not just any kind of cocaine. This stuff is one hundred percent pure super strength and deadly as hell."

Knight was perplexed by Sloan's statement. It defied the age-old practice of diluting the product by distributors and then dealers. He raised his hand.

"Sir, what you just said contradicts how dealers have done things for years. Dealers always cut their product," Knight said. "Baking powder, laundry detergent, laxatives, anesthetics or cretin, stuff like that, to make more money. You're telling us this new stuff is pure? Hell, the average user couldn't afford to pay what the suppliers would have to charge to make a profit."

"Very astute, Sergeant Knight. You're absolutely right. We're not dealing with the average junkie here. We're talking about kids from expensive colleges and universities, trust fund babies, the millennial generation, you know. Now, add in the trend toward younger hedge fund managers and dot.com instant millionaires. It's a new paradigm we're dealing with, gentlemen."

Caruthers made careful notes on his notepad. He had his own set of questions.

"Agent Sloan, this issue as it applies to cities in other states is clearly not our responsibility. Our jurisdiction is strictly within the boundaries of Charleston city limits. How are we supposed to help you?"

Sloan looked toward Chief MacMurray.

"Chief, would you like to answer that question?"

"Red, as of now and for the foreseeable future, you and your team are assigned to the DEA, answerable to Senior Agent Sloan." The chief let his words sink in before continuing. "Agent Sloan and I go way back. We were in the same Army Ranger Unit going into Panama after Noriega. I trust him, and he trusts me. A seminar on Drug Interdiction in Washington, D.C. brought us together. I told him if he ever needed my help, all he had to do was call. This rest is history. Any questions?"

With hesitation, Caruthers said, "When do we start?"

"For starters, you'll be working normal eight to five. At least you'll start at eight. See you tomorrow."

That brought chuckles from everyone.

～

THE MEN SEEMED to have taken quickly to Ryan Callahan. He had an engaging personality with a smile to match and enough humility not to try and outdo the others with his own war stories. With the return of Caruthers and his sergeants, the cleaning supplies were quickly put away, tables rearranged, and weapons secured. Ryan closed the Drug Enforcement Task Force Orientation binder Root had given him earlier. Never known to be long-winded, Caruthers started to brief his men.

"All right, here's the long and short of it. Effective 0800 tomorrow morning, we will be assigned as a special unit to the DEA. There have been a number of deaths attributed to a strand of one hundred percent cocaine. We will be assisting the DEA in this operation and taking directions from Senior Agent Jerry Sloan. He'll address you tomorrow on the specifics. Finish up your business here and get out. Oh, make that 0745 tomorrow and have your shit together."

His smile told his team they didn't need the prompt. Root opened his locker and grabbed his duty bag. He unzipped it and pulled out a brown paper bag. He reached in and took out two large macadamia white chocolate cookies.

"No need to save these until morning," he chuckled, placing one entire cookie in his mouth.

With his head tilted backward, his chin munched slowly and deliberately. A muffled, "Mm-mm," came from his closed mouth. Callahan thought Root was in some sugar-induced trance.

"Must be good," Ryan asked.

Not willing to rush his enjoyment to answer Callahan's question, Root savored every last morsel.

"Uh-huh, they are. Care for one?" Root asked, extending the brown bag to Ryan

Callahan had no appetite for sweets at that moment. His mind was whirling with anticipation over working with the DEA. All he could think of was, could he measure up to the expectations of everyone?

~

THURSDAY MORNING, Callahan had set his alarm early to ensure he would arrive at work at least fifteen minutes earlier than directed by his lieutenant. If four years in the Marine Corps had taught him anything about punctuality, it was "on time" meant being early. The Mr. Coffee his mother had given him for a house warming present emanated its aroma of fresh brew throughout the house. After turning on the lamp next to his bed, he rubbed his eyes, stretched, and then headed to the bathroom. After a Navy shower and quick shave, Callahan returned to his bedroom to dress. Once suitably attired in his black cargo pants and shirt, he carried his duty belt with him to the kitchen, where he poured himself a cup of coffee. He sat at the kitchen table, taking time to enjoy the last of his mother's batch of cookies. After dispatching the last one, Callahan rose and went to the kitchen cupboard. He took out a large, insulated coffee mug, filling it to the top, leaving enough room for a dash of half and half. Duly caffeinated, he grabbed his jacket hanging on the back of the kitchen chair and headed out the door. Glancing at his watch, he knew he could make the thirty-minute drive to police headquarters with fifteen minutes to spare. At 0730 hours, Ryan Callahan stood in front of the Narcotics Task Force room. A feeling of smugness came over him as he opened the door.

"You're late," smiled Willie Root, taking a sip from his coffee mug.

"Are you kidding me?" said a dejected Callahan, again looking at his watch.

"If I get here first, you're late. If you get here first, you're on time," chuckled Root, as he pulled out a chair for his new partner.

Callahan gave a sheepish nod.

"Don't worry, kid. You won't learn everything in one day," said Root.

Ryan had just settled into his chair when the door opened, and the rest of the men began arriving. Some mumbled at the early arrival time Caruthers had set. Others came in munching on a morning danish from "Dunkin" and holding a large cup of their brand of coffee. Casual acknowledgments to others were made with nods and fist bumps. There was barely enough time to enjoy one more bite or sip of coffee before the door opened.

Lieutenant Caruthers, and a stranger, walked to the front of the room.

"Gentlemen, this is DEA Senior Agent Jerry Sloan, our new boss. He'll brief you on our new mission."

With his normal suit and tie gone, Sloan dressed in a black tactical jumpsuit similar to Caruthers' team with the exception of the gold letters DEA on the back. He had a five o'clock shadow and wore a black wool cap. Sloan exuded a sense of "one of us" that the men appreciated. He addressed the men.

"Good morning. What I'm about to share with you is to be considered highly confidential and not to be discussed with anyone outside this room."

That not so subtle admonition drove everyone's alert meter to ten.

Sloan had made reproductions of information he had received in the middle of the night from DEA Headquarters. He started passing them out to the men, explaining their meaning as he went.

"This piece of paper may be the puzzle solver," Sloan said. "A US Coast Guard Cutter in the Caribbean thinks they've broken a code used by the Colombian Drug Cartel. Essentially, the numbers represent the longitude and latitude of cities on one of the charts I've given you. They span the entire east coast and parts of the Gulf Coast. The repetitive letters spell out the word 'El Nino.' What exactly that means, we don't know."

Always the cerebral one, Sergeant Knight asked, "Could it refer to weather patterns, Agent?"

"Maybe, Sergeant. I've tasked the National Weather Bureau to chart the last three years of storm patterns to see if there's any relation between them and an El Nino. What we've got to worry about is 187 miles of pristine coastline to monitor. The Coast Guard has assigned two cutters to the DEA to monitor ship traffic as far as 100 miles off the coast. We have to be the eyes and ears onshore."

Knight's hand went up again.

"Are you expecting the contraband to arrive aboard ship in Charleston Harbor or drop off points along the coast?"

"We have to be prepared for either, Sergeant."

Caruthers sensed Knight's uneasiness at being referred to by his rank. It had been Caruthers' philosophy to refer to his men by their first names. He felt it created a closer sense of team.

"Jerry, we are not much to stand on rank formality around here."

Reading into Caruthers' words, Sloan nodded.

Looking to Caruthers, Marty asked, "Red, can the port authority get us a list of upcoming arrivals with foreign registry, particularly South American or Panamanian? It might eliminate wasting our resources."

Sloan smiled to himself at Knight's thought process. He'd like to have him on his DEA team. Caruthers stepped into the back corner of the room to make the call. When he closed his phone, he called out, "They'll fax it over in a few minutes, Marty."

In the interim, Caruthers had his two squads divide themselves into teams of two, with instructions to prepare for an all-night operation. A sense of adrenaline began to flow through Callahan's veins. For his partner Root, there was a different response. He seemed methodical as he began packing his duty bag.

"You don't seem too excited about this, Willie?"

"Never did like night ops much. My body takes too long to recuperate.

The fax machine beeped, and slowly a piece of paper eased its way out of the slot.

Caruthers glanced at the paper, then handed it to Sloan before addressing his men, a professional courtesy on his part.

"Well, what do you know," Sloan said with a wide grin on his face. "Could we get any luckier? In the next five days, only one ship, La Novia, with Panamanian registration, is scheduled to arrive in Charleston harbor on the fifteenth, this Saturday, at midnight."

The smile on his face told everyone that Caruthers was pleased with the arrival date and time. His men would have an unexpected day off, and he would have ample time to develop an ops plan with his sergeants.

"Jerry, how soon can you get us an overview of the harbor?"

Before Sloan could reply, Knight said, "Already on it, Red." Knight had uncoiled an electric cord, plugging one end into his laptop and the other end into the PowerPoint projector. His fingers moved rapidly across the keyboard of his laptop computer. Knight pressed the enter button. Instantly, a GPS image of Charleston harbor appeared on the wall. Everyone focused on the map.

"Any ideas, Red?" asked Sloan, giving deference to the street experience of Caruthers.

Red took several minutes studying the image on the wall. His eyes strained to catch the smallest detail. The long harbor had berthing locations on both sides, each with one-way entry points, no two-way traffic.

"One way in, one way out," he said. A faint smile appeared on his face.

"It's probably the port authority's way of controlling traffic congestion at shift changes," Knight mused.

"The berth assignment of the La Novia?" asked Red. His eyes still fixated on the image on the wall.

Sloan double-checked the fax.

"Berth 10B, right here," answered Sloan, pointing to the location on the image.

The small smile on his face began to grow.

"That's the last unloading berth before exiting the facility on the western side. It's the fastest way for the ship to get back to sea and the fastest way for any contraband to get out of the facility."

The directions from Caruthers came fast and furious.

"Derek, I want your team to cover the entrance to the western pier. Have two of your men at the entrance shack three hours ahead of the ship's 1400 hours arrival time. Be alert to any strange looking vehicles coming in prior to arrival time."

Without taking his eyes off the chart, he asked, "Jerry, can you arrange for those assigned to the entrance and exit gates to have port authority uniforms?"

"Consider it done."

"Okay then, Derek, position your men accordingly along the wharf. Marty, I want you to take the eastern end of the pier, two men on the exit gate. Like Derek, position your men accordingly in and around the ship's location. I want both snipers on the rooftops nearest the entrance and exit locations, and Marty, I want copies of this map for everyone ASAP. Derek and Marty, I want your schematics before you leave tonight. The rest of you, it's Thursday. I'll see everyone Saturday here at 2100 hours, sharp."

For the first time, a smile came over Root's face. "Now you're happy?" quizzed Ryan.

"You bet," Root replied. There's time for me to help my wife with her school project on Friday."

"Need any help?" Ryan asked as he tended to his own duty bag.

The offhand remark surprised Root. He glanced askance at Ryan, repeating, "Help?"

To clarify, Ryan responded, "Well, I am your partner, and partners help each other, don't they? So yes, can I help?"

"Ever hear of the Special Olympics?"

"Sure, but only in the news. Some sort of competition for handicapped kids, right?"

Root smiled. "A little bit more than that, Ryan. My wife is a special education teacher at Weatherby School. It's on the campus of Jefferson Junior High. Weatherby School is on the far end of the campus, the corner of Fifth and Wilson, to be exact. See you there, 2:00 p.m. tomorrow. We'll do a little coaching."

Ryan Callahan's future was about to change in ways he could have never imagined.

6

THE UNTHINKABLE

Upon returning from their trip to the market, Eddy placed several shopping bags on the counter. Maddy had accompanied Eddy on his trip to the market and seemed in an unusual state of awareness, even remembering where certain food items were located. Even more surprising, she had asked if they could stop at "Nibs" for a milkshake on the way home. Nibs was a retro version of a sixties hamburger stand, complete with young girls on roller skates taking orders from parked cars and '50s-'60s Doo-Wop music blasting over outside speakers. It had been one of Tina's favorite places to go as a young child. She had been fascinated by the young girls whirling between parked cars on roller skates holding trays over their heads with any combination of fries, burgers, and Nibs landmark malted shakes. Eddy pulled slowly into a parking slot. The regular lunchtime crowd had not arrived.

"Shall we eat inside or make it more like the old days and eat in the car?" Eddy asked.

Maddy's head was swaying the saxophone-driven rhythm of an old Bobby Darin hit, "Splish Splash." Her eyes were closed, and her head swayed side to side. Her finger and thumb snapped to the rhythm as she sang along.

"Oh, no. Can't we just sit here and listen to the music while we wait?"

Eddy was pleased with her answer. He, too, felt the need to enjoy memories of the past, a past where the future was something to be dreamed of, not dreaded as was his present situation. He reached over to hold Maddy's hand and said, "You bet we can."

The irony that she could remember a song nearly sixty years old and yet struggle to recall events as recent as yesterday had not escaped Eddy. Reality can only be ignored for so long. The call had to be made. Eddy's thoughts were interrupted as a young carhop, complete with a Nibs visor, Nibs signature white blouse with a high starched collar, and red midi-skirt, rolled up to the driver's door. Nibs' original owner's son had provided all the carhops with a headset to get orders in and out faster, a sign of the changing times.

"Welcome to Nibs. Can I take your order?"

Knowing her favorite, Eddy ordered.

"One strawberry malt and one double cheeseburger with no onions and no pickles, to go, please."

Maddy added quickly, "Could I have extra malt in the shake?"

The carhop nodded, then called in the order.

"One strawberry, extra malt, one double cheese, no onions, no pickles, to go."

Maddy leaned back against the headrest. "I love this place, Eddy. So many memories."

Eddy was suddenly alerted to the realization that Maddy had some momentary grasp of her past, of their past. He would not lose the opportunity to keep her in that moment. One recollection could lead to another and another. Optimism would prove to be a fickle god.

"Remember the time Tina knocked the tray off the door sending three cheeseburgers, fries, and drinks sailing through the air?"

"I loved that song," she sighed. The past was slowly slipping away. His heart ached. If only she could stay in the moment. Over the loudspeaker, you could hear the sound of a quarter dropping into a coin slot and then the sound of an Elvis Presley song. With the last refrain of "In the Ghetto," the carhop appeared with their order. Eddy gave her a rather generous tip and then headed out of the parking lot. As he did, Maddy woke from her semi-conscious trip down memory lane. She straightened herself. Her eyes had a look of panic in them. Her face froze as if something terrible had just happened.

"Why are we at the hospital?" she gasped.

Choosing not to overreact and thus exacerbate her already spiked anxiety, Eddy responded, "We stopped at Nibs. I got you that strawberry malt you wanted."

Her eyes seemed alert, but her response indicated otherwise.

"What strawberry malt?"

The unthinkable had become a reality. The unavoidable was at hand, and Eddy Pinafore could no longer ignore it. There would come a time when he would no longer be able to care for his beloved Maddy on his own. That time would be sooner than later. The ride home was a somber one. Eddy Pinafore thoughtfully began making a mental list of all the decisions that would have to be made to find a suitable place for his wife. Maddy sat quietly, her lips repeatedly opening as she appeared to be trying to say something. The words never came.

～

It was two days before Eddy would have a chance to follow-up on the brief phone call he had made to Magnolia Gardens after his shopping trip with his wife. Eddy placed a call to one of his old golfing buddies, Jim Hill. Fortunately, Jim's wife, Sandy, answered the phone. After all, it was her help he was seeking.

"Sandy Hill."

"Hi, Sandy. Eddy Pinafore."

"My gosh, Eddy. It's good to hear your voice. How are you and Maddy doing?"

At the sound of her question, Eddy suddenly felt trapped between having to reveal the truth behind his call and wanting to keep private his living hell.

"I'm fine, Sandy, but Maddy's had some health issues lately. That's why I'm calling. I was wondering if you could spend a couple of hours with her tomorrow. I need to look into something without worrying her unnecessarily.

"Of course, I will, Eddy. Our bridge club really misses her. She had such a wit about her. She brightened up the game like nobody's business. We all knew something was wrong when she started forgetting who bid what and what suit to follow. What can I do to help?"

"If you could come by about ten a.m. and spend a couple of hours with her, I'd really appreciate it."

"Does she still like to quilt?"

"Occasionally, yes," Eddy answered. "She had been working on a quilt for our granddaughter, Missy, but never got around to finishing it."

"Then quilting it is," Sandy replied enthusiastically. "It will be so much fun being together again. See you at ten."

Eddy hoped for such an outcome. Maddy needed something to be happy about, something to bring out her old spirit.

~

"Oh, Eddy, I'm so excited. I haven't seen Sandy in ages. It will be so much fun getting together again," Maddy replied when Eddy told her of Sandy's visit that morning.

Eddy allowed himself to smile. At the moment, she was aware, anticipating a visit from an old friend she remembered.

"I've got to get my quilting bag out. Do you remember where I put it?"

That momentary sag in his spirits quickly dissipated when she responded, "I remember. It's in the back bedroom."

Eddy left Sandy and Maddy sitting on the living room couch. A large piece of material was spread between them. With their quilting bags by their sides, each began working on attaching a square of colored cloth. Working their needles carefully from the bottom up through the material, the two began sharing old memories. Keeping in mind that Maddy had exhibited some memory issues in the past, Sandy did more narrating than asking questions. Though not a trained professional, Sandy skillfully infiltrated the conversation with sufficient clues that Maddy never realized she was practically being fed the answers. Eddy stood in the doorway, savoring the gleeful banter between the two before leaving for Magnolia Gardens.

~

The hour drive across town gave Eddy Pinafore pause to remember the lost years. Following his return from his Seal Team's ill-fated dark ops mission in the Middle East, Eddy Pinafore had suffered the loss of his left arm, right leg, and a horribly scarred face. Letters he had received from Maddy saying she had something to tell him tore at his heart but went unanswered. He didn't need the additional torture of hearing she had found someone else. He never wrote her of the extent of his injuries. Suicide would have been a better option than losing her because of the ugliness of his injuries. When

Maddy's closest friend, Kristin Andrews, tracked him down and told him what Maddy had gone through, Eddy Pinafore was ashamed of himself. He had failed in his commitment to her. He had doubted the depth of her commitment to him. Their reunion brought him more happiness than he thought humanly possible. The opportunity to adopt three-month-old Mary fulfilled Maddy's dream of having a family—a dream previously thought impossible due to an assault she had written Eddy about in letters he had never opened. So deep in thought was he that a couple of times, the honking of a passing motorist alerted him he was drifting out of his lane. Having lost her once, the drive to Magnolia Gardens took on a new purpose. It was no longer about Maddy—it was about them. With steel determination, he would never allow them to be apart again.

~

THE DRIVE UP Magnolia Lane to the Gardens was as beautiful as he had remembered. The magnolia tree in front of the entrance loomed large over the circular driveway. Its limbs full of white and purplish blooms cast a shadow almost 40′ wide. The marble columns outside the bricked entrance were as stately as ever. It had been over twenty years since Eddy relinquished his temporary position as Executive Director. There was little chance any of the staff on hand would remember him or Maddy, and Eddy needed an inside source of support. Fortunately, Samantha Callahan had returned as the acting Executive Director following the death of her husband, Mike, a sergeant in the Charleston Police Force. Samantha had started out as a volunteer under Maddy's tutelage. Eddy would call in a favor, but in Samantha's mind, it was hardly necessary.

As the automatic double glass doors closed behind him, Eddy paused to look at a portrait of Jane Kilgore hanging on the wall. At the bottom of the gold-gilded frame, the brass plate read, "In grateful appreciation for her dedication and service." When Maddy had retired as Executive Director, Jane Kilgore had agreed to be her temporary replacement. As it turned out, temporary turned out to be five years. Eddy continued down the hallway, noting that the furniture and decoration changes still reflected that home-style environment for which the Gardens were famous. The rounded raised counter where visitors used to check-in had been replaced by a custom-made Queen Ann table. It gives the area a more open look, according to the decorator. The small matching coffee table with two over-stuffed chairs beckoned any visitor to sit. The receptionist no longer wore nursing scrubs, but rather a more comfortable yet professional blouse and pants combination.

"May I help you?" the receptionist said, extending her hand to greet Eddy.

"Yes," replied Eddy after taking her hand in his. "My name is Eddy Pinafore. I have an appointment to see Samantha Callahan."

An iPad had replaced the old computer tower and monitor. With a quick swipe of her fingers, the receptionist replied with a smile, "Yes, I'll see you to her office."

Noting her name tag, Eddy replied, "Thank you, Janine. But I know the way."

Eddy proceeded down the hallway. He felt a sense of familiarity as he headed to what had been his old office. As he approached the closed door, he heard a raised voice from inside.

"You tell that arrogant son-of-a-bitch never to step foot on these grounds again," the voice raged, followed by the slamming of the telephone.

Eddy Pinafore paused then knocked gently, hoping to give Samantha a moment to defuse her obvious anger. There was no response. He waited a moment, then knocked again. This time a little more forceful.

"Come in," a voice called out, somewhat calmer than the profanity-laced tone he had just heard.

On the north side of fifty, the years had been good to Samantha. A devotee of yoga and an avid cyclist, Samantha's body had little of the unwanted flab that haunted most women her age. She wore her hair in a pixie style akin to Liza Minnelli. She favored jade teardrop earrings with a gold knotted choker chain necklace. Her ebony eyes came right out of a John Keane picture. Through tear reddened eyes, Samantha said, "My God, it's good to see you, Eddy. Give this friend a hug!"

Eddy held her with his one arm, gently patting her back as any father would to an upset child. Setting aside his own agenda for the moment, Eddy said, "Would you like to talk about it?"

Her sigh spoke volumes.

Eddy realized getting to the bottom of Samantha's emotional tirade would have to be addressed before he could broach the purpose of his visit. Eddy took her hand in his, saying, "Samantha, let's have a seat. Take a deep breath and start from the beginning, ok?"

Once seated, Samantha's temper seemed to subside, though her body remained rigid as her revulsion to her previous call had not ebbed.

"About six months ago, the Board of Directors was approached by an agent representing a large development company. They were interested in purchasing Magnolia Gardens: the buildings, the grounds, everything. It seems they had this grandiose plan for a mega-development, and they wanted this property."

Eddy was not surprised that the Board had finally been approached by someone who was interested in Magnolia Gardens. The five-plus acres it occupied and the adjoining ten acres the Garden owned had great investment potential, in his opinion.

"What was the Board's response?"

"Thank God, it was no!" Samantha said. "From its inception, Magnolia Gardens has always been dedicated to the quality of life for the aged, so that in the remaining years of their lives, our residents would always be treated with compassion and care. Their dignity would never be compromised. You can't put a dollar price on that."

If that was the Board's response, Eddy wondered why the upsetting phone call.

"With that kind of negative reception from the Board, why continue to contact you?"

Samantha bolted to her feet.

"The first time he came here, I took an immediate dislike to him. He was so arrogant and smug. He didn't seem to care about the residents or their families. For several months, every visit was the same. He would have this look on his face like, 'Why don't you just give in and accept my offer.' It was like nothing I said mattered. Honestly, Eddy, I wanted to slap the shit out of him. When the bastard tried to bribe me, his precise words being that I would be amply compensated for my efforts, I told him to never call here again."

Realizing the civility of her language had slipped a bit, she quickly added, "Sorry, Eddy. I've developed a bit of a potty mouth." Eddy grinned. After twenty-five years in the Navy, Eddy Pinafore was no stranger to profanity. He found Samantha's outburst comically refreshing in this age of feminine equality.

Somewhat puzzled, Eddy asked, "If you told him never to call again, who was that on the phone?"

"Someone called Arthur Ashcroft. He said he worked for Atlantic Financial, Inc. His company was behind the efforts to buy Magnolia Gardens. He was apologizing for his agent's behavior and assured me he had only the best interests of our residents in mind.

Hoping to soothe Samantha's mind, Eddy said, "My guess is the Board will continue to take the moral high ground. Even in my time here as the Executive Director, they always seemed dedicated to the altruistic values that made Magnolia Gardens what it is today."

Realizing that she had pretty much monopolized the conversation up to that point, she said, "Enough of my business. What brought you here?"

Suddenly Eddy Pinafore couldn't remember why he was there. His mind suddenly fixated on twenty-five years of dreams with the woman he loved. It replayed everything, starting with the visit from Kristin Andrews and the discovery that Maddy still cared about him, the elation when the adoption of their daughter, Tina, was finalized. Eddy and Maddy embraced the responsibilities of parenthood. The memories of Tina's first words, her first steps were as vivid in his mind as the day they happened. There was the laughter of children at birthday parties, pool gatherings and barbecues with friends, and vacations on the coast. The family album provided volumes of pictures documenting a lifetime of milestones. Eddy didn't need to look at the pictures to see them in his mind. After Tina had moved out, he and Maddy would sometimes go through the album, turning pages of faded yellow paper glued with pictures of every phase of their lives. Maddy would coo over how sweet Tina looked in the team pictures when she played youth sports. Eddy reveled in remembering the competitive outburst of his daughter. There were endless discussions that Tina would find someone who would love her and her daughter Missy. Eddy and Maddy had gleefully anticipated the day when Maddy could help Tina plan her wedding, and Eddy would have an opportunity to walk his daughter down the aisle to the waiting arms of her husband-to-be.

They spoke at length of those golden years and what they would do. There would be travel to Europe, something of which Maddy had always dreamed. Eddy wanted that small summer cabin near Lake Swanson they had once seen in a real estate magazine. Their lives would be the fulfillment of all their dreams, the probable and the improbable. His eyes reflected the desperation of a man seeking to hold on to something that might never be. There was no controlling his emotions at this point. His eyes moistened. His throat constricted as he tried to get the words out.

"Maddy has had some issues in the last few years, serious issues that, in time, I won't be able to deal with on my own. Considering her years working here and mine, I was wondering if there was any way to reserve a place here at Magnolia Gardens.

Samantha didn't need to hear the unsaid details behind, "Some issues." She worked with individuals with deteriorating mental capabilities on a daily basis. Hearing it was someone as near and dear to her heart as Madeline broke her heart. Madeline had nurtured her from being a volunteer to becoming Director of Volunteer Services and ultimately endorsed her selection by the Board to become the Executive Director at Magnolia Gardens. She gave Eddy the assurance he so desperately needed to hear.

"Eddy, there will always be a place for Maddy here at the Gardens."

His response was not what Samantha expected.

"I'm not asking just for Maddy, Samantha," he said. "I'm asking for both of us."

7

PROMISE KEPT

Ryan sipped the last of his Acai drink. He had taken a liking to the concoction of the popular health berry, granola, milk, and bananas. He entered the address of Weatherby School into his phone's GPS. He had seen children with disabilities before, sometimes on the street, sometimes in stores, but nothing longer than a fleeting glance. He never gave much thought to a child whose body had spasms with cerebral palsy or whose crippled body needed leg braces and crutches to walk. Ryan was beginning to have misgivings about offering his help to his new partner. Would he have the heart for it? Would he be able to look past their disabilities and see what was special about them? Remembering Root's words about coaching, Ryan wore his running shoes, nylon jogging shorts, and OD green t-shirt. Like his father before him, when he had been discharged from the active-duty Marines, Ryan had joined the local Marine Corps Reserve Unit, a military police unit specializing in background investigations. He finished his coffee, then opened the dishwasher to see if it was full. *Good,* he thought, seeing a couple of empty spaces, *I can wait another day,* as he set his cup in one of the two open spaces in the top tray. He grabbed his Marine Corps windbreaker and headed out the door.

The music from his favorite radio station played classic country songs, another habit he had picked up from his father, while periodically being interrupted by an annoying Siri who told him to turn left in fifty yards or take the next exit. At last, Siri said, "Your destination is on your right."

Ryan recognized Root's cream-colored Chevrolet SUV and pulled to the curb behind it. He was somewhat perplexed by what he saw—a series of portable buildings, a large playground area with numerous kickballs of different sizes scattered about, a downsized baseball diamond, and a huge grass area, all enclosed by a cyclone fence. The main school campus was nearly fifty yards away. *Why contain these kids within a fenced area,* he thought, as he approached the main gate. He pressed the speaker button. A voice answered, "Weatherby School."

Ryan answered, his words tenuous with curiosity. *What have I gotten myself into,* he thought?

"Yes, my name is Ryan Callahan. I'm here to see Willie Root."

"Please come in. The office is the first building on the left," said the voice.

The lock clicked as the gate swung open. Then came a reminder.

"Please make sure you secure the gate."

Ryan made a quick assessment of the buildings. Each had ramps instead of steps. All the doors appeared extra wide. As Ryan opened the door to the office, he was greeted by brightly colored finger paintings on every wall. Letters hung underneath the countertop reading, "A Smile Brings Happiness." Ryan waited while the heavyset woman behind the counter finished her telephone call. She looked up at Ryan and signaled,

"Just a moment." Ryan nodded back. There was a young boy sitting in a chair leafing through a magazine. Ryan thought he was in his teens. The boy's thick tongue continuously moved in and out of his mouth. He was a little on the heavy side. Black rimmed glasses awkwardly balanced on his roundish face with almond-like eyes. After finishing her call, the woman looked up.

"May I help you?" she asked. Her desk plate read, "Mrs. Payne."

"Yes, Mrs. Payne," replied Ryan. "I'm supposed to meet a Willie Root here. Do you know where I can find him?"

The woman rose from her chair slowly. Her obesity necessitated her using a cane for support. She awkwardly made her way to the counter. Somewhat out of breath but smiling, the woman responded. "I'm Freda Payne—welcome to Weatherby School. Willie told us to expect you."

Payne turned to the boy in the chair,

"Jimmy, would you take Mr. Callahan to Mrs. Root's classroom?" she asked.

The young boy gleefully obeyed, bored with having nothing to do but look at magazines he couldn't comprehend. He came over to Ryan.

"My name is Jimmy Rose. I'm the escort today," he said proudly as if he had been appointed to some lofty position.

Ryan had to struggle to understand the boy whose speech was affected by his disability. The boy extended his hand to Ryan. Not wanting to disappoint the boy, Ryan took the boy's hand in his. He felt ashamed of his uneasiness to make contact with the gleeful boy.

"I'm Ryan."

After his enthusiastic greeting, Jimmy said, "Follow me."

Using the handrail, Jimmy walked down the ramp to the office. His eyes focused on his every step. They came to a classroom with a sign on the door reading, "Mrs. Root, Primary Class."

"That's Mrs. Roo's classroom," Jimmy said, unable to pronounce the "t" in Root. "It's for the small kids." He pointed to the next classroom. "I'm in the classroom for the older kids in there." The sign on the door read, "Mrs. Royce, Intermediate Class." His face beamed with an exalted sense of pride. He dutifully knocked on the door before opening it.

As Jimmy stepped inside, he called out, "Mrs. Roo. It's me, Jimmy."

The scene before Ryan appeared to be complete chaos. In one corner of the room were large floor mats. Three children were flopping on a figure wrapped in a large blanket as if it were a super-sized beanbag chair. All were gleefully laughing and giggling as they landed on the mysterious mound covered by a blanket, none more so than an undersized girl with blonde hair. She had a brace on her left leg, but more noticeable was her left arm, which ended just past the elbow. There were two large round tables, no more than two feet tall. Children were spaced evenly around each table, sitting on the tiniest of plastic molded chairs. An attractive black woman with sparkles of gray hair in her closely trimmed Afro sat on a small round stool on rollers. She deftly maneuvered around each table, constantly offering encouragement and praise for the activity underway. Around the walls hung large plastic letters of the alphabet. Below each letter was a picture of an object starting with that letter. One wall was covered with poster papers with unintelligible figures in finger paint. Names were printed at the bottom. In the far corner was another large floor mat. A young woman, probably in her early twenties, Ryan guessed, was working with three children on flexibility. She alternated between the three, gently bending legs forward and back as they laid on their backs. Her long hair was formed into a bun to prevent clinging fingers from grabbing it. She wore pale blue nurse's scrubs.

"I'll be right back, children," the black woman said, adding, "Sharon, would you mind taking over here?" Looking at Callahan, Eva Root identified the young woman enthusiastically, "Sharon is doing her internship in Physical Therapy through the University of South Carolina. She's the greatest!"

The young girl smiled at Eva in response to the compliment.

The young woman working with the children on the mat replied, "Sure. Okay, let's everyone get up and take your seat at the table."

Sharon helped one boy put on his leg braces, then got him to his feet.

The black woman called out, "Willie, your partner's here!" while walking to Callahan.

In a most pleasant voice, she said, "I'm Willie's wife, Eva, and you must be Ryan. Willie's told me a little about you. I'd like to introduce you to my class, if that's OK?"

Ryan nodded.

"Listen up, everyone. I want all of you to meet Ryan. He's going to help coach you for the Special Olympics. So, let's everyone say hi to Coach Ryan."

A chorus of happy sounds resounded throughout the room. Some were difficult to understand due to speech problems. Others clapped their hands, and some just grunted a smiling approval.

Ryan offered a smile, hiding his apprehension about coaching children with disabilities he knew nothing about. Strangely, there seemed to be one universal characteristic of the classroom. Everyone seemed genuinely happy despite their physical or mental impairments. It struck a note in Ryan's heart that would resonate later. Unraveling himself from the large blanket that had covered him, Willie Root appeared, saying,

"Hey, partner. I see you made it." Almost immediately, the young blonde girl jumped at him again as Root sat on the floor.

"One more time, Willie. Please!"

Willie grunted as he absorbed the unexpected impact, and like a giant teddy bear, Root hugged her gently, saying, "Okay, Missy, that was the last time. We have to get ready for practice."

"Can I run, Willie? Please, can I run?" Missy pleaded. She was as anxious as a youngster waiting for a ride at an amusement park

"Sure, Missy. You can run, but my friend Ryan and I have to set up the equipment first. Mrs. Eva will bring you out when school is over. We'll start then, Okay?"

With the promise of a dream to be fulfilled, Missy hobbled over to her teacher, almost falling over with excitement.

"Mrs. Eva, Mrs. Eva, I get to run today!"

"Well, isn't this a special day for you, Missy! Let's have a seat until recess time," Eva Root responded.

At six-feet-five, Willie looked like Gulliver in the land of the Lilliputians. When he stood up, a couple of die-hards still clung to his leg, pleading for more jumping time. His huge hands carefully pried their tiny fingers from his sweatpants. These kids may have special needs, but gripping power wasn't one of them.

"Ryan, come with me and grab that ball bag by the door on your way out."

The large net bag contained several softballs and small to medium kickballs. With the bag in hand, Ryan obediently followed Root out the door to the field behind the classroom.

∼

"PRETTY IMPRESSIVE, HUH?" said Root, admiring his handiwork and that of many other volunteers. "We put this together ourselves, that is, me and a number of parent volunteers. It took us the better part of four months of long weekends."

The design reminded Ryan of something out of "It's a Small World" in Disneyland. It was a large hexagonal area, probably thirty feet across, covered with redwood bark chips. He was amazed at the intricate detail of the playground equipment. Everything was scaled down for small children. There were metal horses atop springs for the kids to ride, along with two fifteen-foot-long wooden bridges supported by lengths of chain to challenge their sense of balance. The bridges were only inches off the ground to minimize any injures if a child fell. Along another side of the hexagon were several sets of swings with basket-type seats and safety straps to keep the kids from falling out. Next to the swings was a maze of elevated narrow ramps going left and then right before leading up to a square platform about five feet off the ground. Multi-colored hard plastic handrails provided support. The platform was enclosed with a colorful four-foot-high railing, again for safety. In the center of the hexagon was a large merry-go-round. There were no horses, only lengths of metal handrails about five inches from the surface for the kids to hold on to or just sit if they so chose.

"This is impressive," said Ryan as he gazed over the various types of adaptive equipment."

Root smiled at the compliment.

"The one for the intermediate children between ten and eighteen followed the same principle, to challenge the kids motor and sensory deficits. We just had to make the equipment bigger and stronger," Root said, pointing to another hexagonal area about twenty feet away. "We better get ready," Root said, looking at his watch. "Eva will have her brood out here any minute."

"What do you need me to do?" asked Ryan, who now was a little more at ease with the task at hand thanks to Root's seemingly knowledgeable explanation of the specialized equipment.

"Grab the ball bag and follow me," Root said, as he walked about ten feet from the edge of the play area.

"Put the softballs here along with those wire stakes with the flags on top. We practice the softball throw here. The kids throw the ball, and you mark where the ball landed with a wire stake. Be aware that direction is not necessarily in their repertoire. You never know exactly where that ball will land."

Root took several more steps and said, "Take out the tent pegs and stake out the strip of white canvass. We are doing the standing jump here."

Continuing his walk, Root stopped several feet away.

"Here is where we practice running, with a little twist. There's a thirty-foot long section of rope and a small section of PVC pipe in the bag. Drop them here, and I'll be right back."

Walking over to a large plastic storage shed next to the cyclone fence bordering the sidewalk, Root opened it and took out two large coffee cans with two sections of PVC pipe about three foot long cemented into each can. He carried them back to where Ryan was waiting. Setting one can down, Root said, "Take this other can and pace off about thirty yards and set it down. The primary kids only run twenty-five yards. Tie off one end of the rope to the first PVC section, run the rope through that five-inch section of PVC pipe, and then tie off the rope to the other coffee can pipe."

Seeing that Ryan seemed perplexed about the purpose of the rope through the small section of PVC, Root explained.

"Some of our kids are visually impaired. They hold on to the small section of pipe and run. The PVC guides them as they run."

Ryan was intrigued by this, but his curiosity was really piqued by Root's explanation of the small battery-operated beeper at the bottom of the bag.

"This baby is for our hearing-impaired kids. The trick is to get everyone to be quiet when they run. You'll run ahead of them, sounding the beeper every few seconds. The kids run toward the sound. Simple, huh?" said Root.

The ringing of the school bell alerted Root that school was out for recess.

"OK, they're on the way. It's a little bit like herding cats at first, but Eva and Sharon have a schedule of what each kid is supposed to practice. We do the rest."

"How long does practice last?" asked Ryan.

"Until an hour before the buses arrive. We only practice three events because of the kid's ages." replied Root.

Good, Ryan thought, *plenty of time to see his mom and still finish packing for the next day's assignment.*

The therapist aide, Sharon, soon appeared with a clipboard in hand. She called out each child's name and where they were supposed to stand.

"Billy, Susie, Carrie, and Matty, stand here by the baseball throw. Missy, George, Arty, and Sammy stand by Ryan for running. Danny, Marty, Gertrude, and Jack, you guys go to Willie for standing jump."

With a collective scream of excitement as if the gates to "It's a Small World" at Disneyland had just opened, the children hurried to their assigned places.

"You'll handle the running, Sharon will do the standing jump, and I'll take the softball throw," Root told Ryan.

Looking at the foursome awaiting his instruction, Ryan asked timidly, "Do I use a stopwatch, and what do I actually coach them to do?"

Root laughed at his partner's shyness.

"Simple as pie, Buddy. Say, 'On your mark, get set, go.' Then lots of encouragement. Effort is everything; time means nothing."

Ryan soon saw the wisdom in Root's instructions. He put his four charges in a line.

"Are we ready!" he asked with planned excitement.

Missy shouted above the others, "Let's run! Let's run!" George, one of the three visually impaired students in the class, echoed Missy. He teetered precariously forward and back, straining to see the finish line through thick black horn-rimmed glasses. If his mental impairments weren't enough of a challenge, little Arty suffered from crippling osteoarthritis. His legs were horribly bowed, and he walked stooped forward. Standing without falling was difficult, much less running. He hollered, "Ready!" Sammy, the only African American child, stood next to Missy. Oversize bib overalls shrouded his obese body. His malformed jawbone hampered speech development. Sammy's smile was his way of communicating. He smiled a lot with Ryan coaching him.

"Okay then, when I say 'Go,' run to where I'll be standing."

Ryan walked to the end of the thirty-foot rope, then hollered back to them, "Ready, Set, Go!"

The children's efforts at running resembled a fast walk more than a run. Like George and Arthur, some had no stamina and took several stops to catch a somewhat exaggerated breath rate. Sam, almost eleven, had few ambulatory issues and finished first. Missy, on the other hand, took a few steps and fell flat on her face. She rolled to one side and struggled to her feet. She took a few more steps and fell again. This pattern was repeated numerous times until she reached Ryan and the other kids at the end.

Adhering to Willie's advice, Ryan told all the kids that they did great. Somewhat doubting his words, Missy announced, "I fell a lot, didn't I, Coach Ryan. I tried my best, but I just kept falling."

"Not a problem, Missy, you ran great. Let's do it again."

With more shouts of approval, the kids walked back to the

starting line. The results of their second attempt were much the same as the first. Focusing on Missy, Ryan noticed that Missy moved her leg with the brace straight forward when she tried to run. This motion caused her foot to catch on the grass and resulted in her falling forward. The prolonged time it took Missy to get to the end gave Ryan time to assess Missy's running. He had an idea. Ryan knelt down next to Missy.

"Missy, when you run, I want you to swing your leg out. Don't move it straight forward. Like this," he said.

Ryan stood up and swung his leg out to the side and then forward several times for Missy to see. Missy watched. From the expression on her face, the connection between mind and muscle had not been made. Ryan said, "Let me move your leg, Okay?"

With a smiling nod, Ryan gently placed one hand on Missy's ankle and the other on her shoulder. He moved the leg out to the side a few inches, then slowly arched it forward. He repeated this several times.

"Now, you stand still and try it."

Unsure of her balance, Missy held Ryan's hand and repeated the sequence. With each effort came words of praise and encouragement from Ryan.

"That's great. Let's try the run one more time."

Ryan lined the kids up, and this time stood by their side.

"Ready, set, go!"

For the first four steps, Missy did fine. No stumbling, no falling. Then her tiny mind seemed to forget Ryan's instructions, and she fell. He was immediately at her side, lifting her up.

"That's it," he found himself shouting. "Keep it up!"

And so, the little girl did, falling two more times before getting to the finish line.

Exhilarated, she screeched with the excitement of a child seeing Mickey Mouse at Disneyland, "I ran, didn't I? I ran!"

"Yes, you did, Missy. You ran!" cheered Ryan, who unexpectedly found himself kneeling down and giving the child a hug.

For Ryan Callahan, a new world had opened up before him, a world of Herculean efforts where running times meant nothing, where the standing jump success was measured in the smallest of increments, and the softball toss was where the throw was just as likely to go left or right as straight ahead. This was a world where success was measured in the effort and not the result. He would be changed forever.

8

THE ARROGANCE OF WEALTH

He raged when he read the letter. Who in the hell did she think she was threatening to take him to court for child support? The threat of being sued meant nothing to Trevor Barrington. His family had a wealth of attorneys to deal with such matters. What angered him was the emergence of what he had considered a mere dalliance with an old college girlfriend at a time when he needed to focus all of his attention and energy on his future. There had been an option she could have taken to end the unwanted pregnancy. It was her decision not to take it, and as far as Trevor Barrington was concerned, she owned the consequences of that decision, not he.

Ask the average South Carolinian if they recognize the name "Paris Barrington," and they'd probably say he was some soap opera villain. Now, if your income exceeded three commas, your answer would be completely different. Paris Barrington was a billionaire developer of global gated conclaves for the rich and famous. His latest project would only add to his long list of pedigreed creations. A pedigree that his son, Trevor

Barrington, was most anxious to see completed to feed his Machiavellian plan for success.

Barrington's private residence was a posh twenty-acre estate in Port Royal, South Carolina, though working from his New York headquarters rarely allowed him to spend more than a day or two there every couple of weeks. His son, Trevor, had attended the prestigious Porter-Gaud Prep School in Charleston. Like his father, he had enrolled in Furman University, a benefit of his father's money rather than his own academic abilities. Despite two drug rehab episodes, the younger Barrington managed to graduate and, with his father's influence, was accepted into the MBA program at Furman. The Barringtons had one child, something for which Hildegard Barrington had been eternally grateful. Had it been a girl, she would have been pressured to have another child and maybe another until she had provided Paris with a male offspring to carry on the Barrington name. With enough money for a live-in nanny and boarding schools from the age of ten, her son was more of a stranger than a treasured gift from God.

That morning Paris Barrington had a meeting with his head of project development, Arthur Ashcroft, at "The Towers," Barrington's corporate office in Columbia, South Carolina. His penthouse apartment afforded him the opportunity to spend fourteen hours a day on his work and to avoid those incredibly insincere goodbye "air kisses" from his wife in the morning. The private elevator accessed a large conference room with ceiling to floor windows and the most incredible view of Charleston Bay. When Paris exited the elevator, he found his son, Trevor, and Ashcroft waiting for him.

"The caterer sent these up for you," Trevor said, referring to a cart with freshly brewed Colombian coffee and an array of fresh fruits and yogurt.

Paris had always had the internal discipline to take care of himself, something his son lacked, to his eternal disappointment. His terse response hardly acknowledged his son's presence.

"Coffee and a Chobani."

Arthur Ashcroft studied his boss, trying to gauge his readiness to discuss a mega-development project with him, much less his son's anticipated role in the project. Paris Barrington had a reputation for being short on pleasantries. His looks only added to that reputation. He preferred to wear black suits with a narrow purple tie. Entirely gray since the age of thirty-five, his hair was stylishly trimmed short. He wore black horn-rimmed glasses, which he repeatedly took on and off when concentrating. He had a rather chiseled face and a pronounced proboscis. Nearly six feet tall, his slight frame only added to his Gothic appearance.

He walked over to the display of his latest project, taking off his glasses and holding them in his hand. There was little sign of the awkward movement in his right leg, which he had developed as a youth, resulting from a series of childhood seizures. The symptoms only appeared if he was on his feet for long periods of time. The muscles in his face tensed as he slowly walked around the ten square foot model, looking for that "what if" possibility that might ruin the project. You didn't enter into the company of the world's wealthiest billionaires by assuming others had done their jobs. After his review, he was pleased conceptually. The ten-story luxury hotel was the cornerstone of the development. He loved the placement of luxurious custom homes and condos lining what would surely be a championship golf course. The two-story shopping mall would rival Rodeo Drive in Hollywood. Every high-end retailer from Tiffany's to Versace was lining up for secured sales space.

"Your thoughts?" Arthur asked. Despite his years of association with Paris Barrington, Ashcroft still found it difficult to gauge the man. He kept his thoughts to himself, making any sense of collaboration impossible.

With a noticeable gleam of self-adulation, Barrington smirked, "This should certainly trump that alligator-infested swamp called Mar-a-Lago." Barrington had an immense disdain for its developer. The two had been bitter business rivals for years. Whereas Barrington let the presence of the family name speak for itself, his business nemesis, the self-anointed "King of the Deal," was ubiquitous in newspapers and publications surrounding his developments.

With the lack of any critical comments, Ashcroft's confidence rose. Only two small stumbling blocks remained, which he was sure were of no consequence. Always the man in the background, Ashcroft made sure his name and picture were in newspapers and on the news as the frontman for the "Nirvana" project. He had grown tired of being referred to as "Barrington's second hand." He wanted public admiration for this project for himself. But this time, Arthur Ashcroft had a different agenda. One which would require a different public face.

"Where are you in securing the properties I need?" Barrington said, sipping his coffee, now sufficiently cool to drink.

Barrington's imperious nature had drained the energy from many who had worked for him over the years. Like a human sponge, he had an insatiable appetite for his ego to be fed. Everything was "I" when it came to Paris Barrington. Much to the senior Barrington's surprise, it was his son who picked up a small remote control and pressed the "on" button. On the far wall, a fifteen-foot screen rolled down the wall. Every property needed to complete "Nirvana" was delineated by dotted lines and colored, green indicating it was secured and red if unsecured. Trevor stood confidently before his father. He had spent months studying the project under the tutelage of Arthur Ashcroft. This was his opportunity to prove to his father that he had the acumen and shrewdness to be part of this endeavor.

"Father, if I might interject at this point. I have worked

closely with Arthur for the past months on this project. I know it almost as well as he does."

A confident smile spread across his face. The son would apply even more adoration for his ego-driven father.

"You have created a business empire second to none. You are revered by some and feared by others as a great financier. If I'm to ever to follow in your footsteps, I need an opportunity to demonstrate to you my capabilities."

His indulgent words struck a note with his father. A nod from Ashcroft to the elder Barrington secured Trevor's opportunity. The father took a seat and replied caustically, "Show me."

With his laser pen, Trevor pointed to several units colored red.

"These are all small to medium family ranches, none of which are under the Williamson Act. Once we put the right price on the table, they'll sell," said a confident son.

Paris Barrington pointed to a sizeable five-acre parcel in the upper right corner of the proposed development.

"And this one?" he asked.

Trevor chose his words carefully. If his father knew his preemptive efforts had already failed, the young Barrington would be relegated to a mere office boy for the rest of his life, and he had too much at stake to have that happen.

"This one may be problematic, father," he answered. "It may give us some difficulty. But I know I can do this, father. You can count on me."

His eyes focused on his father like laser beams, steeled in determination to succeed. It was a trait his father had used over the years. Almost satanic in its influence, the gaze paralyzed those he confronted into submission. Paris Barrington had become a victim of himself.

"Yes, of course, you can," Paris said as if he had awoken from a trance. "

Trevor continued.

"It's an assisted living facility with almost two hundred residents. The place offers independent living apartments, assisted living areas, skilled nursing, and a memory care unit. The place is called Magnolia Gardens."

"What's the corporate structure?" Barrington asked, more interested in the business model than the trivial matter of the displacement of aged residents. The sheer scope of "Nirvana" had forced Paris Barrington to borrow extensively from several of the wealthiest union pension funds in the nation, not to mention the millions invested by dozens of venture capitalists. This project had to succeed. He had been so confident in its success; Barrington had avoided the more traditional approach to financing the project through municipal bonds and other sources of public monies. He chose instead to use borrowed private money. Unlike public financing, where he could default and leave the public to deal with the consequences, his sources would demand payment, no matter what.

Despite being leery that his son had the business acumen to handle the acquisition of these last two pieces of property, Paris Barrington succumbed to his son's guile.

~

TREVOR BARRINGTON WAS NOT BORN in the south. He had little appreciation for the devotion to family that runs deep in many multi-generational families south of the Mason-Dixon line. He had been raised in the affluence of Darien, Connecticut. His parents enrolled him in Porter-Gaud Prep School in Charleston, intent on Trevor eventually attending Furman, an exclusive private university in South Carolina. He attained his bachelor's degree in economics and a subsequent MBA. Upon graduation, Trevor had joined his father's development company. Those early years were spent struggling to live up to the Barrington name. Projects such as Nirvana required patience and the skill to read people. Both were virtues Trevor Barrington lacked. He preferred relying on being Paris Barrington's son for success rather than hard work. But young Barrington was not stupid. He knew that at some point, he would have to show his father that he was more than capable of assuming greater responsibilities. Paris Barrington was hesitant to give his son the lead in property acquisitions for his newest project, but with Ashcroft's assurance, he allowed Trevor to handle such matters. When it came to dealing face to face with people, people like Cletus Edwards, Trevor Barrington was at a distinct disadvantage. A man of simple tastes, Cletus's simple manner and homespun wisdom was a perfect foil for the inflated ego of Trevor Barrington.

~

CLETUS EDWARDS' two hundred acres was critical to the success of Paris Barrington's mega-development, almost as critical as the much smaller parcel some assisted living facility occupied. Arthur Ashcroft's senior assistant, Sidney Melton, had failed in three previous meetings with Cletus Edwards to reach an agreement for the sale of Edwards' property. Unusual for Melton, who had an uncanny ability to find that hidden thread of greed in prospective sellers. The silver Bugatti proceeded down the delta highway. Charleston Bay inlet on the right, and acres of farmland to the left. A sea breeze created constant lapping of white caps against the levee's side. That same breeze blew a shimmering sea of green silage intended to feed Edwards' three hundred head of dairy cattle. Beyond that were two hundred acres of farmland divided into sugar beets, soybeans, and wheat.

Good God, could this possibly be the right place? Trevor Barrington thought to himself, referring to a sign that read, "Edwards Road."

He slowed long enough to double-check his GPS, then turned. The rhythmic hum of the Bugatti's Michelin tires on the highway soon gave way to the crumbling monotony of tires on a gravel-based country road. The dusty rooster tail created by the sports car was a built-in alarm system alerting Edwards of company. A mile away on a rising knoll stood Cletus Edwards's home, originally built by Cletus's father, Preston Edwards.

The land was once considered to be unfarmable due to the constant flooding of winter storms and hurricanes. Preston Edwards never made it out of high school, but he was intuitively brilliant. He was the son of a sharecropper who worked twelve-hour days, six days a week, and still barely managed to make ends meet. Preston inherited his father's work ethic and his mother's ability to squeeze a nickel into a dime, a perfect combination. At sixteen, Preston began driving a truck for a local cotton processing plant. He saved every nickel and penny he made. By his twenty-first birthday, he bought two more trucks, and by the time he was twenty-five, he had a small fleet of trucks. He was going to be more than just the son of a sharecropper. By the early thirties, he knew that FDR's effort to employ a chronically out-of-work population in public works projects would likely result in massive levee construction throughout the south. Gambling every dollar he had saved plus taking advantage of newly available low-interest government loans for farmers, Preston secured some two hundred acres of delta bottomland. Eventually, those levees created the richest farming soil around and the beginnings of Edwards Farms, Inc.

~

HAZEL EDWARDS WATCHED the approaching car from her kitchen window. The dishes could wait. Placing the towel over her shoulder, she walked out to the front porch. Her husband,

Cletus, was enjoying a glass of iced tea, a reward for repairing a leaky kitchen sink.

"Another stranger taking a wrong turn?" she asked, closely monitoring the approaching rooster tail of dust.

Slow to answer, yet habitually polite as was his ingrained manner, Cletus uttered, "No, Ma'am. I believe it's someone from that Barrington company wanting to buy our farm."

She groaned, having grown weary of such calls repeatedly over the last several months. "Another one of those bankers trying to get his talons in our land." Cletus was reserved and gentle. His spouse was anything but gentle.

Preston Edwards had always regretted not finishing high school, much less college. He wished there had been money to send his boys to college. Instead, Preston passed on to his sons every bit of knowledge he had amassed over the years. By their early twenties, both boys knew much about the growth of foreign markets, the profitability of having your own processing and distribution facilities, mechanization, and the maze of government subsidies needed to hedge against falling prices. To judge Cletus Edwards by his appearance would be a costly mistake. Behind the white shirt with sleeves rolled up to the elbows, suspenders holding up his tan work pants and supporting a noticeable potbelly, was a mind keen on the science and finances of corporate farming.

Rising from his rocker and adjusting the wide suspenders supporting his work pants, he walked to the porch's handrail. Nothing in his simple mannerisms or appearance would reflect the natural cunning this man possessed. As the silver Bugatti came to a stop, the first thing that raised Cletus's curiosity was what kind of a man drives a car whose door opens straight up? The second mistake the driver made was dressing like he was making a presentation to the Board of Directors of some company instead of meeting a man more rooted in judging a man by the grit in his eyes and the strength of his handshake.

Edwards had expected an older man, silver-haired and wearing glasses, not this youngster who more resembled a model in some magazine.

After sizing the man up for a few moments, he greeted the corporate piranha in a seemingly friendly, homespun manner.

"Welcome to our little farm, Mr. Barrington."

Trevor buttoned his $400 Armani suit coat, then gently tapped his Versace shoes on the flagstaff walkway. His black leather valise hung from his shoulders.

"Trevor Barrington and thank you," smiled Barrington, extending his hand to Edwards.

As they shook hands, Edwards made a mental note; *smooth hands, no callouses.* Cletus had sealed many a deal with a handshake on his front porch. Though he had no intention of making any deal with his visitor, he would extend him the courtesy of a chair to sit on and a glass of sweet tea.

"Let's sit on the porch. Too nice a day to be inside," Cletus said, leading his visitor up the four steps to a spacious wraparound lanai, something Hazel had insisted on when they had the family home remodeled some years back.

Cletus sat in his customary rocking chair and began a slow rhythmic back and forth motion. He prepared his mind to hear a proposal to sell his property, one that he had heard and rejected three times before.

"My wife has brewed up a batch of sweet tea, and I would be happy to share a tall glass with you."

"Thank you so much," responded Barrington, trying to be hospitable at the thought of drinking his least favorite beverage.

Unintentional or not, Cletus was deftly preparing a clever trap for the young Barrington, a man whose hubris would quickly become his undoing.

"Mother, could you bring Mr. Barrington and me a couple of sweet teas with plenty of ice?"

Mother Edwards was a typically hospitable southern belle, but she bristled at the thought of serving his man. Without responding, Hazel Edwards turned and returned to the kitchen.

Barrington tried to make himself comfortable in the tall back wooden chair next to a small wooden table made from a slab of Magnolia wood. Unlike Cletus's rocker, which had seat and back cushions, Barrington's chair was bare hardwood. The small table was nowhere near big enough for him to display the financial reports he had prepared. As he momentarily stared at it, Cletus seemed to enjoy the puzzled look on the young man's furrowed brow. Hazel used her foot to open the screen door. She had a tray with two tall glasses of her homemade sweet tea and a small plate with freshly baked cornbread muffins. Now to Barrington's dismay, there was even less room to display his financial manipulations.

"I'm sure you must be hungry," Hazel said, smiling at Barrington as she set the muffins on the table. "And these should quench your thirst," she added, setting the two glasses of sweet tea next to the muffins. Hazel walked over to Cletus and kissed him on the forehead.

"I've got shopping to do, so I'll leave you to your guest."

She quickly disappeared into the house, seemingly interested in other things. But before she left, Barrington moved to display uncommon civility. Attempting to stand up, the legs of his chair caught on the edge of a small rug it rested on, causing him to stumble backward. Hazel was not someone to relish in an other's misfortune, but she could not help but be amused by this man's clumsy behavior.

She managed to say, "Don't bother, Mr. Barrington. You just enjoy your tea and muffins," Hazel replied to an obviously embarrassed Barrington.

Cletus chuckled to himself. His father had taught him to keep his business adversaries distracted as a means of keeping them off balance. The stiff-backed chair and rug had worked perfectly. Cletus unwrapped a muffin and took a bite. He closed his eyes and tilted his head skyward as the muffin dissolved in his mouth.

"Heaven, sheer heaven, Mr. Barrington," he moaned. "You should try yours while they're warm," he said, playing the country bumpkin with consummate skill.

Not wanting to appear unappreciative, Barrington began to peel off the paper muffin cup. Hazel had placed a pad of butter on each muffin top, which had melted down the sides of the muffin. The melted butter made removing the paper cup quite messy. He brought the muffin to his mouth and took a carefully measured bite. Despite holding his hand under the muffin to catch any falling crumbs, the inevitable happened. Several butter-soaked crumbs landed on his lap. He awkwardly tried to brush them aside, only to exacerbate the stains on his pants. This was Cletus's opening.

"So, Mr. Barrington, you didn't drive all the way out here just to enjoy the farm and relax on my porch. You look like a man with 'land' on your mind."

"As a matter of fact, I am Cletus. I can call you, Cletus?"

"Absolutely, Trevor, or do you prefer Trev?" Cletus replied, assuming the familiarization of Barrington's formal name would be bothersome to him. Cletus was right. Barrington cleared his throat before answering with a lie.

"If you prefer."

The young Barrington was clearly backpedaling, and Cletus hadn't even gotten started.

Barrington picked up his valise, which rested on the deck of the porch next to his chair. Trevor placed it on his lap, loosened the straps, and withdrew a thick folder. At first, he looked for space on the small table to display the multitude of reports. Seeing there was none, he rested the file on his lap. Tapping the file with his fingers, Barrington began his doomed presentation.

In his usual deft manner, he was unaware that his ploy was already doomed.

"Cletus, what I've prepared for your consideration is a debt to profit analysis of your farm's worth, taking into account an appraisal of the land's worth, current contracts, projected income for the next five years; factoring in optimal weather conditions, the value of all existing mechanized machinery, processing and distribution facilities and the assumption of all existing debts."

The work had been complied by others who gave the young Barrington a cursory though adequate summary of its contents. He thrust the file into Cletus's hands in what he considered to be an act of triumph.

"My father's company is prepared to offer you twice the value of all your assets."

Cletus looked at Barrington with the mournful eyes of a basset hound.

"Goodness, Trev, this land is all I have to pass along to my children and their children. It's their heritage. Is twice its value really enough?"

His throat cracked with artificial emotion as he slowly reeled in his company like a barker at the country fair.

"May I have that file back?" he asked while taking a pen from his jacket pocket.

Cletus complied. Barrington scribbled a note on the file and signed it. Handing it back to Cletus, he said, "This number should help satisfy your doubts."

He had written, "Three times the assessed value."

Satisfied he had toyed with him enough, Cletus said, "There's something I want to give you, Trev."

Cletus excused himself and went inside. Within moments, he returned, carrying a large manila envelope.

"This is a report I've compiled of my farm's value and the

price I've set on it. Why don't you look at it, and we'll talk later?"

So, the old man has a price, Trevor thought. *They all do.*

Confident the deal was done, Barrington said, "Deal, Cletus," and extended his hand to Edwards.

After shaking hands, Trevor thanked Cletus for his time and walked down the steps to his Bugatti. He turned back for one last wave before getting into the car. Cletus reciprocated as he watched the Italian sports car head down the gravel road to the highway. On his way back into the house, Cletus dropped Barrington's report into the trash can. Once back on the highway, Barrington opened Cletus's envelope. He took out a single piece of paper and read it.

"This land is the history of my family going back three generations. It is the future history for generations to come of Edwards' children. Its value is priceless."

A crumpled piece of paper flew out the driver's window of the Bugatti as it increased its speed.

9

THE MISSION

As he pulled into the parking lot behind Police Headquarters, Ryan Callahan parked his truck. The light mist from a dense fog necessitated Callahan using his wipers on low. The flapping ends of rubber on both wipers were a stark reminder to get new wipers before the existing wiper blades etched the glass. As he exited his truck, Ryan felt the bone-chilling cold. A moonless night shrouded in dark rain-bearing clouds and the falling mist would make this operation very uncomfortable. He hurried up the back steps, then swiped his ID card through the security slot on the wall. Once inside, he waved to the duty officer assigned to the rear entrance and then headed down the hallway to the Drug Task Force office. Remembering his words about being on time, the one face he hoped not to see as he opened the door was Willie Root. Ryan smiled more because of Root's absence than the greeting of his fellow team members.

"Callahan, this is for you. Make your notes accordingly," said Sergeant Knight, handing him a printout of the pier. As he scanned the document, noting the location of the numbered berths and building numbers, the door opened, and Root made his arrival.

"Root," Knight called out. "This is for you. Your partner already has his."

Root nodded, then sat down next to Callahan. Without looking up from the diagram, Root said, "Now you're on time."

Ryan smiled to himself. He studied the diagram Sergeant Knight had given him. By name, Knight had indicated where each man of his team was to position himself. Ryan would be positioned atop the last building directly across from 10B, the berth for the La Novia. Root was assigned a position on the ground directly below Ryan. He would wear a windbreaker with lettering on the back reading "Port Security." Such men were commonplace on the docks and would not draw unwarranted attention.

Every operation of the Drug Task Force had an inherent danger to it. Serious injury and even death was a possibility. But this assignment had an added element of danger, considering the team would be facing a ruthless and murderous South American drug cartel. Savage brutality and senseless bloodshed was their trademark. As each man studied his handout, their minds ignored the omnipresent thought of *what if*. The silence of such mortal thoughts was broken with the entry of Lieutenant Red Caruthers and DEA agent Jerry Sloan. Sloan spoke first. His demeanor was in stark contrast to his easygoing style in their preliminary planning session.

"You all have your diagrams, right?" he asked authoritatively.

Some nodded. Others held up their copies.

"Good. Let's proceed. Outside is a Port Authority ten-passenger van. There are Port Authority jackets for everyone except for Reed and Callahan—as snipers, you won't need them. Sergeant Olson, you drive. At the west gate, drop off your designated gate personnel. Proceed down the wharf intermittently dropping off those wearing Port Authority jackets, leaving the last two men for the east gate. Then proceed around the back of Building #10 and drop off Callahan, then to the back of Building #1 and drop off Reed. Callahan and Reed, there are exterior access stairs for you to make your way to the rooftop. Lieutenant Caruthers, myself, and Sergeant Knight will be right behind the van in a modified unmarked DEA SUV."

Looking at Knight, Sloan added, "Sergeant, that vehicle has every electronic and communication device known to mankind. You'll be monitored by a Coast Guard Shore Security Force and additional DEA resources."

Knight savored the opportunity to work with such sophisticated equipment. Sloan was anxious to finish his final briefing, but he knew every detail was essential and not to rush for the sake of expediency.

"This is most important, men. You on the west gate pay particular attention to any vehicle entering before the La Novia docking at twenty-two hundred hours. Once the ship docks, lower the gate barrier, lock it, and carefully make your way down the wharf to berth 10B. We don't know what to expect, so be suspect of anything and everything. Lt. Caruthers, do you have anything to add?"

"Communications will be critical. Reed and Callahan, your night vision goggles are our eyes in the sky. I want a SITREP (situation report) every five minutes from your locations."

Never one for sentimentality, Caruthers added, "Lastly, I want to see every one of your ugly mugs Monday morning, so be careful."

Looking at his wristwatch, Caruthers said, "Alright, I have 2024. On my mark, 2025." He watched the second hand on his watch move agonizingly slow until it reached 2025. "Mark."

Sloan withdrew his Glock from its holster. He grabbed the slide with his thumb and forefinger, drew it back, and racked a round. Reholstering it, he announced, "Load up!"

Sloan's operation plan started without a hitch. Sergeant Olson dropped off Harrison and Woodson at the entrance gate. Midway down the mile-long wharf, he dropped off Edwards, Hanson, and Popkey in their Port Security jackets. Driving slowly, Olson reached the east exit gate, where he dropped off Ortega and Hodgner. Turning right past the gate, he drove behind the long line of warehouses, dropping off Callahan first and then Reed at the end. At the end of the line of warehouses, Olson turned right and parked next to the black SUV containing Sloan, Caruthers, and Sergeant Knight. After a few minutes, Sloan turned to the back of the vehicle, where Knight was seated in front of a panel of radios and computer screens. "Now, Sergeant." Knight nodded, then spoke into his microphone headset.

"Key your radio once if you are in position."

A series of clicks came over the radio.

"Now we wait," said Sloan.

The massive lighting system did its best to illuminate the wharf despite the moonless night's dark clouds and misting rain. Neither Callahan nor Reed needed their night vision goggles, not yet, at least. Reed spotted the freighter first.

"She's here," he said softly into his radio.

The La Novia moved slowly down the deep draft channel. As she neared berth 10B, her captain angled her slowly to the right. After a series of forward and backward movements, the ship came to a rest. Almost immediately, its cranes, under direction from a ground supervisor, began unloading the first of a dozen cargo containers. Ordinarily, this would take about twelve hours, but the ground supervisor was only interested in the first container, XQ-109.

Watching from the bridge, the captain smiled. His work would soon be done. He took out his cell phone, pressed contacts, then favorites.

"Esta Abajo."

The call set in motion another operational plan. Two white cargo vans approached the western gate. Mike Harrison stepped out of the booth with a clipboard in hand.

"May I ask your destination, sir?" he asked.

"My crew is headed to building 10B, a small pick up job," the man replied with a smile, hoping to ease any apprehension on the gate guard's part.

It didn't work. The answer triggered an alert in Harrison.

Stepping out of the gate booth, Harrison waved the man and his vehicles through. "Last building on your right, sir. Can't miss it." Back inside, he told his partner, Barry Woodson, "They're here." Woodson grabbed his radio and notified Sergeant Knight.

Once the two vans reached the area adjacent to berth 10B, the driver picked up his radio.

"Ahora!"

At that moment, an accomplice positioned a block away from the electrical power transfer station started his car. As he approached the transfer station, he stopped. He quickly exited his vehicle and threw a package the size of an adobe brick over the fence. As he drove away, he detonated the package containing C4. The massive fireball lit up the sky. The port went dark.

~

HARRISON AND WOODSON immediately exited the gate booth, guns drawn, searching the darkness for any sign of danger. Ortega and Hodgner did the same at the east gate. Callahan and Reed immediately activated their night vision goggles, scanning up and down the wharf. Lieutenant Caruthers immediately shouted into his headset.

"Be alert, be alert. Emergency power will take four to five minutes to kick in. It's going down."

Callahan's hand tightened on his Barrett M82 sniper rifle. His eyes focused intently through his goggles. There it was, right in front of him on the ground. Four men, dressed in dark attire, had opened the door to a cargo van and were hastily throwing large duffel bags into the two vans.

Callahan spoke urgently into his headset, "Red, my POS (position). I make out at least six men, probably armed, loading what looks to be duffel bags from a cargo unit into white vans."

"Everyone to the east gate! Now!" Caruthers hollered into his headset. "Nobody leaves this wharf, understand!"

No response was necessary. All weapons were on ready. Eddy Popkey and Barry Woodson moved quickly and stealthily down the wharf. They were about fifty yards from the white vans when Caruthers radioed to hold their positions. Callahan wondered how much longer he would have to hold his fire. The captain of the La Novia had made his way down the gangplank to a parked Mercedes sedan waiting for him. He got inside. The keys were in the ignition. He drove slowly toward the gate, not wanting to attract unnecessary attention from the gate guards now standing outside their booth. One of the guards waved for him to stop. Rolling down his window, he asked what the problem was.

"We've lost electrical power, sir. No one is to leave until power is restored, and I'll need to see your ID."

With a chuckle meant to be reassuring, the captain said, "No problem. I've got it in the glove compartment. Emergency power will probably kick on soon."

As the glove department door flipped up, its small light exposed the handle of a handgun. As the captain's hand grasped its handle, Hodgner's partner yelled, "Gun." The captain was dead before his gun fell harmlessly to the floorboard. The sedan lurched forward, then stopped. The captain slumped against the steering wheel, blood gushing from his mouth. The gunfire alerted the men loading the vans to imminent danger. Through his goggles, Callahan could see them yelling at each other. Panic had set in. Through his headset, he could hear Sloan and Caruthers hollering instructions to the men.

"Police. Put your weapons down and get on the ground."

Repeated similar requests went unheeded. Three of the men pivoted and sprayed the area with deadly fire from their automatic rifles. Callahan's instincts took over. He quickly took out two of the three shooters, then focused on the three in front of the cargo unit. Two were dead before they hit the ground. The third had already dropped to the ground, hoping to survive the carnage that had cost two of his accomplices their lives.

Over his headset, Caruthers hollered, "Give me a headcount."

Everyone knew the absence of one name meant trouble.

"Find Root!" hollered Caruthers.

Callahan slung his rifle over his shoulder and raced to the stairs leading to the ground. The adrenaline rush blocked everything from his mind except to find his partner. With their weapons at the ready, Caruthers and the others moved with maximum speed down the wharf, pausing only to clear any open area between cargo units before proceeding. Red Caruthers moved with the determined purpose of a commander searching for a missing comrade. No one had ever died on his watch, and he wasn't about to let it happen now. He willed it not to happen. The other members of the Task Force hid their anxiety as they called out Root's name. Caruthers' voice bellowed through the darkness, "Root! Root!" A sudden movement to his right caught his attention. Just as quickly, he recognized Root's body next to a stack of wooden pallets. Ryan Callahan was at his side.

"Got him!" screamed Caruthers, using his flashlight to signal Root's location to the others.

Callahan had used his balaclava to slow the bleeding from a gaping hole in Root's left thigh.

"Willie, talk to me! Talk to me!" Callahan pleaded as he watched his partner's lifeblood seep through his fingers.

Knight dropped to his knees next to Root's body. He tore open his field medical kit. A trained paramedic, he quickly applied a compression bandage to the wound. He could feel a broken femur bone. His next move was to jab a morphine syrette into Root's thigh to relieve the pain. After checking Root's carotid artery, Knight said," He's lost a lot of blood, but he's got a strong pulse, Ryan. He's going to be OK.

The team allowed themselves a brief moment of relief before Sloan's voice interrupted their thoughts.

"I just got off the phone with the Port Authority. It seems someone in a black SUV tossed a package, probably C4, into the electrical yard supplying power to the harbor area. They're checking the security cameras now to ID the driver. It took about four minutes for the emergency generators to kick in. That was their window of opportunity. About a block away, police found a black SUV crashed off the road. The driver had been shot, but he's in stable condition at Charleston Memorial."

The wailing of the ambulance's siren announced their presence. Red Caruthers leaned against the side of the cargo unit, instinctively patting his jacket pocket for a pack of cigarettes, a habit he had quit twenty-five years ago.

"I don't know how much more of this shit I can take," he sighed.

Jerry Sloan looked at him.

"What? The fun's just beginning. Let's find out who these guys are!"

The mastermind behind the failed attempt to smuggle in cocaine had yet another plan for that dark night. With a moonless night and any light from a galaxy of stars hidden by dark clouds and low hanging fog, a black SUV proceeded down the levy road. When the farmlands owned by Cletus Edwards appeared on the right, the vehicle suddenly stopped. A figure quickly jumped out of the back seat and slid down the landward side of the levy. He used his hands to burrow a small indentation in the bank, pushed in a small package, and then hurried back to the waiting vehicle. Two hundred yards down the road, it happened again, and again, and again until nearly a thousand yards of levy road had passed.

The ominous silence of the darkness was shattered by a series of thundering explosions that woke anyone within miles of that section of the levy road, including Cletus and Hazel Edwards.

"Goodness gracious, Cletus, what was that?" Hazel gasped as she bolted upright in bed.

Cletus had already thrown off his covers and was standing at the bedroom window looking down from their hilltop house toward the levy highway. A minimalist when it came to words, Cletus responded, "Not good." He hurriedly put on his work pants and boots. Bare-chested, he moved as quickly as a man in his sixties could down the stairs. He grabbed a set of keys off the stand in the foyer and bolted out the door to his nearby Dodge truck. He had gone about fifty yards down the road leading to the highway when he slammed on his brakes. The roar of rushing water pushed the night air like a wind storm. He jumped out of his truck. Standing by the front grill, Edwards felt the rush of chilled air and the unmistakable odor of saltwater. He ran back to his truck and grabbed a high-powered LED lamp he carried for emergencies. Slowly moving it back and forth into the darkness, the devastation before him caused him to utter a heavenly cry, "Oh my God!" Millions of gallons of seawater were pouring across his farmland through several breaches in the levy road.

Within hours, only Edwards' house was spared, along with three storage facilities further up the hill. Knowing the farthest parts of his farm would not escape the flooding seawater, Cletus Edwards slumped against the hood of his truck. His life's work laid ravaged before him. The land his father and grandfather had farmed and that Cletus had hoped to pass along to his children was ruined. It could take years to undo the saline poison seeping into the soil. That dogged determination to overcome nature's forces, which every farmer has, now seemed like a mountain too high to climb, a river too wide to cross. Further down the road, the black SUV slowed down. The driver pulled out his cell phone.

"Dice a el nino que esta hecho!"

10

THE FACE OF GOLIATH

A bigail Strauss started her day as usual. As Sheldon Sutro's administrative assistant, her first duty of the day was to sort through Mr. Sutro's mail, review its contents and determine if a lower-level staffer could handle the issue. Starting as a paralegal, Abigail had worked for the firm for nearly thirty years, forsaking marriage and family for the pursuit of corporate status. In the eyes of the firm's fifty-plus associates, she was the real power behind the throne and literally controlled all access to the founding partners. After reading the letter from Matthew Adams, she immediately buzzed Sheldon Sutro on the intercom. Never assuming her years of service entitled her to use first names, she said, "Mr. Sutro, I have something here that I think needs your personal attention."

"Certainly, Abigail. Please come in."

Befitting his position as founder of Sutro, Bellow, and Finestein, Sheldon Sutro's office reigned over New York City as if he were Zeus sitting atop Mount Olympus. On a clear day, the view from the thirtieth floor of the Barrington Towers extended from the Hudson River on the west to Long Island

and the Statue of Liberty on the east. The corner office's twelve-foot ceiling with glass windows on two sides made the entrance seem like one was stepping out to the very edge of the world.

Abigail Strauss's attire was a bit Gothic in appearance by her own choice. She kept her long brown hair pulled back into a carefully woven bun. Nearly fifty years old, she had managed to keep a somewhat shapely appearance even with the unavoidable few extra pounds aging brought. Makeup could not hide the crow's feet in the corners of her eyes. Complete with a neutral shade of lipstick, Abigail Strauss bore a remarkable resemblance to the woman in Grant Wood's iconic *American Gothic*. She was obsessed with a regimen of tasteless health food, vegetables, and Chobani yogurt. Her standard choice of professional wear was a black or dark blue pants suit, professionally fitted, with gold buttons engraved with the firm's initials on the jacket. Her black-rimmed reading glasses hung from a twenty-four-karat gold chain she could not afford to buy. She was never without her Franklin Day Planner. She rarely hurried, preferring to walk with a determined gait accentuated by the sound her Un Cosmo Step shoes made on the marble tile floor. Younger associates joked among themselves that she sounded like the Grim Reaper approaching.

Dutifully she knocked on the solid glass door of Sutro's office. He waved for her to enter. Pushing on the silver door bar, she approached his desk, standing off to the side like some confidant to a medieval king. She had Matthew Adams' correspondence in her hand.

"What is it, Abigail?"

"Mr. Barrington's son, Trevor, and that unpleasant incident several years ago. The young girl has retained an attorney and is seeking child support."

Sutro took the letter from her, reading it carefully. His firm had been bailing Trevor Barrington out of trouble since he was in prep school.

"I told Paris and his wife, Hildegard, to settle this matter and pay the young woman whatever she wanted. Hildegard was adamantly opposed to any payment. According to her, the young woman's situation was an embarrassment to the Barrington family's name. The boy received several letters from the woman seeking support. I advised Trevor not to reply."

At first, Sheldon Sutro seemed almost sympathetic to the woman's plight. Then the cold-hearted pragmatism of the ruthless attorney Sutro was famous for took over.

"What do we know about this Matthew Adams? What kind of an attorney is he?"

Strauss had done her homework.

"He's a graduate of the University of Alabama Law School. He opened his own practice several years ago, dealing mostly with the indigent and poor. As an aside, his grandfather is Morris Dees, the Southern Poverty Law Office Morris Dees."

A smirk came over Sutro's face. "Another do-gooder. What a waste of a law degree! So, Abigail, who do you suggest we assign this to?"

Having completed a recent review of each associates' annual performance evaluation for possible bonuses, the perfect person came to mind.

"Amanda Boyle. She's been with us for just over a year. Her boss describes her as dedicated, focused, detail-oriented, and hardcore when needed, with impeccable credentials. First in her class at Harvard Law, she was only the second woman since Susan Estrich to chair the Harvard Law Review."

"Fine," Sutro replied. "Make sure she understands I want her to execute every legal maneuver she can to squash this issue. Delay it under any pretense until this Matthew Adams gives up."

∼

AMANDA BOYLE often ate her lunch at her desk, not that she was opposed to the company of other associates. However, conversations about who got assigned what case, and gossip about who was up for the next partnership, bored her to death. In addition to different dreams, Amanda Boyle came from a completely contrary background to that of her blue blood peers. Their path to Sutro, Bellow, and Finestein started at exclusive prep schools and the country's most elite law schools. Amanda's biggest obstacle at Harvard wasn't her commoner background. It was her looks. She was tall for a woman, just over six feet tall, and her auburn hair had a natural sheen. She kept it long, causing a seductive sway whenever she walked. With that height came a model's body, high cheekbones offsetting sparkling green eyes, and a complexion needing nothing more than basic makeup to highlight her features. Amanda's inherited trait from her mother caused her brothers' numerous fights in high school over crude "tatas" remarks from more testosterone-laden adolescents than she cared to remember. Her stunning physical attributes gave rise to that "Good Ole Boy" speculation from her male counterparts that she would be on the short path to a partnership.

The last of five children and the only girl born to Peter and Katherine O'Boyle, Amanda was raised in South Boston, where her father owned a popular bar and buffet called "O'Boyle's." O'Boyle's was famous for its corn beef and cabbage and infamous for being a popular eatery for James "Whitey" Bulger, King of the Irish Mob in South Boston. Her two older brothers, Sean and Peter Jr, were part of Boston's finest. Sean was a detective, and Peter Jr., a lieutenant on the Boston Police Force. Ian was a special agent with the FBI. Michael, or Mickey as he was nicknamed by his brothers, helped his father run the family business.

Amanda had her brother's toughness of being a "Southie," a reference to a Boston neighborhood where disputes were just as likely to be settled with fists or guns. But she also had her mother's heart that rallied to the support of any underdog she read about or heard about. Upon graduation from law school, Amanda's passionate desire was to work for an international human rights organization. She had been inspired by the work of Princess Diana and Amal Clooney, wife of actor George Clooney. However, having amassed over eight hundred thousand dollars in student loans between undergraduate and law school, pragmatism, not idealism, ruled the day. The offer from Sutro, Bellow, and Finestein paid nearly three times what she had been offered by several human rights organizations. With hard work, a little luck, and saving every dollar she could, Amanda calculated she could have most of her student loan debt paid off in five years.

The irony that the cost of her dreams was steeped in pragmatism did not escape Amanda O'Boyle. However, it had been a long time since she lived in South Boston. During her undergraduate years, she took summer classes and had part times jobs for additional support. Three years at Harvard Law were not much different, though her mother made a painful observation on a rare visit home. On the drive home from a funeral for some second cousin on her mother's side of the family, her mother commented, "You seemed different today, honey," her mother said, as she maneuvered off the interstate from New Jersey where the funeral had taken place.

"I guess I wasn't very talkative, Mom, but I barely remember any of that side of the family."

Amanda's attention was more drawn to the deteriorating neighborhoods in the distance, neighborhoods much like the one she had called home.

"Oh, I didn't mean you didn't talk much. I mean, you sounded different when you talked. If I didn't know any better, I would have never guessed you were a Southie."

"Oh, Mom, I'll always remember my roots," Amanda said, her words half masking the truth of her mother's remarks.

Truth be told, Amanda O'Boyle had made a decision upon her arrival at Harvard, which would have crushed her mother, had she known. Her harsh Bostonian accent and quickness to respond aggressively, sometimes too aggressively, drew negative attention to her in seminar classes. Amanda was looked down on by some students who conveyed an unsaid message that she belonged at Fitchburg State College, but not the hallowed halls of a prestigious Ivy League school like Harvard. Losing her pronounced accent and dropping the "O" from her last name were the first steps in her transformation to prove she belonged. A beep from the phone on her desk caused her to put the last of her sandwich down. Amanda saw the name "Strauss." She dabbed the edges of her mouth with a paper napkin and picked up the phone.

"Amanda Boyle."

"Yes, Amanda, Abigail Strauss. Could you come to my office, please? I have an assignment for you from Mr. Sutro."

The name Sutro caused an immediate adrenaline rush in Boyle. Had her Harvard Law Degree finally warranted attention from the top, or was that "Good Ole Boy" speculation about to come true?

"I'm on my way, Ms. Strauss."

The ride up the elevator to Strauss's office was short, but sufficient time for her to ponder the reason for the call. Amanda's assignments were typically given to her by her supervising attorney, Harold Cutter. This was either the "Kiss of Death" meeting where she's told, "Thank you for your services...." or something very different from her standard assignments. She could not imagine how different.

∼

STEPPING OUT OF THE ELEVATOR, Amanda was greeted by Hazel Worthington, the longtime receptionist and heir apparent to Abigail Strauss when and if she ever retired. Unfortunately, Hazel Worthington flaunted all the presumed importance she felt befitted her position. On hearing the chime of the elevator door open, she looked up from her rather ordinary mahogany desk. Worthington wanted an area that, at least in appearance, would indicate a person of some importance worked there. She had managed to secure a small table and chair to simulate a waiting area. She had a desk extension added to her oversized computer screen. She detested the word receptionist, preferring to use the rather ostentatious phrase, "Office Director." Her failed attempt at self-aggrandizement resulted in behind-her-back ridicule from others. Preoccupied with establishing her own sphere of importance, Worthington had failed to acquaint herself with the associates' names and faces.

"May I help you?" she asked as Amanda approached her desk.

"I'm here to see Ms. Strauss," Amanda answered.

"One moment. I'll see if she's in. And your name is?"

Really, Amanda thought, *do you think I can't see her through the glass walls of her office?* She hated the stratified air at her firm, which, when breathed in, made the sycophants of the world feel superior.

"Amanda Boyle. I work here and oh! There she is in her office now. Thank you so much," replied Boyle.

She walked right past Worthington, leaving her fumbling with the numbers of her desk phone to alert Strauss of her presence. Unlike her male counterparts, Amanda had no fear of Abigail Strauss. Growing up with four brothers, she was well acquainted with the art of intimidation, something Strauss had perfected to an art. Amanda pushed the glass door open without knocking and announced, "You wanted to see me, Abigail?"

Without looking up from the papers she was pursuing, Strauss replied, "Yes, Amanda, have a seat."

She took a chair at an expensive Victorian desk that Strauss felt added to her status.

"Mr. Sutro has a very sensitive matter he wants you to handle," Strauss said, holding the envelope from Matthew Adams.

"Well, let's take a look at this sensitive matter," Boyle said.

Boyle remained seated, forcing Strauss to get up from her desk and bring the papers to her rather than vice-versa. This was Amanda's perfect and subtle example of the art of intimidation. Strauss's face grimaced at this ever so subtle but obvious slight. After handing the envelope to Boyle, Strauss returned to her chair behind her desk, akin to a throne from which she ruled. She gave Amanda several minutes to look over the documents before speaking.

"Mr. Sutro would like you to make this matter disappear, through whatever means necessary. It concerns Trevor Barrington, the son of Mr. Sutro's close friend, Paris Barrington."

Sensing Strauss knew more than she was saying, Amanda asked, "Are you familiar with this matter?"

Sheldon Sutro valued Abigail Strauss for her organizational skills. What he valued more was her ability to keep secret the firm's indiscretions, both moral and ethical. She would not betray that confidence.

"The matter is over seven years old. I really can't recall."

"Well, just looking at this letter, I can tell you that this young woman, Mary T. Pinafore, is claiming that Trevor Barrington, no doubt Paris Barrington's son, is the father of her child, a Melissa Pinafore, age seven."

Amanda waited to see what kind of reaction her speculation would generate. Abigail Strauss remained unresponsive, her lips pursed, her eyes squinting in the face of Boyle's rather impudent language.

"If you don't recall the details of this situation, Abigail, who can I talk to who can enlighten me? I don't like surprises from opposing counsel."

"Such details are irrelevant at this point, Ms. Boyle. What you need to know is Mr. Sutro wants you to use the vast resources of this firm to bury this crusading neophyte in motions until he quits."

The ruthlessness of Strauss's words aroused a passion in Amanda. Staring Strauss directly in the face, there was a calm, almost defiant tone to her words.

"There is no such thing as an irrelevant detail, Abigail. I'll find out what I need to know."

Abigail Strauss and, by extension Sheldon Sutro had made a serious mistake.

~

AMANDA BOYLE STRODE across the tarmac to the Gulfstream G650 luxury jet awaiting her, a corporate perk of working at Sutro, Bellow, and Finestein. She was met at the bottom of the steps by a silver-haired man in a dark blue uniform suit, complete with golden epaulets and gold stripes at his sleeves. His white cap rested snugly on his head. He identified himself as Captain Stevens.

"May I take your briefcase for you, Ms. Boyle?"

"Thank you, Captain Stevens, but I can manage," she replied as she started up the boarding steps. She intended to use the hour and a half flight time to Charleston to research South Carolina Family Case Law. Amanda sat in one of the twin cushioned white leather chairs, a glass table in front of her as a work or dining space. The flight attendant presented her with a menu of in-flight meals from which to choose and a beverage list that included everything from the most expensive liquors to imported bottles of water. She set her briefcase in the empty chair and adjusted her seat belt. This was just one of the many benefits of working for a high-priced New York City law firm. In conjunction with everything else that went on at the firm, there were perks that could negatively affect one's value system. The lone flight attendant, a dark-skinned young man in his twenties named Armand, approached Amanda.

"May I get you a water, Ms. Boyle? Perhaps a bottle of Veen or Bling H20, or the favorite of Mr. Sutro himself, Fillico?" His tone was a bit pretentious, as if mimicking a waiter in some five-star restaurant.

With equal snobbery, Amanda replied, "Thank you, Armand, but I'd prefer a Coca Cola diet if you have it, in a bottle not can, and with a straw."

Keenly aware Boyle was mocking his waiter-like presentation of choices, Armand offered a quick apology. An embarrassed look came across his face. He bent slightly at the waist.

"Sorry if I sounded a bit snooty, Ms. Boyle. The bosses seem to like being treated that way."

Like most of her colleagues at Sutro, Bellow, and Finestein, Boyle had begun to feel her Harvard Law Degree entitled her to be treated like a divine emissary. However, a more profound feeling left her feeling guilty for talking down to the young man.

"No, it's I who should apologize to you, Armand. I seem to have forgotten my manners. Juxtaposed to how my peers want to be treated, my mother from South Boston would be appalled at my acting like I was from Beacon Hill."

A grin suddenly appeared on Armand's face. He turned his head quickly toward the cabin, then back to Boyle whispering, "Roxbury High."

With the glint of an Irish leprechaun in her eye, Boyle whispered back, "Jamaica Plain."

The two enjoyed a silent chuckle at their common backgrounds. Amanda now reassessed her attendant.

"Is flight attendant your career destination, or do you have higher aspirations?"

"God, no!" he replied. "I've had a lifetime of serving the pretentious and obnoxious. I started law school at Boston College last spring. This job pays really, really well, and law school costs a really, really lot of money."

Amanda nodded in agreement.

"Working at Sutro, Bellow, and Finestein will strengthen your resume."

Again, with a glance toward the cockpit, Armand looked back at Amanda, then pointed to a couple of lights on either side of the cockpit door. Tapping at his ear, then his eye to indicate there were listening devices and cameras, he bent forward. Speaking softly, he said, "Working for them won't impress the folks at Dougherty, Street, and Chambers. They specialize in human rights litigation. That's my passion."

Hearing the young man's dream, she remembered a quote from Martin Luther King in a first-year law school class, "Justice denied anywhere diminishes justice everywhere." Boyle saw her own dreams in Armand's eyes, dreams she had sold under the pretext of paying off her student loans. She smiled approvingly, though inwardly, her self-betrayal began to eat at her. Amanda opened her briefcase and took out a business card. She handed it to Armand.

"Keep this handy."

With a bit of a magician's flare, Armand quickly snapped his personal card from his vest pocket. It was printed with the Gold Eagle of Boston College and read, "Armand Ortiz, Law School, Boston College."

Smiling sheepishly, he said, "My mom likes to show it around the neighborhood, if you know what I mean."

Amanda thought of her law degree from Harvard that still hung over the bar at the family restaurant, and the betrayal she had perpetrated on her own blood. Her family had been so proud of her when she graduated from law school.

"Never forget the guy who can't afford your best," her father had told her on graduation day.

The uneasiness of that memory awoke a disturbing realization. She had lost focus of her real dream, the love of defending the helpless, the poor, those societal castaways who would have no hope at all, were it not for some neophyte crusader, as Abigail Strauss so crudely put it.

11

THE QUEST FOR JUSTICE

C ourt was not in session on Fridays, affording Matthew Adams time to catch up on paperwork and research. This particular Friday was unusually quiet as his receptionist, Rose, had called in sick. With only a solitary light illuminating the hallway, and no one sitting at his receptionist's desk, anyone looking through the front window would assume his law office was closed. In his solitude, he sipped the Latte Mocha he had purchased from the Starbucks across the street. The contents of the envelope he had received from Sutro, Bellows, and Finestien, lay spread across his desk. Whoever this attorney was, they were trying every legal maneuver possible to make the case go away. There were multiple motions beginning with, "There is no evidence that Paris Barrington is, in fact, the father of the child in question. Anybody's name can be put on a birth certificate," the letter stated. Another motion petitioned the court to move the case to Family Court in Connecticut, as that was the defendant's legal residence. Another was to order the plaintiff to cease from any further attempts to extort monies from the Barrington family. The attorney went on to argue that the mother of Trevor Barrington was now under a doctor's care for hypertension and any number of other psycho-babble illnesses brought on by the false allegations made against her son. Finally, the attorney argued that Adams' request for a DNA test to prove paternity was an outrageous and egregious violation of her client's constitutional rights. Adams let this last motion drop onto his desk. He leaned back in his black leather high-back ergonomically designed chair. Its lumbar and neck supports eased the tension from stooping over his desk for long hours at a time. It baffled Adams that a family like the Barringtons, with more money than a hundred families could spend in a lifetime, maybe two lifetimes, was so determined to fight this issue. *Hell,* he thought, *the attorney's fees alone would amount to more than what she was requesting in child support.* But this is Trevor Barrington, the son of billionaire developer Paris Barrington. Paris Barrington had more commas in his net worth than some foreign countries. Adams realized his case lacked any prima facie evidence to support his claim that Trevor Barrington was the child's father. If only he had DNA evidence, but that would require the defendant's cooperation, and that seemed highly unlikely, given the mound of motions sitting on his desk. He needed to talk with his client. Tina Pinafore needed to be prepared for what was to come.

∾

THE RECREATION CENTER for Adults with Disabilities was located on the edge of Old Town Charleston, South Carolina. Originally it was called the Downtown Men's Athletic Club, obviously in a time when the Virginia Slims cigarette advertisement telling women "You've come a long way baby," would be unthinkable on Madison Ave. Equality between the sexes did not exist on the plane of social consciousness.

The Men's Athletic Club was founded in the late forties by William R. Spritz, a billionaire shipbuilder and philanthropist from New York who had moved to Charleston following WWII to escape the harsh northern winters. The two-story red brick building housed offices, a full gymnasium, steam baths made with imported Italian white marble, and sauna and massage rooms lined with Indian Teak. William R. Spritz had imported a noted French chef of the day, Francois Archambeau, to head the kitchen staff. His signature dish was Oysters Bienville, and a Manhattan made with Old Overholt Whiskey. The elegance of the dining room was the envy of every restaurateur in Charleston. Eighteen-foot walls of rich mahogany displayed reproductions such famous sea paintings as Willaert's' *Stormy Seas*, Bakhuizen's *Ships in Distress off a Rocky Coast*, Aivazovsky's *The Ninth Wave*, and Cranes' *Neptune's Horses* were on display to whet the viewer's artistic appetite. To be invited to lunch at the Men's Club was a much-sought-after honor.

Spritz made sure every room and wall were adorned with paintings and artifacts representing different periods of the American shipping industry's majestic past. There were two outside swimming pools, one of Olympic size and one shallower in-depth, designed more for beginning swimmers and children. The pool area was surrounded by an expansive grass area with picnic tables and a large softball field. In the seventies, Sarah Broadbent bore William Spritz his fourth grandchild, a son named Randolph, his grandfather's middle name. Shortly after birth, young Randolph was diagnosed with Tay Sachs disease, a disorder that attacks spinal and brain cells. The impact of the child's birth brought a shocking awareness to the Spritz family that would ultimately cause a significant shift in their philanthropic endeavors—the utter lack of recreational facilities and programs for disabled children. The Spritz Family Foundation phased out the Downtown Men's Athletic Club and established the Recreation Center for the Handicapped. Decades before handicap accessibility became law, the Spritz family had the foresight to install wheelchair ramps, widened doors, and adapted restroom facilities. The center had its own physical therapists, speech therapists, and a work program designed for mentally and physically impaired adults. Tina Pinafore headed the work program. She coordinated several work crews contracted to perform minor landscaping work around the city. Tina was particularly proud of the contract she had secured with the College of Charleston to assemble sets of plastic utensils for the college's dining halls. She was a passionate believer that the disabled were far more able than the credit they were given.

She was nearly finished with her lunch when her cell phone pinged. The caller ID caused her stomach to knot. It read "Adams, M," her attorney. She let it go to voice mail then listened to his message. He told her he wanted to talk with her that afternoon about what to expect when they went to court the following Tuesday. It had been over seven years since her last encounter with Trevor's mother and father, and no amount of time would ever erase the memory of their invective response to her pregnancy. Tina glanced at her Franklin Day Planner. She had no meetings in the afternoon. After a quick call to her supervisor to take the rest of the day off, she drove across town to her parent's house. Tina began to doubt whether or not it was all worth it. Even if she were to prevail, any child support would probably end when Missy was eighteen. Sure, she intended to put it in a savings fund for Missy should the day ever come when Tina was not around to care for her, but she could save some on her own and avoid the emotional confrontation ahead of her. Tina was going to ask her dad to pick up Missy from school so she could keep her sudden appointment with Adams at three p.m. She also needed his wisdom. In recent months, Tina had developed an even greater respect for her father, considering her mother's condition. He was never cross with her forgetfulness. If her mom needed to be corrected, her father always took the blame; maybe he hadn't told her after all, or perhaps he was the one who didn't write the date on the calendar in the kitchen. Whatever the reason, her father was endlessly patient with her mother. More than ever, she realized how lucky her mother was to be loved by him. Too protective of her own heart to admit it, but in some hidden recess of her heart, she could only wish to find a man like her father. In a most inauspicious way, Tina Pinafore would do just that.

∼

"I'M sorry to be so tired lately, Eddy," Maddy said as she sat on her bedside, taking off her shoes. "I don't know what's the matter with me."

Her smile revealed a weariness about her. Her eyes looked fatigued, and her gait had become slower and more deliberate. When she and Eddy went for their daily walk, Maddy paused more frequently, staring at familiar sights as if she was seeing them for the first time.

"Nonsense, sweetheart," Eddy said as he unfolded the multi-colored afghan her knitting group had made for her as a gift and laid it across her. "We're in our seventies. We're entitled to be tired and take an afternoon nap. It's a reward for living this long," he joked. His self-deception would not last long.

"I suppose," responded Maddy, smiling in return as she laid her head down on her pillow. As her eyes closed, she said, "I love you, Eddy."

Eddy sat on the bed next to her. He gently stroked her brunette hair, now more gray than brunette. He leaned down to kiss her on the cheek. "I love you more," he whispered. He remained at her side, contemplating their life together, all that had been, all that could have been. Whoever said life is not fair had only scratched the surface of human suffering. There was nothing fair in Maddy being the victim of a savage sexual assault, leaving her unable to bear children. Eddy Pinafore thought he knew the risks in becoming a Navy Seal. But he had no idea how unfair the Gods of War were in deciding who lives and who dies, who comes home unscathed, and who comes home missing body parts. Despite all the unfairness they had endured, somehow, Eddy Pinafore and Maddy Orsini were reunited and later blessed with a beautiful daughter. All those memories were as vivid in his mind as the day they happened. His wife, Maddy, was fighting a losing battle retaining such memories, and that was unfair in his mind. She deserved better. There was nothing he could do about it except be there for her. Once assured she was asleep, Eddy rose. He walked to the double french doors that opened onto the patio and slowly drew closed the flounced ruffle drapes to mute any disturbing light from the afternoon sun. Despite a thick Safavieh Shag rug, Eddy stepped gingerly across the carpet to the bedroom door lest even the softest shuffle sound disturb Maddy. Taking hold of the antique crystal doorknob, he turned to take one last look at his wife, then gently pulled the door shut.

~

EDDY HAD JUST SETTLED into his favorite chair, a rich brown leather Patrick High Back Club chair intentionally designed with lower-than-normal armrests, which Eddy found accommodating to his prosthetic arm. He was intent on finishing a book on the Morality of American Politics by his favorite author, R. Mattison Gordon. Eddy found Gordon's conclusions to be analytical and well thought out, unlike the emotional and pitifully biased thoughts of current commentators on American politics. Hearing a soft rapping on his front door, his irritation at the interruption elicited a mild expletive as he snapped his book closed. His annoyance quickly subsided when he saw his daughter's face through the peephole in the door.

"To what do I owe this pleasant surprise?" he said as he opened the door for his daughter, Tina.

Her feigned smile as she gave her father a short-lived hug alerted Eddy that Tina's visit was more than a welfare check on her mother.

"Daddy, I need to talk to you," she said.

Her tone was not angry or aggressive, but rather fatigued, almost defeatist in spirit. Eddy could tell from her reddened eyes she had been crying. Her face looked tired, like someone who had been reliving a bad dream.

"Let's have a seat on the couch, and you tell me what's going on," Eddy said, hoping his words of concern would ease whatever was troubling his daughter.

Tina let her purse fall carelessly to the floor. Other than a jingling of keys, it made little sound on impact. Tina put her hands on her forehead and slowly moved them to the back of her head as if she could push out the tension within her. She rested her head on the back of the couch. Her eyes stared straight ahead, focused on nothing in particular.

"It's this whole attorney thing over Missy's child support," she sighed. "The attorney called me. He wants to meet today to go over what to expect when we go to court this Tuesday. Daddy, just what am I supposed to expect?" she pleaded. Her voice began to quiver, the flow of her words interrupted by a constricted throat. "I'm not asking for a king's ransom, just what's fair, and help with Missy's medical bills." The purging of this pent-up anxiety brought a rush of tears from Tina.

Eddy's heart ached at the pain his daughter was experiencing. He also felt a father's rage at the person responsible for it. In a different time and different place, he would have beaten Trevor Barrington to within an inch of his life and loved every minute of it, despite the consequences. But that was fantasy, and this was the real world. Setting his book on the white marble end table next to his chair, he rose from his chair and moved to the couch, sitting next to Tina. He handed her a much-needed handkerchief, then put his arm around her shoulders.

"Honey, I'm not an attorney, so I don't know what Mr. Adams is speculating. Just remember what he told you. Paris Barrington may be Goliath, but he is your David. That sounds like something to put your trust in, in my opinion."

Tina nestled in the security of her father's arms. She used his handkerchief to wipe the remaining tears from her cheeks. For a moment, she thought, *why couldn't she just stay here and let someone else go to court for her.* Her breathing became more controlled. Her mind became less muddled with emotion and filled with more resolve, the type of determination her father had always displayed throughout his life. Tina sat up and kissed her father on the cheek.

"Thanks, Dad, I needed to hear that, "she said, as she reached for her purse. "I'm on my way to see my David." Almost forgetting, she quickly added, "Oh, could you pick up Missy at school for me? I'm not sure how long this meeting will take."

"Of course," smiled Eddy. "You focus on this meeting. Don't worry about Missy."

A new guardian angel for Missy was on the horizon.

12

THE SECOND DAVID

Ryan Callahan had promised his partner, Willie, that he would not abandon the kids at Weatherly School in practicing for the Special Olympics. With a fractured femur bone surgically held together by several titanium rods, and the femoral artery stitched back together, Willie would be confined to bed in his home for three to five weeks, according to the doctor. The Charleston Police Department had its own fitness center on the bottom floor of the adjacent building next to the city parking lot. Ryan was religious in maintaining his daily one-and-a-half-hour regimen of aerobics and weights. With his last set of squats done, he wiped his face with a damp gym towel hanging over his shoulder. He glanced at his watch. *Damn!* If he was to make it to the school on time, he would have no time for a shower. He threw his towel into his gym bag and raced to his truck in the parking lot. He wasted no time in getting to the school. It was two forty-five when Ryan pulled up in front of Weatherby School. As Ryan approached the school office, he saw Mrs. Payne, the secretary, standing with her back to the corner of the building, waving her left hand in front of her face trying to eliminate the last puff of cigarette smoke. She held her right hand behind her back, obviously holding the carcinogenic source of a habit she had unsuccessfully tried for years to break. Ryan chuckled to himself at her awkwardness when she realized she had been exposed as a closet smoker. Freda quickly dropped her cigarette to the ground and twisted her shoe on it.

"I'm trying to quit, honestly," she said, her inner strength once again foiled by her addiction to such a nasty habit.

"No judgment," smiled Ryan. "I'm just here to check in and work with the kids."

Eased that her secret habit would remain so, at least for the time being, Freda said, "I'll sign you in. Eva has taken some time off to take care of Willie. The district sent us a substitute teacher fresh out of school. Her name's Courtney. She's got a different way of looking at our kids. Personally, I find it refreshing," smiled Payne.

Ryan made no comment. He was too new at working with these kids himself to get caught up in someone's pedagogy. He found the substitute teacher out on the playground. She had long dark hair and wore black horn-rimmed glasses. From her clothing, Ryan judged she was more interested in functionality than the latest styles in Cosmopolitan and certainly not at all concerned with political correctness. Her long hair formed a ponytail wrapped by a plain rubber band. She wore a visor cap embroidered with letters reading, "So What!" Her black T-shirt was equally defiant. Large white letters read, "Don't Tell Me What I Can't Do!" A pair of loose-fitting denim jeans with sandals made from pieces of old tire tread finished her outfit.

As he approached, he called out, "You must be Courtney. I'm Ryan. I'm sort of the substitute coach."

She eyed him before answering, "And I'm Courtney, sort of the substitute teacher," she wisecracked.

Courtney rose to her feet and extended a firm hand to Ryan. Her comic sarcasm appealed to Ryan. At the sound of his voice, several of the kids greeted him like he was some returning war hero. Shouts of, "Coach Ryan! Coach Ryan," filled the air. Ryan had come to love their spontaneous exuberance, the loudest being little Missy, the girl Ryan was allowing to run.

"Can I run?! Can I run?! Coach Ryan."

"First, let's check with your teacher, Missy."

Courtney said, "Mrs. Root didn't leave me much of a lesson plan. I'll follow your lead."

With that vote of approval, Ryan set about arranging the running area, the broad jump spot, and the softball throw. Courtney glanced up at a cloudless sky and squinted at the brightness of the afternoon sun. "Good thing I brought these," she said, holding up a bottle of sunscreen and pointing to a small cooler filled with ice and bottled water. She had taken some adaptive PE classes in school and was well familiar with the activities at hand. Each child got a generous dose of the creamy sun protector on their faces and necks. Soon she and Ryan had the kids rotating through the three stations like kids changing rides at Disneyland. Courtney made sure every child got maximum praise and encouragement. Ryan liked that. Her spirit was so contagious the kids began cheering for each other. Ryan's attention was drawn to watching Missy run. She was more confident in her ability to run than he was. There were still falls, bruised knees, and an occasional tear. With every fall, Ryan was at her side in an instant. He never babied her but rather offered constant support for her efforts, dismissing any boo-boo or owie with that trite Marine Corps expression, "No pain, no gain."

By the end of the forty-five-minute practice session, Missy's nylon pants and shoes were dutifully adorned with grass smears. Her Minnie Mouse t-shirt was also stained with grass along with noticeable perspiration stains. George's glasses were wet with drops of sweat, and Little Arty's face was flushed from his Herculean efforts. Even Sammy's exertion gave his ebony skin an unmistakable redness. Ryan had all the kids sitting in the shade of the large Magnolia tree. They were emptying their water bottles as fast as they could swallow. Ryan was giving everyone praise for their efforts and projected Gold Medals for everyone at the county's Special Olympics, a month away.

WITH THE END of the school day nearing, parents began arriving to pick up their children. Clusters of moms chatted with each other about anything and everything while waiting for their children to come out of the gate. A few buses with hydraulic equipment to load students who used wheelchairs and others with mobility issues had moved to an area marked "Bus loading only," along the curb outside Weatherby school. The presence of another adult standing on the sidewalk next to the cyclone fence should hardly have attracted anyone's attention. However, this adult happened to be wearing walking shorts, which highlighted a prosthetic leg. A gray t-shirt announced to all a missing left arm. His attire was well-suited to the warm spring temperatures but only served to draw unwanted stares from the waiting people.

The stranger on the sidewalk leaning against the cyclone fence had been watching much of the children's practice. His tolerance for such behavior had changed over the years from "They're just curious" to an almost defiant posture. Rather than hide his disabilities, Eddy Pinafore intentionally wore clothing that blared out, "Yes, I'm different, and it's alright to ask me about it." His heart swelled with pride with every step one of the children took. *She can. She really can,* he thought. *I knew it!* Eddy Pinafore always felt more comfortable in casual clothing, even at the risk of exposing his disabilities. Though his bitterness for the way the government and the Navy had covered up the disastrous Seal mission that cost the lives of all of his team had never ebbed, Eddy had never lost his love for the Seals. He proudly wore a gray t-shirt with the word Seal across the front and their famous trident pin below it. Khaki walking shorts completed his ensemble that day.

Almost from the start of practice, Ryan had noticed a man standing against the fence, watching the kids, his kids. Ryan's eyes constantly checked on him. He also took mental notice of all the children, making sure no one had suddenly disappeared. With his police background, nothing good came from an older man watching kids play at school. Ryan walked inconspicuously to the man's location. It was then he noticed the absence of the man's left arm and a prosthetic leg. It was difficult not to, momentarily, focus on the man's handicaps.

"Is there something I can help you with, sir?" Ryan asked politely.

Annoyed at the implication that he needed help because of his obvious disabilities, Eddy answered rather firmly, "No! I'm just here to pick up my granddaughter."

A sense of relief came over Ryan. "Which one is she, and I'll bring her over to you."

"You were just holding her, Missy Pinafore."

Relieved that the man wasn't some sort of child stalker, Ryan answered, "Let me get her for you, sir. I'll be right back."

Ryan headed back to the group. He picked up Missy, who was unsuccessfully trying to wipe off a grass stain from her pants.

"Missy, your grandfather is here to get you."

That announcement brought a smile to her face. As they neared the fence gate, Missy yelled out, "Papa! Papa! Did you see me run!?"

"Yes, I did, sweetheart! You looked great!" His scarred face beamed with unabated pride.

Ryan opened the gate and surrendered the child to Eddy's waiting arm. Feeling the need to explain his questioning him,

Ryan said rather sheepishly, "My name is Ryan Callahan. I'm volunteering here to help the kids get ready for the Special Olympics. I am still learning the names of the staff, let alone the names of parents and family members."

Sensing Ryan's discomfort, Eddy offered a bit of reassurance.

"No need to apologize, Ryan. My name is Eddy, and I appreciate your alertness."

Ryan could not help but notice the Seal insignia on the man's t-shirt.

"You were a Seal?" asked Ryan with admiration.

Eddy allowed himself an all too infrequent smile at the mention of his Navy service. There was no such thing as water under the bridge for Eddy Pinafore. Every step on his prosthetic leg, every morning shave, every adaptation made for his prosthetic arm was a reminder of the price of his service.

"Yes, I was," responded Eddy, giving no further details.

"Marine Corps," smiled Ryan, offering his hand as a congratulatory gesture.

"How could I tell?" replied Eddy to the man wearing a sweat-stained USMC t-shirt.

Looking down at his own t-shirt, Ryan smiled at his faux pas.

"Then my granddaughter's in good hands," Eddy said, shaking Ryan's hand.

"I'll see you next week, Missy," Ryan said, as Eddy put his granddaughter into the front seat of his sedan. With the innocence of a child, Missy responded, "I love you, Coach Ryan."

13

TENUOUS HEARTS

A t home, standing in his driveway, the dented right front wheel well appeared bigger and bigger, and with it his anger. *What kind of scumbag hits your truck then drives off without leaving a note, even if all it said was sorry,* he thought. Ryan had immediately contacted his insurance agent when he discovered his truck had been hit while parked in the city parking lot next to police headquarters. He had taken a picture of the damaged truck and texted it to him. His policy would cover the damage, but he was still out the deductible, five hundred dollars. With this preying on his mind, his body craved rest from the twenty-mile training hike his unit conducted on the Sunday weekend drill with the Marine Corps Reserve. The pinging of his cell phone was about to bring some relief to the truck issue and complicate his life beyond belief. His caller ID indicated the call was from the Charleston PD. He answered accordingly.

"Officer Callahan."

"Callahan, this is Officer Woodrow. I've got some good news for you."

Officer Woodrow, Woody to his friends, was somewhat of a

computer geek assigned to the department's IT division. There wasn't anything about computer-related technology he didn't know.

"What's up, Woody? You working weekdays now?" quizzed Ryan.

"The price one pays for being an IT genius," chuckled the officer who was the father of four children and busier at home than he ever was at work. "Listen, I was going over the tapes from the security cameras and discovered the culprit behind your truck incident."

"You're kidding me!" exclaimed an excited Callahan. "I'd love the chance for some parking lot therapy with that piece of shit!"

"Afraid that's not going to happen, ole buddy. Your piece of shit is a she."

"You got to be kidding me!" responded Callahan. "A woman ought to be more responsible."

"Don't be too quick to judge, pal. The tape shows her getting out of her car, walking over to your truck to see the damage, then hurrying across the street. Thanks to our department's philosophy to buy cheap, the camera's pictures are grainy and don't give much detail about the woman. I'm texting you some pictures and driver information I got off the license plate."

"Thanks, Woody," responded Callahan.

As promised, within a minute, his phone pinged again. Several pictures appeared showing precisely what the officer had told Ryan. The imagery was low, but Ryan could tell the woman appeared to be carrying a large purse hanging from her shoulder. She wore her hair short, but not in any perceivable style. The vehicle was registered to a Mary T. Pinafore. Ryan found himself staring at the image of the woman. His mind wondered. *What did she really look like? "Why didn't she leave a note? Where was she going in such a hurry?"* At least he had the information from her driver's license to go on. For the moment, it could wait. The long weekend drill left Ryan needing to rest his mind from the Marine Corps and his truck. He tossed his duty bag, uniform, and boots in the spare bedroom, not bothering to put anything in its proper place. For the moment, all he wanted was a cold beer and a place to decompress from the weekend's activities. He walked to the kitchen and opened the refrigerator. Everything in it pointed to a bachelor living there; a six-pack of Heineken, a random assortment of sodas and bottled water, several bowls of leftover meals, all with blotches of blue fuzz adorning the surface, and an eclectic array of hot sauces. He grabbed a bottle of Heineken. The bottle opener still laid on the counter from his last thirst-quenching beverage. After disposing of the cap in a small garbage can under the sink, he made his way to the living room couch. Setting aside his guitar, which he had left on the couch, he grabbed the TV remote control and allowed his weary body to plop down on the well-worn cloth sectional couch—a moving in gift from his mother. He quickly went to his favorite channel, ESPN. Ryan was more than a sports fanatic. If there was a game on, it didn't matter who was playing whom, North Dakota State versus Little Sisters of the Poor, Ryan would watch it. It brought back wonderful memories of him and his dad watching the NFL games on Sunday and Monday night, an event his mother had found particularly unbearable. "Not another game!" she would groan.

Setting the refrigerator on eight kept the bottled beer to a chilled perfection. Ryan took a long pull of his Heineken, then settled back on his couch. It was then he noticed the piece of paper he had placed under the strings of his guitar. Though hardly a professional songwriter and nothing more than a novice at the guitar, Ryan did enjoy playing with words to the greatest song the world would never hear. A few minutes of listening to Stephen A. Austin, an ESPN commentator, was all

Ryan could handle. He muted the TV and reached for his guitar. This would be much more therapeutic than the TV. Not long after he started helping the children at Weatherly School prepare for the Special Olympics, Ryan had been playing with the lyrics to a simple melody that spoke to the range of disabilities the children had and the hopes their parents had for them. He opened the folded piece of paper and laid it on the aged coffee table in front of the couch, another gift from his mother and one that Ryan cherished. Many a snack was shared with his dad on that table while watching TV as a kid. He had the simplest of chord progressions and perhaps even simpler lyrics, but they had moved his heart. He started to play while reading the words written on the paper. "You're not the image of what your parents thought you'd be. Sometimes I often wonder what it is you really see." He tried several combinations of words before jotting the final selection on the paper. There was an inner satisfaction that Ryan felt, not only from working with special needs children but also in acknowledging the struggles they faced. With one last inspiration, the first verse was complete. He set his guitar down and sipped his beer. He was content with his progress, not realizing that more inspiration would soon follow.

∼

THE FOLLOWING day greeted Ryan with what he hated most about police work; reports, then more reports. Following the incident at the Harbor, everyone had turned in rough copies of their reports. After reviewing them, Ryan's team leader, Sergeant Marty Knight, had sequestered his team in a small conference room at police headquarters. Those more senior on the team knew exactly what was coming. Being the newest member of the team, Ryan was mildly irked at what he perceived as Knight's obsessive attention to detail. After all, he was no rookie fresh out of the academy, with five years on the force plus another five years as a Marine Corps staff NCO. Certainly, he knew something about report writing. Begrudgingly, he took a seat at one of several small tables.

"First time at this, Callahan?" asked Ed Popkey, one of his B Squad teammates.

His frustration with the meeting had not subsided.

"A bit of an overkill, don't you think?" responded Callahan.

Popkey was surprisingly amused at Callahan's naivete to the potential of a poorly worded or incorrectly filled out report. Knight would soon educate the rookie member of the team. Knight rose from his seat in the front of the room. He walked to each member of his team, placing their reports face down in front of them. When he was finished, he addressed them.

"Before you turn your report over, listen carefully to what I have to say. Your reports, as written, will be scrutinized by a plethora of attorneys, some for us, some for defendant's counsel, if there are any. Your credibility can be damaged by a single unfilled box, a simple misspelling, or verb usage, which could be misconstrued as being out of control. Please look at my suggested changes and if you have any questions, ask me. I'm here until you're done."

With that, Ryan turned his report over. With a yellow highlighter, Knight had diligently marked every mistake he felt Ryan had made. There were way too many for Callahan's ego to accept. With pen in hand, he painstakingly and grudgingly went line by line through his three-page report. By the time he had finished with the first page, his inflated sense of competence had begun to crumble. His RDO (regular days off) box was incorrectly filled out. Of all things, he had omitted the last digit of his badge number. There were half a dozen highlighted misspellings along with several word usage questions.

Along with their original reports, Knight had given each member of his team new report forms to fill out. Setting his hurt feelings aside, Ryan began to correct his original report, though he kept some of his original language. When he turned in his revised report, he defended some of his choices.

"Sarge, I didn't make all of your suggested language changes. I think I wrote exactly what was going through my mind."

Knight smiled at the mettle his newest member displayed.

"The operative word in my instructions is suggested, Ryan. You have to be comfortable with what you wrote, how you wrote it, and be prepared to defend it if necessary. I've seen a lot worse. Keep up the good work."

His smile gave Ryan a renewed sense of approval. Not wanting to reveal the complete truth behind his next request, Ryan said, "Sarge, I've got an accident report Office Woodrow from IT gave me that I need to follow up on."

No rookie himself, Knight knew there was more to Ryan's request than he was being told. Trust is a two-way street, especially on his team. He asked for it from his men, and they deserved it in return.

"Go. Take care of business," Knight said.

~

UNLIKE NEWER HOUSING DEVELOPMENTS, which had quaint names such as Palmetto Gardens or Coastal Meadows, the area of Callahan's search consisted of older craftsman homes with neatly manicured lawns and aged but well-maintained houses. Ryan made a note of the older model cars in the driveways of many homes. With the absence of bicycles and other children's toys left out by their absent-minded users, he assumed there were few children in the neighborhood. He was pleased to see signs indicating this was a "Neighborhood Watch" community. His GPS led him to Mercy Lane. Moving slowly down Mercy Lane, he scanned the house numbers, checking addresses for

4131A. He found 4131, then 4132, but no 4131A. The mid-morning hour found several homeowners sitting on their porches with their morning coffee, reading the morning paper. Others were walking their dogs, giving both owner and pet some much-needed exercise. At a loss, he pulled to the curb. As Ryan exited his patrol car, an older man approached him. He wore a broad straw hat for protection from the rising sun and carried a pair of hedge trimmers in his hand. The glistening perspiration on his forehead suggested to Ryan the gentleman was looking for an excuse to take a break from his yard work.

"Can I help you, officer?" he asked, taking a blue bandana from his rear pocket to dab his moistening forehead.

"Yes, I'm looking for 4131 A Mercy Lane," replied Ryan.

The older man smiled at the perplexed look on Ryan's face.

"Lots of folks have that problem. 4131A is a small cottage behind my house. I never bothered to have the numbers put on my house."

"Well, I'm looking for a Mary Pinafore," continued Ryan, as he glanced down at the text message on his phone.

A worried expression formed on the man's face.

"I rent the cottage out to Tina Pinafore. Is there some sort of problem? I think of her and her daughter as my own family," replied the gentleman.

"You said Tina," responded Ryan. "My information says a Mary Pinafore lives here."

Smiling, the older man said, "Oh, Mary goes by Tina. If I may ask, what seems to be the problem?"

Preferring to leave his personal involvement in the matter private, Ryan replied, "Ms. Pinafore may have been involved in a hit-and-run accident. I just need to clear up a few facts."

"That doesn't sound like my Tina," queried the man.

"People do strange things under stress," replied Ryan, knowing that what had transpired was a stretch to fit the definition of a hit-and-run incident. "I'm sure the matter can be cleared up easily."

"Tina is a single mother and the most responsible young adult I've ever met. I'm sure if she can help you in any way, she will. She works at the Recreational Center for the Handicapped in Old Town."

"The old Downtown Athletic Club?"

"That's it," replied the man.

"I appreciate your help, sir," said Ryan, touching the bill of his hat as a thank you.

~

IT WAS ALMOST eleven when Ryan pulled his patrol car to the curb in front of the Recreation Center for the Handicapped. The sight of the old two-story brick building brought back memories of his father bringing him here as a young child to swim in the indoor plunge and father-son baseball games in the summer. The then chief of police had taken a liking to Ryan's father, Mike, and his precocious son and allowed Ryan's father to take advantage of the chief's membership. The old man had given Ryan a bit more information than what was listed on the driver's info Officer Woodrow had given him. She was a single mother, not much to go on, but it was something. Ryan paused in front of the aged structure to soak in a few more memories before entering. Automatic doors, making wheelchair accessibility easier, opened as he approached. A pleasant-looking young woman in a wheelchair sat behind a rather large table serving as a receptionist's desk. Her name tag read, "Phyllis."

"May I help you?" she asked.

"Yes, I'm looking for a Tina Pinafore," Ryan replied.

"Her office is right down the hallway to the right. I'll show you the way," she replied with a smile.

"No bother, Phyllis, I'm sure I can find it on my own."

Smiling at the use of her first name, she responded, "Oh, it's no bother. I could use the exercise." She wheeled her chair from behind the table. "This way."

Smudges from rubber-tipped canes, crutches, wheelchair tires, and any number of other mobility devices marred the black and white tiled floor. Phyllis stopped in front of the first door on the right. The nameplate on the door read, "Tina Pinafore, Director of Work Activities."

"This is it," she said, then quickly added, "There's no problem, is there? Tina's a wonderful person." The look of angst on her face made Ryan rue the subterfuge he had allowed to continue. What was waiting for him inside would only exacerbate that feeling.

Ryan knocked on the door. A muffled sound came from inside.

"Come in, please."

As he entered, he quickly scanned the interior. It was a small office with a tiled floor that matched the hallway. Several gray metal file cabinets were aligned along the right wall. On the left wall was a large eraser board with work schedules for the month neatly noted with a blue sharpie. A round table sat to the left of a cluttered desk. The table legs and the front of the dark stained desk had countless chips and dings, no doubt the result of contacts with mobility devices. A young woman stood facing a window to the back of the building. Her arms were folded. Ryan could see a handkerchief in her left hand.

"My name is Officer Callahan from the Charleston PD. I'm looking for a Tina Pinafore."

When she turned around, Ryan Callahan was, for the first time in his life, speechless. Forgetting the bloodshot eyes, the result of continuous sobbing, or the streaked makeup from the flow of tears that had poured down her cheeks, before him stood the most beautiful woman Ryan Callahan had ever seen. Her brown eyes stared at him like a puppy begging to be picked up. Her blonde hair hung in a short bob cut, olive complexion, and a small mole on her left cheek left him thinking he was looking at a young Sophia Loren. She wore a modest white cotton blouse with a black skirt, but there was no hiding the fact that she had a model's figure. Her lips quivered as she spoke.

"I'm Tina Pinafore. You're here to see me. My landlord, Fred, called me."

That would explain the tears and angst in her voice. Fred had undoubtedly made it sound like she was about to be put on the FBI's Most Wanted List. Before he could answer her, she blurted out, "Am I in serious trouble?" She paused momentarily, then cried, "I don't think I can handle much more!" An eruption of tears soon followed.

Though he knew precious little about the woman or the circumstances of her emotional outbreak, the primal male instinct to protect her tore at Ryan.

"Ms. Pinafore, I'm not here to arrest you. I only want to clear up the incident in the city parking lot a few days ago involving your car. That's all," Ryan replied, hoping his words would have a soothing effect on her emotional trauma. "Could we just sit down and talk about it?"

Without saying a word, Tina pointed to the small table. Ryan pulled out a chair for her and then seated himself. As she took a seat, she made one final pass with her handkerchief, dabbing the flow of tears.

"I'm sorry. I must look a mess," she mumbled apologetically.

"Not at all. I think you look fine," Ryan answered, hoping he had not sounded too forward.

Taking a deep breath, she said, "Let's get started. What do you need to know?"

Ryan placed his cell phone on the table. He pressed "photos," then turned the phone so she could see.

"The security camera shows you pulling into this parking slot. The right front bumper of your Subaru struck a pickup truck that had backed in and was parked next to you. You're seen getting out of your car. You walked over to the pickup truck apparently to see what damage you caused, then hurried out of view, heading across the street."

Her finger scrolled through each picture. He was right, but the pictures didn't capture her intentions. She sought to make amends.

"I know this looks bad. I had intended to leave a note on the truck's windshield, but I was already running late for an appointment with my attorney, whose office is just across the street. When I was finished with my appointment, I came back, but by then, the pickup truck had left. As I remember, the damage looked minimal, but I know now that doesn't excuse anything," she quickly added.

Already feeling smitten, her contrition only added to the confluence of emotions Ryan was experiencing. Her next question eliminated any chance of Ryan being able to shortcut the emotional meeting.

"How much damage did I do?" she asked, staring at a photo of the right front fender area.

In his haste to soothe her anxiety, he replied, "The insurance company quoted fifteen hundred dollars..." Before he could continue, she gasped, "My God, I can't afford that, not with everything else on my plate." Tears soon returned to her reddened eyes.

Ryan blurted out, "The deductible is only five hundred dollars, and I can cover that. You don't need to worry about it."

Shocked at his admission, Tina looked up. "This is your truck!? I hit your truck?"

"Yes, you did."

She tilted her head slightly. Feeling both wonderment and confusion, she said, "I don't understand."

Ryan put his phone back in his pocket. He preferred her focus on him and not the embarrassing and incriminating photos.

"Because the security cameras caught this on tape, a police report was filed. Being that my truck was involved, I was given a heads-up, and I thought I could resolve this without any fuss. I went by your house earlier to see you but your landlord, Fred, told me you were at work. He said some pretty flattering things about you being a single mother and very responsible. I wanted to prevent anything from getting out of hand with the police and insurance bureaucracy being what it is, so I came here to fix things. Of course, when I got here, you were already pretty upset between this and whatever else was filling your plate. I should have told you right from the start. I'm..."

The look in his eyes only served to amplify the sincerity of his words. This unexpected explanation caught Tina Pinafore off guard. She was not used to such consideration, given her current situation with her child's father, and certainly did not expect it from the good looking, blue-eyed policeman sitting across from her. She quickly dismissed the sudden cardiac skip in her pulse as an anatomic abnormality.

"I don't know what to say, Officer Callahan. I really don't," she said in utter amazement.

"I think Ryan would be in order, don't you? After all, it appears there's no issue at all, right?"

For the first time since receiving her landlord's call, Tina Pinafore felt she could afford to smile. When she did, she was met with a smile in return that activated that cardiac impulse again. Their eyes locked for an embarrassingly long moment before Tina asked, "What happens now?"

With more than a modicum of pretentiousness, Ryan said, "In police work, there's always some kind of follow-up investigation. To keep things simple and uncomplicated, I was wondering if perhaps you'd be up for pizza some time, just to make sure we've got all the I's dotted and T's crossed?"

This time Tina Pinafore enjoyed her cardiac disruption.

Tina added her own bit of comedic repartee with a nod of her head and an uncontrollable smile forming on her face.

"Yes, of course, paperwork and bureaucracy being what it is."

As he stood up, Ryan said, "Say six o'clock tomorrow night. We could go to Gino's over on sixth."

"Okay. But just to keep things uncomplicated, what with police work, you know, why don't I meet you there?"

Neither realized just how complicated things were about to get.

14

THE DATE

The child sat mesmerized as she watched her mother painstakingly apply her makeup. Mascara, eyeliner, a few gentle strokes of facial powder, and a delicately applied lip gloss to her light-toned pink lipstick had taken the better part of half an hour to apply. After receiving his phone call setting the time for their simple, uncomplicated meeting for pizza, Tina underwent a wave of emotional conflict. It left her tantalized by the expectation of their meeting, yet somewhat embarrassed by the titillating feeling of the man-woman attraction she was experiencing. She remembered their meeting in her office. There was no question his smile was captivating, and his deep blue eyes emanated a rather sexual overtone, whether intended or not. It was an overtone that Tina found surprisingly inviting. Discounting the times some friend wanted her to meet someone from work who was single or the bachelor out of town who was visiting, she could not remember the last time she had been on a date, an actual date, just her and the guy with no prying eyes of friends or family.

She placed the cap on the tube of lip gloss and gently pressed her lips together. Standing in front of the mirror above her vanity, Tina exclaimed, "There, what do you think?" turning her head from side to side along with her body. Her Calvin Klein jeans fit just short of skin-tight, a feature that soothed Tina's sometimes fragile ego. She wore a black elbow-length silk blouse opened between the elbow and shoulder, provocative yet not overly sexual.

With one arm, Missy had been playing with her own little girls' makeup kit, a present from her grandmother for her sixth birthday.

"How do I look?" she countered, nudging her mother so she could look in the mirror, completely ignoring her mother's question and emulating her mother's head movement.

In that moment, Tina forgot about her daughter's disability. She saw a beautiful young child whose naiveness to her physical state left Tina, loving her more than ever.

"You look beautiful, Missy," Tina exclaimed. "Get your coat. Fred and Willa are going to babysit you tonight."

Despite her mild cognitive limitations, Missy was no different than other girls her age when they try to assert that they no longer need certain parental protections. She boldly announced to her mother with an unabated tone of indignation, "Mom, I don't need a babysitter; I'm almost eight!" Her childish features wore a look of grim determination.

Missy's impish defiance touched Tina's heart. Her daughter had no idea her limitations required a different level of parental oversight. Tina realized Missy needed an explanation that was less demeaning in her eyes. She picked her daughter up and set her on her lap.

"Missy, Friday is Fred's night to bowl with his friends, and Willa will be all alone. You wouldn't want her to be alone, would you? I thought that you could, like, babysit her. You know, kinda keep her company until Fred gets home."

Suddenly empowered with adult responsibility, Missy stiffened her posture and proudly announced, "That's a great idea, Mom. I'll babysit Willa."

With that proclamation, she slid off her mother's lap and went to her bedroom to retrieve her coat. When she returned, she stated rather directly, "Mom, we better hurry. Willa needs me."

"Yes, she does, sweetheart," replied a smiling mother.

It wasn't often that she was able to turn the tide in such a positive manner. For the moment, she was quite satisfied that she had brightened her daughter's day while fulfilling her parental responsibilities.

Tina and Missy walked down the driveway to Fred and Willa's house. After carefully explaining the ruse to Willa, she hugged her daughter and left. While standing on the front porch, she heard Willa said, "I'm so thankful I have someone to be with me tonight, Missy. Would you like to help me make some cookies? What kind should we bake, chocolate chip or peanut butter?"

There was a bit of twitterpation in her heart as Tina drove across town to Gino's Pizzeria, a feeling that evoked conflicting emotions, anticipation, and apprehension. One moment she wondered, *"What the hell am I doing?"* The next moment, *"Do I look alright?"* Adding to that, cross-town traffic was particularly heavy, ensuring she would be late. What a way to start a first date, she thought.

He was the one who had insisted on keeping things simple, uncomplicated. Then why was he feeling like he was getting ready for the Senior Prom? He turned his head from side to side while facing the mirror. He hoped his high and tight haircut wasn't too extreme. After a quick roll of Old Spice underarm deodorant and a splash of Jovan cologne, he dressed. Pizza meant casual, but he was not leaving "casual" to chance. With his best formfitting blue jeans on, tan cowboy boots, and maroon polo shirt embroidered with "USMC" in gold letters, he made one last final inspection in front of the mirror in his bedroom. *This was as good as it gets,* he thought, with hopeful optimism.

～

GINO'S PIZZERIA was in Old Town Charleston. The area was referred to as "Old Town" not because it was in the gentrified, redeveloped section of Charleston, but because it was genuinely in the older part of Charleston. What had once been the business hub of Charleston had been long abandoned by its commercial residents. The remaining tenants were generational owners who had been too stubborn to move after the last recession. They remembered the old days when their shops and cafes were filled with a voracious lunchtime crowd and weekend nights with families whose children many owners knew by name. Gino's Pizzeria was one of those places. Gino Santini had started his family business in the early '50s. The two-story red brick building sat on the corner of 5th and Elm, one of the few businesses with its own parking in the back. The top story was a small three-bedroom apartment where Gino and his wife, Silvia, had raised their three children, Salvatore Jr., Maria, and Peter. When the old man died from a heart attack in the early '80s, his oldest boy, Salvatore, nicknamed Sal, took over the family business. His sister, Maria, had married shortly after their father's death and moved to Florida. Her brother, Peter, had no desire to be involved in the business. His passion was art. After receiving a degree in Art History from the University of South Carolina, Peter moved to Florence, Italy, where he restored old paintings.

Sal was smart enough to realize the generations of returning customers did so because of the ambiance and the food. He wisely did nothing to change either. There were no booths along the wall. His dad couldn't afford them back in the day. In their place were eight-foot-long wooden tables salvaged from the nearby Naval yard. Round wooden tables occupied the center of the restaurant, another salvage job from the Navy's decision to remold their decades-old mess halls. Every table had its classic red and white checkered tablecloth with twine wrapped Chianti bottles serving as candle holders. The red brick walls had brass covered lamps resting on protruding bricks. That was one new touch Sal had added.

The floor consisted of thick planks of shiplap siding where cleaning up spilled drinks and crumbs of food or bits of salad required nothing more than a push broom and wet mop. He left his father's old photos of family members from Italy, some working in vineyards, others in fish markets or standing by their fishing boats. As for the food, twin brick pizza ovens, hand made by his dad, continued making their landmark pizzas the old fashion way. No thin crust to satisfy calorie counters or double stuffed cheese edges. Sal's crusts were brushed with a butter, garlic, and fennel concoction and baked to a golden brown. Their soup of the day changed weekly after careful proportions of beans, sausage, and vegetables were added daily to stretch out the contents until Saturday, when a new batch would be started. His mother's recipes for any number of pasta dishes had been preserved on old parched yellow pages, which she had used to create them. Sal's only addition to these time-honored recipes was oven-baked garlic bread, either in small loaves or twists. The twists were the kids' favorite. There was one more reason Ryan Callahan devotedly visited Gino's several times a month. Salvatore Santini Jr. was a former Marine who had lost his left leg below the knee in the bombing of the US Embassy in Beirut in 1983.

∼

PULLING into the parking lot behind the building, Ryan made his way in through the back kitchen door, a favor extended from one Marine to another Marine. An old creaky screen door announced anyone's entry with a loud slam. The spring-loaded hinges had not worked in years.

"I thought that was you," smiled Sal, extending a hand covered with flour and red sauce. "Semper Fi." Ryan clasped his hand and echoed the time-honored Marine to Marine greeting.

"Any of the boys with you?" I can put a couple of tables together," Sal said, as accommodating as ever.

"No, just me and a friend," responded Ryan, knowing full well Sal's prying nature would not accept his clearly guarded answer.

Sal took the towel off his shoulder and tossed it onto the worktable. He folded his arms and glared at Ryan.

"Friend my ass, old buddy. Don't bullshit the bull! Who is she?"

There was no way to avoid telling him about Tina. He gave him as brief a version absent the part about her eyes, face, smile, and build as he believed Sal would accept.

"Sounds like a ten, Ryan," smiled Sal.

"More like a twelve," chuckled Ryan. "She is supposed to meet me here around six."

"Just my luck," glowed Sal. "Listen, the wife forgot to pick up a dozen loaves of french bread today. Could you do me a favor and make a quick trip over to Mario's Bakery and pick them up? I'll call Mario to expect you. He's only three blocks over on Stanton. You can make it before she even gets here."

Not anxious to miss Tina's arrival, Ryan was not about to disappoint a fellow Marine's need for help.

"You call now!" Ryan said as he turned and practically ran to his truck.

~

THE LAST WORD from Siri was, "Your destination is on your right." Tina pulled to the curb. Overhead lights shone down on a white oval sign trimmed in green, reading "Gino's Pizzeria." The sign had two small Italian flags at each end. *Casual and uncomplicated, this is it, she thought.* Gazing through the glass windows on either side of the front door, Tina would see this was the kind of place her mom and dad would take her to as a kid. Nothing pretentious, it was family and child friendly and had really good food. As she got to the front door, she took a closer view of the interior, hoping to see where he was sitting. He wasn't there. Maybe he had been slowed by traffic, like her. She started to turn back to her car, deciding to wait until she saw him arrive when a man's voice called out, "Tina, come on in. Ryan will be right back."

Sal had been standing at the front door watching for a single woman approaching his establishment. After calling out her name, Sal stood by the open door.

"Excuse me?" Tina asked the strange man who seemed to know her. Her natural defensiveness went into full play.

Sal recognized her discomfort and immediately set about putting the young woman at ease.

"My name's Sal. I own this place. Ryan's running an errand for me. He'll be right back. Please come inside. I've got a special table reserved for you two."

It was hard to turn down's the man's request. His smile was as big as the overhead sign, and he was clearly sincere in his tone. He was tall with fully gray hair trimmed short on the sides. His maroon polo shirt with the name "Gino's" embroidered on it fit rather snugly on a well-developed chest, broad shoulders, and bulging biceps. *He was no stranger to the gym,* Tina thought.

Still not completely sure, she approached him cautiously, asking, "So Sal, how do you know my name?"

Sal stared momentarily at the woman. Ryan was right. She was a knockout. He hoped for Ryan's sake her beauty was not just skin deep. He was unabashedly protective of his younger fellow Marine. He had seen Ryan and his friends come in with girls on their arms before. Most were lookers, but few were keepers, in his opinion.

"Ryan told me about you. It wasn't hard to spot you from his description."

Somewhat embarrassed by his answer, Tina shyly asked, "And just how did he describe me?" Her coyness betrayed a fragile ego.

Realizing he may have set his friend up for a failed date, Sal smiled, "You know, eyes, smile, those kinds of things."

His evasiveness intrigued Tina. She knew there was more, but she wasn't about to press him. She'd leave that to Ryan. Tina followed the owner inside, where he had set aside a table marked "Reserved."

"Can I get you something to drink?" I've got beer, wine, soft drinks, you name it."

Since Ryan had apparently told Sal so much about her, two can play the same game.

"What would Ryan order?"

Sal smiled outwardly. "Most guys think pizza and beer is a God-given decree. Truth be told, Ryan likes one of our imported red wines. His favorite is a Pinot."

"Then Pinot it is," Tina replied with a beguiling smile. "And please join me. I hate sitting alone."

As Sal headed to the wine rack behind the counter, Tina noticed his obvious limp. It was a limp she had grown up watching. Sal walked exactly like her father. He soon returned with an opened bottle of Pinot and three glasses. He set them on the table and took a seat across from Tina. The bottle was carefully wrapped with a white cloth napkin tucked in at the bottom of the bottle. Sal carefully poured each a glass. He held his glass and toasted, "Salute."

Tina tapped her glass to his and enjoyed her first sip of what she found to be a surprisingly delightful choice of wines.

"Just how you did meet my buddy? He's not exactly a player, if you get my drift."

Tina dabbed her lips with her napkin. "The short version is I kind of hit his truck in a city parking lot. Security cameras caught it, and a cop friend of his gave him the photos. He came to my work to let me know what had happened. There was no way I could afford to pay for the repairs, much less pay his deductible. I got a little emotional and..."

Sal finished her sentence. "And he said not to worry. He'd take care of it himself."

Tina nodded, and Sal smiled. "That's Ryan. He's got a huge heart. He even trains with me when I'm preparing for a marathon. When the job permits, we lift weights at Planet Fitness."

Without thinking, Tina expressed her surprise. Wide-eyed, much as a child, she exclaimed, "A marathon? How could that be possible? I saw you limp." Then, instantly realizing her obvious faux pas, she shifted to a much needed, if inadequate, apology.

"I'm so sorry. I didn't mean to pry. Running, much less a marathon seems an impossibility. Please forgive me!"

Her eyes started moistening, and tears from a woman were one thing Sal could not handle. He recognized instantly the embarrassment she felt.

"Don't let it bother you, young lady. I was a young Marine in Beirut when terrorists bombed the US Embassy. Two hundred and twenty Marines died that day. I lived but got this." He reached down and tapped his leg.

"And you run marathons?" she asked in amazement.

"Tina, this doesn't define who I am or what I can do. It's not a limitation on what I can do. It's motivation. Ryan understands that, and I love the guy for that. "

Sal's emotional words struck a chord with Tina, considering her objection to her daughter's wanting to run. Her heart was certainly affected by the affection shown toward the man who was her date. Perhaps this was the time to learn a little more about him.

"I'm intrigued," she said, with a beguiling wink and a twinkle in her eye. "What else can you tell me about him?"

Just then, a woman came around from behind the counter. She had a shirt matching Sal's with the added words, "The Boss" under the business's name. She looked to be in her early fifties, quite trim and fit, Tina thought. She had a certain natural beauty that required minimum makeup to accentuate her high cheekbones, ebony eyes, and movie star smile. She came up to their table. "Honey, Ryan's here with the bread."

"Tina, this is my wife, Bella. Bell, this is Ryan's friend, Tina."

Before she spoke, the brief pause told Tina she was getting the once-over look of approval from another protective friend of Ryan's.

"Honey, that boy's a keeper, and he plays the guitar," she said as if she was revealing some secret she would only share with someone special.

"Geez, Bella. This is only their first date," groaned an exasperated Sal.

"I'm just saying," Bella smirked while winking at Tina. Then she whispered, "By the way, his favorite pizza is the gourmet chicken with anchovies."

Tina smiled at yet another revelation and replied, "Thanks, girl to girl," and gave Bella a wink in return.

An obviously embarrassed Ryan hurried to the table.

"I'm really sorry to be late, but Sal asked for a favor, and it took longer than I expected."

"No apologies necessary. Sal and Bella kept me company," Tina replied. Her smile eased his apprehension and confirmed his prior assessment of her beauty.

Relieved, Ryan took a seat at the table.

"Would you like something to drink?"

Preoccupied with lingering guilt over his late arrival, Ryan did not notice the bottle of Pinot and glass on the table. His nervousness was clearly evidenced by his unnecessary questions about having a beverage when it was already right there before them.

Tina seemed to relish in his awkwardness. "You need to take a deep breath and relax. Your favorite Pinot is right here, and it's delicious, I might add." Tina then took the bottle and poured a glass for him.

"I thought that was supposed to be my job?" said Ryan.

"You can order the pizza. That will make us even," Tina said with a chuckle as they raised their glasses to each other.

"Do you like pepperoni?" He asked.

Everyone seemed to relish pepperoni, yet Tina allowed her true feelings on the matter to show.

"A little too greasy for me."

"How about Italian sausage with mushrooms, olives, and peppers?"

"Really not much of a meat-eater," Tina said, clearly toying with the young man. Not wanting to prolong the torture, she said coyly, "I know this is kind of unusual for a girl, but that gourmet chicken with anchovies sounds great." She absolutely relished this deception!

"You're kidding," Ryan said. "I don't think anyone here orders the gourmet chicken with anchovies but me." He tilted his head slightly, then looked at Bella and Sal, who were pretending to wait on customers while keeping an eye on them. Realizing that the joke was on him, Ryan moaned, "Sal told you that's my favorite, didn't he?"

He didn't mind the deception, he thought.

"No, actually it was Bella, but I really do like anchovies," she added to validate her selection.

"Wow, isn't anything a secret anymore?"

Tina smiled. His fake sense of betrayal struck a comedic note with her. Her comfort zone began to grow. She became a little more inquisitive.

"So, do the Charleston police chase down every hit and run driver with as much tenacity as you?"

Embarrassed by her directness, a sheepish grin formed on his face.

"Not exactly, but this was more than just a hit and run as you put it."

"How so?"

"The camera footage also showed you hurrying out of the parking lot and across the street to a law office. I figured it had to be something pretty important, or you would have left a note or something. Besides, Matthew Adams has a pretty good reputation among some people I know.

Tina felt uneasy, expecting he was going to ask more questions. She was saved by the arrival of the large gourmet chicken pizza.

Setting it on the table, Sal announced, "Mangiare!"

Ryan politely offered Tina the first piece.

Tina bent forward slightly and inhaled deeply. She closed her eyes. The aroma of the butter-basted crust with fennel and crushed garlic demanded a moment of appreciation. She was happy to provide that moment.

"That smells absolutely divine. Forgive my manners," she said, as her acrylic nails carefully picked up a thinly sliced piece of anchovy. Carefully placing it in her mouth, she swallowed. "And it tastes even better!" she added. The expression on her youthful face demonstrated this was no deception.

Using her fork, Tina slid a piece of Sal's creation on to her plate. Ryan added a bit more wine to their glasses and took a slice of pizza himself. After each had taken their first bite, Ryan's a bit more manly than Tina's petite sample, a short silence followed. Their palettes were electrified with the savory flavor of the gourmet selection. Tina took a sip of her wine. First they started slowly at. "So why did you decide to become a police officer? Does the profession run in your family?"

As Ryan wiped his mouth with his napkin, his memories flowed easily and with pride. He would have no difficulty in telling this tale.

"As a kid, I used to love listening to my dad tell me stories about being in the Marines and later being a cop. I wanted to be just like him. I even took up playing the guitar though I'm not very good at it. It kind of puts me in a different place, if you know what I mean. After high school, I enlisted in the Marines, something my mom prayed over for four long years, as she puts it. My dad was killed in the line of duty just before my enlistment was up with the Marines. I never wanted to be anything but a cop and to be as good a cop as he was. When I joined the department, my mother went ballistic. All she could think about was getting that call in the middle of the night that I had been hurt or, worse, killed. I hated the pain it caused her. I think in time she got over it, at least I hope so."

As he spoke, Tina felt the urge to take hold of his hand and assure him his mother was fine with his decision. She, too, had memories of her mother telling her stories, though somewhat abbreviated, about her father and how her mother worried about him when he was in the Navy. She denied her feelings for the time being.

Ryan had not talked about his father and mother for a long time. Even when fellow officers would ask if he were Sergeant Mike Callahan's son, Ryan would merely nod. He kept his memories close to him, but this woman was different. He felt completely at ease, sharing them with her. He finished his first slice, then asked Tina, "How about you? What was your growing up like, and how did you come to work at the Rec Center?"

Unashamed to show her hunger or appreciation for Ryan's favorite pizza, Tina had already started on her second piece. She held up one finger indicating—let me swallow first before answering. She was enjoying her wine as much as the food and took a healthy sip before wiping her mouth with her napkin.

"I had a pretty normal upbringing. My dad was a little different from other kids' dads in that he only had one arm and one leg. It never stopped him from coaching my girls' sports teams growing up and taking the family on camping and fishing trips. He even plays golf. A couple of summers when I was a teenager, we rented a cabin on Lake Marion. We would go fishing in the morning, just him and me. Mom stayed back and would have breakfast ready for us when we got back. Her blueberry pancakes with coconut syrup were fantastic. After high school, I started at the University of South Carolina. I met somebody." She paused, "Things changed after that." Her voice noticeably dropped off with this last sentence.

She stopped abruptly, wishing she hadn't said so much and hoping he would not want her to go on. Hiding a secret is a hard thing to do. A glance, a head twist, there is always something that shows there's more to tell. Ryan sensed this, wisely choosing not to ask more. It was the only way to protect her from further revealing anything more hurtful.

"And your job at the Rec Center?"

She had been attracted to him from the moment he came into her office. He had exposed feelings that she had denied for too long; the need to have someone to talk to, someone interested in her and her dreams, someone she could care for, and not just as a friend. He already knew she was a single mother, thanks to her landlord. That alone would have been enough to scare off some men but throw in a child with special needs, and you could pretty much guarantee you'd never see the guy again.

"That's going to take more than a few sentences to explain."

Her terse answer told him he had broached a subject too sensitive to talk about, at least for here and now. He desperately wanted to assure her his question was not meant to pry. He was nervous again.

"Sorry, I'd didn't mean to pry into your private life. Let's talk about other things."

Through the bottle of wine and a few more pieces of pizza, their time was spent sharing small anecdotes about their growing up, high school stories, and the dreams of adolescents on the verge of adulthood.

"Guess what? With Sal and your father, we share some things in common," Ryan said.

"Probably," Tina replied, wishing there was more time to do just that, share.

The evening could have gone on for hours as far as Ryan was concerned. He wished now that he had picked her up at her home. It would have given him even more time to be with her. Though she was in no hurry to end the evening, Tina had to get home and relieve her neighbor, Willa, from her babysitting job. Tina decided now was as good a time as ever. She looked intently into his eyes and stated, "I've really enjoyed this evening, Ryan," placing her hand on his.

"Me too," he replied, realizing his Cinderella was about to hurry down the palace steps—he quickly added, "Listen, I'd like to do this again if you would?"

"You mean pizza at Gino's?" she asked, with an amusing twist to her smile.

"Oh no," he answered hurriedly. "I meant maybe lunch or take in a movie, or go to a River Dogs game?"

He clearly wanted to establish alternatives for another meeting. She found his eagerness endearing in an old-fashioned kind of way.

"Call me when you decide where we're going," she replied, with a beguiling smile.

There was no denying she wanted to see him again. An all too apparent squeeze of his hand was her affirmation of those feelings. Ryan took his wallet out and placed two twenties on the table. With her hand in his, they headed to the door. Ryan escorted her across the street to her car. There was more than a yearning to take her in his arms and kiss her. As archaic as it seemed, chivalry dictated "first date" and "first kiss" should not happen at the same time. But this was not England under King Arthur. Ryan Callahan had no interest in playing the devoted servant to the queen—Lancelot. As they got to her car door, Ryan said, "I wasn't kidding, Tina, I really would like to see you again. He released her hand and placed his hands on her elbows, pulling her slowly closer. Her arms moved instantly to his broad shoulders. Tina had no intention of playing the maiden in waiting—Guinevere.

"If I haven't already told you, I had a wonderful time tonight." With that proclamation, her lips met his with a subtle movement meant to be polite, but leaving no doubt politeness was not her future intent.

15

A FATHER'S DOUBLE BURDEN

I t was early Saturday morning, about seven a.m., when a call came in on Eddy's cell phone, interrupting his morning routine of coffee and the newspaper before his wife awoke.

"Let me check on your mom," he whispered into his phone.

Tina remained curled up on her living room couch, a cup of coffee delicately balancing on her lap, her bathrobe pulled tight. Her daughter was still asleep, affording Tina some quiet time to call her father. It had been years since they had had a father-daughter talk. The unexpected arousal of conflicting emotions from her meeting with the police officer necessitated the call to her father. Eddy's moccasins muffled the sound of his awkward gait down the hallway to his bedroom. The door was slightly ajar, allowing him to get a glimpse of his sleeping wife. She looked so peaceful. Even in her declining state, Eddy Pinafore felt that never-ending love for her. He turned and headed back to the living room.

"Okay. She's still sleeping. Now, tell me about this date you had."

"It wasn't really a date, Daddy, more like a first meeting," replied his daughter, still in a state of denial about Friday night at Gino's. She didn't want her father to get an impression different from the one she wished to project.

Eddy smiled at the linguistic manipulation his daughter had applied to her evening with the young police officer.

"As I understand it," he said, "you had already met him at your office when he came to see you about the damage to his truck, right? So, this was really your second meeting."

"If you're going to get technical, yes, Daddy, it was our second meeting," answered Tina in a firm tone.

She was seldom flippant with her father, but she was in no mood for his teasing. The basis for her terse response had more to do with the possibility of a third or fourth date than her father's mathematical accuracy. His comical nitpicking had been misunderstood.

"Honey, I was only kidding. Tell me about him."

Tina relaxed her guard, which came naturally when talking with her dad.

"Daddy, it's been so long since I've felt any kind of desire or attraction to date someone. I'm kinda in this quandary. I'm not sure I can trust my emotions considering what happened the last time I did."

"Oh, Tina. Trusting your emotions had nothing to do with Missy's father. It was what you based your emotions on. Yes, superficially, there was cause to be attracted to Trevor. Certainly, he was good looking, and he had plenty of money to spend on you, but did he ever make you feel wanted or that being with you was the most important thing in the world to him?"

Tina took a sip of her coffee, trying to digest her father's words. It took no time at all for her mind to traverse seven years of memories. It was always being at five-star restaurants, exclusive country clubs, and driving the most expensive cars that appealed to Trevor Barrington. Having a beautiful woman on his arm like Tina was like wearing a thousand-dollar Rolex or a custom-made Armani suit. She was nothing more than an accessory to him, a showpiece.

"Daddy, it would be so easy just to trust my heart. He's kind. He's sincere. He listens. We laugh together. There's nothing phony or pretentious about him. I think he's your kind of guy. But he doesn't know that much about me."

Her eyes began to moisten. She stifled the urge to cry. Eddy had no problem reading between the lines.

"So, he doesn't know that you have a child?"

"Oh, no. He knew from my landlord that I was a single mother. He just never asked about that."

"Maybe you're what's important to him. Did you ever think of that?"

Tina allowed herself a brief moment of fantasy. Even if he was all she thought he was, could she trust his heart with her child, a childlike Missy?

"Maybe, Daddy, but then there's Missy."

That was a topic close to Eddy Pinafore's heart. He could not, would not tolerate anyone ever viewing his granddaughter as anything but a special child of God.

"Honey, give yourself a little time to gauge his feelings for you and yours for him. If he's all you think he is, it will become clear very soon."

Tina took a tissue from a small box on the end table next to the couch. She dabbed her eyes from the tears that were entirely out of her control. Wishing to change the subject, she gently asked, "How's mom doing these days?" she asked, moving to an even more sensitive issue.

Eddy rested his phone on his lap to sip his coffee before it got cold.

"Sorry for the delay, but I hate cold coffee," he replied after taking a sip. "She's pretty much the same. We don't do walks in the morning anymore, but she does enjoy it when I take her shopping. I think seeing other people, even if she doesn't know them, gives her a feeling of normalcy. Memory is a continuing issue, and frankly, at times, I'm terrified that one day she won't remember me. Other days, I'm amazed at what she still remembers."

Tear ducts opened for both Eddy and his daughter. Tina hated to ask the question her father had never talked about with her.

"Daddy, have you planned for the day when Mom doesn't remember you? How will you take care of her?"

Eddy Pinafore knew that day was inevitable, but it was still difficult for him to talk about it. His plan pertained to both of them. The dryness in his throat caused his words to sound raspy, an indicator of the emotion of the topic.

He cleared his throat.

"Yes, sweetheart, I have. I've talked with Magnolia Gardens, and they've assured me there will be a place for both of us when the time comes. Your mom has a long history there. It would kind of be like going home, so to speak."

Tina's memories of being taken there as a young child and seeing the tenderness and compassion shown to the residents did little to assuage the feeling that her mother and father would become part of that aged generation of people who are forgotten, even as they forget themselves. It was useless to plead, but she had to.

"Daddy, what can I do?"

Eddy knew there was nothing anybody could do. He was fortunate even to have the option of a place like Magnolia Gardens. So many others in their position would languish in understaffed care homes where their identity consisted of the person in room number six. He was careful in his response, yet his answer was simple and direct.

"Honey, just love her and remember her."

The undeniable shuffling of her slippers on the tile floor told

Eddy his wife had risen and was making her way down the hallway. He could hear his daughter crying over the phone and knew this was no time to be talking with her mother.

"Honey, I hear your mom coming. Let me call you later. Love you."

Another tissue fell onto a pile of already discarded, dampened reminders of their conversation. Thankfully Missy was still asleep, affording Tina additional time to herself. Having set her phone on vibrate, Tina leaned her head against the back of the couch and closed her eyes, retreating into memories of what used to be. The subtle vibration of her phone caused her eyes to open. She looked at her phone. *What's he doing calling this early?* She thought, seeing his name on Caller ID. She tried to shift emotional gears.

16

THE CALL

"What a pleasant surprise this early in the morning," she said, as she cleared her throat.

"I hope it's not too early, but you did say to call when I made up my mind, didn't you?"

It took a moment for her to remember her response to Ryan's multiple-choice offer for their next meeting, and she smiled to herself. The sound of his voice helped ease the pessimism of her previous phone call to one of anticipation.

"Now that you mention it, I do."

She took one last tissue to dab her eyes as she awaited his decision. *It's a good thing we're not using face time*, she thought.

"Well, I thought to keep it simple and uncomplicated, we could go on a picnic, maybe do a little fishing if it's alright with you? Alberta Lake is only an hour away, and I know Fish and Game has planted it recently."

She felt that small but undeniable cardiac impulse. A feeling of warmth came over her causing her to nestle even deeper into the softness of her couch. He made "simple and uncomplicated" sound endearing and special, and he made her sound special.

"You never mentioned fishing as a hobby," she replied in a coy manner. She sounded like some femme fatale in an old spy movie, trying to seduce information from her prey.

"One of my many secrets," he replied with an audible chuckle in his voice. He was much more relaxed than last night.

"Touché," Tina answered. "As a matter of fact, I'd love to go fishing, and I can't remember the last time I was on a picnic, but there are a couple of obstacles. One, I don't even own fishing gear, and two, I'll have to arrange for a babysitter."

These were trivial matters to Ryan, whose only thoughts were to spend time with Tina. The prospect of involving himself in an activity that was not police work, yet he still enjoyed, was captivating.

"I've got plenty of gear for both of us, and you can bring your child along too. Maybe I could teach him a thing or two about fishing."

Are you kidding me? Tina thought. *This kind of thing only happens in a Hallmark movie.* Sobriety began to curb her enthusiasm.

"Well, he is a she, and it's not as simple as you think." Even as she said this, Tina yearned for an outside activity such as this that would both pleasure and teach her child.

"What's not simple about teaching a kid to fish?" answered Ryan, completely not sensing her hesitancy about bringing her child. "My dad did it all the time with some of my friends."

"That's very sweet of you, Ryan, but I really think another time would be better."

So, she thinks there will be another time. He was trying hard not to be offended by her rejection but was agitated by her taking such a kind offer so lightly.

"You're the boss. Listen, I'll start getting the gear together. Would a couple of hours give you enough time to find that babysitter?" Looking at his watch, he added, "I'll pick you up around ten."

"Okay, I'll call and make the sitter arrangements."

That titillation in her heart returned as she answered, "See you then."

~

NEVER ONE TO BE AN EARLY riser, Missy was awakened by the giddy laughter coming from the living room. She crawled out from beneath the warmth of her Ariel comforter, grabbed her Princess Gomu blanket, and shuffled awkwardly into the living room with her leg brace in hand. Seeing her daughter standing in front of her rubbing her sleepy eyes, Tina said, "Oh, my baby. Come sit with mommy." She patted the couch invitingly.

Obediently, Missy crawled up on the couch and nestled next to her mother, emitting that sigh of security a child gets when cuddled in their parent's arms. Tina stroked her baby's hair, now matted from a night of deep sleep.

"Let me put this on," Tina said, taking the brace Missy had placed on the coffee table.

Putting the horse before the cart, she asked, "How would you like to spend some time with Papa and Nana?" Missy's intellectual disabilities by no means kept her from connecting certain dots. Papa and Nana's house meant blueberry pancakes for starters and, later, if she was lucky, Nana's special cookies. Her doziness immediately gave way to the thought of sweets.

"Can Papa make pancakes for me?" she pleaded. Her eyes widened with anticipation.

"Let's ask," Tina replied as she dialed her father's number.

After asking her father if he could watch Missy for the day without giving away any crucial details other than, "I'll explain later," Tina hurriedly went to her bedroom and changed into clothes more appropriate than her terry cloth bathrobe. Then she went to Missy's room and packed a small tote bag with a change of clothes and a few of her favorite toys. When she returned to the living room, she announced, "I forgot. Yes, papa will make you blueberry pancakes!"

With that assurance, Missy quickly got off the couch and bolted for the front door, her mother not far behind. Tina passed every speed limit sign as if it were a suggestion on the way to her father's house.

～

"THANKS, DADDY," Tina said, as she gave her father a hug and a kiss on the cheek. "I know this is unexpected, but something came up at the last minute."

Remembering the tenor of their recent conversation, Eddy smiled.

"Going to check out those feelings?"

Tina nodded, then knelt to face her daughter.

"You be a good girl for Papa and Nana, okay?"

More concerned about her impending feast than a prolonged mother-daughter good-bye, Missy sputtered, "I will, I will!" then turned to her grandfather and screeched, "Pancakes!"

Eddy smiled at his daughter.

"Go! Go! And I want a report later, understand."

～

HER RESPONSE SENT Ryan into warp speed. It was not overconfidence that caused him to hook up his seventeen-foot War Eagle out-board the night before. It was a gamble that their last good-bye kiss good-bye was a prelude to the future. He was right. His rods and tackle box were permanently stored on the boat. He added a small propane barbecue, two beach chairs, a large blanket, and his Ozark Trail ice chest. He had already showered and shaved while waiting for the appropriate time to call, not too early but not too late. He checked the contents of a wicker picnic basket, a housewarming gift from his mother, and one he never thought he would have occasion to use, silverware, napkins, and wine glasses. He checked the list he had made the night before, noting items he had to get at Pete's Deli on the way; a pack of sweet Italian sausages, a pint of potato salad, a twin pack of small mustard and mayo bottles, a half dozen large hot dog buns, and a cup of cured Italian olives. As an alternative to the sausage, he'd also get a selection of cold cuts, prosciutto, mortadella, salami, some sliced Swiss cheese, and a couple of Pete's sourdough rolls that he bakes daily. Better to be prepared, he thought.

With his survey complete, he checked the weather for the umpteenth time on his phone; clear and sunny, temperature in the mid-eighties. *Perfect!* He thought.

∾

PERFECT! She thought as she did a once over in front of her bathroom mirror. She had hesitated to wear her Calvin Klein jeans. After all, she had already worn them on their first date, but what man would ever notice that. Her gray University of South Carolina tee-shirt was attractively tight. The matching sweatshirt was tied around her neck. Tina was her own worst critic when it came to makeup. There were repeated stares into the mirror to check for the slightest flaw in her mascara, eyeliner, lipstick, and whatever else she could spot. She paused, momentarily falling into that temporary funk; what if things didn't work out. She placed her hands on the edge of her vanity. What's the point of all this if he's not... then she remembered her father's words; take the time to gauge his feelings and your feelings. She took a deep breath and said to the image in the mirror, "Alright, Tina, let's see what this guy's got!"

17

AN IDEA TOO LATE

Eddy Pinafore was not naive to his wife's condition. Even without a doctor's diagnosis, he had read enough to know that dementia was slowly ravaging Maddy's mind. At best, her memories were fractured. She tired at Eddy's prompting her to remember things, prompts that led to tears of frustration on her part, and that was unbearable for her husband of some twenty-five years. Even with the obvious staring him in the face, Eddy would not give in without trying one more time. He had taken to the internet searching for articles about dementia, its root causes, and possible remedies. One name kept appearing with astounding regularity, Doctor Shane Tipton. Doctor Tipton had long ago retired from active practice and now devoted most of his time as a consultant with the Bright Focus Foundation, a non-profit foundation specializing in dementia, Alzheimer's disease, and macular degeneration. He was the neurosurgeon who had helped with the treatment plan for Jane Lincoln after the tragic accident that took her husband Daniel's life and left Jane in a vegetative state. Eddy doubted the doctor would remember them, but it was worth a try for Maddy's sake. Eddy had been trying for months to get an appointment with the renowned doctor. The phone call that Doctor Tipton finally had an opening was a two-edged sword for Eddy Pinafore. It could confirm his amateurish diagnosis, or it could lead to some slim possibility of hope. Eddy prepared for the former.

For some time, Maddy Pinafore had suffered through long periods of lethargic behavior. Any attempts by Eddy to bring his wife out of these funks of depression proved fruitless, frequently resulting in episodes of frustrating tears where Maddy would blurt out, "What's wrong with me, Eddy?" It was following one of those events that Eddy suggested they see a doctor about Maddy's condition. In a rare moment of coherent thought, she responded, "Yes."

Doctor Tipton still maintained an office in the Center for Neurological Studies in Charleston, South Carolina, a research center affiliated with the University of South Carolina. At Doctor Tipton's request, all of Maddy's medical records had been sent to his office.

∽

MADDY STARED into the mirror over her bedroom vanity. Her eyesight had degraded due to her macular degeneration. She no longer labored over eyeliner or mascara. A bit of facial powder and lipstick was the limit of her ability. Her feminine ego would not allow her to ask her husband for help applying makeup, for which Eddy was eternally grateful. She turned her head slowly to the left, then the right, and then she stopped, staring straight ahead. Bewildered at her fresh image, Maddy asked, "Are we going somewhere, Eddy?"

Eddy was sitting on the side of the bed, adjusting his prosthetic leg. He had sometimes taken the easy way out when asked such a question and answered, "Yes," a short answer with no explanation, neither of which she would remember.

From his recent readings, Eddy had decided that a more detailed answer was the better approach. Simply and naively, he thought that maybe a word or a phrase might ignite some connection within her fractured memories.

"Yes, we are sweetheart. We're going to see Doctor Tipton, the doctor who tended to Jane after her accident and arranged for her to go to Magnolia Gardens."

Maddy smiled into the mirror.

"That's nice."

Eddy said nothing. It would serve no earthly purpose to disrupt the pleasantry of whatever imagery his wife had in mind. With his prosthetic firmly in place, Eddy slipped on his khaki pants and then stepped into his tan loafers with tassels across the arches. He tucked in his red polo shirt, and with one hand, deftly secured the top button. He walked over to their closet and slid open the door.

"Would you like your black jacket or the yellow sweater?"

"Oh, I think I'll wear my yellow sweater. It goes well with my floral blouse, don't you think?"

Taking the sweater off its hanger, Eddy responded, "Absolutely," but thought, *"Yes, if you were wearing your floral blouse."* Another unnecessary correction.

Eddy slipped on a gray windbreaker, then picked up a cane leaning against the nightstand next to Maddy's side of the bed. Due to her failing eyesight, Maddy experienced difficulty seeing uneven surfaces on walkways and sidewalks. The use of a cane afforded her some assurance of not falling. Eddy's arm did the rest. He walked over to Maddy and helped her with her sweater.

"I've got your cane right here," he said, holding it out for her to grab. "We'd better be on our way."

Maddy failed to respond to Eddy's smile, partially due to her diminishing eyesight and partially due to a mind that could no longer comprehend the depth of the love it represented.

They made their way down the hallway into the living room. As they approached the dining area, Maddy asked, "Are we going to have breakfast before we leave?"

Eddy looked at the two plates, still on the table. One had a half-eaten piece of toast and some leftover scrambled eggs. The other plate had only a bit of toast on it.

"I can make you something if you're still hungry?"

"Oh, don't you bother, sweetheart. I don't seem to have much of an appetite," Maddy answered.

Eddy smiled as he held open the front door.

AFTER GETTING Maddy safely belted in the passenger seat of their Honda Accord, Eddy walked around to the driver's side. As he got in, he placed Maddy's cane next to her side. With his seat belt clipped in, he started the car. He pressed Sirius XM radio, which was preset to "Hits of the Seventies," a time when Eddy and Maddy idyllically planned for their future, their family-to-be, a time when Eddy thought of his career as a Navy Seal being some grand adventure where he would conquer all dangers, defeat all foes, all in the name of defending America. The words of Neil Young's "Heart of Gold" mesmerized him back to that time. He glanced at Maddy, whose head swayed gently left and right to the melodic sound of Young's voice. Eddy hoped that she had at least some remembrance of the song, but then probably not.

Eddy checked the radio clock as he pulled into the parking lot of the Center for Neurological Studies. It read 1:30 p.m. Surprisingly, Maddy had stayed awake during the forty-five-minute drive to Doctor Tipton's office. Apparently, the music selection had kept Maddy's focus sufficiently alert that she fought the urge to doze off. They had plenty of time to navigate the long curved pathway, consisting of exposed aggregate, from the parking lot to the entrance doors. Maddy would need the extra time, as walking on the uneven surface was time-consuming, to say the least. Reaching the front doors, Eddy wondered what degree of alertness Maddy would have for the doctor. In an instant, he had his answer. As they crossed the threshold, Maddy said, "What movie are we seeing?"

"A romance, sweetheart."

Maddy smiled. Eddy scanned the walls looking for a directory. The foyer lacked the traditional receptionist station with a woman wearing a headset and a computer in front of her window. There was no accompanying sitting area with small tables and chairs for patients awaiting their appointment. Instead, A matronly looking lady with silver hair sat behind a small card table-sized desk. She wore a powder blue smock and a name tag reading, "Nora." Her reading glasses hung from her neck on a golden braid. A laminated sheet of paper lay in front of her. A sign on the desk edge read, "Information Center." Despite her apparent advanced age, a bit of rouge on each cheek, a dab of facial powder, and a thin line of red lipstick indicated Nora still tended to her public appearance.

"May I help you?" she asked.

"Yes, we're here to see Doctor Tipton," Eddy answered.

"He's down the hallway to your left. Suite 101," smiled Nora.

"Thank you so much."

With Maddy on his arm, Eddy proceeded across a nearly empty foyer to the hallway. The first office on their right was Doctor Tipton's. Eddy paused to look at the photograph on the wall next to the door. The name beneath it read, "Shane Tipton, MD." His silver hair was cropped short like a flattop, a hairstyle long since out of style. He had high cheekbones that narrowed to a chiseled chin. His hazel eyes hardly did justice to the kindness of the old doctor. Eddy opened the door and led Maddy inside. The waiting room, if you could call it that, more resembled a small reading room than a holding area for patients. An aquarium nearly 8' long, 2' deep, and 3' tall occupied one wall. A vast variety of fish swimming through and around various rock formations was mesmerizing. Sunken lights only added to the brilliance of the occupants. A mahogany bookcase spanned the opposite wall. Eddy surveyed its shelves. A voracious reader himself, he marveled at the eclectic collection, historical and political anthologies from medieval Europe, and row after row of the greatest American authors, poets, and historians, names like Pond, Cummings, Whitman, Poe, Melville, Twain, Faulkner, Steinbeck, and Vonnegut. There were two strategically placed highbacked tan chairs at either end of the bookcase, obviously intended for the curious reader to use. A small tan leather couch occupied the last wall, affording whoever sat there a beautiful view of the aquarium and a most impressive reading selection to occupy their time before seeing the doctor. Eddy was leading Maddy to the leather couch when a door opened.

"I hope I haven't kept you waiting. When someone enters the waiting area, it sounds an alarm in my office. I was preoccupied momentarily with a phone call. I assume you are Eddy and Maddy Pinafore? I'm Shane Tipton."

Eddy thought the doctor was near his age, mid-seventies. His shoulders were slightly stooped. He had a most engaging personality. The gracious doctor offered his hand first to Eddy and then to Maddy. Eddy noticed the doctor had a malformed pinkie finger on one hand. Eddy had seen older golfers with similar such injuries.

"Play a lot of golf?" Eddy asked, alluding to the doctor's finger.

Smiling, Tipton replied, "No. The results of an old man thinking he could still play basketball with young men. Shall we go into my office?" Seeing the cane in Maddy's hand, Tipton offered her his arm.

"Maddy, allow me," he said.

Maddy blushed at the gesture of politeness extended by the doctor. Tipton guided Maddy through the door and into his office. Eddy dutifully followed. It was the most un-doctor-like office Eddy Pinafore had ever seen. There were no certificates or licenses displayed on the walls, no panels to read x-rays, no small stool on rollers, or a reclining table for a patient to sit on. Tipton's desk was rather unassuming, like something purchased at Wal-Mart. A large laptop computer occupied the center of the desk with a Tiffany lamp at its side. Much like the furniture in the waiting room, Tipton had a somewhat larger tan leather couch. In front of the couch was a glass top oval table. Two very comfortable looking stuffed leather chairs were positioned on each end of the table. Against a far wall was the only item clearly not intended for patient comfort. Eddy recognized the eighty-two-inch ZD Net computer, one of the largest business models on the market. Tipton led Maddy to the couch.

"Why don't you and your husband sit here? I'll take a chair."

With Eddy and Maddy comfortably positioned, Tipton slid his chair closer.

"I'm not one to stand on formality, so if it's okay with you, please call me Shane."

Eddy smiled with a nod, and surprisingly, so did Maddy. *Could this be one of those moments he had hoped for?*

"When my nurse told me your last name, I must admit I didn't remember you at first. But your records indicated I had a patient some years ago who was a good friend of yours. If I recall correctly, her name was Jane Lincoln."

Tipton wisely chose not to go into any details of the case. He also knew his next question would be pivotal in getting information without being insulting. He leaned forward and addressed Maddy directly.

"So, Maddy, tell me why you're here today."

Eddy instinctively took hold of her hand as Maddy looked

at Tipton and said, "I'm sorry, but do I know you?" The gentle tentativeness in her voice spoke volumes for the doctor who specialized in gerontology.

Tipton smiled.

"My name is Shane. I'm going to be your doctor. I'd like to ask you a few questions if that's okay with you?"

Maddy looked at Eddy. She seemed confused, as if she needed his approval.

Eddy answered for her.

"Of course, you can."

"Great. There's one thing, though. I need Eddy to sign some papers. Maddy, would it be alright with you if I took your husband into the other room for a moment?"

Maddy looked at the doctor. "Shane, your name is Shane, right?"

When he answered yes, Maddy's eyes brightened. She stunned Eddy with what she said next.

"But bring him back, remember you're my doctor."

There was an impish grin on Maddy's face. Eddy had seen these moments of coherence before. They were fleeting at best, but even false hope was better than no hope. Once in the other office, Tipton revealed his plan to Eddy.

"I'm going to administer a test to your wife. It's called the Mini-Mental Status Exam. It will measure your wife's ability to understand time, date, and location. It will also measure her ability to remember objects, words and perform simple math calculations. I need her answers to be free of any hesitancy or reliance on you for help. Your mere presence during the test will draw her attention to you and away from the question, so it's important you wait out here. Does that make sense to you?"

"Perfect sense," replied Eddy.

Tipton returned to his office, leaving Eddy to ponder the amazing collection of sea life in the aquarium. After half an hour, Tipton had his answer, but he would need one more test to confirm his suspicions. He brought Maddy out to the waiting area. She was giggling about something Tipton had said to her. A nurse soon appeared. She had a small rolling tray with a couple of vials and a syringe on it.

"Eddy, we're all done. I need this nurse to draw some blood from Maddy for one last test. Maybe we could talk in my office?"

"Maddy, my name is Kristin. Why don't you have a seat right here? This will only take a minute."

Maddy seemed perfectly at ease with the request, thanks to the calming tone of the nurse. Tipton waved to Eddy to follow him into his office. Once inside, Tipton had Eddy take a seat. Tipton's hazel eyes betrayed the bad news he was about to deliver. It was times like this that made Tipton wish he had become a pediatrician delivering a healthy baby to some joyously happy new parents. His field of expertise dealt with people on the other end of life's spectrum where good news was qualified by phrases like, "We can make her comfortable" or "There are no bad memories for her anymore."

"Eddy, you have a lovely wife. I'm sure what I'm about to tell you will come as no surprise. The Mini-Mental Status Test results indicate your wife has severe cognitive impairment; in other words, she's suffering from dementia. Her blood test will most surely show high levels of trans fats. It's probably been coming on for the last few years. Have you considered what to do when you can no longer care for her by yourself?"

The confirmation of his worst fears was like a stake being driven into his heart. Eddy Pinafore had spent the better part of twenty plus years living without the dream of his life after the failed mission that had cost the lives of all his Seal teammates and left him a double amputee. Then through a miracle of God, he and Maddy were brought together to fulfill their life's dream of marriage and a family. Now he was losing her again, and there was nothing he could do about it. How much more did

God think he could handle? With what little resolve he had left, Eddy answered, "Yes, I've made plans to move us to Magnolia Gardens. Maddy was once the executive director there. They've secured a small apartment for us when the time comes."

"That's good to hear, Eddy. In the meantime, what are you going to do?"

The resignation in his voice seemed void of emotion.

"Love her. Take care of her. What else is there?"

Tipton knew what he was about to tell Eddy Pinafore would sound absolutely crazy. He hoped his own deeply held faith would provide Eddy some consolation.

"Eddy, there is something I'm going to recommend you do. I want you and Maddy to go on a road trip. I want the two of you to revisit some places that held special memories for the two of you. Relive those memories once again with her. I would offer this one caution. Don't use the word remember in any context, not 'I remember when,' not 'do you remember when.' Her struggle, when cued to remember, will only frustrate her and you."

Eddy sat there, flabbergasted. As far as he was concerned, that was an exercise in futility, and a very painful one at that, considering the good doctor had told him his wife had severe cognitive impairment. His answer had a noticeable tone of frustration.

"How does that help Maddy, considering her condition?"

"Even with her condition, there's a possibility of some sudden resurrection of a memory long forgotten, if for only a second or two. It will be momentary at best. Mostly though, Eddy, it will help you. The time you take with Maddy to go back to where those memories were formed will help you focus on the fullness of your lives together and not the ending."

For Eddy Pinafore, one thing was certain. The future was dim, and any chance at all of brightening it was worth a try.

18

A SPECIAL PLACE

There was a sense of exhilaration as Ryan headed to pick up Tina, and it had nothing to do with fishing or a picnic. He just wanted to be with her. It was an unusual feeling for the good-looking bachelor who had dated some in the past. Those were times when having a girl on your arm meant you weren't the fifth wheel, so to speak, and sometimes it meant friends with benefits, which wasn't bad either. But this time, things were different. There would be no getting out of bed and leaving before the sun came up, more like enjoying the sunrise together. He made a beeline to Pete's Deli to pick up a couple of bags of ice and the food items for the picnic, then to Tina's place. His hand tapped nervously on the steering wheel to the beat of Paul van Dyk's hit, "Nothing but You."

Pulling up to the curb in front of her place, he was greeted with a surprise. She was already outside, waiting on the steps of her landlord's house. *She looks beautiful,* he thought, as he exited his truck. He was earnestly trying not to be nervous, but it was no use.

"Am I late?" he asked, worried that he had taken too much time getting things together.

"No, I'm early," she smiled. "Too nice of a day to wait inside."

He held open the passenger door.

"Those jeans look familiar. Gino's, right?"

She remembered his stare the night they met at Gino's.

"Yes." The smile accompanying her answer registered a ten on her approval meter.

Glancing at all the gear in the boat, Tina mockingly stated, "This is a day trip, isn't it?"

A childish grin formed on his face. "Just want to be prepared," he replied.

One thing he wasn't prepared for was the hug she gave him before getting in the truck. Not a quick "thank you" type of hug, but a prolonged hug that left Ryan hoping this moment would not end.

"Thanks for being so thoughtful," she whispered in his ear.

True to the forecast, the mid-morning temperature was in the low sixties. Ryan left the windows down. The airflow provided a coolness both seemed to enjoy as they headed to the crosstown freeway. Curiosity was getting the best of Tina.

"What made you decide on fishing and a picnic? They're kind of old-fashioned choices, but in a good way," she said with a reassuring smile.

Checking the traffic as he headed up the on-ramp, he said, "You said how much you loved it when your father used to take you fishing on summer vacations. My mom was especially fond of picnics with my dad when I was a kid. I sort of combined the two."

He listens, she thought. Tina filed that away for future consideration.

"There's coffee in the thermos in the console, with French Vanilla creamer, if you'd like some."

"I did short myself of my normal two cups this morning, thanks." The thoughtful consideration brought another smile to her face.

Ryan lifted the lid of the console, and Tina retrieved the thermos. As she poured a portion into the thermos' top, she savored the aroma of the brew.

"Hot coffee with French Vanilla creamer, my favorite," she sighed.

"I know," Ryan replied. "I saw a bowl of creamers in your office the day I came to see you. Certain things kind of stick with me."

As Tina enjoyed her coffee, she noted that she was actually enjoying the quiet periods between them.

For Tina Pinafore, Ryan Callahan was slowly proving her father right. She enjoyed her coffee. She enjoyed the quiet between the two more, no forced conversation to fill the awkwardness between two near strangers. He didn't feel like a stranger to her. In fact, eerily so, he seemed to be drawing her heart closer and closer to his. Nearly ten miles outside of Charleston, Alberta Lake lay in the middle of some 150 square miles of land purchased by a private conservation group devoted to preserving some semblance of the local area's natural ecological environment. The 100-acre lake was regularly stocked with twenty-one varieties of fish, making it ideal for anglers of all ages. Ski boats and powerboats were prohibited; only four-stroke engines were allowed for ecological purposes. There were two small sandy beaches on either side of the boat launch with roped-off swimming areas. There were also a limited number of campsites available for overnight stays. Except for one area known as Boulder Cove, the shoreline consisted of marshy bogs home to a variety of ducks and geese along with bass.

"Here we are," Ryan announced as he exited the crosstown freeway. The overhead sign read, "Alberta Lake, one mile."

The serenity of the view was in stark comparison to downtown Charleston's commercial structures or the residential developments that surrounded the city central. The entrance road wove through a forest of densely populated bristlecone pine trees, eventually coming to a large, graveled area. Tina rolled down her window, closed her eyes, and inhaled. The sweet butterscotch aroma of the bristlecone pine sap filled her nostrils. The melodic sounds of the Red Crossbill that nested within its branches seemed to alert the surrounding wildlife another intruder was entering their territory. Ryan parked in front of a small general store made of logs, with a cedar-shingled roof covered with moss. The sign over the wooden porch read, "Paradise Lost." Ryan said, "We need to get a launch permit and a box of nightcrawlers, and there's a restroom inside if you need it." Tina got out of the truck, arched her back, and sighed, "This is absolutely beautiful!"

Ryan had hoped she would think so. This had been a special place to him, and Tina was about to discover yet another facet of his charm. Ryan noticed the large number of cars in the parking lot. What pleased him was the relatively few boat trailers. *More of the lake for just the two of them,* he thought. The log handrails with nails pounded in at odd intervals to hold fishing poles, and crooked steps leading up to the doors hadn't changed in years. Nor, did it seem, had the squeaky hinges on the double screen doors. As they entered, the owner called out, "I'll be damned if it isn't little Ryan Callahan. My god, boy, I haven't seen you in years."

A short, older bald-headed man came out from around the counter. He wore tan work pants held up by red suspenders, black boots, and a checkered flannel shirt with its sleeves rolled up to the elbows. Ryan bent slightly forward as he and the shorter man hugged. The man stepped back and announced, "I haven't seen you since your father died. What's kept you away?"

"I don't know, Mick. This was such a special place for me and my dad. I guess I needed a special reason to come back."

"Well, you're here, and that's all that matters," smiled the old man as he gave Ryan another hug. "And who do we have here?" he asked, looking at Tina.

"Tina, meet Mickey Donovan, Mick for short. Mick and my father were cops together on the Charleston PD."

Tina extended her hand. "Mickey, it's a pleasure to meet you."

"Young lady, you can call me Mick, just like Ryan and Big Mike used to do, and a hug, not a handshake, is the order of the day."

Feeling like she was being initiated into a special kind of club, Tina embraced him. The interior of the store reminded Tina of a similar place on Lake Marion where her family used to vacation in the summer. Old wooden shelves made of cedar planks were stocked with every variety of canned food a camping family could need—potatoes, chili beans, pork and beans, beef stew, hash, and spam. Other shelves held every style of chips and dip imaginable. Behind the counter, Donovan stocked the hard liquor, pints, and fifths of inexpensive booze at twice the regular store's price. Cases of beer were stacked next to twin refrigerators. There were back-to-back metal racks with every candy bar a sweet-toothed kid would want. Next to the candy racks was an old Amana refrigerator filled with ice cream bars and plastic tubs of nightcrawlers.

"Getting ready for the summer rush, Mick?" Ryan asked as he went to the old Amana and took out a tub of nightcrawlers.

"The ownership is planning on expanding the number of overnight camping spots, and that means more hungry and thirsty adults with kids addicted to sugar in any form. Someone has to make a buck. It might as well be me," he laughed. As Ryan was paying for the worms, he said, "See you at the dock."

Ignoring Ryan, Mick looked at Tina and smiled.

"Young lady, it was a pleasure to meet you."

"The pleasure was all mine, Mick, especially if I can get another hug."

Mick's bald head appeared to blush with embarrassment as he reached over the counter to accommodate Tina's request. When they got to the truck, Ryan placed the worms in his ice chest. As they got in the truck, Tina asked, "There's more to this place than just fishing, isn't there?" Ryan started his vehicle but didn't answer Tina's question. For a moment, he stared straight ahead. He lightly bit down on his lower lip. He idolized his father. He was the reason why Ryan joined the Marine Corps out of high school and later became a police officer. You could fish anywhere, on any lake, any stream. That's not what made it special. It was who you were with and the memories you made. He would wait to answer her completely. "Yeah! There is."

Ryan drove to the launch ramp. He made a long looping approach, and once there, skillfully backed the boat to the water's edge where Mick was waiting. He uncoupled the boat and held onto a rope that was attached to a bow cleat. When Ryan stepped onto the floating dock, he took the rope from Donovan.

"See you later, Mick."

Donovan got in Ryan's truck and pulled forward slowly until the boat floated free of the trailer. He leaned out the window and shouted, "Call me when you're ready." He drove up the ramp to the boat parking area. Ryan pulled the boat close to the dock's edge.

"Okay, hop in," he said, extending his hand to Tina to use for balance.

Ignoring his gesture of help, Tina put one foot on the boat's side and then adeptly put her other foot onto the middle seat and then stood on the deck of the boat.

She looked up at Ryan. Her hands placed on her hips and said in mock defiance, "This isn't my first rodeo, cowboy!"

Ryan shook his head in comic relief. He stepped into the boat and headed to the rear seat. He had paid extra for an electric ignition that he dearly loved, compared to multiple pulls on a starter cord of a stubborn engine. Once it started, he gave the throttle a little juice before kicking it into gear.

"Have a seat and enjoy the ride," he said.

Once outside the buoy markers indicating to boaters to make no wake, Ryan gave the throttle another twist. The four-cycle Evinrude engine whined as it began to propel the War Eagle out into open water. The layers of her hair quivered gently in the breeze. At one point, the boat's bow slapped the water creating a cool spray to Tina's face. She started to giggle then looked back at Ryan.

"Hey, I worked hard on this makeup, Mister!"

"And you look beautiful, too!" Ryan was glad he said that. He was not always so quick on the uptake.

The twenty-minute drive to Boulder Cove afforded Ryan an opportunity to recall those special times with his father, times when valuable lessons were passed from one generation to another. He learned patience does not just apply to fishing and to appreciate where you are, not just why you are there. Even more valuable, never forget to bring toilet paper. Tina's thoughts were more centered on the present. The water was like glass. The cool breeze off the water relieved the warmth reflecting on her face from the noontime sun. An occasional passing cloud caused the waterfowl to venture out of the marshy shoreline only to hasten back when the sun reappeared. Tina wished she had sat next to Ryan rather than sitting alone on the middle seat, ignoring the principle of keeping the boat balanced.

"That's us to the right," Ryan called out.

A huge granite boulder some twenty-feet high extended out from the shoreline. On the other side of the boulder was a small sandy beach. On the other side of the beach was a thicket of spiny cottonwood trees reaching the water's edge. The unobservant boater could easily miss seeing the beach as they passed by. As Ryan reached the sandy shoreline, he gave the engine a little extra boost, putting the boat securely on land.

"Give me your hand," he said to Tina, "I'll help you out."

With an amusing smirk on her face, she looked at Ryan and said, "Kind of the opposite of getting in, isn't it?"

She walked to the bow, carefully avoiding all the stuff Ryan had brought. Very gracefully, she hopped off onto the beach.

"How was that?" she smiled at Ryan.

"Will the surprises never end?" he quipped.

It took Ryan about thirty minutes to offload the boat and arrange the picnic setting. Two corkscrew metal rods near the shoreline held the two fishing rods. Further up and next to the boulder, Ryan had spread out the beach blanket. The chairs were side by side, the chest next to them. In front of the ice chest was the wicker picnic basket. Just in front of the basket was the small propane barbecue. After surveying the scene with a critical eye, he asked, "What's missing?"

"Are you kidding!" replied Tina, who thought she was in the middle of a scene for a Hallmark movie.

"Good, then let's get those rods in the water."

Ryan got the nightcrawlers from the ice chest and walked down to the rod holders. He dug through the damp loam soil to find a fat one. Releasing the hook from the eyelet, he skewered the worm onto the hook, then moved the red and white bobber up the line about four feet. He then baited Tina's rod, for which she was very grateful.

"Thanks," she said, holding up both hands to display her long acrylic nails. "These make that kind of difficult." Not that she was all that interested in handling a worm under any circumstances.

Handing her a rod, he said, "Now cast this bad boy and put the bobber near the end of the boulder."

There are some things like riding a bicycle that one never forgets. Casting a fishing rod isn't one of them. Tina drew her rod back over her shoulder and cast forward. The red and white bobber wrapped itself around the end of her rod.

Seeing the tangled mess, Ryan apologetically said, "I should have told you to flip your bail."

"Yeah, the bail?" Tina replied, looking completely lost at Ryan's instruction.

"It happens to the best of us," said Ryan, hoping not to crush her enthusiasm.

He took the rod from her, untangled the line, then returned it to her, tapping the curved metal bail as a reminder. This time her cast was perfect. Inwardly, Tina sighed, *Thank God!* Outwardly she merely smiled. Ryan cast his rod not four feet from where Tina's bobber landed. He placed his rod in the holder. Tina followed his example.

"Are you thirsty or hungry?" he asked.

"A little of both," she replied with a smile.

"I came prepared," he joked.

They headed back to their beach chairs. Ryan opened the wicker basket and the ice chest. Flipping a cloth towel over his arm and with the most pretentious impression of a professional waiter she had ever heard said, "For your dining pleasure, I have Italian sausages to barbecue or a fine selection of imported deli cold cuts, complete with Po' Boy rolls baked fresh this morning. From our beverage list, may I suggest an ice-cold Heineken or a room temperature Pinot Noir?"

Unable to contain her laughter, Tina was barely able to indicate she'd take the Heineken.

He handed Tina her bottle. Tipping their bottle tops together, each enjoyed that first ice-cold swig. Taking advantage of the moment, Tina asked, "I take it from Mick you haven't been back here since your dad died. Why is that?"

Ryan took another swig of his beer and swallowed slowly,

letting the cold liquid soothe his constricting throat muscles. He rubbed the cold bottle across his forehead as if to numb some sort of emerging pain. He stared off across the water.

"This place was our special place. I don't think he ever took my mom here. At least if he did, he never mentioned it to me. This was where I got those father-son talks that embarrassed me no end to hear and were totally unnecessary to a teenager who thought he knew everything. When that phase passed, we had our man-to-man talks, talks about what direction to take with my life, what real happiness means, and the mark you want to leave on this earth when you're gone. I wasn't out of high school long when I realized how smart my father had gotten in such a short time. Once after getting a Dear John letter when I was in the Marines, I asked him how he knew mom was the woman he wanted to marry since my selection process was clearly faulty. I never forgot what he told me. It was their first date, and dad took mom to a restaurant he had never been to before. It was some small, inexpensive mom and pop's place that specialized in Greek food. He said he couldn't afford a really fancy place. Anyway, he said the way she smiled at him made him think he was in a four-star restaurant and the sound of her voice made the food taste like he was eating a gourmet meal. She made that restaurant seem special, not the other way around."

His small oratory caused his throat to beg for another swallow of beer.

"Sorry," he said, looking at Tina. "I didn't mean to ramble on and on."

Silent tears belied the emotions Tina tried desperately to control. Seeing the results of his answer, he reached over and took her hand in his. "I'm so sorry," he said, "I never meant to upset you."

Tina shook her head slowly and got enough control of her

emotions to utter, "No, that was beautiful," before more silent tears appeared.

Seeing the need to change the conversation, Ryan said, "You did say you were hungry too, right?"

Another nod.

"Okay, barbecued Italian sausages or deli cold cuts on fresh-baked Po' Boy buns. Your pick?"

The anticipated aroma of barbecued sausages won out over the deli cold cuts.

"I pick Italian sausages." Leaning forward in her chair, she added, "Can I help?"

"I got this under control. You relax."

This was the kind of pampering to warm any woman's heart. For Tina Pinafore, she had never been treated like this, but it was certainly something she could get used to. Ryan moved the wicker picnic basket to his right. He lifted the top of the ice chest and took out four of Pete's finest sausages wrapped in white butcher paper and set them in front of the barbecue. Next came Pete's sourdough rolls. With a twist of the black handle on the propane tank to "On" and a press of the red ignition button, Ryan had a flame. He set the flame on low, then laid the sausages on the grill. Stretching his long legs out straight, he proudly stated, "It doesn't get any better than this!" *Oh yes, it could,* Tina thought, allowing her imagination to drift off to some erotic love scene on a deserted island. Ryan broached a subject he knew would be a sensitive one, but it couldn't stay in the background forever.

"I don't mean to pry, but I know you have a child, yet you've never mentioned your ex," Ryan asked.

She knew this question would come sooner or later, but she was savoring the euphoria of the moment. That was soon to be disrupted. Ryan reached out with a barbecue fork and carefully rolled the sausages over a quarter turn.

Tina brought her feet together and rested her elbows on her

knees. She raised her bottle to her lips and said, "He's not in the picture."

Ryan had known a few friends who had gotten divorces. Child custody and visitations were always contentious issues. Motivated by admitted jealous curiosity, he continued.

"That's unusual, considering fights over child custody and visitations are pretty typical in most divorces."

"In this case, there wasn't a divorce or fights about custody or visitation."

There was a deep hurt in her words that made Ryan feel tremendously guilty for even asking the question in the first place. The last thing he ever wanted to do was to hurt her.

He took her hand in his, "Look, Tina, I'm sorry for asking. It's really none of my business."

As their interlocking fingers gently squeezed together, she felt the sincerity in his heart. Still, she questioned whether she wanted to open up that part of her past, especially when it involved the humiliating rejection of the man she thought loved her, and the abandonment of their unborn child. Her father's advice suddenly became harder to accept, to trust your feelings, and trust in his. She turned to him and saw the longing for forgiveness in his eyes. *Oh, you are so wrong, Ryan,* she thought. *I want it to be your business! I want everything about me and my past to be your business!*

As she stood up, she continued to hold on to Ryan's hand, causing him to rise. This was the moment she decided to act on her father's advice; besides, she had a Plan B. *I survived rejection once before. I can survive it again if I have to.* She took both of his hands in hers, placing them on his chest.

"We met when I was a sophomore in college. He was a senior and came from a very wealthy family. We were in love, or so I thought. Anyway, I got pregnant. I thought I was the luckiest woman on the face of the earth, that is until my pediatrician recommended an amniocentesis test near the end of my first trimester. The test results showed there was a possibility the child might be born with developmental issues. He and his family wanted me to get an abortion. Long story short, I refused and never heard from him again. So, it's my daughter and me. There, now you know."

Ryan could tell from the resignation in her voice she expected him to say something polite, something neutral and noncommittal, then disappear from her life forever. He had no intention of fulfilling that prophecy. He let go of her hands and placed his on her shoulders. His blue eyes stared intently into hers. His affirmation caused her heart to stop, but not the unexpected flow of tears that now ran down both of her cheeks.

"How could anyone fall in love with you and not love what that created?"

Tina tilted her head upward to rebut the naiveness of his words when his lips met hers. She quickly succumbed to the sensuality of the movement of their lips together and sunk deeper into his arms. Her hands tightened around his neck. His arms engulfed her body till she could feel his heartbeat. The rapidly rising sense of mutual arousal was interrupted by the passing of a small outboard whose obnoxious driver insisted on honking his horn at the impassioned couple on the beach. This was a moment neither wanted to waste by reacting to the intrusive passerby. But for the need to breathe, their embrace would have continued till who knows when.

Tina rested her head against Ryan's chest, hoping she had not misunderstood the message behind his words or that cardiac eruption that caused her to take a deep breath following his kiss. She would not be disappointed. He placed both hands on her face and spoke squarely to her heart.

"Let me tell you something. You're not alone in this anymore."

The rapture that engulfed her left her speechless. Her father had been right. But there was something he needed to hear, and soon, or the afternoon picnic would end quickly.

"Ryan, I think the sausages are burning."

"Damn," he shouted as he turned his attention to the barbecue. Dark smoke rose from the sausages, which were covered with a darkened char. Juice oozed out of cracks in the skin. He dropped to his knees and, using his fingers, snatched the now near inedible meal off the grill and onto a paper plate. With the mournful look of a stray puppy, he said, "Is well done okay for you?"

Hardly able to contain her laughter, Tina knelt next to him and replied, "I love well done." Then she renewed their previous embrace.

Somehow Ryan had managed to salvage the sausages, and along with toasted sourdough buns and potato salad, he had indeed created a tasteful meal. Rather than more emotional revelations, each wisely took advantage to appreciate the moment. There would be profound consequences for both. There were sweet smiles back and forth as if to assure one and another there were no regrets for misspoken words or intentions. It was Tina who brought them back to reality.

"Ryan, are you sure you hooked up my bobber correctly?"

"Of course, I've done that a thousand times. Why?" he asked, looking at her.

"Because it's gone."

Ryan immediately shifted his attention to the two rods secured in their holders near the water's edge. Indeed, her bobber was gone, but the erratic movement of the rod tip explained it all.

"You got a fish! You got a fish!"

They bolted to the shoreline. Ryan quickly yanked the rod from its holder and gave it to Tina.

"Start reeling!"

In quick succession, he barked out more orders.

"Keep your rod tip up!" "Don't reel if he's taking out line!"

Ryan's bobber floated lifelessly on the surface. He quickly reeled it in to avoid their two lines getting tangled up. The surface suddenly exploded as a monster trout flipped over and over in the air. Tina screamed with excitement, almost tipping over backward. Ryan reached for the net next to his rod holder. He could see the trout tiring as Tina continued to reel.

"You've almost got him!" Ryan assured her as he watched the fish cease its struggle. He reached down in the water and brought the net up with its prize inside.

"Nice catch," Ryan said.

"It was all the bobber and worm," laughed Tina, deferring credit to Ryan.

With the fish cleaned and on ice, Ryan took her hand in his.

"You've made this place special again," Ryan said. "That means a lot to me. I hope we can do this again and soon."

She had no words to describe the emotional void he had filled in her life, no words to describe the frail grasp on her future she hoped was there. She had made herself vulnerable, and he had made her feel safe and protected. More than anything else, she wished for a tomorrow with him. With more daring than their brief times together warranted, Tina Pinafore pushed her father's words to the limit.

"I'd like us to make a lot of places special."

Ryan Callahan wanted this woman now. He wanted her tomorrow. He wanted her for the rest of his life. His arms encircled her. Her arms tightened around his neck. The last words he spoke before his lips met hers were, "And I want a future with you."

19

THE ROAD TRIP

By the time he had gotten home from their appointment with Doctor Tipton, Eddie had begun to think Tipton's idea was not such a good thing. Their past had more than its share of unspeakable horror and tragedy—the failed Seal mission where only Eddy survived—if you could call losing an arm, a leg, and a horribly scarred face surviving—and Madeline's savage sexual assault which had robbed her of ever being able to bear children. And then there were the twenty-plus years apart where Eddy had foolishly thought his injuries would have been too graphic for Maddy to accept, years when the Navy refused to acknowledge the mission due to political overtones at the time. This topic Eddy could not have broached with her even if he'd wanted to. Worse than the injuries he had suffered, his heart was crushed by her letters saying there was something she needed to tell him. Did he really need to see her only to hear she had found someone else? Isn't that what every soldier thinks when he gets such a foreboding correspondence? For Maddy, the Navy's years of stonewalling, refusing to tell her anything about her fiancé, left her with the only conclusion possible; he had died, a victim of a black ops mission gone bad. For Eddy, any place or thing that might conjure up those memories again would be like revisiting Hell, or at least their own personal version thereof.

Maddy's downward slide into dementia was hellishly frustrating for Eddy Pinafore. Even more discouraging were those moments when Maddy seemed lucid and aware. Admittedly, they were fleeting, but soon there would be no moments at all. Eddy would savor every one of them. He had made mental notes of places they could visit. The two of greatest significance were their small house in Oceana, near Little Creek, Virginia, where he had been assigned to Seal Team Six. This was a home where dreams of marriage and a family were made. Then there was Eddy's brother's home where he and Maddy had been married. Several others were eliminated due to Maddy's waning endurance and lack of mental acuity.

∾

By noon, the day was warm. With typical southern humidity raising his thirst, Eddy headed to the kitchen to make his concoction of Border Buttermilk to accompany the salami sandwiches Maddy had insisting on making. It was one of those moments. He emptied the contents of a can of Minute Made frozen lemonade into a glass pitcher filled with ice cubes. After adding the appropriate amount of water, he stirred the contents vigorously with a large wooden spoon. He plucked several sprigs of fresh mint growing in a bed in a greenhouse window over the kitchen sink and laid them next to the glasses. After rubbing the rim with a sprig of mint, he filled the glass with lemonade. He poured a healthy dose of Don Julio Tequila, which he kept for auspicious occasions, in the other glass. He brought them to the patio where Maddy was awaiting their lunch. There the AC maintained a pleasantly cool seventy-eight degrees. He set the glasses on the round, wrought iron table and pulled out a chair.

"To quench your thirst," he said, graciously.

"And for you," Maddy replied, pointing with pride to a plate with his salami sandwich and a couple of the baby dill pickles she had made. It made a pleasant and inviting picture.

At that moment, his hope had become a reality. Maddy was Maddy once again. A feeling of contentment, the likes of which were all too infrequent in Eddy's life, settled on him. He smiled and took a sip of his lemonade. *A bit heavy on the Tequila,* he thought. Maddy sipped hers.

"Eddy, this is delicious," she said, as she waved a sprig of mint under her nose. "Try your sandwich."

Whole wheat, how in the world did she remember that? He thought as he raised the sandwich to his mouth. He chewed slowly. His eyes closed; the better to enjoy the missing imported salami Maddy had forgotten to put in his sandwich.

"That might be the best salami sandwich I've ever had, honey."

As self-serving as the words may have sounded, he meant every one of them.

The compliment brought a smile to Maddy's face, something he had not often seen in the recent past. Now was the time to broach the subject of a road trip, he thought. Maybe better as a declaration and not as a question; less of a challenge for her diminishing cognitive abilities.

"I want us to go on a trip," he said, after taking the last bite of his salami-less sandwich.

"A trip?" That staring gaze, the result of dementia, had returned. It clouded the present and isolated Maddy from taking part in the plans.

Eddy continued as if he hadn't seen it.

"Yes, I want us to go back to Little Creek and see the old

house where I proposed to you and then to my brother's house where we got married."

Maddy sat there as if she hadn't heard a word he had said.

"It won't be long, a couple of days at the most."

He continued with the plan as if she was following every word. Why not? They were taking the trip, whether she understood or not. And if she never remembered a thing about it, at least Eddy would. He would have this last opportunity to remember with her at his side.

"We can pack tomorrow morning, Maddy, and be on our way by noon?"

"Pack?"

Ignoring the pain in his heart, Eddy calmly repeated the plan for their trip, with every word a smile, and with every word the agony of experiencing the inevitable.

~

IT WAS WELL past noon by the time Eddy had his 2010 Ford Fiesta packed with their clothes for the trip. Following breakfast, there was a repeat conversation about their journey. Patiently, Eddy went over the whats and the whys. Again, Maddy was very gracious, not because she understood but because Eddy said he wanted to take the trip. Packing for his wife was easy but repetitive. Eddy would lay several choices of blouses on the bed and tell Maddy, "Pick the one you want." Her prolonged stare at the selections before her clearly indicated to Eddy that Maddy had no idea what she was looking at or why. He would gently say, "You'll look great in these two," which he would then fold and place in her suitcase. This process was repeated with pants, sweaters, and jackets. It was a miracle to Eddy that even when not prompted, Maddy remembered what cosmetic items to take. He accepted these minor recollections with thankfulness. Because of the late start, Eddy had made a simple lunch for them so they wouldn't have to stop on the drive.

The mid-week traffic on I-77 north to Little Creek consisted mainly of big semis hauling their freight to their northern destinations. Eddy's Ford Fiesta cruised along at sixty-five without a problem. His Sirius Radio was preset to the seventies. The nostalgic melodies affected Maddy like a mild tranquilizer. Her head leaned back against the headrest of her seat. Her eyes were closed. The occasional smile or tapping of her fingers on the console gave Eddy pause that maybe Tipton had been right. For some brief nanosecond, maybe she had remembered. Four hours later, they pulled into the Holiday Inn parking lot in Little Creek, Virginia. It was no four-star establishment, but it did afford Eddy a comfortable room and a nearby Waffle House restaurant for meals.

~

IT WAS NOT difficult to understand the state of obesity of southern people given the items on the Waffle House menu— anything and everything on the breakfast menu that could be deep-fried was. With a plethora of choices, Eddy ordered for Maddy; scrambled eggs, wheat toast, and a small bowl of fresh fruit for her, two eggs over easy, country spuds crispy, and sausage links for him. Maddy seemed distracted throughout breakfast by the multitude of seagulls feasting on all sorts of food they had scavenged from two nearby dumpsters. Eddy enjoyed his coffee while gazing at the perpetual look of wonderment in Maddy's eyes as she focused on something as simple as birds eating. He hoped the rest of the day would provide her that same pleasure.

It had been fifty years, but Eddy still remembered the way to 32 Ascot Way, Oceana, Virginia. The quaint looking beach cottage, now a summer rental, had undergone a complete renovation. Gone was the small grassy front lawn, replaced by a redwood deck. Several wet towels hung over the railing. Scattered sandals covered with sand were strewn about. A small propane barbecue and a couple of folding chairs occupied the far corner. Ironically, the original yellow paint remained unchanged. Eddy took a few minutes to stare at the place where so many dreams filled the nights and where their futures were planned.

"We're here, Maddy. Shall we get out?" he announced as he opened the driver's door.

"Where?" she asked. At first, she looked straight ahead as if she had no understanding of what "where" meant.

"Our old place on Ascot," Eddy replied.

Maddy turned toward the house. For a few seconds, there was an intense focus. Then came that questioning look on her face that told Eddy Maddy didn't remember where she was or its significance. Eddy walked around to Maddy's door and opened it.

"Let's take a closer look, shall we?"

Eddy helped Maddy out of the car. He handed her the cane, and taking her other arm in his, walked around the front of the car to the sidewalk. Eddy had not intentionally tried to stimulate Maddy's memory, but he could not help but vocalize his own.

"Man, do I remember those barbecues with the team. I never realized how much beer a thirsty Seal can drink." A smile formed on his face. "And Chief Madigan, God knows what that man couldn't do with hot coals and rib-eye steaks! I wonder if the old barbecue is still in the back yard?" With no car in the driveway, Eddy surmised no one was home. "Come on, let's see," he said mischievously. He and Maddy walked slowly up the driveway. When they got to the backyard, Eddy gasped in amazement.

"I don't believe it!" he exclaimed. There it was, their old

barbecue made out of stacked shale stepping stones crudely held together by a very sloppy application of cement. The barbecue had been a weekend project with some Seal team-mates. The sides weren't level, and the front leaned backward slightly. All that was attributed to the amount of beer they drank and not their lack of masonry skills. Eddy glanced at the back of the house where their bedroom used to be. In that moment of nostalgia, Eddy's memories shifted to another type. He slipped his arm around Maddy's shoulders and leaned over to whisper in her ear.

"I loved loving you when 'Just You And Me' played on the radio."

Maddy said nothing, but for Eddy, the moment fulfilled Doctor Tipton's prophecy that the trip might do Eddy more good than Maddy. Eddy took Maddy's arm, and they walked back down the driveway to their car. Once Maddy was seated, Eddy straightened up and took one last look at the old house. Suddenly, he felt like he was in another place, in another time with the person he loved. There was no doubt what he heard from Maddy's lips. "You are my love....you are my love...," she mumbled. The start of the first line of 'Just You And Me."

During the drive to Beaufort, South Carolina, Maddy dozed off and on into a semi-sleep, a habit that had become common for her whether in the car or at home. Eddy seemed content with the thought that maybe Maddy had remembered some-thing about their old house and what took place there. After all, what was it that Doctor Tipton had said about a sudden resur-rection of a lost memory, even if for only a second or two? Eddy had called ahead to his cousin, Andy, about their visit and to alert him as to Maddy's condition. It was more of an edited version than a detailed recitation of the past few years. Eddy was glad he had taken that approach. His cousin was more interested in telling Eddy about his decision to sell his home and move into a nearby Senior Living Community called

Sonora Hills. As he pulled to the curb in front of his cousin's home, any feeling of being happy to be there and see his cousin quickly faded. The once attractive Tudor house was badly in need of a paint job. The old white stucco was cracked and faded. The brown window trim and shutters were splintered and discolored. The folded metal walker next to the front door did not bode well for his cousin's health. Eddy elected to walk up the cement driveway after getting Maddy out of the car and avoid the old earthen pathway now covered with wood mulch. It was a certain disaster for Maddy to navigate even with Eddy's help. Her gait was slower than normal as she placed her cane a few feet ahead of her and shuffled a step or two and started over again. It was humanly impossible not to get a little frustrated with her slowness, though Eddy tried to keep this all too human failing to a minimum.

After a rap or two on the old English style door with its rough-hewn lumber and black wrought iron bracing, a voice called out, "Coming." It took a minute or so for the door to open. His cousin, Andy, stood before them. His shoulders were noticeably slumped forward, and he was leaning on a cane. He looked tired, and the five o'clock shadow of a beard indicated that simple task had become a bit of a chore for him.

"Gosh, Eddy! It's good to see you two again! Please come in," Andy said, clearly happy to have the company. He reached out to hug Maddy, who seemed totally detached from the present. Maddy might as well have been a storefront mannequin from the way she reacted to his embrace.

"I need to get her to the couch. She's a bit fatigued from the drive down from Little Creek," Eddy said.

Andy nodded and moved into the living room. With Maddy comfortably seated on the couch, Andy took his place in his favorite La-Z-Boy recliner.

"Gee, Eddy, what's it been? Six maybe seven years, at least," Andy said, with no tone of recrimination in his voice.

"I know," sighed Eddy. "When our granddaughter was born, more of our time was spent helping Tina raise her."

"How is that little darling!?" Andy said. He genuinely cared for the child, never forgetting to send a birthday card or a Christmas present.

"As well as she can be, considering her disabilities," Eddy replied. "But tell me about you. Why the move to that senior community?"

"As you might see," patting his cane, "That TIA put a real crimp in my ability to get around. Can't tend to the house or the yard the way I used to. It only made sense to move someplace where all that's taken care of for me."

"I suppose," replied Eddy, knowing he had made similar plans for himself and Maddy.

Noticing that Maddy sat silently with her hands folded on her lap, Andy nodded toward her and said, "I was so sad to hear about... you know."

Eddy gave his cousin an appreciative smile.

"In the beginning, I thought that's what happens when you get old. You forget a little here, a little there. In Maddy's case, it got worse."

The sound of her name elicited an inconsequential turn of her head. Whatever had they been saying was merely tones with no meaning whatsoever to her. A sweet smile was her only reaction, a reaction without understanding or comprehension.

"Which brings me to why we're here, besides seeing you. Andy, is that gazebo still in the backyard?"

"Sure, but it's hardly in the condition it was when you and Maddy got married in it," reminisced Andy.

"I'd like to take Maddy out to see it," asked Eddy.

"Okay, but as I said, it's not what it used to be."

Andy rose from his chair and headed through the kitchen to the double french doors leading to the patio. Eddy helped

Maddy to her feet. "There's something I want you to see, sweetheart," he said.

Maddy looked at him with that sweet, sweet smile and complied. They followed Andy to the backyard patio. It was still where Eddy remembered it, in the corner of the yard surrounded by a high cinder block wall. Other than its location, not much else was the same. Except for the deck, nothing remained of the beautiful old structure. The cedar-shingled roof was gone, along with the ornately carved handrails. The planking on the floor was faded, and in a few places, it looked like the ends of several planks had worked their way loose. This was now, but what Eddy remembered was the old, the place where Eddy Pinafore and Madeline O'Connor exchanged their wedding vows.

He took Maddy's hand in his. "Sweetheart, come with me," he said.

With that ever-present smile, Maddy looked at him with questioning eyes. Eddy reassured her. "Come on, you'll see."

Eddy carefully guided Maddy across a lawn badly in need of cutting. He helped her step up into the gazebo. Time had certainly taken its toll on the structure as well as the couple now standing in it. But for one of them, nothing had changed. It was still a beautiful setting, and she was still the most beautiful woman he had ever met. Eddy reached out and took her hand. It was as if it were yesterday, but this time Eddy spoke the words.

"Do you Alan Edward Pinafore take this woman to be your lawfully wedded wife?"

"I do."

"Do you Madeline Mary O'Connor take this man to be your lawfully wedded husband?"

"I do."

He tilted her head upward and kissed her with all the love and affection that comes with a lifetime of devotion. He then turned Maddy to the imaginary crowd of friends and proudly announced, "May I present Mr. and Mrs. Edward Pinafore!"

Eddy smiled at his cousin, who stood clapping on the edge of the patio. He guided Maddy across the lawn and onto the patio, where they paused for one last glimpse of their wedding site. As they turned around to go back inside, Maddy suddenly stopped. She didn't look at anyone. She stood there for a moment, and then that sweet smile appeared once more. A voice so soft and tender whispered the words. "I do."

In less than a second, a dream had come true, then faded in even less time. So far, the trip had only been of any benefit to Eddie. It had confirmed Maddy's situation was every bit as dire as he believed. It was difficult not to be depressed.

20

DECEIT AND GREED

The letter from her Board of Directors caused Samantha Callahan to question the faith she had placed in them. After initially crumpling and discarding it into the trash can next to her desk, she retrieved it. Most of the day staff were gone, leaving Samantha in a position to enjoy a glass of wine from a bottle of Windy Oaks Pinot Noir, which she kept in a large oak cabinet in her office. After pouring herself a healthy drink of the velvet nectar, she carefully smoothed out the crumpled piece of paper and then walked out of the double french doors of her office to the lanai. At one end of the lanai against the backdrop of a trellis woven with Jasmine blossoms, was a small wrought iron table with a frosted glass top. Without the double thick padding on the seat and back, the iron-framed chair seemed more like a medieval torture device than her favorite resting spot. The coolness of the late afternoon breeze helped soothe the ire raging inside her. Her glass of Pinot would have a similar effect. As she read the letter again, she thought to herself, *How could they? How could they possibly consider selling Magnolia Gardens? Why else would they want to discuss with her the five-year financial report they had asked her to put together?* She placed the letter on the table and took a sip of wine. Her face tensed with determination. Was there any expense in the past few years that could have raised a red flag for the Board? Not operationally speaking, she was sure of that. Arthur Ashcroft was nothing like Paris Barrington's son Trevor Barrington, the individual the senior Barrington had initially entrusted with the responsibility to acquire Magnolia Gardens. With the cunning of a King Cobra, he would stare down his opponent until he saw the slightest flaw in their defense, and then he would strike. His other great skill was his ruthlessness, which he learned at the side of Paris Barrington. If human suffering was the cost of success, so be it. Samantha Callahan was determined to do her due diligence before she met with the Board of Directors in four days. Unbeknownst to Samantha, someone else had also done his homework.

∾

"THANK YOU SO MUCH, Doctor Calhoun. I was sure you would find my offer intriguing in light of the circumstances outlined in my proposal."

After hanging up the phone, Arthur Ashcroft smiled to himself, an uncommon event for his face. His Machiavellian plot was nearly complete. Dr. William Calhoun was the last of the five members of the Board of Directors of Magnolia Gardens he had contacted. If he had to judge, he had three members solidly supporting his proposal and two others who could not be bought. That was fine by Ashcroft. All he needed was a plurality for the purchase of Magnolia Gardens to be approved. The Cletus Edwards property had been secured at a fraction of the cost he had initially offered to Edwards for his land. The acquisition of the Magnolia Gardens property would be no different.

The Oxford, one of the most expensive apartment buildings

on the upper east side, had been home to Arthur Ashcroft for the last three years. Though he could easily afford the apartment, the ultra-wealthy owners still required letters of recommendation. This process helped maintain the building's reputation for exclusivity. To breach that barrier, he had needed the recommendation of his employer, Paris Barrington, a recommendation that he loathed to request. It wasn't enough that he, Arthur Ashcroft, had made Barrington billions as his head of development; he still lived under the shadow of the billionaire. The Oxford was a thirty-story apartment building with a magnificent view of Central Park and the Hudson River. Ownership kept the penthouse level for their own lavish affairs. Arthur Ashcroft had the apartment just below. The ceiling to floor windows on one wall offered a panoramic view fit for a Hollywood movie. The view over the eight hundred and forty-three-acre greenery of Central Park was fitting of King Arthur ruling over his kingdom. For years, Arthur Ashcroft had been an avid collector of Chinese art. He had developed his avocation for the work of the ancients while spearheading the development of two of Paris Barrington's hallmark projects in Hong Kong and on the island of Macao. The hallway of his apartment had several works of calligraphy by the Chinese artist Wang Xizhi. At his request, the old white floor tile, which looked all too antiseptic to Ashcroft, had been replaced with rich mahogany wood. Each of the other three walls had its own unique theme. On one wall hung a painting by Lou Zhongli, a master of Chinese realism, Fang Chuxiong's exquisite ink and brushwork, and He Jiaying with his modernistic figures and female nudes in Chinese ink wash. Centered under these paintings was a small cherry wood table ornately decorated with mother of pearl inlay displaying a Qianlong Dynasty porcelain vase. On a second wall were several large paintings Ashcroft had commissioned himself of numerous Paris Barrington's developments. These developments had Barrington's name on them, but in reality, they were the result of Arthur Ashcroft's sweat and tears. It was his determination that brought these projects into being, not the braggadocious and obnoxious rantings of Paris Barrington. These paintings served to fuel Arthur Ashcroft's ambition to be second-to-none, including Paris Barrington, but also reinforced his own egotistical perception that he, like Cardinal Richelieu, was the real power behind the throne. Though Richelieu had failed to unseat King Louis, Ashcroft was driven to succeed where the Cardinal had failed.

On a wall behind the sofa hung a picture of Qinghai Lake, the largest saltwater lake in China. Ashcroft walked over to the painting. Reaching under the bottom of the frame, he pressed a button. The picture retracted upward, revealing an inset bar complete with Waterford crystal glasses on two, one-inch-thick glass shelves supported by golden dragon head brackets. The bottom shelf displayed an array of the finest liquors, the likes of Crown Royal, Old Forester, Belvedere Vodka, Roku Gin, and Pasion Azteca tequila. The bar top was made of black marble set into a cherry wood frame. An automatic icemaker maintained a ready source of ice cubes. The back of the bar was an enormous piece of glass etched with the image of the Great Wall. Prestigious as his address was, and as magnificent as was the view, Ashcroft still had not made it to the top. But not for long, he mused, as he filled a glass of Baccarat Crystal to the halfway point with Glenfiddich dark whiskey. He settled onto a couch of soft brown Italian leather and mused over his most recent accomplishment, with a satanic smirk of satisfaction on his face.

~

IT WAS NOT difficult for a man of Arthur Ashcroft's many skills to acquire a copy of the paperwork that created the Limited Liability Company known as Magnolia Gardens L.L.C. Formed some thirty years ago by five rather wealthy philanthropic physicians. There had been several new partners over the years. As members passed on, there was no lack of interested parties seeking to become members of its Board of Directors. This was due in part to those original members who had doubled their original buy-in of five hundred thousand dollars. To force a sale of Magnolia Gardens, Ashcroft would need the support of three of the Board's five members. Another of Arthur Ashcroft's dubious skill sets was his ability to dig up the most humiliating and embarrassing secrets people would rather take to their graves than have revealed.

Of the five-member Board of Directors of Magnolia Gardens, William Abernathy and R. Mattison Gordon were dedicated to the cause of eldercare. The wealth he had acquired as head of Abernathy Accounting Inc., one of Charleston's largest public accounting firms, had not dulled his sense of humanity. R. Mattison Gordon, a prolific writer of screenplays satirizing American political history, had watched his own father pass away in a care facility, making Magnolia Gardens all the more special to him. Making a profit off their membership would be unconscionable to them, a thought process absolutely foreign to the materialistic Ashcroft. Doctor Anthony Abrams and Doctor Mathew Singer were the bleeding victims a piranha such as Ashcroft made a living devouring. Doctor Abrams considered himself a self-anointed stock market expert and had done quite well for himself over the years. However, a third divorce and children in expensive private colleges soon took a drain on his resources. Would an offer to buy into Paris Barrington's Nirvana development at a ridiculously low price be enough to sway him? Matthew Singer's problem was due to an addiction to any and every speculative land scheme that he came across. Whether it was that island paradise golf course and hotel, he sank a hundred thousand dollars into or that investment company promising a ten percent return on your money due to their recently patented idea for converting refuse into fuel for electrical energy, Singer had a predilection for picking losers. The Nirvana project was no "oceanfront property in Arizona" scheme. Ashcroft had sent Singer the prospectus and the anticipated worth of his participation. Ashcroft hoped the gambler's appetite for a sure thing would be enough. That left Ashcroft facing two members committed to keeping their memberships and two looking for an option to sell, at the right price, of course. That left Doctor Drake Calhoun as the lynchpin to Ashcroft's plan.

Like the other two members of the Board, Drake Calhoun was faced with his own financial crisis. The good doctor owned over twenty-five medical clinics throughout the south. His problem was that his clinics were overselling oxycodone, fentanyl, and any other number of opiates. Due to the nation-wide opiate epidemic, the FDA had begun requiring pharma-ceutical companies to report purchases of over a thousand pills in a month to any medical distributors. It had taken months for FDA auditors to identify Health Clinics of America and its CEO, Doctor Drake Calhoun, as a major source of excessive purchases. His lavish lifestyle aside, the prospect of spending decades in prison was worthy of contemplating suicide. That was until he received a letter from Arthur Ashcroft. In the letter, Ashcroft offered Calhoun the chance of a lifetime. Would the good doctor consider selling his membership in Magnolia Gardens L.L.C. in return for which Ashcroft guaranteed any problems with the FDA would go away? A consortium of drug manufacturers, headed by Ashcroft, would purchase all his clinics, and all records of prescription sales would be taken care of discretely. The board of directors' meeting would reveal to Samantha Callahan the lack of a moral conscience some can sink to and the strength of moral fiber in others.

SAMANTHA CALLAHAN HAD SPENT the better part of two weeks practically married to the Xerox Work Center printer in her office. In preparation for the Board of Directors meeting, Samantha had prepared a detailed cost analysis of Magnolia Gardens' operations for the last five years, precisely as ordered by the Board. In her relatively brief tenure as the Executive Director, Samantha Callahan had managed to keep operations under budget and yet still received accolades from the National Association of Assisted Living Facilities, including two years running as Executive Director of the year. She added one extra element, one she had hoped would sway the Board from the possibility of selling Magnolia Gardens. At the end of each year's summation, she had attached a section of all the letters of gratitude and appreciation the Gardens had received from its residents' families. Samantha was not above tugging at their heartstrings if it meant keeping Magnolia Gardens operational. She placed the last of five copies of the voluminous production on a cart and proceeded down the hallway to the library, where the Board of Directors' quarterly meeting was to take place.

Her staff had prepared the room exactly as she had requested. A large circular oak table was in the middle of the room. It was set with three large crystal pitchers of ice water, crystal tumblers, and five legal size note pads. In front of each of the five chairs was a copy of Samantha's work. Against the far wall hung a projection screen on which Samantha would display her PowerPoint presentation. She had spent hours developing her display, minimizing areas marked red and maximizing blue areas. If lack of fiscal stability was driving some notion to sell Magnolia Gardens, Samantha Callahan had done everything possible to show the board members that retention, not liquidation, was the smart decision. A small podium stood near the round table, and on it were her notes. She was doing one last review when the first board members arrived, William Abernathy and R. Mattison Gordon. The two were in quite a jovial mood as they entered the library. Having just come from work, Abernathy was smartly dressed in an expensive two-piece Armani suit.

A starched white shirt with french cuffs, a blue silk tie, and a monogrammed handkerchief were fitting accoutrements to the custom-made Italian suit. Abernathy hated the phrase "Clothes make the man," but he realized the adage had some validity when dealing with clients. Impressions be damned, Gordon's attire was chosen for its simplicity and his favorite movie character, Indiana Jones. His brown Fedora fit rather firmly, causing his silver-gray hair to curl at the ends. His brown jacket marked with wear marks on the elbows covered a tan safari shirt. Only his khaki pants appeared without wrinkles. The two men were chuckling about a recent commentary in an article about Gordon in the New York Times, calling him the "Petulant Pen of American Politics."

"This could put you right up there with William F. Buckley," Abernathy said, handing Gordon a copy of the article he had brought him.

"That remains to be seen," grinned Gordon, as he delicately stroked his silver mustache. Though not one to seek adulation, Gordon did enjoy the notoriety of the moment. Truth be known, Gordon was far more interested in stimulating the minds of his readers than gaining their praise.

"Good afternoon, Samantha. You've done a nice job arranging this meeting," Abernathy said, as they drew near the table. "Any particular seat we need to take?"

"No, Mr. Abernathy. It's my hope the circular design will promote equality of thought rather than an implied sense of status."

Gordon smiled to himself at Samantha's analogy. If nothing else, the round table would expose the facial expression of each member's inner feelings.

"Nice approach," stated the man of few words.

Shyly, Samantha replied, "Thank you, Mr. Gordon."

With that, Doctor Anthony Abrams and Doctor Matthew Singer made their entrance, closely followed by Doctor Drake Calhoun. All three seemed absorbed in their own thoughts, acknowledging Samantha with a simple, "Samantha," before taking their seats at the table. Ironically, Calhoun seemed out of sorts. He looked as though he wanted a seat as far away from the others as possible, but Samantha's purposeful selection of a round table prevented that from happening. His face looked fatigued. Deep-set eyes reflected a recent lack of sleep. The beginning of a five o'clock shadow indicated he had been neglecting his personal appearance. Anthony Abrams wore a rather foreboding black doubled breast suit more appropriate for a funeral. Despite being tailor-made, the jacket could not hide the noticeable extra poundage he had put on recently. He walked with the swagger of a man more bent on delivering a message than listening to one. Matthew Singer was rather peculiarly dressed. His day at Mercy General as an orthopedic surgeon consisted of a series of operations that had started at seven o'clock in the morning. At day's end, he put on khaki slacks, a blue windbreaker, and a crew-neck wool sweater. His desire was to end this meeting as soon as possible and get home to a double martini. Abernathy, who had been selected by the other board members to chair their meetings, if only in a procedural sense, greeted the three members.

"Anthony, Matthew, Drake, good to see y' all," he said in his thick southern accent.

"Yes, as always," replied Abrams, with Singer nodding a similar sentiment. Drake Calhoun avoided any eye contact with Abernathy, instead raising his head slightly.

"Gentlemen, shall we defer to Samantha for her presentation."

With that introduction, Samantha directed the members to the projection screen on the wall. Slightly inconvenienced by the table shape, the two doctors had to angle their chairs to see the screen. Picking up the clicker, Samantha began.

"Gentlemen, as you requested, here is the financial analysis for the last five years of Magnolia Gardens. Shall we begin?"

Drake Calhoun was more focused on the tabletop than the screen containing Samantha's information. The two doctors' attention to the details on the screen was sporadic, to put it mildly. They might as well have been looking at a magazine in the waiting room of a doctor's office for all the attention they were giving to Samantha's presentation. From her position, Samantha could see the indifference on their faces. This was disconcerting to her, to say the least. Contrary to their fellow board members, Abernathy and Gordon made notes on their pads while periodically flipping through corresponding pages in the folders in front of them, nodding to each other several times over strategic points Samantha had made. *They're getting it,* she thought. Drake Calhoun might as well have been a stranger brought in off the streets to occupy a seat at the table for all the thought he was giving Samantha. At the end of each year's report, Samantha directed the members to look at the bottom of the last page, where she had emphasized in bold colors the past year's profitability. When she was finished, she placed the clicker on the podium. Her demeanor was assertive yet polite.

"Gentlemen, I hope you can see that operationally, Magnolia Gardens is making money, and thus there is no need to consider Mr. Ashcroft's proposal."

Her bluntness caught the board members off guard. Poised to strike like a coiled viper, Doctor Abrams retorted, "As you so clearly stated in your report, Magnolia Gardens is making a profit, and those of us who are partners in Magnolia Gardens L.L.C do so for the same reason, the humanitarian care of the elderly aside." He firmly placed his pen on the oak table surface to emphasize his point, making a purposeful affront to Samantha.

Seeing the need to soften his colleague's words, Doctor Singer noted, "Samantha, we are all concerned about the welfare of the residents. I think Mr. Ashcroft's offer to find alternative placements for them and to pay the first year's cost more than generous."

"Better said than I," replied a weakly apologetic Abrams.

The hypocrisy at the table frustrated Gordon, who had a firmly planted moral compass when it came to right and wrong. Never one to mince his words, Gordon made his disdain quite clear. Having been bored too many times with the two men's business ventures, good and bad, Gordon was in no mood to be gracious or understanding.

"If either of you two consider your membership on this board as an investment vehicle, you, Anthony, should have stayed with your stock market speculation, and you, Matthew, should keep looking for that deal that's too good to be true."

Gordon's affront brought a volcanic reaction from both men. Abrams shot up from his chair. Barely five-feet-five, his Napoleonic nature erupted. His blood pressure soared. His eyes bulged with rage. He pounded his fist on the table, shouting, "I've never been so insulted in my entire life. Who do you think you are to talk to me in that insulting manner!"

Gordon calmly eyed the man, knowing his bombastic reaction was meant for show. He smiled inwardly while stroking his mustache. His opening remarks were not the end of the salvo he had created for his two fellow board members.

"Why don't you sit down, Anthony, and consider the veracity of my words. It would serve you well," smirked Gordon.

Despite the rage boiling inside him, Abrams felt neutered by Gordon's response. He slumped down onto his chair.

Matthew Singer directed his anger at Gordon's judgmental

words more personally. He rose from his chair. Though he hated Gordon's implication that he was nothing more than a get rich schemer, what he hated more was that Gordon was right. Reasoning was beyond his capability. All Matthew Singer wanted at that moment was some primordial sense of satisfaction. Stretching his five-foot-ten stature to the maximum in some juvenile attempt at intimidating Gordon, Singer's rant resonated through the library room.

"You dare challenge my sense of integrity. You pompous, arrogant asshole! You're lucky I don't take you down a notch right here and now!"

Gordon's eyes narrowed as he stared at Singer. His lips pursed while his jaw jutted slightly forward. His deep baritone voice answered Singer's challenge.

"Matthew, that would be a decision you would deeply regret. As I told Anthony, consider what your membership was intended to produce, quality care for an aging population who have no one to rely on but others."

A rational thought process was beyond Singer's capability. He rudely slid his packet across the table and stormed out of the room. As he got to the door, he turned around and, in one last defiant outburst, shouted, "I vote to accept Mr. Ashcroft's offer. You'll have my letter to that effect tomorrow."

Those around the table sat silent for several minutes. It was clear to Abrams and Gordon, who was in favor of accepting Arthur Ashcroft's offer and who was not. Drake Calhoun was the last remaining hurdle. Like the Judas he was, Calhoun was prepared to sacrifice those who most desperately needed his voice. He calmly stood up.

"I want to thank you, Samantha, for an excellent and thorough presentation. Let me be perfectly clear when I say I want nothing more than the best for the residents at Magnolia Gardens. Yes, Mr. Ashcroft's offer includes a buyout for our memberships in Magnolia Gardens L.L.C. However, his commitment to ensuring continued quality care for the residents assures me we are not abandoning them just for monetary gain. I am saddened with my decision because I know change is difficult, but I believe accepting Mr. Ashcroft's offer is in everyone's best interest. William, you'll have my letter of acceptance of the offer tomorrow. Now, I must excuse myself. Again, thank you, Samantha."

When the door closed behind him, Samantha Callahan took a seat at the table. Devastated by what had just occurred, she saw a lifetime of work and commitment to the elderly vanish in front of her. Unable to retain any semblance of composure, she burst into tears. Anthony Abernathy was not nearly as surprised by the outcome of the meeting as Samantha. His contacts in the financial world let it be known to him the monetary struggles of the three in favor of the sale. Based on those contacts, he also suspected that Arthur Ashcroft had made some sort of sweetheart deal beneficial to Abrams, Singer, and Calhoun. All that meant nothing now. Pursuant to Ashcroft's offer, there would be a six-month grace period before any residents had to move, giving their families at least a modicum of time to prepare their loved ones for the move. Turning his attention to the near-hysterical Samantha, Abernathy walked over to her chair. He put his arm around her shoulder. Tears had washed away almost all of the woman's makeup. She looked up at Abernathy with bloodshot and swollen eyes. Her hand clenched a tear-soaked handkerchief. Though well-intended, his words brought little solace to the grief-stricken woman.

"Samantha, you've done a magnificent job here. Never doubt that for a moment. There are just some things out of our control."

Emotions had robbed her of the ability to speak. Her eyes screamed, "Why? Could I have done more?"

Gordon rose from his chair and walked over to Abernathy

and Samantha. Gordon's emotional control could seem uncaring to others, but just the opposite was true. His was a steeled response, meant to motivate, not console.

"Samantha, the fight is never over until you quit. Are you prepared to quit?"

Her hands clenched her tear-filled handkerchief even tighter. She looked at Gordon. A clearness in her eyes appeared. The constrictions in her throat eased due to the resurgence of a determined will.

"No," she responded defiantly, "I definitely am not," she said.

21

SEEDS OF BETRAYAL

With control of Magnolia Gardens, L.L.C. in sight, Arthur Ashcroft savored his second tumbler of Glenfiddich dark whiskey. Acquiring the property which Magnolia Gardens occupied was the last step in conjunction with the Edwards farmlands needed to make Paris Barrington's project, Nirvana, a reality. Staring out his apartment window, the mid-afternoon sun glistened over the New York skyline, leaving Ashcroft feeling like the proverbial Greek God. Hidden within the Barrington chain of luxury resorts was a Trojan horse discretely constructed with the guile of a Machiavellian prince. This horse would bring Ashcroft more money than he had ever made in his life, enough money to ensure he would never have to be beholden to Paris Barrington again. A telephone call was about to crush that dream and Arthur Ashcroft with it. His extra cell phone on the table rang. He grimaced when he saw the Caller ID.

"Yes," Ashcroft replied, refusing to say his name and further buy into the caller's juvenile sense of theatrics.

"It's me, Hector."

"I know," said an exasperated Ashcroft. "I can read."

The caller felt insulted by Ashcroft's tone, as well he should be. In all their previous meetings, Ashcroft had talked down to him as if he were a common field hand. Those who had made that mistake in the past had paid for it with their lives. This time the roles were reversed. He spoke in perfect English, clear, decisive, and leaving no doubt as to his intent.

"I want my money."

The business Ashcroft had created was not unlike investing in the stock market. Yes, at times, one may lose money, but in the long run, multi-millions were to be made. Obviously, this ingrate did not understand the simplest of investment strategies.

Ashcroft was in no mood to be diplomatic, a mistake he would soon regret.

"Listen, I've told you in the past who to deal with when it came to our business."

"Yes, you did, Arthur, and I did as you suggested. The problem is that person pissed in his pants when I talked to him. He cried like a bitch, saying there was no way he could get that kind of money from his family. So now I'm talking to you."

There was silence from Ashcroft. The spineless off-spring of the great Paris Barrington had come to Ashcroft with a plan to make millions smuggling in cocaine and distributing it through the multiple mega-resorts belonging to his father. The rich and wealthy would pay premium dollar for the purest of the drug. Their first few ventures worked perfectly, but small successes were not enough for Trevor Barrington. He wanted a really big score, one worth millions. Ashcroft had advised him against the plan. It was too risky bringing in that amount of cocaine, but the young Barrington had ignored him. Now his Colombian partner wanted his money, ten million dollars to be exact.

Arthur Ashcroft had played for big stakes with some of the

world's largest financial power brokers, where the making of a deal would hinge on a twitch of a lip or a blink of the eye, where a gut check had to be made with every proposal and counterproposal. Ashcroft had relished in that kind of "Let's see who blinks first" environment. The coldness in the words of his caller left no doubt in Ashcroft's mind that diplomacy, not confrontation, was the better course of action. Still confident he would broker a deal, he said, "Of course, the unfortunate results of our venture cannot be overlooked. Let me suggest that I arrange for another shipment. I will pay double the going rate on arrival, and you will make your money back and then some."

There was a frustration in the caller's words that left no doubt Ashcroft's offer was not acceptable.

"Arthur, you do not understand. This is not negotiable. Do you understand me! This is my final offer. You have thirty days, and no more, to arrange for payment, or I will make arrangements to liquidate a bad investment decision."

The phone went dead, and with it, his stomach wretched up a vile substance. Judas got his thirty pieces of silver, and Arthur Ashcroft got his thirty days. Betrayal would be their shared fate.

~

ARTHUR ASHCROFT WAS A VERY wealthy man, but he was not "get ten million dollars at the drop of a hat" wealthy. He had made his fortune using other people's money, and this would be no different. The only question was whose money. He quickly changed clothing after the gastro-eruption following the phone call. Staring into the bathroom mirror, he adjusted his navy-blue Armani tie and smiled at the irony. The source of his salvation would come from the very man he had grown to despise. Atlantic Financial Services, L.L.C. was the money holding corporation for Paris Barrington's investors. It operated similar to a legal Ponzi scheme. Investors were promised an annual payment of ten percent provided they leave their funds with Atlantic Financial for a minimum of three years. As long as the interest payments never exceeded thirty percent of the corpus (body of money), Ashcroft was playing with safe money. He then used those funds to leverage other financial institutions to make his loads. He picked up his phone. The continuous dial tone aggravated Ashcroft to no end. Who did the arrogant asshole think was calling him anyway, some Robocaller about a home security system?

Finally. "What," followed by the sound of a long inhaling breath.

Shit, do you need that stuff in the daytime too, he thought?

"We need to talk. Meet me at Atlantic Financials' office in thirty minutes."

The giddy laughter in the background, followed by the sound of a hand slapping bare flesh, told Ashcroft he was interrupting another afternoon dalliance of the young lothario. The young man's predilection for erotica made Ashcroft envious as he remembered his younger days experimenting in many a menage a trois with the sexual experimentalists of the seventies, but that was then, and this was now.

"Now?" The inquisitive response irked Ashcroft even more.

"Yes, now! Get rid of your love toy or toys, whichever the case may be, and meet me there!"

Ashcroft's phone went dead. Unfazed, his mind went into survival mode. There were more than hurt feelings to be concerned about here. He called for his car service, then headed to his private elevator.

~

HIS DRIVER WAS WAITING for him when Ashcroft came out of the double gold-plated revolving doors of the apartment building. A tall man dressed in a black double-breasted suit, with a black hat, and wearing sunglasses awaited him.

"Thank you, James," Ashcroft said, as he slid into the back seat of the plush Lincoln Limousine. Adjusting his seat belt, Ashcroft settled into the expensive leather seat.

The window between the driver's seat and the rear of the town car slid open.

"Your destination, sir?"

"Atlantic Financial, James."

The small window slid shut. Ashcroft mused over his strategy. His signature would not be found on any of the paperwork, only that of his dupe. Should plans go awry, Ashcroft had a plan B—another scapegoat would be offered to his demanding caller. The confidence of the ruthless manipulator grew. Ashcroft's vehicle dutifully took its place in the slow-moving traffic. Fortunately, they only had four blocks to travel. Omni Plaza was one of the dozens of high-priced business buildings in New York City's financial district. The driver pulled to the curb. So accustomed to being waited on, Ashcroft waited until the driver came to the door and opened it for his passenger.

"I shouldn't be long, James," Ashcroft said, leaving his driver waiting at the curb.

Paris Barrington had a penchant for being at the top, literally. The offices of Atlantic Finances occupied the entire top floor of the twenty-story structure. Ashcroft headed directly to the elevators, bypassing the concierge standing behind a podium as if he were about to make a speech. It was late in the afternoon, yet surprisingly there was little traffic in the lobby. The majority of tenants were financial service firms, hedge fund managers, and investment firms. Their employees didn't know the meaning of a normal workday. They were the hungriest of the hungry, the most ambitious of the corporate ladder climbers. They worked until the last phone call was made, the final email was sent or answered regardless of the time zone, and the fax machines stopped. They took whatever work remained and went home to continue their upward climb. Upon exiting the elevator, Ashcroft faced frosted double glass doors.

In gold letters, the words Atlantic Financial L.L.C. were printed. The large foyer was elegantly decorated with Sauder Palladia furniture. Against either wall was a small sofa of expensive Italian leather and an ornately carved cherrywood table. The receptionist sat behind a vintage Jonathan Charles Buckingham desk. The nameplate read, "Andrea Fleming." Befitting the image Paris Barrington sought to portray, the receptionist was stylishly dressed in a Rebecca Taylor suit. A white blouse was opened displaying a Joan of Arc cameo trimmed in gold, resting at the top of an intriguing cleavage line. Her ebony hair hung to shoulder length with its ends slightly flipped upward. She had stunning hazel eyes along with a creamy complexion.

"Good afternoon, Mr. Ashcroft. You have a guest waiting for you," she said.

"Thank you, Andrea," he replied, inwardly hoping his guest hadn't tried to make the receptionist another conquest.

Ashcroft proceeded down a short hallway to his office. The door was ajar. As he entered, he saw his guest lounging in Ashcroft's desk chair. The abruptness of Ashcroft's call left his guest little time for appropriate dress. His brown hair had grown long and desperately needed a trim. His eyes appeared dilated and bloodshot, no doubt the result of the recent use of his favorite stimulant. His wrinkled Cuccinelli leisure suit had no doubt been picked up off the floor. Ashcroft placed his briefcase on his desk and said, "You'll find a chair at the table more suitable." His office was spacious though hardly ostentatious.

He had a corner office with two windows overlooking the mega-metropolis of financial institutions below. His long Sauder Palladia desk was decorated with two computers one on each end. His name in gold letters against a cherrywood backing was front and center on the desk. A Wildwood counter-weight lamp rested on his right.

With an insolent shrug of his shoulders, his guest spun the chair around slowly and moved to the oval conference table near the window. To emphasize his rankled ego, he pulled out a chair and placed both feet on the tabletop. Ashcroft withheld his surging rage at such adolescent behavior. *It's business; forget everything else,* he told himself. Opening his briefcase, Ashcroft took out a file and went to the table. He stood there for a moment, waiting for the arrogant one to remove his feet from the table. With another shrug, the feet came down.

"Okay, Arthur. Why the big hurry?"

Maintain your composure. He reminded himself.

"I had a conversation with your partner today."

Barrington's face went flush. His brown eyes dilated as panic consumed every fiber of his body. He laid his head on the table. His body began to tremble with small whimpering sounds. He knew the fate that awaited him at the hand of Hector Paz. In his vulnerability, Arthur Ashcroft saw the answer. Barrington raised his head, "What did he want?"

"The money you owe him. Ten million to be exact," replied the master manipulator.

"Where am I going to get that kind of money?"

It was a ploy, but one necessary to impress upon the young Barrington that Ashcroft was his way out of this mess. The ruse was not wasted on Barrington.

"Please, Arthur, help me!"

The master manipulator began to create a way out not only for Trevor Barrington but also for himself. His voice softened. His words sounded caring and concerned.

"Are you prepared to do whatever is necessary?"

Without thinking, Barrington answered, "Yes."

Ashcroft smiled.

"Remember how you wanted to get out from underneath your father's name, be your own man, make your own money. That's why we set this account up in the first place, remember!"

Adding one last inducement for the desperate Barrington, Ashcroft remarked, "You've got several million in the account from our previous ventures with Mr. Paz. You'll be well taken care of, Trevor."

The young man stood up and walked over to the window. Everything he had ever wanted, to be free of his old man and the tightly controlled trust fund that had supported his lifestyle, had been in reach. Desperation strangled his words.

"What do I need to do?"

Ashcroft smiled. His plan was nearly in place.

"Your father had asked me many times to get you into the family business. I told him I would, which is why I added your name to be authorized to transfer funds between accounts under the control of Atlantic Financial."

Ashcroft sat down next to him and opened the file he had in front of him.

"This document authorizes Atlantic Financial to transfer ten million dollars from its general fund to this account." Ashcroft's pen pointed to an account titled "Strategic Planning." In case you're even remotely interested, monies flow in and out of this account during project development."

Ashcroft laid his pen on the paperwork. Knowing his father's penchant for scrutiny, the young man asked, "What if Father sees this transfer and starts to ask questions?"

"Your father had so many accounts intricately woven within the structure of Atlantic Financial. I can easily explain it if necessary."

With that assurance, the young man picked up the pen and signed his signature, "Trevor P. Barrington."

He laid the pen on the table. Picking up his pen and the signed document, Ashcroft reached into his briefcase, which lay on the table. He removed a 9MM pistol. Young Barrington stared at it in disbelief.

"What's that for?"

"That, Trevor, is your way out from under your father, that is, if you have the nerve to take it. Eliminate Mr. Paz, and the ten million dollars is yours and with it the freedom you deserve. Use it when he shows up at the airport."

Trevor Barrington had been humiliated and degraded by his father for years. He was never worthy of being Paris Barrington's son or sharing in his family's wealth. This was his opportunity to be free of that shame. He slowly reached for the pistol and placed it in his jacket pocket. Ashcroft smiled.

"Have your phone handy. Things are going to move quickly in the next few days and weeks. When it's over, you'll be your own man, Trevor. By the way, do you still have that fancy sports car?"

"The Bugatti? Yes."

If he only knew, Ashcroft thought, keeping his smile within. He walked to the door and opened it. "I'll be in touch."

His arrogance was gone. That perpetual Barrington confidence had vanished. As he got to the door, Trevor turned and said, "Thank you, Arthur."

Alone in his office, Arthur Ashcroft laid out the rest of his plan. First, create a number of false accounts to move the money in and out of before the final withdrawal. That would take several weeks. The last thing Ashcroft needed was to arouse the curious eye of one of Atlantic Financials' internal auditors. Lastly, a phone call to his other partner advising him of the pickup point and who would be waiting for him. A small private airport outside of Charleston, Laurel Hills, would serve the purpose. It had the capability of landing small jets. Payment would come from a man in a silver Italian convertible.

~

IT HAD BEEN ALMOST two weeks since the meeting of the Board of Directors of Magnolia Gardens, and Arthur Ashcroft's carefully crafted plan to force the sale of the property was beginning to unravel. The first sign of trouble was a frantic phone call from Drake Calhoun.

"Arthur, we've got a problem."

He went on to explain that the big PHARMA consortium put together to purchase his chain of medical clinics was rescinding their offer. It seems a number of states Attorneys General had filed suit in federal court seeking an injunction to close all Health Clinics of America in their jurisdiction pending the outcome of their own investigations into the excessive sale of prescription drugs. Facing that obstacle, the drug consortium rescinded their purchase offer.

"What am I supposed to do? I agreed to accept your offer to Magnolia Gardens. Now, what with all this litigation, my legal fees are going to soar! I'm afraid I'll have to rescind my letter of acceptance to the board. Certainly, you understand my predicament?"

Compassion and understanding were not in Arthur Ashcroft's DNA. His reply left Drake Calhoun feeling like he was floating on a raft out in the Atlantic.

"What I understand, Drake, is that I have a notarized letter signed by you authorizing the Board of Directors to accept my offer. Anything beyond that is not of my concern."

A sense of betrayal raged within Calhoun. He was not a complex or a sophisticated man, but he had a strong sense of survival. He also knew Ashcroft and how he would have to deal with him.

"Well Arthur, what I understand, you son-of-a-bitch, is I'm looking at the letter you wrote me!"

The egotism and pretentiousness that was Arthur Ashcroft's persona were beginning to unravel. The predator had become the prey.

22

COURT

Tina could not get the memory of her time with Ryan at Boulder Cove out of her mind even as she drove to the courthouse for her child support hearing. There had been something magical about it, and if she had judged him correctly, magical for him as well. Pulling into the city parking lot across the street from the courthouse brought Tina back to the emotionally charged meeting she was about to attend. Against her better judgment, she did as her attorney requested and brought Missy with her. Tina opened the side passenger door and gently unbuckled the seat belt from her sleeping daughter's car seat. The drive was a natural anesthetic for a small child forced to get up earlier than normal. Rubbing her eyes, Missy grumbled, "Why do we have to be here?"

Trying not to chide her, Tina told her the minimum with a smile, "Sweetheart, Mommy has to get some special papers signed for you, and then I'll get you to school."

The thought of school and her friends returned a smile to the little girl's face.

"I get to run!" she exclaimed excitedly.

Paying no attention to something she had explicitly told the school not to allow, Tina said, "Sure, baby," as she focused on looking for the sign reading, "Handicapped Entrance."

~

THE SILVER VOLVO SUV turned into the courthouse parking lot. The driver was looking for a slot that read "For Attorneys Only." Amanda Boyle didn't have to look long. The first dozen or so slots on the left as she drove in were so designated. She checked her watch, eight-thirty a.m. *Good,* she thought, *I've got plenty of time.* She had flown down the day before from New York and had not gotten a good night's sleep as promised by the local Embassy Suites. She took a small mirror from her purse for a final check of her makeup. *Professional, but not overdone,* she mused. She moved the mirror a little farther away to scan her hair. Near shoulder length Auburn hair, neatly trimmed, and with a natural sway when she walked — *it is fine,* she thought. Leaving her purse in the car, she took her black valise with its long shoulder strap and headed to the courthouse steps. Her Bamboo Fibre suit was a perfect match to offset the rising humidity. Normally, she looked forward to the adversarial roles played out by opposing attorneys. Facts of the case aside, the ego boost for winning was a huge rush. It fueled many a bloodthirsty law school student's ego. This case was different. Her directions were to delay with superfluous motions, not argue the merits of the case. The reawakening of her original desire to become a lawyer in the first place only added to her disgust. Considering the vast assets of her firm, she stepped with confidence up the courthouse steps and into the foyer. She faced a line of elevators. Off to the side was a portable stand with a sign indicating which courts were in session that day. She paused momentarily until she saw Family Court #4, third floor. Then she headed to the first open elevator.

~

SITTING on a bench in the hallway on the fourth floor, Tina nervously glanced at her watch. *He said to be there early, so where is he,* she thought, looking at the elevator doors. By now, Missy was wide awake and full of nervous energy. Not satisfied sitting next to her mother, Missy had secured permission from her mother to walk along the black and white tiled floor. She seemed perfectly content to crisscross her feet from white tile to black tile. In time, this bored the young child, who saw the hallway as the perfect place to practice running. Between worrying about her attorney and fantasizing about Ryan, Tina did not notice her daughter gleefully sweeping her leg out as Ryan had taught her, alternating landing her braced leg on a black tile and then a white tile. Had Tina noticed her, she would have also seen that her daughter was not walking but moving with surprising speed.

~

AMANDA STEPPED into the hallway as the elevator door opened, pausing to look at another sign directing her to Family Court #4. That pause led to an inevitable collision between her and the young girl practicing running. The impact caused Amanda's leg to buckle, sending her to her knees and spilling the contents of her valise. Next to Amanda lay a crying young girl, more surprised than hurt, holding on to her leg brace. Ignoring her papers, Amanda immediately took the young girl into her arms.

"I'm so sorry, sweetheart, are you okay? I didn't even see you."

Missy's intellectual impairment prevented her from fully understanding the question. Her frustration resulted in a stuttered response.

"Ma...Ma...Uh...Uh!"

Amanda immediately sensed the young child was different and would require a more simplified approach.

"My name's Amanda. What's your name?"

Amanda barely made out "Missy" as the child turned her head in every direction, looking for her mother. As soothing as Amanda's words were, and the softness of the arms holding her, what any child at that moment needed was her mother. Missy cried out, "Mumma! Mumma!" The words echoed through the hallway. Instinctively, Tina jumped to her feet and headed toward a small crowd assembled in front of the elevator doors. Amanda struggled to her feet, holding on to the child whose head turned left and right looking for her mother. Seeing her daughter safe in the arms of a stranger, Tina gasped, "Missy, Baby, what happened?" Amanda handed the child to her mother.

"I'm so sorry. It's entirely my fault," Amanda said. "I should have been paying more attention when I stepped out of the elevator. My name is Amanda Boyle. Is there anything I can do?"

As Tina swayed back and forth in an attempt to calm her daughter's somewhat melodramatic sobbing, she said, "I'm Tina Pinafore, Missy's mother. She'll be fine. She's got a bit of a stubborn side when it comes to running, and I'm afraid I was preoccupied with the thought of having to be in court today. Do you mind if we sit down? She's a load even at seven."

Despite her intellectual limitations, Missy was quite aware she would be eight on her next birthday. She audaciously corrected her mother.

"Mommy, I'm almost eight!"

"Of course, sweetheart," Tina said, as she rolled her eyes upward in silent exasperation.

Amanda allowed herself a sigh of relief. She knelt down to gather up the papers that had fallen from her valise when she collided with the child and followed mother and daughter to their bench farther down the hallway. As Tina and Missy took their place on the bench, Tina noticed the woman was limping as she walked.

"Did you hurt yourself?" Tina asked.

Not wanting to cause her any more anxiety, Amanda ignored the pain of a twisted ankle and lied.

"Oh, no. I'm breaking in a new pair of heels, and they're not being very cooperative."

Amanda searched through her valise. *There you are,* she thought, pulling out a plastic popup container of orange-flavored Pez candies. She shook a couple into her hand.

"I normally take a few before I head into court. Would Missy like some?"

Inquiring eyes stared at the two pill-shaped objects in Amanda's hand.

"They're candy," she said, with a smile to Missy.

"Say thank you, Missy," Tina prompted her daughter, who was ravenously crunching on her treat.

With a final swallow, Missy said, "Thank you."

"Missy, I have to be going now. Would you like the rest of the candies? I've got another one in my car."

Tina smiled appreciatively as an eager Missy held out her hand.

"From one friend to another," Amanda said, handing over the Pez container.

"Thank you, Amanda, that's very kind," responded Tina.

"You're welcome. I've got to straighten up a bit. I hope your day goes well," Amanda replied as she stood up and headed to the restrooms. As she disappeared into a maze of people getting off the elevators, a man hurriedly approached them.

"I'm sorry to be late, Tina," an out of breath Matthew Adams said. "I was held up by another client."

Mildly irritated that his late arrival had contributed to Missy's accident, Tina was a bit terse.

"Let's keep this about us."

"Of course," replied Adams, seeing that any further explanation would be fruitless. "Did you bring the letters I asked for?"

Grudgingly, Tina opened her purse and retrieved a small bundle of letters tied with a pink ribbon. As she handed them to Adams, she implored, "I wish these didn't have to be read in court. It was another time, and their contents are very private."

"I understand, Tina. I really do, but I need something to show the court a prior romantic interest existed other than your word."

Tina put her arms around Missy's shoulder.

"She won't have to testify, will she?"

"In all likelihood, no. I only want the judge to see the purpose of your request for support, and yes, I admit it's a sleazy attempt to get the judge's sympathy."

Looking at his watch, Adams said, "Let's go in. Remember, the judge is only going to rule on our motions. It's not the end of the world."

Family Court #4 lacked the large galley of a criminal court and no spacious jury box seen on TV crime shows. There were two rows of benches on either side of the aisle. In front of them, there were two five-foot dark mahogany tables. They faced the judge's bench, which sat on a raised stage. Adams made no eye contact with the attorney sitting to his left as he guided Tina and Missy to their table on the right. The two women could not have acted more differently. Missy gleefully chewed each of the remaining Pez candies. Tina looked like she was awaiting the dentist to call her in for a root canal without anesthesia.

"Remember, try not to react to anything the judge says," Adams whispered in a cautious tone.

With that, a side door opened, and the judge entered the

courtroom. He took two steps to the podium floor, then took his seat behind the bench. He had a rather scholarly appearance. His silver hair was cut short, and he wore a Sean Connery style silver stubble of a beard. Black-rimmed reading glasses hung from a cord around his neck. After glancing down at a stack of papers he brought in with him, he looked at both counsels.

"Mr. Adams, you are here to represent the plaintiff, Ms. Mary T. Pinafore, is that correct?"

Adams stood up and responded, "Yes, Your Honor."

The judge then looked at the other attorney.

"You must be counsel for Mr. Trevor Barrington, the defendant in this matter?"

Amanda rose. "Yes, Judge Kotowski. Amanda Boyle."

The judge smiled. "Not many people can pronounce my name."

"I have several friends from Greenpoint, your honor."

Judge Kotowski chuckled to himself at the reference to "Little Poland," the New York area where he grew up.

The judge's smiling acknowledgment was not a good sign to Adams.

Tina was more than shocked as she jerked her head in the direction of the opposing attorney. *You were so kind to my daughter, and yet you represent that son-of-a-bitch of a father!*

"Well then, let's get started, shall we?

Before he could say anything more, the judge was distracted by the young child sitting at the plaintiff's table. She was waving her hand in the air in the direction of opposing counsel. There was precious little not to adore about the young girl with a half-developed arm and wearing a leg brace. Her smile was angelic. Ringlets of blonde hair bobbed as her head moved back and forth.

"You seem to have a friend, Ms. Boyle," smiled the judge, who was intrigued by such an unusual interruption in his court.

"If it please the court, may I have a moment?" Amanda asked.

"By all means," replied the judge, who could hardly contain his laughter.

Amanda approached the plaintiff's table. She knelt down in front of the girl and smiled. Sweetly, she asked, "The judge said I could have a moment with you. What is it?"

Missy held her hand open, revealing a nearly empty container of her orange Pez candy.

"Want one?" she whispered softly. "They're almost gone."

No amount of courtroom etiquette could keep a tear from rolling down Amanda's cheek.

"Thank you, sweetheart. I really would," Amanda whispered back.

Then looking up to the judge, Missy said with great emphasis, "That's all."

With proper judicial decorum, the judge looked at Missy and declared, "Thank you, young lady. You may take your seat."

Clearly, his heart was captured by Missy, and that was good for Matthew Adams and not so good for Amanda Boyle.

"Mr. Adams, I've reviewed your request for an order of paternity naming Trevor Barrington as the father, and a judgment in an unspecified amount for future medical costs, is that correct?"

"Yes, your honor."

"You're not asking for future custodial expenses, only future medical expenses?"

"That's correct, your honor."

The judge let his glasses slide to the end of his nose as he sat back in his chair. His hand wrestled with the papers submitted by Adams.

"The decision to impose parental responsibility on another person is one I do not take lightly, Mr. Adams. I have a birth certificate with Mr. Trevor Barrington listed as the father but without his signature. I've carefully read Ms. Pinafore's deposition that speaks eloquently to a deep-felt relationship between her and Mr. Barrington. Neither of these documents can definitely name Mr. Barrington as the father. Do you have anything else to substantiate your claim?"

Adams rose. "May I approach the bench?"

The judge nodded. As Adams approached the bench, so did Boyle.

Handing the letters to the judge, Adams said, "These are copies of correspondence between my client and the defendant which speak without question to their long and intense sexual relationship, one in which they both speak of marriage. These letters are all dated prior to the birth of my client's child."

Boyle spoke up immediately. "Your Honor, this is the first I've heard of such letters. Even at face value, they certainly do not exclude the possibility of other sexual liaisons the plaintiff may have had at the same time."

The judge handed the letters to Boyle. "For your perusal, Ms. Boyle. You two may take your seats."

Adams knew it was a leap of faith for the judge to rule in his favor at this time. At best, he could stall for more time, but then what. The attorney part of Amanda Boyle felt smugly confident. When she would read the letters later, revulsion would be a more apt description of her feelings.

"Mr. Adams, paternity must be determined by the most precise and definitive information available, that being a DNA test. Ms. Boyle, your argument against a mandatory DNA is not persuasive in light of current case law. My objective is not to avoid making a difficult decision but to ensure that my decision is fair to all parties and in keeping with not only the letter of the law but the spirit of the law. Mr. Adams, you don't, at this point, have sufficient evidence to show that the defendant is the father of your client's child. Ms. Boyle, you seem opposed to the only method that would show your client is not the father, namely a DNA test. Therefore, I am directing the court to order the defendant, Trevor Barrington, to submit to a DNA test within the week. Failure to comply with the order and I will rule that Mr. Barrington is the presumptive father of the child in question. That, Ms. Boyle, will mean your client will be held responsible for past child support, past, current, and future medical expenses and all such expenses incurred for the well-being of the child."

"Your Honor, my client is currently out of the country on family business. His mother is under a doctor's care in a sanitarium in Switzerland. He is needed there to oversee her treatment."

Amanda's brief time with Missy and her mother in the hallway and her quick scan of one of the letters written by her client to Missy's mother left Amanda with no doubt about the authenticity of paternity. Sickened by her lie and nauseated by her legal obligation to zealously represent her client, Amanda abhorred the thought of returning to work in New York. The judge's qualifying remarks did little to absolve her sense of self-betrayal.

'I will hold my order for the DNA test in abeyance for thirty days. At that time, I want an expected return date to this country. Am I clear, Ms. Boyle?"

"Yes, your honor."

"Then I think we are finished here."

The judge gathered his papers, stood up, and left the courtroom. Adams turned to Tina. "We have thirty days to come up with something. I feel good about that."

Tina had a fatalistic smirk on her face.

"Well, I don't. The Barringtons' money can drag this out until hell freezes over."

Any argument to the contrary would no doubt be useless,

Adams thought. Suddenly, Amanda Boyle appeared at his table.

"Excuse me, but may I have a word with you when you're finished with your client?"

"Ms. Boyle, may I ask you a question first," Tina said, as she held Missy's hand.

"Certainly."

"Have you ever met Trevor Barrington or his father and mother?"

Uneasy with having allowed herself to be questioned, Amanda said, "No, I haven't."

"You should. What the entitled, the wealthy, the untouchable look like should matter to you."

Tina smiled, and taking Missy by the hand, said to Adams, "We'll talk later, I guess?"

Adams nodded. Tina and Missy proceeded down the aisle to the courtroom door.

Feeling unapologetic, Adams said, "She's got a mind of her own, and she lives what she speaks."

More than Tina's words tore at Amanda Boyle's heart. Her disdain for Abigail Strauss and the Machiavellian power she yielded at Sutro, Bellow, and Finestein was a good place to start. Her direction to make the case go away by any means possible ignored every legal tenant Amanda Boyle held dear. Even harder to swallow was Amanda's shame at denying her Irish name and south Boston roots in order to fit in at Harvard and her high-priced New York law firm. She stood silent as Adams closed his briefcase. Boyle opened her valise, taking out a small wallet. She flipped it open and took out a small black and white snapshot of a group of children ranging from three to about twenty. She placed it in front of Adams.

"This is a family photo of my cousins at some family gathering that I don't remember. This one," she said, pointing to the one in the middle, "with the big smile, is my cousin, Joey. He's the most precious child God ever created. If you can't tell, he has Down syndrome. There isn't anything my family won't do to protect him. And woe to anyone that would ever hurt him."

Boyle put the photo back in the small wallet and returned once again to her adversarial self.

"Neither my client nor his family will ever concede to a DNA test. Proof of his paternity will have to come from another source." She had fulfilled her legal responsibility.

"Any ideas?" Adams asked rhetorically.

As Amanda Boyle placed the documents the judge had given her into her valise, the resurgence of why she wanted to become a lawyer and who she wanted to serve swelled in her heart.

"Not as long as I work at Sutro, Bellow, and Finestein and represent Paris Barrington."

With a sparkle of Irish guile in her eyes, she said, "I'll be in touch."

23

THE ABYSS NEARS

Eddy rose later than usual the day after returning from what he euphemistically called "Their road trip." It had lasted two nights and three days, shorter than expected due to Maddy's lack of stamina and ever-decreasing attention span. Their excursion into the past had its brief moments of happiness for Eddy Pinafore. Maddy's mumbling of the words to "Just You and Me," in the backyard of their first home in Little Creek, and her utterance of "I do," on the patio of Eddy's cousin Andy's house where he and Maddy had been married, had been connections to the past measured in nanoseconds. For the most part, Eddy might as well have been traveling with a store mannequin as a companion. Maddy was responsive to simple directions, but the days of any meaningful conversation between the two were long gone. For Eddy, the road trip had been a two-edged sword. It had brought him back to the happiest times of his life, but it also brought him to the edge of forever loneliness.

Only once in his life had Eddy Pinafore turned against God, even cursed him, for what he perceived that God had put him through. For too many years, he had been haunted by dreams of his Seal team members screaming after their helicopter had been hit by ground fire from Iranian terrorists. Their bodies were torn by shrapnel. Flames from the burning helicopter attacked their flesh like a predator feasting on some bloody prey. The pain caused his body to jerk spasmodically during his sleep. If his dreams weren't horrific enough, the countless surgeries on his arm and leg and multiple skin grafts on his face made life a living hell. There were endless nights when the only voice he heard was his own, screaming for another shot of morphine, then cursing the nurse for refusing to bring it. The ensuing years had brought some measure of happiness into his life in helping disabled veterans like himself adjust to civilian life. Still, nothing compared to the moment when he was reunited with his Maddy. God had given him his dream back— at least that's how he saw it and felt about it. It was difficult to understand God's intentions in the best of times, but this? For over twenty-five years, Eddy Pinafore lived that dream—then God struck him again. Slowly, agonizingly slowly, painfully, God was now taking his dream away again, one memory at a time.

Eddy had elected not to shower or shave so he would not disturb Maddy, who was still sleeping. It took so little to fatigue her these days and so long to recover. Dressed only in a t-shirt and boxers, he rested on the sofa in the living room. His tousled hair and blurred eyes were signs of a restless night. He had underestimated the effects their short sojourn would take on him. As he listened to the brewing coffee drip into its carafe, he rubbed his forehead, still seeking some resolution to his earlier morose theological thoughts about God. All those sanctimonious cliches of life, "Every cloud has a silver lining," or "Look on the bright side," seem void of any true application to his situation. *What silver lining?* He thought. *What bright side?* For Eddy Pinafore, the paradox wasn't "Is the glass half empty or half full?" It was an intellectual treatise that he chose to ignore for the moment. He would have the answer to that question in the next few minutes. He had left their bedroom door ajar specifically to hear for any distress from Maddy. A groan of frustration and anger came from their bedroom. Eddy rose to check on her. He found her sitting on the side of their king-size bed, her back to him. She was struggling with putting on her flower print kimono bathrobe. He walked to her side of the bed.

"Here, let me help you," he said, as he held out the troublesome sleeve for her.

With her bathrobe on, Maddy placed her hand on her nightstand and stood up. She managed to tie a rather clumsy knot before turning to face Eddy. There was that eternal smile and then a pause as she seemingly tried to formulate her thoughts. Eddy put his arms around her.

"Do you know how much I love you?" He whispered as he embraced her, kissing both of her cheeks.

From some far-away place came a spark of memory. With the giddiness of a younger woman in the arms of an amorous younger man, Maddy answered, "Shouldn't I shower first?" At that moment, Eddy embraced his own fantasy.

"I'll have your coffee ready when you're done, darling," Eddy responded.

He left Maddy to her shower, confident that she could perform this simplest of daily hygiene steps. The reality would send Eddy Pinafore to the precipice of hopelessness. As Maddy made her way to the bathroom, Eddy grabbed a clean t-shirt, a fresh pair of underwear, and his favorite Bermuda shorts from his armoire and headed to the guest bathroom to shower and shave. As he stood under the hot water, he slowly adjusted the temperature to cold. He liked the invigoration the temperature change gave him. With his shave completed and a spray of Jovan Musk to his neck, Eddy headed to the kitchen to check on the coffee. As he took down two coffee cups from the cupboard, Eddy realized how much pleasure he derived from the simplest of domestic chores—brewing that perfect pot of coffee, watering the half dozen of Maddy's favorite houseplants, even arranging the small pillows on the couch the way Maddy did. He had decided a breakfast of sliced fruit, scrambled eggs, and sausage patties with whole wheat toast would start their day. He placed two pieces of bread in the toaster and laid the eggs and sausage patties next to the frying pan on the stove. He placed a bowl of Maddy's favorite, sliced strawberries sprinkled with powdered sugar, on the kitchen table. *Now to check on Maddy,* he thought, as he hung a small kitchen towel over his shoulder and walked to their bedroom. The bathroom door was closed. Eddy called out her name.

"Maddy, are you finished? Coffee's done, and I'm ready to make breakfast."

There was no answer, and worse, there was no sound of running water. Eddy moved quickly to the bathroom door and opened it. Maddy was standing in front of the opened shower stall, naked. Her kimono lay at her feet. She was staring straight ahead.

"Sweetheart, didn't you hear me?" Eddy asked, keeping his tone soft and without impatience. "Your coffee's ready, and breakfast won't take long."

Maddy said nothing. Then she slowly looked at him. Tears were flowing down her cheeks. Her eyes reflected abject panic and fear. She tried to speak, but she choked on her words.

"Honey, what is it?" Eddy begged. The terror that had stricken his wife now gripped his heart.

"I don't know."

Terrified for her and horrified at the reality standing before him, Eddy Pinafore froze for the first time in his life. *No, it can't be,* he thought. *Tell me, God— it hasn't come to this,* his mournful soul screamed. Had she been in a different frame of mind, Maddy would have been humiliated at the thought of having her husband bathe her. There was no such realization now.

Eddy forced himself to take control of the situation. He stepped around Maddy, reached inside the shower turning the water on. When it had reached the desired temperature, he took Maddy by the hand and guided her into the shower, leaving the door open. With simple hand movements, he had her stand with her back to the showerhead. Gently, he moved a soapy loofah across her shoulders and down her back. Then he turned her to face the flowing stream of warm water. He soaped the front of her shoulders and neckline, then let the pulsating cascade of water do the rest. Eddy stood there for several minutes hoping Maddy would enjoy the therapeutic effects of the rotating shower head even if she didn't remember those long soaking showers that Eddy used to complain about. Finally, he reached in and turned the water off. After gently drying her with a bath towel, he grabbed her terrycloth bathrobe from the hook behind the bathroom door and helped her into it. Dressing would come later.

"Let's have that coffee now," he said.

There was a lengthy hesitation. Maddy's facial features turned from stoic to convoluted. Finally, she managed a weak, "Okay."

As they made their way down the hallway and into the living room, Maddy paused several times, first looking left and then right at the array of family photographs that hung on both walls. Each time she stopped, she leaned closer to the wall. Her tired eyes squinted. Her brow furrowed with determined effort to recognize the now strangers before her. It was beyond her comprehension, yet the photographs represented a montage of her and Eddy's life journey together, a journey nearing its end. Eddy walked patiently with Maddy as they made their way through the living room and into the kitchen area. Even with a walker, Maddy's stability was tenuous.

A walker would also take the toll of bearing Maddy's weight off him when she leaned on him for additional support.

Once he got her seated at the kitchen table, Eddy went to the living room to retrieve the remote control from the coffee table. He turned on the TV and tuned it to the WCIV, the Charleston ABC affiliate news station. At some point, Eddy would tire of hearing his own voice in solitary conversation with Maddy, and he would need an alternative to her silence. After adjusting the flame under the Calphalon skillet, Eddy announced the menu, "Okay, how about scrambled eggs, toast, and maple-flavored sausage patties, your favorite?" It was more a statement than a question, as he knew Maddy would probably not answer. She didn't. He didn't bother to turn around. Repeating what he had said to get a response would serve no purpose. The sausages went directly into the microwave oven, one less pan to clean. Eddy skillfully cracked five large eggs against the pan's edge and then, using his good hand, adeptly opened the shells and let the eggs fall onto a medium-hot pan with a drizzle of EVOO in it. He pushed down on the toaster button to brown the whole wheat toast, added a little seasoning of salt and pepper to the eggs and an extra ingredient he had failed to mention to Maddy. He took a small plastic bag of Cremini mushrooms out of the vegetable crisper in the refrigerator. It was a small gift he had purchased for himself at a roadside fruit and vegetable stand on their return home. Using the knife in his left hand, he pushed each mushroom up against his prosthetic hand and then carefully sliced it into thin pieces. *Three would be plenty,* he thought, as he slid the sliced delicacy off the cutting board and into the battered eggs in the pan. With near perfect timing, the toaster ejected two faultlessly browned pieces of wheat bread as the microwave signaled the sausages were done. He gave the eggs one final stir and pushed them onto their plates, then came the sausages and the bread. Eddy put one plate and then the other on the table. He hoped she would appreciate his efforts.

"I made this especially for you," he said proudly.

There was no sense waiting for Maddy, who stared down at

her plate as if to say, "What's this?". After a few bites of egg, Eddy proclaimed, "Honey, you really should try these. What a flavor those Creminis add!" Maddy smiled, and then to his delight, she picked up her fork and began to eat. Eddy made idle conversation about the morning news coming over the TV. He caught a brief glimpse as the sports came on, half expecting a caution from Maddy about too many sports in their life. Eddy had convinced himself this truly was a better time. She had finished about half her eggs, half her toast, and didn't touch her sausages. Her sliced strawberries were another story. Did she remember how much she loved them or had she merely enjoyed the heavenly sweetness of their juice combined with the powdered sugar? In either case, they were nearly gone. All that remained of her delight were small spills of powdered sugar on her bathrobe and juice stains from the strawberries that had dripped on her face. Apparently, the use of a napkin was yet another addition to things she forgot. Eddy took his napkin without comment, reached over, and gently dabbed the corners of his wife's mouth. Maddy turned her head to the TV. *It wasn't the content of the story that caught her attention,* Eddy thought, *more likely the motion of the on-scene reporter walking side by side with the Chief of Police trying to get a comment about a reported shooting at a nearby airport involving members of the Charleston PD Drug Task Force.* Eddy took this opportunity to enjoy one more cup of coffee before beginning an unpleasant but necessary task, another indignity for Maddy.

Eddy pulled Maddy's chair away from the table. She was no longer able to scoot her chair by herself. She was dead weight, making a difficult task even more so for a man using one arm. There were bits of scrambled eggs on her lap, along with crumbs from her half-finished piece of toast. *Let them fall,* Eddy thought. *I can get them later.* He moved her walker in front of her.

"Time to get dressed, sweetheart. Put your hands on the walker, and I'll get you to the bedroom."

She paused before looking at him with eyes that seemed to say, "Put my hands where?"

Though his patience level was near empty, there was enough for Eddy to smile at her. He placed one of her hands on the walker and then the other one.

"There, sweetheart."

Maddy began her arduously slow journey to her bedroom with Eddy at her side. Once at the bedside, Eddy asked her to sit down. He took the walker and set it in the corner, and then he walked over to her dresser. For Eddy, the selection of undergarments was simple, whatever was on top. There was no question of color—underpants were underpants, a t-shirt was a t-shirt, but for a woman like Maddy, such was not the case. She was never the one to look plebeian, even when it came to the bare essentials. There was a drawer full of different colored panties and different colored bras. He was sure she would not know the difference, but it was really his impatience at having to suffer the indignity of dressing his own wife that caused Eddy to grab the first thing he saw. He had never placed his own feelings before Maddy's, but this time was different, and he felt ashamed for it. Fortunately, Maddy would at least follow his prompts. He got her underwear on, then her bra. He took her favorite perfume bottle, Elizabeth Taylor's White Diamonds, off her dresser and sprayed a fine mist across her neckline. He selected a pair of peach-colored slacks and a white cotton floral print blouse for her to wear.

With those items of apparel on, Eddy did the best he could at brushing Maddy's hair. Her makeup was another story. He got Maddy to her feet and guided her over to her vanity, gently setting her down on the padded yellow cushion. Several makeup items lay on a glass tray in front of her. Eddy gently placed his arms on her shoulders and whispered softly in her ear, "Honey, I can't do your makeup for you. You'll have to do it. Do you understand me?" As much as dementia had taken hold of her mind, the last vestiges of feminine ego had not acquiesced to the disease. Maddy looked down at the tray of items in front of her. She managed to open her lipstick tube with feeble fingers and apply a thin line of ruby red to her lips. To Eddy's surprise, the application was without a single smear, a bit thick in spots due to her pushing on the tube too hard, but all in all, not bad. With his wife dressed, Eddy placed the walker in front of her and said, "I need to get you into the living room, sweetheart. I've got some chores to do around the house."

In a moment of unexpected and spontaneous clarity, Maddy looked up at her husband and said, "I'll be fine, Eddy." To further indicate her understanding of the coming events, Maddy took hold of her walker and stood up, and headed to the bedroom door. She still needed help navigating the narrow hallway and then finding the couch in the living room. Once seated, Eddy turned the TV to "Jeopardy," her favorite daytime TV show. Confident that she would be fine with the TV on and a stack of magazines on the end table next to her, Eddy proceeded with his work. It took him well over an hour and a half to make the bed, clean up the bathroom, get the breakfast dishes rinsed and into the dishwasher, and vacuum around the kitchen table. By the time he was done, Maddy had dozed off and was soundly sleeping on the couch. Eddy took a seat in his lazy boy chair with its electrically operated foot riser, not that he was tired or needed a rest, but his mind was stuck in a quagmire of decisions to be made, some hypothetical, some real. He closed his eyes. In another time, his mind would dissect each decision, the rationale for making it, and then weigh the possible consequences, making sleep an impossibility. This time though, his brain acted as though it was in a state of cerebral avoidance, no longer willing to deal with such matters. Eddy slept soundly.

~

HE HEARD a knock on the door. As if he was in an out of body experience, he saw himself getting up and walking to the front door. He opened it and saw an older woman standing there, dressed in a powder blue uniform.

"We're here as you requested, Mr. Pinafore."

"Who are you?" he asked, annoyed at the interruption of a stranger at his door.

"Mr. Pinafore, you asked for us to come here," the woman said.

Annoyance turning to anger, Eddy shouted at the woman. His words sounded slurred.

"I don't know who you are and where you came from!"

"I'm Mildred Patterson from the Visiting Angels."

Eddy was jolted into consciousness. The dream had been like a bucket of cool water splashed on a dulled brain. He sat upright. "Where was it? Where did I put it," he mumbled? He was sure he had left it on the end table next to his lazy boy chair. He reached over to a small stack of unopened mail and began sorting through it. He was surprised how much annoying junk mail came to their house. "There you are," he said to himself. It was a brochure for the Visiting Angels he had seen on top of the bookcase in Dr. Tipton's office. It was among many health care businesses dedicated to eldercare. Eddy had taken a copy, knowing there would come a time when their services would be needed.

He usually kept his reading glasses on the end table. When he looked for them, they weren't there. His reading glasses had joined that trio of items that he made sure he had wherever he left the house, keys, wallet, checkbook, glasses. He looked on top of the coffee table, not there. Frustrated that he would have to get out of his chair, he muttered, "Damn it!" More out of reflex than a conscious act, he tapped his shirt pocket. There they were. Eddy expelled a sigh of relief. He put them on, then opened the trifold brochure to acquaint himself with the services they provided before making the call. He went through the entire brochure twice, making sure he hadn't missed anything. *Yes, this is exactly what I need*, he thought. Suddenly he was overcome by a wave of guilt. Had he really found bathing his wife so intolerable, or dressing her such an imposition? *No, of course not*, he thought, continuing this debate between himself and his conscience. But ultimately, being a man of logic, Eddy Pinafore knew that there would be a progression to a task of even greater indignity, incontinency, and that would take an angel of a different sort. Because of the morning events, Eddy had a sense of urgency to make arrangements for this. Now more than ever, he needed to expedite the process for transitioning to Magnolia Gardens.

The next several months would keep Eddy Pinafore busier than he had been in years, and he was going to need help. Thank God for the silence of the electrically operated footrest. The slight drone of the motor did not disturb Maddy. He rose gently and walked carefully across the tile floor to the kitchen. There on the counter was a small black notebook they used for making lists. Eddy grabbed it and a pen from a small wooden box next to it and sat down at the kitchen table. As he began to formalize his mental list of tasks that needed to be done, Eddy was overwhelmed at the enormity of the process. One item led to another and then another. It seemed endless the things that he was facing and facing alone. First, a call to the Visiting Angels, then a call to Samantha Callahan at Magnolia Gardens to schedule their move, but that would mean selling their house and the disposition of years of accumulated possessions that would not fit in their new home. A realtor would have to handle that issue—another call that needed to be made. And then there was Tina. She had told her dad when he first told her of her mother's deteriorating mental condition that whatever was going on in her life, her mom and dad would come first. Unbeknownst to her, that promise would prove to be an enormous challenge in Tina's own quest for happiness.

24

TWO AS ONE

Her workweek had been exhausting and the term "Thank God It's Friday" certainly applied to Tina Pinafore. She had worked all week and several nights at home to complete a grant application to the Abilis Foundation for nearly one hundred thousand dollars to develop work activities for disabled adults. The deadline for submission was today. Tina slipped the forty-page document into a large manila envelope and prepared to head to the post office when there was a knock at her office door. Clearly annoyed by the interruption, she responded to the knock curtly.

"Come in."

She was not anxious to entertain a visitor as she needed her document to be postmarked with Friday's date. Her anxiety rose when her visitor entered her office, but for a very good reason.

"Hi, Kiddo!"

He had christened her with his own special term of endearment after the picnic at Boulder Cove. Since then, every conversation had begun and ended with it, "Hi Kiddo!" or "See you later, Kiddo!" Some special assignment at work had forced

Ryan to work several nights, eliminating any opportunity to see her, so his phone calls became even more special. They had reached a point in their relationship where if they were to go to the next level, one thing for sure had to happen. Ryan needed to know about and meet her daughter, Missy. There would be no future without him embracing her. She hurried to his arms. The privacy of her office enabled them to share a long-overdue embrace and a sensuous kiss that, in the right circumstances, would have resulted in the shedding of clothes and more.

"Missed you," he said, as their lips parted.

"Me too," sighed Tina. "To what do I owe this unexpected pleasure, and I do mean pleasure," as she taunted him by pressing her body against his.

Never in his life would Ryan Callahan have thought he would reject this opportunity, but the office of his girlfriend hardly seemed appropriate for such intimacy. With sufficient embarrassment, he said,

"I was thinking a different time and place."

Okay, sweetheart! she thought, as she giggled and released her arms from his shoulders.

"I stopped by to ask if you'd like to go to Sal and Bella's tomorrow? They've invited us over for a barbecue. Bella said to tell you it's nothing fancy, so dress casual."

Realizing the moment had finally presented itself, Tina faltered a bit.

"Look, Ryan, there's a bit of a complication. My mom and dad are out of town on what my dad called a road trip, so my normal babysitters aren't available. There's no way I could get a replacement on such short notice. I'll have to bring my daughter along."

Without a moment's hesitation, he responded, "Sure, that's no problem."

Maybe not, she thought, but she had no choice now but to tell him about Missy. It had to happen sooner or later.

"You don't understand. She's got special needs, some cognitive impairment, and mobility issues."

Tina felt a twinge of annoyance at being forced to say this much. Realizing he did not fully comprehend the implication of what she had said, Tina turned and walked away. Without turning back to face him, she spoke to the wall as if reciting items off an imaginary list.

"My daughter is developmentally disabled. On top of that, she has a malformed arm and an undeveloped leg joint that requires her to use a brace. She needs help bathing, dressing, eating, you name it. Every phase of her life will require help from someone. So, it's not, 'no problem.'"

Ryan was silent a moment and then said, "Wow, that's a load."

They had only gone out twice and, by all the rules, were taking things one day at a time. It was impetuous, to say the least, for either to feel otherwise, but matters of the heart are not always governed by cautious, thoughtful deliberation. Once smitten, the heart is like a runaway horse. His pause seemed like an eternity, and her heart sank. She turned away from him lest he see the dejection that had overwhelmed her. *Maybe it was too much of a load for him to accept. Better to give him a way out now.*

"Look, Ryan. If you'd rather not, you know, see me anymore, I'll understand. A child like that is a lot to take on."

For Ryan Callahan, it was too late. He had fallen deeply for Tina, and nothing was going to stop him from continuing to see her. Whether it was naiveness on his part or proof that "love is blind," it didn't matter. He couldn't control his heart at this point. He walked up to her, placed his hands on her shoulders, and turned her around to face him. He took her hand before she could wipe away the tears of anticipated disappointment that rolled down her cheeks. She knew what she was about to hear. Tina placed her hands on Ryan's chest and, with one final roll of the dice that would dictate her future, looked into his eyes and asked, "Now, how do you feel?"

"I'm sorry if you thought I meant it would be too much of a load for me. What I meant was that's a huge responsibility for a single parent, but it doesn't scare me from wanting to see you."

∼

"SAL, are you sure there's nothing we can bring? Beer, wine, french bread, what?"

Sal had his phone pinned to his shoulder as he trimmed off the excess fat on two large tri-tip roasts.

"Bring your appetite, Bro. Bella's making macaroni salad with bay shrimp and, for dessert, her famous Tiramisu."

Ryan's mouth began to salivate at the thought of the rich, velvety chocolate dish.

"Listen, Sal, there's going to be three of us. It seems Tina can't get a babysitter for her daughter, so she's coming along."

"That's great. You know how much Bella loves kids."

Ryan thought it best to prepare his friend.

"Sal, the girl has some special needs. Tina said she's got some mobility issues and some cognitive impairment, as she put it. I wanted to prepare you."

"Prepare me for what, Ryan? Sounds like the child is developmentally disabled. We'll treat her like family, like any other kid."

Working at Weatherly School had erased any curiosity Ryan may have had about children with disabilities. Whatever their limitations were, one thing was certain—those kids were not limited in giving the most unconditional love Ryan had ever experienced. If the child was anything like her mother, then what's not to love. Despite Sal's instructions not to bring anything, Ryan stopped by Pete's Deli and bought a couple of loaves of french bread. The aroma of the freshly baked bread soon filled the cab of his truck. On the way to Tina's place, Ryan couldn't help but wonder how the girl would take to him. From what Tina had said, it didn't sound like there had ever been a male figure in their lives. A barbecue at Sal and Bella's was an all-day affair, so having been forewarned, Ryan pulled up to Tina's place about eleven a.m. He walked up the drive to the home in the back.

The small mother-in-law cottage behind Fred and Willa's house had a flagstone walkway leading to the front door. Painted yellow with white trim and a cedar shingle roof with patches of moss, it was quaintly Southern in appearance. The grass needed mowing. The flower boxes lining the edge of the porch got the attention the lawn did not. Two large flower pots of Mandevilla Vogue hung from the porch eaves. The flower boxes full of Princess Blush and Princess Dark Lavender verbenas added additional color. A very inexpensive swing set in the front yard was the only sign of a child living there. Ryan approached the door and gently knocked a couple of times. Soon the door opened. Before he could even speak, he had to clear his throat. She couldn't have been more beautiful. There was a faint aroma of Elizabeth Taylor's "White Diamonds." It had been Ryan's mother's favorite. She wore an off-shoulder floral blouse with a small choker chain around her neck. If he had ever seen a more beautiful smile, he couldn't remember when. He stared at her form-fitting jeans that were flared at the bottom and lined with bling.

He choked before muttering, "You look great!"

She smiled before saying, "You don't look so bad yourself." Then she went to him and gave him a quick kiss on the lips. "Come in, please. I'll just be a minute."

Tina headed down a hallway off the living area. The front room was a combination dining area and living room. A small dining table with two chairs occupied part of the living room. There was a small couch and an even smaller coffee table with all the markings of being Early Salvation Army. A medium-sized TV occupied the wall opposite the couch. A Tiffany lamp hung from the center ceiling. On one side of the TV hung several small photographs. Ryan moved slower to look at them when Tina appeared with her daughter in hand.

"Ryan, this is my daughter, Missy."

Before she could say more, the little girl screamed, "Coach! Coach!" and ran to him. Instinctively, he picked the girl up in his arms.

"Missy, I can't believe this!" as he hugged her and she him.

Tina stood there, flabbergasted. She couldn't believe her eyes. If he knew her daughter, why hadn't he said something before now? Tina had never heard her daughter mention Ryan's name. She slumped onto the couch.

"Can someone please explain to me what's going on?"

Ryan carried Missy over to the couch and sat down with Missy between them.

"My partner, Willie Root, asked me to help him out with something. It turns out his wife was a special education teacher at...."

"Weatherly School," Tina answered for him, still thoroughly confused.

"Right," Ryan replied. "It seems he needed some help getting the kids ready for the Special Olympics, so I said I would. Anyway..."

Tina suddenly sat more erect. "Then you're the one who was teaching Missy to run?" She sounded like equal parts of anger and curiosity.

"I am," said Ryan. His eyes pleaded for an opportunity to explain. "But let me explain,"

"Please do," replied Tina, now clearly annoyed with the situation. "I specially told the school not to have Missy run." Her face tightened. Her jaw was clenched, and her lips were pursed. As she crossed her arms, she dared him to tell her a believable story.

"Okay," said Ryan, "But that message never got to me. A week after I started helping Willie, he got wounded on a job. Eva took some time off. Not the principle or the substitute teacher ever said a word to me about not letting Missy run. Honestly, Tina, if I had known, I would never have gone against your wishes. But I didn't know. The ball just got dropped somehow, and Missy wanted to run like the other kids so badly, I took it upon myself to work with her."

Interrupting him, Missy gleefully announced, "Mommy, I can run. I'm good, too."

In her heart, Tina knew Ryan was speaking the truth. That, plus the smile on her daughter's face, gave her pause to think about something Ryan's friend, Sal, had told her the night she and Ryan had pizza at Sal's place. His missing leg didn't define him as a person, and more importantly, it was not a limitation but a motivation for him. Maybe the same could be said of Missy. She put her arm around Missy and pulled her close to her. More than one tear appeared on her cheeks.

"She's my baby. She's all I've got. The thought of her getting hurt, I guess, was too much. I wasn't thinking of her, only me."

Ryan put his arm around her. Tina leaned into his arms and started crying. He kissed her forehead and said, "Tina, she's not all you've got, not anymore."

25

A HEART TO LOVE

"When are you going to put those tri-tips on?" Bella asked nervously as she finished dicing up half a red onion for the macaroni salad. Sal was always amazed even after all these years that Bella could conduct any culinary art and still talk a mile a minute.

"Honey, they only take thirty minutes. There's plenty of time once they get here."

His sigh indicated that small bit of husband-wife frustration that occurs after twenty-five years of marriage. Sal loved his wife dearly, but after the billionth time of barbecuing tri-tip roasts, she shouldn't have to ask that question. Sal had the two roasts in a large Ziploc bag marinating in a combination of olive oil, crushed garlic, and red wine. The final ingredient, a healthy layer of Montreal Hickory Rub, would go on right before he hung them in the smoker. "Do you think he's has fallen for her?" asked Sal, referring to Ryan and Tina.

"Yes, Ryan has fallen for Tina. I could see it in his eyes that night at the restaurant. Now, do not pester either one of them with questions about their future, do you hear me, Sal Santini!"

"Yes, Your Majesty!" answered the queen's obedient

servant.

Sal was saved from any further royal mandates with the opening of the front door and the announcement, "We're here!"

Sal and Bella looked at each other with gleeful delight. Bella hurriedly straightened her summer dress and followed Sal into the living room. Standing in the living room was Ryan with a paper bag from Pete's Deli with a couple of loaves of French bread. Tina was standing next to him with Missy at her side. Despite Ryan's assurance that Sal and Bella would treat Missy like any other child, Tina had her misgivings, causing her smile to appear a bit forced.

"Sal, Bella, you know Tina, and this is her daughter, Missy."

The sight of a physical handicap was hardly novel to Sal or Bella. The child's smile overwhelmed them.

Bella extended her hand to the child and said, "Well, Missy, I'm Bella. I hope we can be friends?"

Then a very gregarious Missy said, "Sure," and smiling broadly, shook Bella's hand.

Sal's greeting was a bit more personal. He knelt in front of the child.

"Missy, I'm Italian, so I give hugs to my new friends, and my friends give me hugs. So, if we're going to be friends, guess what I get?" He opened up his arms to supply the obvious answer.

Missy looked up questioningly to her mother.

"Am I Italian?"

Her question sent everyone into laughter, which only added to the child's dilemma.

"No, sweetheart," responded Tina as she patted her daughter's head. "But I think Sal still expects something."

Whatever her mental impairments were, Missy was able to make this simple deduction.

"Hugs!" Missy called out, completely ignoring her mother's previous warning to use her inside voice.

With formalities out of the way, Ryan handed Bella the paper bag. Before she had a chance to scold him, Ryan quickly threw Tina under the bus.

"She insisted we bring something."

Looking at Tina, Bella slowly shook her head from side to side and replied, "Sweetheart, I don't think he's telling the truth, but thank you just the same."

Sal and Bella's home was located in what the locals referred to as "Little Italy," about a ten square block area of old homes consisting of red brick houses on some blocks and early Craftsman houses in the new area. Bella and Sal had a corner Craftsman, specifically picked out because the lot was level to the sidewalk and required no modifications for Sal's prosthetic leg. The house had an open porch with Sal's favorite rattan chair and sofa set. Sal had built raised flower beds on either side of the walkway. It would mean less kneeling for him and Bella. Redwood mulch occupied what would have been a lawn —an accommodation Bella had insisted on due to Sal's leg, though it grated on him that she thought he even needed a modification at all.

"Okay, let me give you the cook's tour, and then it's off to the back yard," instructed Sal.

The smallish living room had wood floors, a large area rug in front of a sectional sofa with leg lifts on each end. Sal's gift to himself was a fifty-two-inch LCD TV on the wall opposite the sofa. They breezed through the three bedrooms, the master with Bella's prized en suite, one which they used as an office for Sal, the other for visitors, and another full bath. Bella had insisted on specific upgraded kitchen amenities, such as a six-burner gas stove, an island with twin farm sinks, and an over-head wrought iron rack for pots and pans. That, along with her high-tech touch dishwasher and the refrigerator-freezer combination, made Bella a happy wife. The backyard was Sal's creation. A large pergola shadowed a twenty by fifteen-foot cement patio. His barrel smoker was off to one side. Sal and his father had built a thirteen by ninety-one-foot bocce ball court along the left fence. The traditional Italian lawn game had afforded the two many hours of father-son time, not to count the profanity-laced arguments over illegal throws. On the other side of the yard, Sal had a forty-eight by six-foot horseshoe pit. No family gathering was ever complete without a champion being crowned for each game.

They stopped in the kitchen. Tina could see the makings for the macaroni salad.

"Is there anything I can help with, Bella?" Tina asked, feeling guilty she had not insisted on bringing more than French bread.

"All I've got to do is mix the macaroni salad."

"Then please, let me help," Tina implored.

"Ryan, grab two bottles of red off the rack in the corner and follow me. I'll bring the glasses. The women have work to do."

Had Sal's chauvinistic remark been taken seriously, Bella would have thrown the french bread at him. Instead, he was greeted with a much less hostile remark.

"Please go. What we've got to do is much too complicated for your feeble minds to understand!"

Leaving the women chuckling at their now exposed mental deficiencies, Sal and Ryan headed to the backyard. The eight-foot wooden table and its benches were made of shiplap planking. Bella had set a long red and white tablecloth with a bouquet of yellow mums in the center. Ryan placed the bottles on the table and pulled out the bench. Sal sat opposite him, the wine glasses tinkling as he set them on the table.

"So, she's pretty special, isn't she?" he grinned at Ryan.

Pleading ignorance to a question he knew he could not avoid, Ryan answered, "What are you talking about?"

"Do I have to explain?

A smile spread across his face. He leaned forward as if he

was about to reveal a deep secret.

"She's more than special, Sal, much more."

"Child and everything?" Sal asked. With the wisdom of experience, he added, "Not questioning, only verifying."

"That kid gives unconditional love. What more can I say?"

"That calls for a toast," smiled Sal, who quickly realized he had left the wine opener inside. Ryan followed him back into the house.

Bella and Tina were standing next to the island. Missy sat on a tall stool chair. In front of them sat a large ceramic bowl, a big spoon, a chopping board with diced red onions on it, and a jar of mayonnaise.

"Pay attention, you two. We're about to mix the macaroni salad."

Forcing themselves to look like the class dunces, Sal and Ryan stood still looking like Stan Laurel of Laurel and Hardy.

Bella poured the cooled macaroni into the bowl, followed by the red onions. Then she added a cup of mayonnaise. Noting the young girl's rapt attention, she inquired, "Missy, would you like to stir?"

Eager to please her new friend, Missy took hold of the long wooden spoon. She struggled to hold the bowl still with the nub of an elbow on her other hand. The bowl kept slipping out of what little grasp she had. She was determined to do it, but with every slip, her determination became frustration, and with frustration would come eventual tears. Bella sensed it along with everyone else.

"Excuse me for a second," she said as she left the kitchen.

Tina took the spoon from Missy. "But Mom, I ca..." Her stutter had returned with a vengeance.

"I know, sweetheart. Some other time."

Bella returned from her bedroom. She had a tube sock she had cut in half and an eight-inch section of four-inch-wide Velcro strapping.

"Hold out your arm, Missy," Bella said.

Obediently and with pooled up tears in her eyes, Missy extended her arm. Bella slipped the tube sock over the nub end of her arm, and then she placed the handle of the spoon against her arm.

"Can you hold the handle right here with your other arm?" Bela asked, pointing to a spot near the end of the handle.

Missy nodded, doing as she was asked. Bella then gently but snugly wrapped the Velcro strap around Missy's upper arm, covering most of the handle.

"There, now try stirring," Bella beamed.

With the spoon end extending about eight inches below the stub of her elbow, Missy pushed the spoon end into the salad and, holding the bowl with her other arm, slowly began to stir. With the Velcro strapping doing its job, Missy was able to navigate through the ingredients with ease. The child was so excited with her accomplishment, she shouted joyfully, "I'm stirring!" bringing both arms into the air and splattering Bella and Tina with macaroni salad off the end of her spoon.

"That's what I call adapt, improvise, and overcome!" shouted Sal, with a beaming Ryan by his side.

"It's a Marine thing, Tina. Pay them no attention," Bella explained.

Sal walked over to a clearly moved Tina and put his arms around her shoulders. With the soft whisper of wisdom, Sal said, "Never think what she can't do, think why can't she."

With the salad chilling in the refrigerator, the women joined the boys in the back yard. Ryan poured two more glasses of wine. Handing the marinating tri-tips to Sal, Bella chided him, "Remember these?"

With a shrug of his shoulders as if to say, "See what I have to put up with?" Sal took the roasts from her and walked over to the smoker, then smartly retorted, "Yes, I remembered, see the coals are ready." With that, Sal put a steel hook through the end of each roast, then hung them on a crossbar centered over the flaming coal box at the bottom of the barrel. He placed the lid of the barrel on top, then proudly announced, "Dinner will be served in thirty minutes!"

The plate of antipasti that Bella had prepared provided the perfect accoutrements to the afternoon meal. The platter contained rolls of thinly sliced Genoa Salami, garlic stuffed olives, chunks of Feta and Blue cheese, and sweet cherry tomatoes stuffed with brie cheese. There was an additional plate with cubes of french bread and a small bowl of olive oil and balsamic vinegar. *This was a meal in itself,* Tina thought. Then she was reminded of what awaited them as the aroma from the smoker wafted in their direction. The time quickly passed as Sal and Ryan reveled in their Marine Corps experiences. Bella barely had a moment to tell Tina about their three children. Sal made a point of talking about the occasions Ryan came to his aid or some other former Marine or a stranger on the street, for that matter. There was a gentle squeeze of Ryan's leg with each story or a look of admiration that Tina made no attempt to hide.

When his internal clock sounded thirty minutes, Sal got up from the table and walked over to the smoker. He took the lid off and, with a fork, lifted each roast off the spit and onto the cutting board Ryan was holding. That was Bella's cue to pick up the paper plates used for the antipasti. Sal had the roasts sliced and sitting center table when Bella and Tina returned with the salad and sliced french bread, fresh plates, and silverware. Once seated at the table, Bella placed her elbows on the table and interlaced her fingers. The others followed suit. Even little Missy partook by holding her elbow in her other hand, the sight of which brought tears to Bella's eyes.

"Sal, would you please say grace."

Sal nodded. With heads bowed, he began.

"Bless us O Lord and these Thy gifts which we are about to receive from Thy bounty through Christ Our Lord, Amen."

What followed was organized confusion and multiple requests to pass the same food. "Where's the salt and pepper" was answered with a point of the finger since mouths were filled with food. No meal would be complete without Bella's cautioning Sal to watch his bread intake and not use too much salt due to his high blood pressure. His answer to dietary caution was a shrug of his shoulders. In the Santini family, talking with food in your mouth was completely acceptable, especially when complimenting the chef. With his first bite of roast and a rather big one at that, Ryan managed to say, "Sal, so good!" before Bella cautioned him, "Ryan, how many times do I have to remind you. Chew first, then talk."

In comic exasperation, Bella said, "That boy will be the death of me!"

"Don't worry, I'll work on him," Tina assured Bella.

Her response was one more piece of the jigsaw puzzle that fit perfectly in Ryan's future. Tina was amazed that two people could use their hands when talking as much as Sal and Bella Santini. Every compliment from "great food" to "what an idiot he is" seemed to have the same movement, fingers pressed against the thumb, and then the hand springs open. It seemed totally unnecessary to wait to say something where others were talking because interrupting was perfectly acceptable, even necessary at times. Always, sounds of laughter and expressions of love dominated everything.

"Sal, Bella, I can't thank you enough for having us over today. Mostly, thank you for accepting Missy and treating her the way you did," said Tina, as she reached across the table to hold Bella's hand.

"She's so lovable, Tina. I can tell you she's got a special place in Sal's heart too."

Tina glanced over at Ryan, who was engaged in a game of olive soccer with Missy as they flicked a black olive back and forth between them. There was an inner sense of tranquility and peace Tina had never felt before. Her heart spoke to God. *If this is real, I never want it to end, and if it's a dream, I never want to wake up.*

"Are you ready for a whipping, Ryan?" Sal grinned as he pointed to the Bocce ball court.

"Good Lord, Tina. That's our cue to clean up. When those two get to playing Bocce Ball, any sense of decorum and propriety goes out the window."

"Bring it on!" challenged Ryan.

Sal headed over to the Bocce Ball court. He set the four green balls to the left and the four red balls to the right. Looking over to Ryan, he said, "Who throws the rock?"

"Your court, your throw."

With a sly smile on his face, Sal grasped the white ball known as the pallino or rock. He swayed his arm back and forth a couple of times, then lobbed the white ball down the court, being careful to make sure he crossed the mid-court line. The rock came to rest about two feet from the backboard. Then he reached down and picked up a red ball. Repeating the same throwing motion, he carefully rolled the ball down the slate court to within an inch of the white ball. *Perfect*, he thought.

"Okay, hotshot. Let's see what you got!" gloated Sal, as he waved his arm down the direction of the court.

Ryan was no stranger to playing Bocce Ball since he had known Sal for over five years. Those classic games that ran past midnight with copious amounts of red wine consumed were, no doubt, not remembered fondly by their neighbors. Unfortunately, he was no stranger to losing to Sal either. Inside the kitchen, Bella had been watching the scene from the kitchen window.

"Tina, you better get over here and see this," she said. Her face glowed with pride. Tina dried her hands with a towel and moved next to Bella.

Ryan reached down and picked up one of his four green

balls. He casually tossed it in the air, taunting Sal with a smile of supreme confidence. Suddenly, Missy cried out, "Can I throw one?" Her newly found eagerness to try anything could not be ignored.

"Honey, do you want me to show you what to do?" asked Sal, sure the young child would accept his offer. But Missy had a different plan in mind. She looked up to Ryan and said, "Coach."

Bella put her arms around Tina's shoulders as Ryan held out the ball in his hand. Both women stifled their tears.

"Okay, now hold the ball exactly like I am," he said, placing the ball in Missy's tiny hand.

Missy carefully cradled the four and a half-inch diameter ball in her hand, barely able to hold it.

"Now, bring your arm back and toss the ball down the middle of the court."

She stared down the court with a fierce look of determination on her face that nearly sent Sal into hysterical laughter. She brought her arm back and then threw the ball wildly into the air. It came to near mid-court, where it careened off the side-board and back onto the court, where it rolled down the court and knocked Sal's red ball to the side.

"Oh, my God!" Bella said as she muffled her voice. Sal's response was more dramatic. He stumbled over to Missy and collapsed onto the ground, shrieking, "I don't believe it. That was amazing, unbelievable."

Ryan yelled, "You did it!" Great!" Missy held up her arms for Ryan to pick her up. And then announced for all to hear, "I did it! I did it!" Ryan then set Missy down, who promptly headed over to Sal's waiting arms.

Now the tears flowed freely down the cheeks of both women. Bella looked at Tina and offered some sage advice.

"Woman to woman, he's not one you want to let get away."

"Woman to woman, I'm not about to let that happen."

26

THE TRAP

For Ian O'Boyle and Jerry Sloan, this meeting was the culmination of months of hard work. Eight-hour days that stretched into sixteen-hour days, weeks without a day off was about to come to fruition. The men of the Drug Task Force were seated before them.

"Gentlemen, you all know DEA Agent Jerry Sloan. Let me also introduce FBI Special Agent Ian O'Boyle. Between them and our own Sergeant Marty Knight, we have been pretty busy this last week or so."

Inquisitive eyes focused on Marty Knight as he shuffled some papers on the table in front of him. Sloan stood first to address the group.

"Keep this word in mind, 'coincidence.' I don't believe for a minute that there are coincidences in our business. Events are always connected but often in ways that are not necessarily evident. Sergeant Knight, why don't you start."

"Thanks, Agent Sloan," Knight said, as he rose and walked over to a dry-erase board on the side wall. Using a black marker, he started jotting down several dates.

"I don't believe in coincidences any more than Agent Sloan,

so pay attention because we're going to be doing some old-fashioned grunt work. The very same night we took down those Colombian drug dealers at the harbor, someone blew up an electrical transfer station that supplied power to the entire Charleston Harbor. We know now that was a ploy to get their cocaine out of the storage containers before the emergency generators kicked on. Oddly enough, that same night, the levee bordering Edwards Farms outside of Charleston was blown up. The ensuing flooding ruined nearly five hundred acres of farm-land. Residue from both explosions was sent to the FBI lab in Quantico, and guess what? Both samples had a unique similar-ity, semolina flour. It was not just any form of semolina flour. To you Anglos, semolina is a flour common in Colombia in the making of C4."

Knight's jab at the ethnicity of those in the meeting was comically out of place, as he was the most white-skinned, Nordic complected person in the room. It inspired Russ Ortega, the only Hispanic on the team, to shout out, "Si, Carnal!"

"Very funny," snapped Knight. "Now pay attention. Police reports indicate that Mr. Cletus Edwards, the owner of Edwards' Farms, had been in negotiations for months with one Trevor Barrington, the son of none other than billionaire devel-oper Paris Barrington. Remember that name, Paris Barrington."

"Now for that coincidence I spoke about," interrupted Sloan. "The DEA checked into the ownership of that Pana-manian Freighter, La Novia, that transported the cocaine to Charleston Harbor. It was a shell company located out of the Cayman Islands. The only problem was that all the Board Members were dead. Coincidence, I don't think so. Anyway, we kept on digging. We bounced from one shell company to another, one country to another, one continent to another. Finally, with the help of Interpol, and the International Maritime Organization, IMO, for short, we got lucky. It seems that there's a shipping company based out of Zurich, Switzerland, named Shazi International. By the way, that's Chinese for fool, and what the connection is there, I have absolutely no idea. To continue, its Chief Operating Officer is listed as Trevor Barrington, son of none other than Paris Barrington. That, my friends, is not a coincidence! I'm going to let FBI Agent O'Boyle take over from here. Agent O'Boyle."

As O'Boyle stood up, there was an obvious tension in the air. To be briefed by a combination of the DEA and FBI meant the investigation had reached a point where things were going to get "Hands-on," as they say. There was no slouching back in their chairs from this point on.

Ian O'Boyle had seen FBI agents speak to multi-law enforcement agency groups before, always with the same disastrous results. Some authoritative asshole from Washington D.C. steps all over the egos of local authorities by announcing, "The FBI will handle this case from here on." He was determined not to make that same mistake.

"Thanks, Jerry. Gentlemen, there's one thing I want to make perfectly clear. This is not some episode of a crime show where the FBI shows up and dictates how things will be handled from here on. This has, from the very beginning, been a team effort. Neither the DEA nor the FBI has forgotten that it was one of your men from the Narcotics Task Force that was wounded on the harbor that night, and that gives you guys an extra chit in the game."

Lieutenant Caruthers and every one of his men had a new appreciation for the FBI, at least for Agent O'Boyle. Their chests swelled with pride. To a man, they were ready.

"Here's what we've got. The FBI lab in Quantico has been very busy going over the evidence in this case. There were numerous cell phones confiscated on the scene. The call records on some were very interesting. At the time, we thought the only survivor was the driver of the vehicle involved in the bombing of the electrical transfer station near the harbor. We were wrong. The driver had been duped into driving by the lure of making some easy money. His passenger, on the other hand, turns out to be the real person of interest. This is what we know about him, and it's not much. He is a very tan dark-haired man with the tattoo of a scorpion on the back of his left hand. With a little help from a source in the Colombian government, we've identified the man with the scorpion tattoo as one Hector Paz, a high-ranking lieutenant in the Medellin Cartel. It's our good fortune that the DEA has an operative in the Colombian National Police. They've been in bed with the Cartel for years. Our source tells us that Paz is most likely hiding out in a cartel safe house behind a Colombian cafe called "La Zamora," a greasy spoon on the corner of 15th and Valencia. The area around Valencia is known to be heavily involved in drug trafficking. There were two cell phones recovered from the black SUV involved. One belonged to the driver; a harmless kid named Ricardo Romo. The other belonged to the passenger who actually threw the bomb. This is where it gets interesting. There were numerous calls made from the suspect's phone during the weeks leading up to the night of the Harbor raid. Those calls were traced to a cell phone registered in the name of Trevor Barrington. Now, over the last few months, Trevor Barrington made over a hundred calls to one Arthur Ashcroft, the head of development for, you guessed it, Paris Barrington.

At this point, Lieutenant Caruthers interjected.

"Assuming you've got something in mind, where do we fit into it?"

"Agent Sloan and I are going to pay a visit to Mr. Arthur Ashcroft's office at Atlantic Financial tomorrow. We've got the subpoenas necessary to seize all his records, computers, etc. Lieutenant Caruthers, we'd like part of your men to stake out the location on 15th and Valencia and the Laurel Hills Airport.

Caruthers looked at Knight. His eyes said it all.

"Got it handled, boss," Knight responded.

"Now, for the rest of you," Caruthers said. "Effective immediately, we're in operational mode. Everyone get your gear ready and station yourselves here. Marty, take whoever you need and get the tactical van up and operational. Olson, split the rest of the men into two teams, one to handle the interviews at the golf course and one to monitor this Paz character. One last thing, no one, and I mean no one is to know about this."

Caruthers look at Sloan and O'Boyle.

"Anything more?"

There was an eagerness in his tone. He was ready, and his men were ready.

~

THE FOLLOWING MORNING RYAN, Russ Ortega, Ed Popkey, and Al Hodgner reported to the Police Department's maintenance yard, where they signed out two unmarked police cars. They had been assigned the surveillance of Hector Paz. Popkey rode with Callahan while Hodgner teamed with Ortega. Sergeant Knight took Rich Reed to help him in the tactical van. Mike Harrison, Billy Edwards, Butch Hanson, and Barry Woodson would handle the surveillance at Laurel Hills airport. FBI Special Agent O'Boyle and DEA Special Agent Jerry Sloan had taken a red-eye to New York City for their unexpected meeting with Arthur Ashcroft.

~

A CHILLY MORNING fog served the surveillance team well as they were able to position themselves without drawing unwanted attention. Ryan and Popkey parked halfway up 15th street above Valencia. This gave them the advantage of observing the front and side of the cafe. "We're set," Ryan said into his headset. Al Hodgner and Russ Ortega parked on 16th and Bay street, a block below Valencia. This position gave them a view of the other side of the cafe and, more importantly, a view of the safe house behind the cafe. "Us too," replied Hodgner. "There's a couple of cars parked in front of the house, a silver Toyota Camry and a black Cadillac Escalade."

"My money's on the Caddy," said Popkey.

Hodgner and Ortega grinned in agreement.

"Now we wait and see," answered Ryan, who was slouched down in his seat trying to get in a quick catnap.

The weather was only slightly better at Laurel Hills airport, but a biting chill was still in the air. The four men in the black SUV in the parking lot exited their vehicle and positioned themselves on either side of the entrance gate. As they waited, the chain-smoking Harrison took advantage of the time to have one more Marlborough.

~

"TIRED?" Sloan asked the FBI agent nursing his Starbucks triple espresso latte, which he had purchased at the airport when they landed.

"This java jolt, and I'll be fine," replied a red-eyed O'Boyle.

Sloan had left nothing to chance. His subpoenas had been issued through DOJ (Department of Justice), the highest-ranking civilian law enforcement agency in the land. He also brought along a dozen DEA and FBI agents to assist. Their plan was simple enough. They would question Arthur Ashcroft about his relationship with Cletus Edwards and the subsequent acquisition of Edward's five-hundred-acre farm. They would then ease into the matter of why one of his employees, Trevor Barrington, was listed as the CEO of a shipping line that owned the La Novia, a Colombian drug freighter. Because Barrington was listed as an account manager for Atlantic Financial, it would be necessary to confiscate any of the office computers to which he had access. More importantly, they didn't want to cast any aspersions about Ashcroft's possible involvement and risk the chance of alerting him to their suspicions. On the ride from the airport, O'Boyle and Sloan went over the plan one more time.

"Exits accounted for?" Sloan asked,

"NYPD has teams covering every exit. Our men are taking care of the front," answered O'Boyle.

"Is Knight up and running?"

"Yes."

"Then let's rain on this man's parade," smiled Sloan.

O'Boyle smiled with the grim determination of a cowboy about ready to leave the chute atop a bucking bronc. Two black SUVs pulled up in front of the Omni Plaza skyscraper causing the uniformed doorman to reach for a phone enclosed in a glass case on the wall next to his station.

"That won't be necessary," called out O'Boyle, "Won't want to spoil our surprise."

The doorman looked askance as an FBI agent walked over and stood beside him. Six men in black vests marked FBI in large white letters followed O'Boyle and Sloan into the lobby, which was crowded with early arrivals for work. They must have thought they'd walked in on the filming of an episode of "Blue Bloods," what with all the police presence. The group took two elevators to the top floor. Entering the frosted double glass doors marked "Atlantic Financial," they were greeted by a receptionist whose name tag read, "Andrea Fleming."

"May I help you gentlemen?" she asked, somewhat flustered by the group of law enforcement crowding her foyer. Her tone was accommodating.

"Yes," smiled a very amenable Jerry Sloan. "We're here to see Mr. Arthur Ashcroft."

"May I ask the nature of your business?" she said most professionally.

"Yes, you may," smiled Sloan, "However, our business would be best kept between Arthur and ourselves."

The use of Ashcroft's first name put the anxious receptionist at ease.

"I understand," Fleming replied. "Let me inform Mr. Ashcroft of your presence."

$\sim$

EVER SINCE HIS conversation with Paz, Arthur Ashcroft had been quietly transferring a million dollars every three to four days through various accounts into an account at Charleston National Bank, to which Trevor Barrington had direct and sole access. This was necessary to avoid any curiosity by the Banking Commission. After waiting for the appropriate amount of time, Trevor Barrington would withdraw the said amount in cash and wait for a call from Ashcroft.

That Friday morning, Ashcroft peered intently at his computer screen. In the box, "From which account," he typed in a twelve-digit number. Then he scrolled over to "To which account" and typed in another twelve-digit number. With a Machiavellian grin, he typed "send." He was almost free of two problems that had proven unnecessary to deal with anymore, and he was one step closer to achieving his dream. The call over his office intercom would soon change that.

"Mr. Ashcroft, you have two visitors here to see you," announced his receptionist.

Anxious to get on with the rest of his plan, Ashcroft rather bluntly responded, "If they don't have an appointment, Andrea, make one for them at a later date and time."

The next voice Ashcroft heard was not that of his receptionist.

"Mr. Ashcroft, this is FBI Special Agent Ian O'Boyle along

with DEA Special Agent Sloan. It is imperative that we speak with you now. I assure you it is of the greatest importance."

Ashcroft was stunned at the FBI agent's announcement. He had done everything possible to cover his illegal activities and divert attention to the young Barrington. Nothing good could come from the FBI prying into his business. He cleared his computer screen. Sounding contrite for his initial response, Ashcroft pleasantly responded, "Please, Andrea, send the gentlemen in," he replied.

Ashcroft greeted the men at his office door.

"Please forgive my abruptness, gentlemen. My schedule doesn't allow for unscheduled visitors, but in your case, obviously, we will make an exception. I'm Arthur Ashcroft. How may I help you?"

"Agent Sloan from the Drug Enforcement Agency and FBI Special Agent Ian O'Boyle," replied Sloan, making the introductions for both men. "We have a few questions for you concerning one of your employees and his connection with a Cletus Edwards. We understand you had been in negotiations with Mr. Edwards over the purchase of his farmland."

Ashcroft gestured to the chairs surrounding a small conference table in his office. As the men sat down, Ashcroft started, "There isn't much to tell you about Mr. Cletus Edwards. Mr. Barrington was very interested in acquiring Mr. Edwards' property for one of his developments. Initially, his son, Trevor, handled the negotiations on behalf of Mr. Barrington. Mr. Edwards was not interested in selling his property, and the negotiations ended amicably."

"Not so amicably for Mr. Edwards. Shortly after your negotiations ended, an explosion blew up the levee protecting the Edwards farmland from the delta. His land was flooded and ruined. Interestingly, a short time later, you were able to acquire Mr. Edwards' land for much less than originally offered, according to our records."

"Yes, ironically, Mr. Edwards' misfortune turned out to be a fortuitous opportunity for Mr. Barrington," responded Ashcroft, with a cold smugness that galled O'Boyle.

The complete lack of empathy in his voice alerted the agents to the vicious human shark they were confronting. Ashcroft continued as if he were in total control of the interview.

"Which employee are you asking about? In this office alone, there are some thirty employees not counting the thousands working at various holdings belonging to my employer, Paris Barrington." Ashcroft smiled with the pleasantry of someone giving an appearance of intending to cooperate fully.

"What can you tell us about Mr. Barrington's son, Trevor Barrington?"

Ashcroft took off his reading glasses and neatly folded them on the table. He shook his head in painful resignation. It was yet another well developed and devious side of Arthur Ashcroft. He relished the opportunity to display it.

"Trevor is a troubled soul," he sighed. "He's been estranged from his parents since college. In an attempt to provide him with some guidance, I put him on as an assistant account manager, hoping to teach him something of his father's business from the ground up, so to speak."

"Do you know much about his private business dealings?"

Playing the part of the unknowing boss, Ashcroft replied, "Trevor has always resented having to live off his trust fund. In recent years, he expressed an interest in venturing off on his own. Why do you ask?" He actually believed that he was manipulating these experienced and capable lawmen.

"So, you won't know anything about him being on the Board of Directors of a shipping company with headquarters in Zurich, Switzerland?"

"Heavens, no!" replied a surprised Ashcroft, belying the treachery in his heart. "Unless he's learned something through osmosis about business that I'm not aware of."

Ashcroft did his best to reflect shock and a little amazement at this revelation. His facade of having no knowledge about anything related to Trevor Barrington was wearing thin with O'Boyle and Sloan.

O'Boyle looked up from his note pad. "Would he have access to any of the computers here?"

"Of course. There's one in his office."

"We'll need to review its contents. Is this acceptable to you, Mr. Ashcroft?"

Ashcroft pushed the button on his intercom.

"Andrea, would you please bring me Trevor's computer from his office?"

He was even more confident that his ploy would succeed. Ashcroft was certain the sophisticated software he had paid a hacker found on the dark web to install on young Barrington's office computer could not be traced back to him. It was indeed a complicated path using multiple IP addresses that even the most skilled computer analyst would find difficult, if not impossible, to track.

"Unfortunately, Mr. Ashcroft, because of Mr. Barrington's son's involvement in the business affairs here as an account manager, as you put it, we'll need access to your data server. Now if you could please have your head of IT meet with our men in the foyer? There's a tremendous amount of data we'll need to download."

For Arthur Ashcroft, this last request was like the proverbial stake being driven through Dracula's chest. He had spent his entire career carefully crafting others to look responsible for his chicanery. Would he now become a victim of his own Trojan Horse? Ashcroft led the men out of his office to his receptionist.

"Andrea, please have Horace Beckworth from IT come here to see these gentlemen."

For the first time, Ashcroft's graciousness was strained and not the least bit sincere. "Is there anything else I can do for you?" Ashcroft asked, with an unintended tone of impatience in his voice.

"No, thank you for all your help," replied O'Boyle with a smugness suggesting, "Gotcha!"

Once back in his office, Ashcroft nervously texted Trevor, "Get the last installment from the bank now and head to Laurel Hills airport. Your man will be waiting for you." He made one more text before leaving. "Your money will be at Laurel Hills airport in one hour."

Once in the elevator, O'Boyle checked his phone, which had buzzed during their interview with Ashcroft. He immediately showed Sloan the text from Lieutenant Caruthers. "Let's make that call."

Sloan nodded as he quickly took out his phone and replied to Lieutenant Caruthers. "It's on!"

INSIDE THE TACTICAL VAN, the computers in front of Knight and Reed began to do their jobs. Red lights appeared from one cell tower to another, indicating that certain phones were now in use. Those were phones for which they had approval for wiretaps. Knight's eyes were focused on directional red lines crisscrossing on the screens. Reed listened intently to the conversations over his headset.

"That's it!" Reed shouted excitedly. "Paz had been told to get to an airport outside of Charleston, Laurel Hills. It's big enough to handle small jets."

His second announcement slammed the door to the trap.

"Holy crap, Ashcroft told the kid to pick up the money from the bank and head to that same airport."

Hearing that transmission, O'Boyle looked at Sloan and asked, "You or me?"

Sloan smiled. "Us."

The two men hurried to the side entrance of the building parking lot and waited. It didn't take long for a chauffeur-driven Lincoln Continental to appear at the exit gate. O'Boyle and Sloan approached the vehicle with guns drawn and holding their badges. The driver' lowered his window. Fear permeated every bone in his body. He raised his hands in the air. O'Boyle and Adams could see the back seat was empty. Shocked that his plan went amiss, O'Boyle stood silent. Adams asked what O'Boyle was unable to, "Where is Arthur Ashcroft?"

ORTEGA PRACTICALLY SHOUTED into his headset, "Callahan, Popkey, you copy that last transmission?"

"10-4," replied Callahan.

"Our suspect is leaving the house now, and he's in a hurry. He's getting in the black Escalade," said Ortega.

Popkey smiled as he took the ten-dollar bill Ryan had begrudgingly handed him. "We'll get ahead of him, so we get to the airport first."

With due haste, Callahan soon had his car on the crosstown freeway headed to the airport. Ortega and Hodgner watched the black Escalade fishtail out of the driveway. The driver, not wanting to take any more time than necessary to arrive at his getaway point, made no attempt to take an evasive route, making the job of the unmarked sedan following him even easier.

~

THIS WAS the moment Trevor Barrington had waited for, the chance to be free of his father and his control. His silver Bugatti convertible sped toward his newfound freedom. A rented locker at the airport held the key to his future. Ten extra-large duffel bags awaited his arrival, and he had no intention of sharing them with his Colombian partner.

Parked opposite the storage locker in an area marked, "Employees Only," Callahan and Popkey waited for the arrival of their target. They didn't have long to wait. A silver Italian Bugatti convertible pulled in front of a line of storage lockers adjacent to the runway. The driver exited his vehicle and went directly to the locker marked 2A.

"So that's our guy," grinned Callahan, not realizing what a role Trevor Barrington had played in his life.

Barrington had just gotten the storage door unlocked when a black Cadillac Escalade roared through the gate and slammed on its brakes next to him. Unnoticed by Paz, a faded brown sedan stopped about thirty yards behind him. Barrington reached slowly for the 9mm Glock in his jacket pocket. As Paz started loading duffel bags onto a metal carrier, Popkey grinned, "Now that's what we call a double in fishing!"

Ortega and Hodgner moved stealthily along the front of the storage lockers, completely unnoticed by the two men loading the duffel bags. Callahan and Popkey approached from the opposite direction, moving carefully in a crouched position along the line of parked employee cars. On Popkey's command, "GO!" the foursome moved in, screaming, "Police, show us your hands and get down on the ground, now!"

Barrington's head swiveled back and forth. His mind raced to figure a way out of the trap. In a futile attempt to escape the police, Barrington bolted for the gate. Unfortunately for him, he ran directly into Callahan. Remembering his wounded partner, Callahan grabbed the attempted runaway and threw him into the cyclone fence, and then slammed him to the ground. A knee to the back elicited a painful scream from Barrington. Callahan put a little extra zip into bending Barrington's arm behind his back, another "Get Even" for his partner. Paz was much more pragmatic. He preferred death to prison. He pulled out the

MAC10, which was strapped to his waist, firing off a burst at the men behind him, and then turned to fire on the two men in front of him. He never got a round off as Eddy Popkey put four rounds center mass into his chest.

"Everyone okay?" Popkey called out.

"Good here!" hollered Ortega and Hodgner.

"How about you," Popkey asked, looking at Callahan.

"Fine," huffed Callahan, slightly winded from the handling of his captive.

The groaning of the captive caused Popkey to ask Callahan," How's he?"

"You two have no idea who you're dealing with!" grimaced a defiant Barrington, thinking one more time his family name would get him out of trouble.

Lucky for him, Ryan Callahan had no idea of Barrington's ties to the love of his life, or Callahan would have rewritten the definition to the term "excessive force."

27

THE FINAL STEPS

After a tour of the house and property, Sharon Burski, a realtor with Berkshire Hathaway Properties, gave Eddy some much needed good news. Eddy had explained to Burski the impending move to Magnolia Gardens and his dilemma of how to handle any movement of furniture lest it detract from the sale of the house. Sharon Burski had managed the sale of Daniel Kilgore's home when he and Jane Lincoln married as well as the sale of their home following Jane's unfortunate demise in a tragic auto accident. She was also their agent when they purchased their current residence. Burski had been a top producer for Berkshire Hathaway for years, as evidenced by the autographed picture of her and Warren Buffet at an awards dinner she kept on her desk at work. With high heels, the five-foot-six Burski could almost look Buffet in the eye. She wore her light brown hair in a pixie cut. Though a bit on the heavy side, Burski's emerald green eyes radiated an attractiveness that brought her unwanted attention from male staff and clients in her heyday. Her computer skills and assertiveness made her the equal of any man in the business. She had built a reputation for being skilled at maneuvering through the complex issues involving the escrow process as well as the even more difficult process of dealing with unrealistic views of both sellers and buyers. Years in the real estate business had taught Burski that the sale of one's home is not always a cut and dried matter. A home is not merely a wood, glass, shingles, and cement structure without feelings or emotional attachment. For many, their homes were places where dreams were dreamt and achieved, where celebrations and disappointments of all types took place. A home can be a symbol of all the joy, happiness, and disappointment that make up life. Burski was keenly aware that many sellers could not separate the emotional value they placed on their home or the sweat equity they put into it from the real market value.

Burski had finished her walk through the house, minus the master bedroom where Maddy was taking her usual midmorning nap. This would not hinder the process, as Burski had pictures and diagrams of the house in her old records. Burski was a hoarder when it came to paperwork from her sales, a real asset when selling the same property several times during its lifetime. Sitting at the kitchen table, Eddy offered Burski a glass of iced tea with a sprig of fresh mint pinched from a plant in the kitchen window herb garden.

"Thank you, Eddy. Let me start by saying how sorry I am about Maddy's condition. It's such a tragedy for both of you."

Eddy took immediate solace in her words. Burski was one of the few who understood that the ravages of dementia take a toll not only on the victims but also on all their loved ones. Her mother had died from the disease, so she knew first hand its devastating effects. As if he had not heard her words, Eddy took his napkin and carefully wiped the chilled sweat off his glass of iced tea, then he softly responded.

"Her dreams, my dreams, hell our dreams! They are all gone!" He paused, slowly turning his glass, not even looking up before he offered one last comment. "I don't bother to dream anymore." At the sound of his own voice, Eddy realized he was groveling in self-pity. He quickly returned to focus on the task at hand. His military training necessitated it, and it was nearly a reflex action.

"Her condition has declined to a point where I can no longer care for her alone. I've got a representative from the Visiting Angels coming by this afternoon to talk about Maddy's needs in the short run. In the long run, I've secured a place at Magnolia Gardens, the assisted living facility where both of us worked. You see the need to sell this house?"

The question was clearly rhetorical to Burski, yet she replied anyway. Looking Eddy squarely in the eyes, she stated, "Of course. That's why I'm here. Shall we get started? There are some preliminaries that cannot be avoided," she said, reaching into a large tan leather satchel she brought with her, and withdrew a stack of forms. She laughed out loud, "It's not like the old days, Eddy, when a handshake and a signature started the process." Her years in the real estate business had given her a sense of what tack to take when dealing with her clients. She sensed a need for levity in this instance.

By his estimate, he signed and had read to him twenty-five forms from the length of the listing period to the use of arbitration if necessary, to any current disclosures with the home, such as termites, leaks, etc. With each signing, Burski laughed, "Just one more." Her laughter brought a sense of pleasantry long missing in the Pinafore residence. Eddy had no idea of the fair market value of his home. The house was paid for, leaving Eddy to believe the sale would bring a tidy profit. He was not disappointed.

"Have you formulated any value for your home?" asked Burski, knowing only she had the genuine answer to that question.

"Not really," replied Eddy, taking a sip of his iced beverage.

"I did the comparisons for your area, and I think you'll be

pleasantly surprised," said Burski as she scanned her notes for the answer. She looked up and responded, "With the accessibility to the golf course and the pool you added, you are looking at something north of five hundred thousand dollars."

That was a bit of good news at a time when nothing good was happening in his life. He smiled briefly; then, he seemed to sink into a depressed state. One of the many skills Burski had developed over her career as a realtor was to read the faces of her clients, faces that reflected never asked questions. For Eddy Pinafore, that translated to the question of what items do I take to Magnolia Gardens; furniture, keepsakes that held tremendous emotional value, not to mention dishes, appliances, clothing, etc.? And what about all the rest?

"It all seems overwhelming, doesn't it?" said Burski.

Eddy did not like to admit that he was feeling so. His years as an officer made him reject the notion. Again, though, facts were facts. "Beyond overwhelming," responded a still despondent Pinafore.

"So, let's make this a little less overwhelming, shall we?" replied a confident Burski. "Do you need the proceeds of the sale to move to the Gardens?"

"No."

"Do you know what items from this house you'll be taking with you?"

"Kind of, but deciding what to take and what to let go of is the problem, another area where I need help," Eddy replied. Again, he bridled at the necessity of help.

"Then we'll get you some," replied Burski. "Does your daughter, I've forgotten her name, live locally?"

"Her name is Tina, and yes, she is local."

"Alright then, I'll need her number. She and I are going to talk. Between the three of us, that decision can be shared."

Eddy felt an immediate sense of relief. He struggled not to

think about the endless minutiae of other decisions that would need to be made. It was as if Burski had read his mind.

"There's way too much information to process right now. You need to focus on getting you and Maddy to the Gardens. I'm semi-retired now, and I've got plenty of time to deal with that endless list of to-dos that are worrying you. For starters, I'm going to be very aggressive in the asking price. It's not unreasonable to start at six hundred and twenty-five thousand. The logistics of moving can be complicated, so I want plenty of time to help you accomplish that. I'll ask for a sixty-day escrow, which is not out of the question. If any buyer wants more time, that's to our advantage. I've got work at the office to do. Eddy, let me reiterate, you focus on you and Maddy. Leave the sale of the house and all the details to me, okay?"

Feeling like a giant weight had been lifted off his chest, Eddy sighed deeply. He had no words to express his gratitude adequately, but he had to try.

"You've been such a good friend to Maddy and me. Where do I start?" said a mournful Pinafore.

Burski smiled as she placed the mountain of papers Eddy had signed back into her satchel. "Helping people is an underappreciated reward in this business."

WITH BURSKI'S DEPARTURE, Eddy settled into his lazy-boy chair. Despite Burski's enthusiasm over the prospects of selling his home, he quickly found himself slipping back into a depressed state of mind. Tina's phone call would soon lift his spirits.

"Hi sweetheart," the familiar voice said in his usual reassuring baritone voice.

Good, he's home, she thought as her frustration started to ebb.

"Daddy, I tried several times to reach you but no answer. Is everything okay?"

"I'm sorry, Tina. I had a real estate agent named Sharon

Burski over for an evaluation of the home. Do you remember her?"

"Vaguely," replied Tina. "But Daddy, why a realtor? What's going on?"

Oblivious to the growing emotional entanglement her daughter and her boyfriend were embarking upon, Eddy felt a twinge of resentment at having to retell his daughter of the plans to move to Magnolia Gardens when the time came and that the time had come.

"Honey, your mom's condition has declined to the point where I cannot care for her alone. I've arranged for an agent from "Visiting Angels." Her name is Paula. She will come twice a day, once in the morning to help shower and dress your mom, and again in the afternoon for three hours to free me up to attend to other things. Sharon Burski will handle the sale of the house, and she's going to be calling you for help. That won't be a problem, will it?" Normally it might be a rhetorical question, but he knew that working full time and caring for Missy left Tina with precious little extra time.

Tina Pinafore was immediately engulfed with an agonizing sense of guilt and failure. Enraptured by her growing relationship with Ryan, Tina had not given much thought to her mother or her father for a couple of months. Guilt-ridden, she quickly replied, "Oh Daddy, of course it won't be a problem. I never expected things to go bad so fast."

"Neither did I, sweetheart, but be that as it may, the inevitable has arrived, and I, we, have to deal with it. I've got a lot to go over with you."

And I've got a lot to go over with you, Tina thought. "Daddy, I've got tomorrow off. Could you come by here, and we can talk about the move?"

"How about in the morning? Paula from Visiting Angels starts tomorrow. She'll be here from 8-11a.m. How's that sound?"

"Perfect!" she responded with more glee in her voice than Eddy thought appropriate. There was nothing happy about what was taking place in his life. Eddy would soon learn the source of Tina's excitement.

Eddy had set his alarm for 7 a.m. That would give him an hour to get Maddy up, showered, and dressed by the time of the 'Visiting Angel' Paula Gotten's anticipated arrival. Surprisingly, Maddy was quite responsive to his prompts. She smiled throughout her shower, unaware of the indignity Eddy felt for her and for himself. Once dressed and with the aid of her walker, Eddy got Maddy to the couch in the living room just as the doorbell rang.

She's here, Eddy thought, grateful that his wife was presentable, at least as best as Eddy could make her.

Eddy made his way to the door and opened it.

"Hello, Paula. You're right on time," Eddy smiled. From their previous meeting, Eddy had found Paula Gotten to have an engaging personality, with a genuine sense of caring for her clients. She made sure Eddy gave her a list of names of family and friends, special occasions throughout his marriage to Maddy, and favorite foods and activities of Maddy.

"No angel wants to be late," she quipped as she looked upward as if to indicate some celestial supervisor was monitoring her schedule.

Paula Gotten was dressed in a fresh set of nurse's scrubs and towing a small piece of luggage, complete with a change of clothes for her, an assortment of feminine hygiene items for Maddy, and several things to be used for physical therapy. These included nerf balls to develop hand strength and a couple of rubber belts for arm and leg exercises. Her slightly graying brown hair, matronly figure, and eyeglasses attached to a silver chain around her neck gave her an appearance of maturity Eddy Pinafore appreciated. Paula Gotten had over twenty-five years of experience working with elderly patients, which gave her the confidence to take control of her visits quickly.

"Let me say hello to Maddy," she said, brushing by Eddy as if he were a hallway piece of furniture. Paula made her way to the couch with her luggage in tow. She took a seat next to Maddy.

"Hello, Maddy. I'm Paula. Remember me from yesterday? I'm going to be spending some time with you this morning. Your husband has some errands to run today."

Maddy turned to the strange voice and said, "Paula?"

"Good, you remembered," Paula replied, taking Maddy's answer as a fact, not a question.

Paula looked at Eddy and nodded toward the doorway, indicating this would be a good time to leave. Her smile told him she had things under control. Eddy gave Maddy a loving smile, then took his windbreaker off the coat rack and proceeded out the door as quickly and inconspicuously as possible.

～

THE KNOCK at her door interrupted Tina's hurried attempt to make her house presentable before her father's arrival. She opened the door to Ryan Callahan, holding a box of Krispy Kreme doughnuts. The aroma of the freshly baked artery cloggers engulfed Tina's small living room.

"A treat for Missy and you," he said with a sheepish grin.

In mock disdain, Tina stood there with her hands on her hips.

"And you, of course, won't be having any of them, now would you?"

With an innocent shrug of his shoulders, the doughnut boy replied, "Only after you and Missy have had your fill."

Tina forced him to hold the box with one hand as she

quickly engulfed him with a very passionate good morning kiss.

When they parted, Ryan gasped, "Wow, I wonder what would have happened if I had brought a full dozen?"

"You wouldn't be holding the box," replied his temptress.

As Ryan entered the front room, he noticed the Oreck vacuum cleaner on the area rug and a can of Pledge on the coffee table with a rag next to it.

"You didn't have to go to all this trouble for me," he said, half-jokingly.

With her mouth nearly full of the gargantuan bite of dough-nut, Tina paused to let the sugary pastry melt slowly across her palate before responding.

"You're right, Mr. Smarty Pants, it's not for you. It's for my dad. He's on his way over as we speak."

With barely a bite of his doughnut gone, Ryan put it back in the box. "Maybe I should come at a different time? I wouldn't want him to get the wrong impression."

Tina found the panic in his voice both amusing and thoughtful.

"He's not an ogre, Ryan. He's a regular guy like you. I've got to get Missy dressed," said Tina, as she finished the last of her doughnut. She quickly grabbed the box of treats, placed them on the kitchen table, then disappeared down the hallway.

Seeing the can of Pledge furniture polish on the coffee table and the uncoiled chord of her Oreck vacuum cleaner next to it, Ryan thought to help Tina with what was obviously a last-minute straightening up before her father's arrival. Ryan threw the dust rag over his shoulder, grabbed the can of Pledge with one hand, and took control of the Oreck with the other hand. He moved the Oreck adroitly around the coffee table, pausing to move a stack of magazines, spray, dust, and move them back. He then proceeded to several plant stands and was about to hit the TV stand when he heard a repeated knocking at the door. Completely forgetting the reason for Maddy's rushed cleanup job in the first place, Ryan called out in an annoying voice, "Hang on. I'll be right there." He turned off the Oreck and went to the door. When he opened it, Ryan and the stranger stood strangely silent as they stared at each other. Each thought the same thing, *I know him from somewhere, but where, and what was his name.* There was an awkward silence. Finally, it was the stranger who answered first.

"If I remember correctly, you're Ryan. You help coach my granddaughter at Weatherby School. Right?"

Ryan had to look no farther than the man's scarred face to remember.

"Yes sir. I'm Ryan. Ryan Callahan."

Suddenly a broad smile appeared on Eddy's face. *So, this is the young man that Tina had talked to him about, the one who seemed so caring and considerate, the one Tina worried about trusting with her heart.*

The cat had truly caught Ryan's tongue. How could he explain being at Tina's home earlier than might be judged appropriate by some and clearly doing cleanup chores? His face turned blush red. He started to mumble as his brain realized no explanation would be sufficient to wipe away a wrong impression. Fortunately for Ryan, Eddy Pinafore came to his rescue. Recognizing the plight that every young man had experienced in some form or fashion for time immemorial, Eddy quickly put Ryan at ease.

"Tina's told me all about you though not specifically by name, but enough to know you've touched her heart and Missy's as well. Nothing could be more important to me, so do you think I can come in now?" laughed Eddy.

His embarrassment lingered despite Tina's father's kind words. Ryan stepped aside and said, "Yes, sir. Please come in." As Eddy crossed the threshold, he asked, "What's that aroma?"

"Some Krispy Kreme Doughnuts I brought over for Tina and Missy."

Eddy ran his tongue over his lips. "God, it's been years since I had one of them. Are there any left?"

"On the kitchen table, sir."

"And is there any coffee?" He asked with a reassuring smile.

"Yes, sir. I put on a fresh pot when I got here," Ryan replied, still a bit tense compared to Eddy's calm demeanor.

"It's been a long time since I was in the navy, so I think you can call me Eddy, Ryan," smiled Tina's father. Eddy headed to the kitchen table. Ryan followed, hoping for an opportunity to tell Tina's father more about his feelings for her. That was not going to happen. Their coffee cups were half emptied as Eddy relished listening to Ryan talk about his job as a member of the Charleston PD Drug Task Force. His laughter echoed down the short hallway, causing Tina's alarm meter to hit ten.

"Daddy, is that you?" The nervousness in her voice caused Eddy to laugh before responding, "Yes, it's me, sweetheart." Ryan, now comfortable that he was not perceived by Eddy as some undeserving scumbag courting his daughter, allowed himself a courtesy chuckle.

The hurried uneven footsteps coming down the hallway belonged to Missy, anxious to see her grandfather and the source of the aroma of fresh doughnuts sweetening the air. Behind her came Tina, more concerned about her father's arrival without a proper explanation of Ryan's presence than about the doughnuts. Her mind raced to find some rationale for a scene that clearly could be misinterpreted. She heard Missy scream with delight at the sight of her grandfather and Ryan sitting at the kitchen table.

"Pa, pa, Ry, Ry," her excitement activated her latent stutter.

Eddy was the first to receive a smothering hug and kiss, followed by Ryan. Only then did Missy turn her attention to the open box of doughnuts. Her eyes opened to the size of saucers.

"For me!" she shrieked as she grabbed at one before waiting for approval.

"Don't you have something to say, Missy?"

A near unintelligible, "Than' ooh," made its way out of the young mouth stuffed with a bite of sweet delightfulness.

"I was hoping to tell you about Ryan first, but apparently, it looks like that isn't necessary," Tina said, as Eddy and Ryan raised their coffee cups to each other.

A broad smile formed on her face. "Daddy, this is Ryan. Ryan, this is my dad, Eddy Pinafore. There, formalities are over."

The three enjoyed a burst of laughter as Tina took a seat at the table. Eddy thoroughly enjoyed listening to Tina describe the current state of her relationship with Ryan, a relationship Eddy had already suspected.

"Well, Ryan, Tina is pretty special to me, as is my granddaughter. You must be special too if you can put up with..."

A firm declaration of "Daddy!" brought an abrupt end to Eddy's soliloquy.

"Can we just talk about mom," said Tina, a bit embarrassed with her father's attempt at humor.

"Unfortunately, yes, honey," responded a now somber sounding Eddy.

Seeing that the conversation was clearly moving in the direction of a sensitive issue, Ryan offered to excuse himself and take Missy with him.

"Daddy, I'd like him to stay if that's okay with you?"

Pleased that his daughter now had someone to share things with, Eddy nodded. He brought Tina up to date with the events of the past several days concerning the increasing care her mother now required. The news of Paula Gotten from Visiting Angels offered Tina only temporary relief. Ryan listened intently to what was obviously the mental and physical decline of Tina's mother.

"Daddy, mom's going to need more than just drop-in visits daily, isn't she?"

"Yes, sweetheart, and that's why the move that we've talked about."

Up till now, Ryan had only been listening, but now he felt he had something to contribute to the conversation.

"Eddy, are you talking about moving Tina's mother to some kind of care facility, because if you are, I may be able to help."

"I appreciate your offer, Ryan, but the place I've picked out is pretty special. It will take both Maddy and myself as residents."

"I understand, Eddy, but the place I'm thinking of is called Magnolia Gardens. My mom is the Executive Director. It's a pretty special place too."

Even advocates of "Six degrees of separation" would find this hard to accept within the realm of impossible possibilities. Eddy was shocked. Tina was as well.

It took a minute or so for Eddy to collect his thoughts. In disbelief, he said, "Your mother is Samantha Callahan?"

"Yes, she is. I'm Ryan Callahan, her son."

His wonderment continued.

"You're the Marine your mother used to brag about so much when she took over for me as the Executive Director?!"

"I'm the one," smiled Ryan, a bit embarrassed by all of this.

"Well, I'll be damned," exclaimed Eddy Pinafore, as he sat back in his chair trying to grasp the improbability of what he had just heard.

"Is there anything else about you I should know?" asked a perplexed Tina, with a pixie-like grin on her face.

"I'm falling in love with you, now that you asked," responded Ryan, no longer willing to keep this emotion to himself.

His pronouncement caused Eddy Pinafore to smile to himself. *You opened the door, Tina,* he thought. For Tina Pinafore, the place and time for this declaration was hardly what she had expected. She would have thought it was more likely in a quiet romantic restaurant over a candlelight dinner. With her father sitting at the table along with her daughter, Tina's normally glib tongue was unable to come up with a suitable response, though in her heart, she screamed, "Me too!" The awkward silence was broken by the innocent one.

"What's love, mommy?" asked the ever-inquisitive Missy.

"We'll talk about that later," smiled Tina, both at Ryan's revelation and her own matching feelings.

IT WAS incumbent on Ryan to look after Missy as the sugar jag from ingesting a whole glazed Krispy Kreme doughnut put the young girl in a random whirl of running, playing on the swing, and throwing a Nerf ball to Ryan with multiple misdirected results. Eddy and Tina spent several hours outlining the many tasks ahead of them. They would start with a visit the next day to Magnolia Gardens to revisit Maddy's old residence to judge what furniture items to take. Eddy forced a rather painful decision on his daughter's shoulders.

"Honey, I want you to have anything from the house you want to keep. You don't have to take anything right away, but you will have to let me know, and the sooner, the better."

For the first time, Tina realized the "I keep this but not that" dilemma facing her father now was facing her. She lived in a very small two-bedroom cottage that barely had room for her meager possessions as it was. What was worse was how do you possibly decide from a lifetime spanning fifty years what to let go of and what to keep? Every picture, every stick of furniture, every object that occupied space in the house she grew up in had some special value to Tina. She agonized at the task ahead of her. Seeing her embroiled in this excruciatingly painful moment, Ryan offered up an alternative.

"Listen, I've got an oversized two-car garage that you could use and a big three-bedroom house for any overflow stuff."

His generosity brought tears to Tina's reddened eyes, and for Eddy, it was a hint to a time when he might not have to worry about his daughter's welfare.

28

REVELATIONS

I t was a process that seemed to have no end, and each step in that process appeared to make minimal progress. For weeks on end, Eddy Pinafore and Tina Pinafore found themselves immersed in the painstaking procedure of going through the house one room at a time, carefully deciding what items to keep, what items to put in storage, and what items to give away. It was impossible to rank their personal possessions in terms of worth—every single thing held enormous emotional value for both father and daughter. Tina had asked her father to take her to Magnolia Gardens to view the one-bedroom suite where they would be living. She believed this would allow her to better understand what would fit and be appropriate for the new surroundings. That visit produced a few surprises.

Tina made arrangements for the school bus to drop Missy off at the after-school program at the Recreation Center for the Handicapped. No one was more elated with the phone call from Eddy Pinafore that he and his daughter were coming over to look over the suite that had been set aside for Eddy and Maddy than Samantha Callahan.

When he had placed the call to Samantha, Eddy had intentionally not mentioned the relationship between Tina's boyfriend and Samantha Callahan. Not sure what Ryan may or may not have told his mother about his feelings for Tina, Eddy felt it best left between the young people. Had he known how close Ryan Callahan was to his mother, Eddy would have taken a much different approach. The first sign of anxiety came on the drive over. Eddy seemed to prattle on and on about how this piece of furniture would be here or there and how this picture or that picture would look best on what wall. Tina sat silently staring out the passenger side window.

"Have you heard a single word I've said?" asked her slightly annoyed father.

Tina continued to be lost in thought but finally turned to her father and asked, "Do you think Ryan told his mom about the extent of our feelings for each other?"

"To answer your question, yes. To what degree he revealed his emotions that I do not know."

"Do you think he told her I have a child, that I never married the father, or about Missy?"

Her rapid-fire questions alerted Eddy to the mounting tension in his daughter's heart. He needed to put his daughter at ease lest meeting Ryan's mother should cause Tina to be overcome with anxiety. Spying a Circle K gas station on the next corner, Eddy pulled in and parked next to the convenience store. He unbuckled his seat belt and turned to face his daughter. He placed a comforting hand on her shoulder. His battle-scarred face reflected sincerity as he asked, "Let me ask you a question. Do you know this man well enough to have faith in his heart?"

Tina seemed perplexed by her father's question. What does trusting Ryan's heart have to do with anything? What she was remembering was meeting Trevor Barrington's mother and father and the scorn and disdain with which his mother treated her. That and her true feelings for Ryan had Tina on the verge of tears. Her voice cracked, and fighting back the tears, she answered.

"Yes, Daddy. I know I haven't known Ryan that long, but we've talked a lot about things that are really important to both of us. I feel secure talking to him. His heart is so transparent I know he's always going to be there."

"Good. Then what say you trust in the heart of the woman who raised the young man, shall we?"

There would be no holding back the floodgate of tears now. Tina unbuckled her seat belt. She leaned over and hugged her father to the point where he had trouble breathing. She managed to mumble, "He's so like you, Daddy!"

"Okay, I love you too! Now let's get going, shall we?"

Eddy had alerted Samantha that he and his daughter would be arriving shortly after nine in the morning. Samantha had said to meet her at the suite, being prepared for them. Driving through the entrance and then along the private road leading to the side entrance to the suite, Tina commented, "My Gosh, Daddy, this place is as beautiful as I remember!" The air was full of the sweetness of blooming Magnolia trees. Adding to that was the intoxicating fragrance of endless trellises of interwoven yellow jasmine blossoms and contrasting red bougainvillea plants serving as borders along the various pathways on the grounds. As they pulled in their private parking slot, Eddy could not help but notice the painters were busily at work. Drop cloths covered the outside shrubbery and walkway, leading to the front door. He had hardly expected the outside to be painted. He was more concerned with the interior color. Eddy and Tina walked gingerly across the drop cloth on the walkway. With the front door open, Eddy called out, "Samantha, it's me, Eddy. Are you in there?"

"Come on in and be surprised," called out a very excited Samantha Callahan.

As Eddy and Tina entered the foyer, they saw that every piece of furniture was gone. Bare walls were being sanded and prepped. The kitchen cabinets had been removed and were stationed on the patio for repainting. Samantha stood in the middle of the living area with the lead painter. He held a large binder of paint samples in his arm. He was in the process of placing several samples one at a time against the wall for Samantha to choose from. When she saw Eddy and Tina standing there, her exuberance burst forth.

"Oh, my dear ones, you're here!" She pulled each one to her for a long and loving hug. First Eddy, and then Tina. "We were about to select the color scheme, but first things first."

Samantha took Tina's hands in hers and announced, "I'm Ryan's mother. It's so good to finally meet you. My boy has been keeping you to himself for way too long." Samantha turned to Eddy. Her face radiated with approval. She shook her head in wonderment. "She is more beautiful than Ryan described, Eddy." Then turning back to Tina, Samantha set the young girl's heart at ease. "My son is very much like his father. I trusted and loved him, and he never let me down, and neither will Ryan."

Samantha gave Tina another hug, more sincere and endearing than the first one. Tina was overwhelmed with emotions. This was not the type of reaction she had expected. It left her wondering if she weren't the lucky one, or was this false sincerity?

"Let me walk you two through the place. After thinking your situation over, I have taken the liberty to make a few modifications I believe you will like..."

Samantha took them to the one and only bedroom first.

"I plan on replacing the sliding doors with accordion doors.

I think it will give you greater access, and I want to widen the bathroom door to make it wheelchair accessible."

Fully understanding the emotionally charged nature of these intended changes, Eddy and Tina surveyed the room and considered the proposed changes. Their smiles were the affirmation for which Samantha had hoped.

"I think those changes will work to our benefit, Samantha," replied Eddy.

Tina stared at the closet first and then the bathroom, visualizing how her mother would access both. "That's perfect for Mom, Mrs. Callahan," she replied.

Unaware of how much Ryan had shared with his mother about his feelings for Tina, Samantha would not allow Tina to continue with such formality.

"Please, Tina, call me Sam. Samantha seems so formal."

Whatever reservations Tina had about being accepted by Ryan's mother vanished in an instant. With that burden lifted, Tina could not help but hug Ryan's mother again.

"I don't know what Ryan's told you about me, but thank you for that," Tina said after releasing Sam from her arms.

"Honey, after I heard that beautiful song he wrote about your daughter, I didn't need to know anything more about you."

As unexpected as Samantha's reaction to meeting Tina was, the announcement that Ryan had written a song about her daughter caused Tina to gasp audibly. "Song, what song? He never told me anything about a song?"

Realizing she had spoken too openly, Sam tried to do damage control.

"Oops! I think I spoke too soon. Listen, Tina, can we keep this song thing between you and me until the time is right for him to tell you about it? I tend to brag too much about him at times."

Samantha had touched a part of Tina's heart, and she was not about to disappoint her.

"Of course," smiled Tina, her mind already working on how to maneuver Ryan into revealing his musical creation.

The tour continued into the kitchen where a new stove and refrigerator were planned and finally into the living room where Eddy had to decide what wall the sixty-five-inch HD TV would go on, then out to the patio.

"I hadn't planned on replacing the double French doors, but they will get a fresh paint job," announced Samantha.

This time it was Eddy who gave out hugs. He put his arm around Samantha. From his moistened eyes, tears began to fall. "Sam, you've made this home again for Maddy and me." His throat constricted with emotion. He tried to say more but was graciously saved by Samantha. "Don't say anything, Eddy. I love both you and Maddy."

Tina had sketched out in a small note pad she had brought with her where she thought different pieces of furniture should go. Remembering Samantha's prompt about titles, she asked, "Sam, would you mind looking at this? I sort of sketched out my plan for the furniture."

Sensing he was now the proverbial "third wheel," Eddy walked out onto the patio. He allowed his mind to drift back to that day when Kristin Andrews reintroduced him to Maddy. Had twenty-five-plus years really gone that fast? His attention was soon diverted to a group of hummingbirds feasting on the nectar of the blossoming Jasmine. He wondered how many generations of such birds had come and gone since that day. Were hummingbirds capable of understanding the past or the present, or were they creatures focused solely on the here and now with no concern about the future? Eddy wondered what it would be like to be a hummingbird. His trip into fantasy land was interrupted when Tina called out, "Dad, I think we're done here."

"Coming." His sense of tranquil contemplation ended.

On the way back to Eddy's house, Tina received a text message from Ryan.

"How about pizza tonight?"

"I'm sorry, Daddy, I have to answer this. It's from Ryan."

Eddy nodded with a smile. Tina's fingers sent her reply. *"Yes. Lots to talk about."*

29

HEARTS CONNECTED

She would have to get Missy from the after-school program at the Recreation Center for the Handicapped, then home to clean up. Still early into their burgeoning relationship, this female of the species wanted her male counterpart to see a desirable, attractive partner. Missy's makeover was simply a change of clothes and a warm washrag to her face. Tina's was a bit more complicated—selecting the right blouse and pants, a quick shower, and the not so quick application of makeup. When she was finished, she made a left turn, then a right turn, in front of her bedroom mirror. The off the shoulder midriff white silk blouse was daring but not overly sexual, and the jeans from J Crew had the right amount of tightness. *This should tantalize his desire button,* she thought. The question had occurred to her if Ryan was taking them to Gino's Pizzeria or if he had another destination in mind. With the knock on her door, she would soon have her answer.

When she opened the door, her guest stood there in stunned silence. He carefully looked Tina over from top to bottom before managing, "Is it my imagination, or do you get better looking each time I see you?"

"I certainly hope so," replied an appreciative Tina. When his hands touched her bare back as he pulled her to him, she instinctively let out an embarrassing moan of delight. The open door hid their embrace from Missy's view, who was engrossed in a children's cartoon show on the TV. If not for a commercial, there was no telling how long the cartoon would have distracted the child. Suddenly relieved of her focus, Missy exclaimed, "Mom, I'm starving!"

That alert broke the romantic moment.

"I'll handle this," smiled Ryan. He stepped inside and announced, "Starving for pizza?"

Missy screeched, "Ryan!" and hobbled around the coffee table to his open arms. Picking her up, he gave her a hug and kisses on both cheeks.

"You smell wonderful. Is that a new perfume you're wearing?"

He spoke as if addressing an adult. His adult humor was lost on her unsophisticated mind.

"No, silly," she said with a tone of misplaced defiance in her voice. "Mommy washed me, that's all!"

Feeling a need to change the direction of the conversation, Tina grabbed Missy's coat off the back of the couch and said, "Maybe we should go have pizza, shall we?"

With another screech of approval, Ryan headed toward his truck, one arm holding Missy, the other arm around Tina. Once seated inside, Tina said, "So where are we going for pizza?"

Staring into his side mirror to check for any oncoming cars and to avoid eye contact with his questioner, Ryan said, "It's a new place in town. I hear the pizza is really great there."

For the moment, Tina accepted his non-committal answer. As they moved farther away from any stores or shopping centers, her curiosity got the best of her. Her eyes scanned both sides of the road for any sign of commercial development.

"What exactly is the name of this new place?"

Ryan could not long keep his secret to himself.

"It's called Ryan's place."

For a nanosecond, Tina's mind accepted the similarity between this new pizzeria's name and his first name as a coincidence. Startled with the realization of the true meaning, Tina turned sharply to Ryan.

"Your place? We're going to have pizza at your place?"

Smiling like the Cheshire cat in Alice and Wonderland, Ryan replied, "Yes, my place. I do have a home, you know. Gino is trying out his "You take it, you bake it" pizza service. What awaits you is a half Chicken and garlic with anchovies and half pepperoni for Missy."

"Peppa...peppa, is my favorite," yelped Missy, as she struggled with her stuttering problem.

Silenced by her wonderment, Tina envisioned what she was about to see.

Her curiosity about Ryan's abode increased as they drove through the pastoral setting outside of Charleston. The area consisted of gently rolling hills with homes scattered about without the definition of a planned development. The houses were older, though a few looked like massive renovations had taken place,

"I would have pictured you as more of a city guy," smiled Tina, as she turned to focus on Ryan.

He smiled and said, "I like the quiet. My job gives me all the excitement I could want. When I get off, I like to give my mind and body a rest."

She started to respond when he interrupted her by exclaiming, "Here we are," pointing to a home off to the right. The house sat on a slight hill. The front lawn was in need of mowing though it hardly detracted from the quaintness of the home. The wraparound front porch was particularly attractive to Tina. Someone, probably a woman, had nicely decorated the porch with hanging flower pots and a double rocker made of wrought iron painted black. Ryan pulled into the driveway, stopping in front of his garage.

"I figured your dad might store items he couldn't part with here," he said before exiting his truck.

Tina gently woke Missy, who had fallen asleep during the peaceful drive. Ryan led them around to the front door. Standing on the porch, he announced, "Here we are," and opened the door. Whatever misconceptions Tina may have had about Ryan's home being some hedonistic bachelor pleasure palace quickly disappeared. The vaulted ceiling made the living room seem even larger. A fairly new eight-foot sofa faced the largest TV screen Tina had ever seen. It was obviously the resting place from which Ryan and his friends watched their favorite sporting events. A long, distressed coffee table made of darkened pine was the home of the TV's remote control. Tina correctly surmised that Ryan had done some housecleaning before their arrival. At the other end of the living room was a lightly stained eight-foot farm style dining table. There were captain chairs at either end and benches along the sides.

"Follow me, and I'll give you the cook's tour. Obviously, this is the living room and dining area. Balancing the ready to bake pizza in one hand, he remarked, "The door to the right is the master bedroom. That china hutch was a housewarming gift from my mother. I've never used any of the dishes."

As she surveyed the entire room, she fantasized about the appearance of the master bedroom. Heading toward the kitchen, she saw a guitar stand in the corner by the china hutch. A piece of paper had been folded and placed between the strings for safekeeping. The kitchen was another source of amazement for Tina. No dirty dishes were left on a small pine kitchen table. Four chairs were neatly pushed in around the table. Open shelves on either side of the kitchen sink held dishes, cups, and saucers. Above a five-burner gas stove hung a wrought iron rack with a trio of skillets hanging from it as well as a kitchen towel, an oversight during Ryan's housecleaning. He set the pizza on the kitchen table. He walked to his right and opened the door.

"This is a Jack and Jill bathroom. Two more bedrooms are on either side, though one is more of a catchall place for my gear," he said with a bit of an embarrassed grin. "Come on, and I'll show you the backyard." They passed through a large laundry room with a washer and dryer on one side. On the opposite side was a deep sink with table surfaces on each side. He held open the screen door for Tina and Missy. The little one was getting a bit fussy as she had expected to eat when they got there. She was more concerned with filling her stomach than the tour Ryan was taking them on. Off the end of the house was a large deck. Ryan pointed to the far end of the porch and nonchalantly said, "A hot tub I rarely use." He walked over to the biggest stainless-steel barbecue she had ever seen and gently patted it.

"This baby, on the other hand, I use all the time. I'm not bragging, but some say my ribs and brisket are the best they've ever had." The swagger-like tone in his voice was unmistakable. Tina noticed deck furniture was nonexistent.

"You stand when you're out here?" she asked, gazing around for someplace to sit.

A bit embarrassed, Ryan replied, "I'm working on that. I got my dad's woodworking tools in the garage. I'm working on a swing and matching chairs right now."

Another hidden talent—Ryan is just full of good surprises.

"Is that where you practice for your games with Sal?" she said, pointing to a very recognizable Bocce Ball court. There were two rounds of pine at either end, each notched out to hold a cold beer and a glass of wine.

"Yeah," he smiled. "Sal helped me put it in on the promise I would practice whenever I could, which hasn't been much lately."

Tina felt a defiant tug on her hand.

"Mommy, when can I eat?" moaned Missy. She had reached the end of her short supply of patience. Her normally pleasant features began to foreshadow what her mother knew was coming.

"You'd better get this one fed, or you'll see a tantrum to end all tantrums."

"Well, let's get this dinner started, shall we, Missy?" said Ryan.

Missy quickly let go of her mother's hand and grabbed on to Ryan's hand. The two chanted, "Pizza, Pizza," as they headed back inside. Ryan removed the pizza from the refrigerator and laid it on the counter. He walked over to the oven and set the temperature for 450 degrees.

"I have beer, wine—red and white, and water. Who wants what?"

Speaking for Missy, Tina said, "Missy will have water, and I'd like wine."

"Pinot, I am guessing," grinned Ryan, as he reached for a bottle of wine from a small wooden wine rack at the end of the counter. He took the opener on a hook on the edge of the wine rack and began peeling off the foil. He carefully inserted a needle into the cork and pressed on the plunger. Slowly the cork rose. Ryan took two glasses from the cabinet over the stove and set them on the table. Seeing that he was busy between the wine and the pizza, Tina asked, "I will take care of Missy. Where are your water glasses?"

"In the cabinet next to the sink," replied Ryan, who by now was placing the pizza in the preheated oven. "Fifteen minutes to heaven," he said, taking one last smell of the unbaked delight. Tina took the smallest glass possible for Missy.

"Ice cubes in the fridge?" she asked.

"Yep, in the freezer," Ryan replied. "Oh, and there are

Macadamia nut cookies for Missy later. They're in that tin next to the refrigerator."

Missy squealed with delight at the expectation of getting her favorite cookies.

"Shall we eat in the kitchen or the dining room?" Ryan asked.

Seizing the moment for a bit of comic smugness, Tina answered, "Clearly, this unique Italian cuisine and imported wine is most aptly suited for a formal dining setting."

Completely missing Tina's left-handed compliment, Ryan replied, "Dining room it is."

He took the opened bottle of Pinot and two glasses and said, "Follow me." Deftly holding the bottle of Pinot in his right hand while cradling the two wine glasses between the fingers of his left hand, Ryan led the way. Once seated at the table, Ryan immediately saw a problem. Missy's chin barely cleared the tabletop. He quickly rose and went to his bedroom. He returned with a pillow.

"Let's try this," he said, and he lifted Missy off the bench. He folded the pillow in half then placed Missy on top of it. A temporary fix at best, but it would do. She was pleased and charmed by the deference shown her daughter. Tina glanced at the bottle of Pinot.

"Isn't that the same brand that we had at Sal's?" Tina asked.

"It sure is," smiled Ryan. "Sal has become something of a wine connoisseur. He found this place in a vintner's magazine advertising a winery somewhere in California called Windy Oaks. Anyway, Sal loves reds, so he ordered a sample box of their reds. He fell in love with their Pinots. He's been serving them at his restaurant ever since."

Raising his glass, Ryan said, "To the pizza and wine." As their glasses touched, he softly added, "and us." That slight addition moved Tina's heart.

Tina gazed around the room. Her mind was three steps

ahead of Ryan's. She imagined what would fit where should she have the opportunity to rearrange things. Ryan asked, "What do you think?" Not exactly a typical bachelor pad, is it?"

"I think I'm surprised again. Your home is beautiful and not at all what I expected."

"I'll take that as a compliment," Ryan replied as he took a sip of his Pinot.

At that moment, the oven bell chimed, indicating their dinner was ready, although the lovely aromas of the pie had already given that fact away.

"I'll be right back," said Ryan.

"I help?" asked Missy, more eager to eat than be of any assistance.

Looking down at Missy's upturned and eager countenance, Ryan said, "You sure can." He took Missy by the hand. Tina followed them.

Ryan pulled the piping hot pizza from the oven and set it on the kitchen table. Then he went to a cabinet next to the kitchen sink. He took out three napkins and handed them to Missy.

"You can put these on the table. Make sure we each get one."

Missy beamed with delight at being trusted with such an important task, at least in her mind.

Realizing she had done practically nothing to contribute to this culinary feast, Tina blurted out, "What can I do?! I can't leave everything up to you entirely."

Sensing Tina's need for participation, Ryan directed her to the china cabinet.

"You could get the dishes from the china cabinet."

"But I thought you said you'd never even used them?" queried Tina.

"My mom told me these would come in handy for that special occasion," grinned Ryan.

"And you call pizza a special occasion?" mocked Tina.

"That depends on what kind of pizza," said Ryan. Raising his glass of wine, he added, "But mostly who you're with."

Usually quick with a comic retort, Tina found herself speechless. Her daughter's presence only added to her inability to respond to how special he had become to her. Taking a pizza cutter from the silverware drawer, Ryan carefully cut the medium-sized pizza into eight pieces. Cheese and tomato sauce oozed onto the baking shell holding their dinner. Ryan carefully lifted it and headed to the dining room table. With Tina's help, Missy had placed a napkin in front of each seat. Tina then helped Missy onto the bench with its folded pillow as a makeshift child seat. Ryan set their meal on the table. Tina leaned forward to smell the aroma rising from freshly baked pizza. This delay only served to aggravate the hungry Missy, who had no problem letting her mother know she would not tolerate any more delays. Her face again adopted less than pleasant features as she demanded, "Mommy," she begged, "Can we eat?"

Sensing a need for immediate action, Ryan carefully removed a slice and set it before Missy. Completely unaware her response was a subtle snub at her mother, Missy replied, "Ooh, thank you, thank you, Ryan!"

Following dinner, Tina retreated to the bathroom where smears of tomato sauce, bits of pepperoni, olives, and mushroom toppings had to be removed from Missy's shirt top. On their return, Missy seemed quite content to browse through a stack of Sports Illustrated magazines Ryan had on the end table along with a Macadamia cookie he had slipped to her in a folded napkin. Her mind was more content with the color photos than any printed content, which was beyond her intellectual grasp. Her sweet tooth was satiated with her cookie treat. Tina snuggled next to Ryan. She kissed him on the cheek while whispering, "Your culinary skills never cease to amaze me."

"Let the amazement continue," quipped Ryan, as he returned Tina's kiss.

Remembering his mother's words of a song he had sung to her; Tina seized the moment.

"Yes, let the amazement continue," she said. "Would you play the song your mother said you played for her?"

Ryan was completely caught off guard by her request. He kept private his sentimentally for the kids at Weatherby School and Missy. He had specifically requested his mother to keep the simple composition between him and her. He hoped he could avoid embarrassing himself.

"It's not really a song," he said.

"Oh please, let's not quibble about semantics," smiled Tina, responding to his childlike awkwardness. "You wrote down words, put them to music, that's a song, Ryan. Besides, I would really love to hear it."

"There's no way out of this, is there?" he asked in one last futile attempt to avoid revealing the feelings that inspired him.

"No, sweetheart, there isn't."

With resignation, Ryan rose and went to the corner of the dining room to get his guitar. He returned and took a position facing Tina on the couch. He took the piece of paper from behind the strings and laid it on the coffee table. He placed the guitar on his knee, strumming each string as he tried to get it in perfect tune. Satisfied it was as good as his untrained ear could get it, he offered this caution.

"Don't expect to hear a professional musician or anything like that. It's simple chords and simple lyrics." His apologetic manner continued unabated.

Ryan slowly started picking the melody with his thumb and fingers. He was right. It was not a complicated arrangement, but its simplicity was enticing. Ryan's soft tenor voice began to sing.

"You're not the image of what your parents thought you'd be,

317

Sometimes I often wonder what is it you really see,
Simple things are maybe things for a mind that never grew,
You always have a smile to give in all you try to do.
Sometimes the only way you move is on legs made out of steel,
Your eyes see only shadows, so your world remains concealed,
Some have twisted bodies that never will respond,
But through all this, you never quit; you just keep moving on.
Some parents often wonder why it's they that had this child,
They hoped and dreamed that theirs would be a model in their eyes.

I hope someday that they will see the beauty with which you live,
You ask so very little yet have so much to give.
Oh, you who were born to be so different, with beauty sometimes hard to see.
And as you greet the day each morning, remember, you're a special Child to God
and me.

With every note, with every word, Tina's heart was impacted. So simple yet so eloquent, he sang of the impact of having a special needs child. Imperfect bodies, imperfect minds that many had prayed would have been different. But in their imperfection, such children exhibit the greatest of human values, determination against impossible odds, achievements measured in the smallest degrees, and where unconditional love is given so freely. There was no need to try and control her emotions. No force on earth could stop the flow of tears, the depth of emotions she felt for the singer of the song, and the deeper appreciation for the gift God had given her.

"Why are you crying, Mommy," Missy asked, pausing for a moment to take a bite of her sweet delight. The child did not like to see her mother cry. She crawled up on the couch to give her mother a hug.

"It's nothing," sobbed Tina, who was desperately trying to retrieve a lace handkerchief from her back pocket. When she finally succeeded and was able to dry the tearful paths running down her cheeks, Tina struggled to say, "Right now, Mommy's heart is so happy, sweetheart!"

Missy stared directly into her mother's eye, trying to sort out how her mom could be happy and still be crying.

"But why? You are still crying," came the innocent reply.

Tina took her beloved child deep into her loving embrace, smiled broadly down at the innocent child, and stated, "Because I have you, honey," Tina answered.

Missy looked at her mother. From a mind challenged by the simplest of tasks and a heart unencumbered by trying to understand complicated human relationships, Missy said, "And you have Ryan too, mommy!"

Tina did not know how to respond. She didn't want to embarrass Ryan by assuming she knew the depth of his feelings for her, but in her heart, she felt, *"I hope so, today, tomorrow, and forever."*

In a joint three-way hug, Ryan answered Missy's question. "Yes, Missy. Mommy does!" Ryan pulled Tina into his arms. Taking his thumb, he gently wiped away the last stubborn tear rolling down her cheek. He whispered softly, "I love you, Tina Pinafore." The ensuing embrace was tempered by the presence of the innocent one though there was no doubt, each wanted it to last longer. Their moment was interrupted with the joyous shout from Missy. "See, we all have each other."

"Yes, we do, sweetheart!" said Tina as she snuggled deep into Ryan's arms, "Yes, we do!"

At Tina's insistence, Ryan serenaded her with several more songs. It was Ryan's good fortune that Tina liked country-western music, so his selection of songs from George Strait, Willie Nelson, and Garth Brooks only endeared him more to her. His fingers had begun to sting from the contact of the steel strings on his guitar, a sign he needed to practice more. When he paused, Tina nodded to him to look at Missy. Her bedtime was long past due, so the little child found comfort sleeping peacefully on the end of the couch. The two adults looked at each other with questioning eyes, each wondering if the other was thinking the same thing. Ryan spoke first.

"I have an extra bedroom. Missy could always sleep there tonight?"

As if she needed any prodding, Tina half-heartedly said, "It does seem a shame to wake her and have you drive us all the way home."

Only too quick to answer. Ryan replied, "Yes, that would be a shame."

One of the trio never woke up as she was transported gently to the extra bedroom and placed in bed. The child slept soundly through the night. The remaining two fell asleep shortly before sunrise. Their night was filled with the rapture of two hearts in consummated love.

30

KARMA

Over the sound of the running water in his bathroom sink, Ryan could hear Tina's voice as she spoke to someone on her cell phone. Her voice sounded irritated, as if she had received unpleasant news. Ryan quickly washed off any traces of shaving cream and patted his face dry with a hand towel hanging next to the sink. He found her sitting cross-legged on the bed, a cup of coffee resting between her legs. The rays of the morning sun shone through the sheers covering the bedroom window, casting a seductive shadow around Tina's bare shoulder. He paused momentarily to appreciate his new love and to listen to the cause of her anxiety.

"No, I don't mean to sound unappreciative of all the work you have done, Matthew, but things have changed. There are more people to consider now, that's all, and of all places, why there?" she said, her voice trailing off so as not to alert Ryan to the purpose of her attorney's call. It was too late.

"I'm no psychic, but that does not sound good for a Saturday morning," Ryan said as he sat on the edge of the bed.

Her legal battle with Missy's father over paternity and help with medical expenses was something she had not shared with

Ryan. Any hope for success seemed dim following their court appearance leaving Tina wishing she had never started the process in the beginning. However, the excitement in Matthew Adams' voice raised an awkward sense of optimism. Her relationship with Ryan had reached a point where there could be no secrets between them, not from the past, not from the present.

"There's something you need to know about Missy's father and me. I had taken Missy to an orthopedic specialist to inquire about the possibility of surgery to correct her leg. The doctor told me a special operation might help her, but it would be expensive and possibly have to be repeated when she grew older. I went to an attorney to force her father to help with present and future medical expenses. When we went to our first court appearance, the judge said that he could not legally force the father to assume any financial responsibility without proof of paternity. When the judge ordered a DNA test from the father, his attorney argued his client was out of the country and not expected back for at least a month. Everything was put in a holding pattern for the foreseeable future."

Tina took a sip of her coffee. Once hot, her beverage had cooled sufficiently for Tina to take a deep gulp. She continued. "That call was from my attorney. He said getting a DNA test was no longer a problem and that I should come to his office he'd tell me the whole story."

She looked up at Ryan. Her sense of embarrassment at the dire situation Ryan was unintentionally being dragged into caused her eyes to pool with tears. She wanted their relationship to be nothing but happy, but of course, this was life.

"This was never something I wanted you to be involved in or to have to worry about, the whole paternity issue and support. You know what I mean?"

Ryan took the coffee cup from her hands and set it on the

lampstand next to the bed. He cuddled her hands in his, like that of a parent protecting a child.

"I don't care about some legal definition of paternity. Her father should be the one who loves her, and she loves back, not some uncaring sperm donor, pardon my language. And what kid doesn't have medical expenses? Now let's get ready for that meeting with your attorney."

His words spoke to an affirmation that she hoped in her heart would be the future for her and Missy. For the next few minutes, Ryan held her in his arms, soothing a heart as it emptied itself of every drop of uncertainty it contained.

~

MATTHEW ADAMS SAT at the conference table in his office. Never in a million years did he think things would turn out the way they had. It was a story he relished in telling his client. The buzz of his intercom signaled the arrival of his guest.

"Ms. Pinafore is here to see you, Mr. Adams," said his receptionist.

"Send her in."

Adams made a habit of keeping his office door open. The sound of multiple footsteps altered him to expect more than one visitor. Adams called out, "Come on in, Tina." Much to his surprise, standing in the open doorway was Tina Pinafore and a young man Adams did not recognize. Tina took care of the introductions.

"Matthew, this is Ryan Callahan, my boyfriend. I brought him along for moral support."

Adams smiled. "Hopefully, the news I'm about to tell you will be all the support you'll need." Recalling the report he had read earlier, Adams mused, "Ryan Callahan? Yes, I'm familiar with that name. Please come in and have a seat."

Ryan looked at Adams and said, "I don't believe we've ever met, Mr. Adams."

"Please, call me Matthew, and no, we haven't met, but I'll get to that." Adams held his hand out, indicating for them to take a seat at his conference table. Skeptical of the unknown, Ryan cautiously pulled out chairs for Tina and himself. Adams sat on the other side of the oak conference table with several manila folders laid open in front of him. He began with a smile.

"You're familiar with the expression six degrees of separation, correct?"

Perplexed by Adams' opening question, Tina replied, "Yes. Why?"

"Because what I'm about to tell you will baffle you. Do you remember what the attorney representing the Barrington family said in court the day of our meeting? She said no way would the family ever agree to a DNA test. That information would have to come from another source," Adams said to Tina.

She nodded, remembering how helpless she felt at the time. Adams continued.

"About a month later, I received a letter from the attorney saying if I wanted proof of paternity, to look no further than the Federal Prison in Bennettsville, South Carolina. After a little research, I discovered that Trevor Barrington was being held in the high-security federal prison following an arrest for the attempted murder of a police officer, drug trafficking, and a plethora of other state and federal charges. Young Barrington and an accomplice were involved in a gunfight with a team of elite police officers at a local airport. Surely you saw it on the local news?' questioned Adams.

"My life in the last several weeks has become very complicated, and I haven't had the time to watch any TV," replied Tina. "Besides, the Trevor Barrington I know is a spineless coward who won't fight with his own mother, much less a police officer!"

The contempt in her voice was pleasing to Ryan, though it did nothing to abate his nervousness that something more revealing was about to emerge. Ryan Callahan was not a believer in coincidences. The hair on the back of his neck bristled at the possibility that Missy's biological father and the man Ryan had fought with at the airport the day of the Drug Task Forces battle with drug dealers was one and the same.

Wanting to stay on track, Adams said, "Back to my original point. As a prisoner in Federal Prison, a swab of Trevor Barrington's DNA was entered into CODIS, the Combined DNA Index System for non-law enforcement people. When I requested that a test be done comparing Mr. Barrington's DNA to the swab I took from Missy's cheek the day of our court hearing, I was referred to an FBI agent by the name of Ian O'Boyle. After explaining the nature of my call, Agent O'Boyle approved my request. The results came back a perfect match."

Tina was not surprised at what she always knew to be true, though the news hardly sent her into running a victory lap around the conference table. It was Ryan's cop's intuition that sensed Tina's attorney was holding back some information.

"There's more, isn't there?" he asked.

Adams glanced at his wristwatch.

"Yes, there is, Ryan, and the person to tell you that should be arriving any minute."

For FBI Agent Ian O'Boyle, the request to meet with Matthew Adams's client was more than rewarding. It was the culmination of a difficult and complicated case and the welcoming back of a prodigal sister. As he pulled to the curb in front of the law office of Matthew Adams, he texted Adams. *"I'm here."*

The pinging of his cell phone brought a smile to the face of Tina's attorney.

"Please excuse me for a moment."

Adams stood up and walked out to the waiting area. In the

brief interlude before Adams returned, Tina sighed, "I don't think I can take many more surprises, Ryan." What she was about to hear would hardly qualify as a surprise.

Adams escorted Ian O'Boyle into his office.

"Tina Pinafore, Ryan Callahan, may I introduce FBI Special Agent Ian O'Boyle. He has the rest of your story."

His deeply ingrained Irish mirth was evidenced by a broad smile on his ruddy face. His large hand gently engulfed Tina's hand. "It's my pleasure, Ms. Pinafore." Turning to Ryan, O'Boyle's grip became firmer. "Nice to put a face to the name, Ryan."

Once again, Ryan and Tina were struck with wonderment. O'Boyle took a seat next to Adams. Looking across the table, O'Boyle made a quick assessment of the two individuals facing him. O'Boyle saw a reflection of a younger version of himself. Ryan was studied in his gaze. His eye movements appeared deliberate, not scattered. He didn't shrink in the presence of an FBI agent. Tina reminded him a bit of his sister; whose beauty was seen as a weakness by some, but belied a presence of a fierce protector beating within her. It was that fierceness that spoke first.

"Matthew, before Mr. O'Boyle gets started, can we return to this DNA issue. Am I looking forward to another day in court with Trevor's attorney, Amanda, whatever her name was, and the judge?"

Both Adams and O'Boyle started laughing. Ryan and Tina looked at each other, aghast that the two would find anything humorous about the situation at hand. O'Boyle knew an explanation was deserving.

"First, my apologies for laughing, but when I explain, I think you'll understand. Mr. Barrington's attorney is Amana Boyle, originally O'Boyle, my sister. Somewhere along her path, she decided to drop any reference to her Irish heritage. Fortunately, she has seen the error of her ways and now goes by

Amanda O'Boyle, a blessing to my brothers and our mother and father."

For Ryan, another coincidence. For Tina, another question.

"Okay, his attorney is Mr. O'Boyle's sister. How does that affect anything?"

It was Adams' turn to explain.

"To your first question. Yes, I will appear before Judge Kotowski with the DNA match and seek the monetary relief requested for past, present, and future medical costs. You and Missy need not attend.

"So, you and his attorney will battle things out?" asked Tina.

With a broad smile, Adams answered, "No, Mr. Barrington will have different counsel. Ms. Amanda O'Boyle is now associated with a new legal firm, Adams, O'Boyle, and Associates."

That irony did not escape Tina, who now burst into laughter. "Well, if that's not a twist of fate."

During this exchange, O'Boyle had surreptitiously turned the opened file in front of him toward Ryan, his finger pointing to a spot on the report. O'Boyle's eyes darted toward Tina and then back to Ryan as if to say, "Does she know?" Ryan gave a subtle shake of his head. O'Boyle skillfully took the lead.

"Matt, I think this is where I take over." Adams nodded. He was most eager to see Tina's reaction to the rest of the story.

O'Boyle leaned forward as if to give greater emphasis to his explanation.

"Tina, let me explain how the charges against Trevor Barrington came to be. For months, the FBI and the DEA have been working on a very confidential case involving the introduction of massive amounts of cocaine into this country. Those involved in this operation were sworn to secrecy, including an elite unit from local law enforcement. If any mention of the operation were to leak out, the lives of innocent people would be jeopardized, and the whole operation would have fallen apart. It's important you know the seriousness of the big picture."

Tina, not accustomed to connecting dots between the seemingly unconnected, replied, "I don't understand."

"As it turned out, this whole drug thing was a family operation," O'Boyle continued. "Trevor Barrington hatched the idea to Arthur Ashcroft, the head of development for the senior Barrington's mega-developments, that his father's luxurious developments were the perfect market for high-grade cocaine. Arthur Ashcroft was the real brains behind the operation; Trevor Barrington was never more than a greedy partner out for a quick buck. Ashcroft siphoned millions of dollars from a couple of dozen accounts of Paris Barrington to finance the projects. Wisely, he made it appear as though Trevor Barrington had completed the transaction for himself, putting the funds into his own private account, all a complete manipulation by Ashcroft.

Listening to the scheme O'Boyle was laying out before her, Tina could not but help feel a little curious about the effects on the Barrington family. Not that she felt any sympathy for either the father or mother, but Tina was keenly aware of the influence of power and money wielded by the Barringtons. Money and power insulate the wealthy from the consequences of their illegal activities.

"His family's money always kept Trevor out of trouble. No doubt it will work for him and his family again," said Tina. Her voice trailed off, resigned in the reality of the double standard for people like the Barringtons.

A smile spread over O'Boyle's face.

"Not this time, Ms. Pinafore. Young Barrington and his accomplice made the unfortunate decision to battle it out with an elite unit from the Drug Enforcement Task Force of the Charleston PD. They lost, and the ten million dollars of cocaine profits Barrington was attempting to get away with will seal his fate, a life term in one of the government's finest federal prisons. As for his father, it seems Mr. Ashcroft provided the federal government with a detailed history of fraudulent accounting practices, insider trading information, intimidation and coercion in property acquisitions for his latest development, and foreign bank accounts with ties to a Colombian drug cartel. The net result is all the assets of the Barrington Company have been seized by the federal government. All his money will only prolong the inevitable, which is a cell next to his son."

Ryan Callahan had been keenly following the breakdown of the actions and consequences of those involved in this complex scheme. There was something missing, or better put, someone missing.

"What about this, Arthur Ashcroft? Did he buy himself some sort of immunity for providing information to the FBI?"

This detail was a source of embarrassment, particularly for Ian O'Boyle, who prided himself on catching the bad guys.

"Actually, Ryan, what he bought was an airline ticket to Japan. It seems that following our attempt to place him under arrest after our interview at his office, Mr. Ashcroft purchased a one-way ticket to Japan. From there, he chartered a private jet for Hong Kong. There was no trace of him after that, but his money left a trail. Mr. Ashcroft transferred some thirty million dollars from an offshore account in the Caymans to a holding company in Macao, a city on the southern coast of China. Paris Barrington had two major developments there, which Ashcroft spearheaded. With his connections there and with no extradition treaty, it appears Arthur Ashcroft has dodged the bullet as they say."

While Ryan was fascinated by this series of events, Tina sat back in her chair. All she had ever wanted was justice for Missy. It was beyond her comprehension that the Barringtons' greed and arrogance would have such widespread devastation. It was only then that Tina remembered something the FBI agent had said about the gunfight with an elite team of officers from a Drug Enforcement Task Force. *It couldn't be,* she thought. *There was no way he could have been involved, secrecy, or not.* The irony of such a possibility brought a smile to her face. She turned to Ryan. The look on her face that said, "You've got to be kidding me!" had O'Boyle and Adams desperately trying to remain stone-faced. Each had wondered at what point Tina would finally link her boyfriend to that elite squad from the Charleston PD.

Ryan braced himself. Would he be challenged with "Why didn't you tell me about this?" or would Tina see this as a weakness in their relationship? He was about to proclaim, "I can explain this," when Tina said, "I don't believe it, not you!" She did not attempt to stifle the laughter that erupted out of her mouth. She was joined by Adams and O'Boyle. All three relished in the irony of the moment. Ryan looked at them with a deer in the headlights stare. Somewhat defensive, he muttered, "I don't get it. What's so funny?"

Tina threw her arms around him and kissed him. She backed off, stared at him, then kissed him again.

"Really, the man I've been battling for child support for Missy; the man who abandoned her and me as unfit to join the Barrington family; and it turns out it's you, the man I love, who arrests him after a gun battle. Geez, Ryan, Hollywood couldn't write a script with that ending."

With any possibility of recrimination gone, Ryan felt an immense sense of relief. He even attempted to join them in their laughter, awkwardly, though. When the laughter finally subsided, Ian O'Boyle made the final salutation to the group.

"Ryan, if you ever decide to give the FBI a try, call me. Tina, if I may make a suggestion. Put Trevor Barrington behind you. You deserve someone much better."

Turning to Adams, O'Boyle said, "Matthew, it's been a pleasure." With a handshake goodbye, Ian O'Boyle left.

Adams smiled and turned to Ryan and Tina. "You can sleep soundly tonight, Tina. David slew Goliath, again."

"Wait till I tell my dad about this! He won't believe it," Tina chuckled.

Savoring Tina's reaction to his role in taking down Trevor Barrington, Ryan felt he'd press his luck with someone else.

"Speaking of your father, there's something I need to tell him as well," said Ryan.

31

IN THE SHADOW OF THE MOON

The perfect plan turned out to be not so perfect, after all. The yard sale, which Sharon Burski saw as an excellent opportunity to dispose of extraneous possessions while making a few dollars, turned out to be a violation of the Home Owners CC&R. The few hours each day Tina was able to devote to helping her father were less than productive. Tina still had to attend to Missy, whose curiosity about the entire process created endless questions. Adding to these misfortunes was Ryan's job change at work. His team had been assigned to work eight to five a.m. Tuesday through Saturday. This cost him much wanted time with Tina and even less time to help with the move. These logistical nightmares had only deepened the depression now crushing Eddy Pinafore. A man whom life had taught to compartmentalize pain and suffering now found life had left him with no safe place. His days and nights were consumed with a sense of failure. He had lost control of the transition to Magnolia Gardens, which had exacerbated the helplessness of watching Maddy's decline into dementia. The few times Ryan had been able to help, he noticed the change in Tina's father. With help from his friends at work,

Ryan had come up with a possible solution to the problem. Besides, there was another issue that needed to be addressed. Monday, Ryan stopped by Eddy's house around noon to talk about both.

As he pulled into the driveway, Ryan saw the open garage door. Eddy was sitting on a lawn chair in the middle of the garage, surrounded by a dozen half-packed storage boxes. Scattered about the garage were stacks of Eddy's attempts to categorize the collection of tools, nuts, and bolts, paint cans, garden implements, you name it that he had accumulated over the years. It was a nearly impossible task. Uncharacteristically, Eddy had a bottle of Heineken in his hand. There was no humidity or heat that day, which would have normally called for such a beverage. Even Eddy's regular positive disposition had been replaced by a more somber and distant temperament. He failed even to acknowledge Ryan as he exited his truck. His focus was on the endless waves moving slowly toward the shore with the incoming tide, as endless as the problems he was now facing.

"Hi, Eddy," Ryan called out.

Eddy jerked his head toward Ryan as if the sound of a slamming door had brought him out of his mental drifting. His lethargic attempt to stand was a testament to his state of mental and physical energy. He set his bottle of Heineken on the concrete floor then slowly stood up. His shoulders were no longer squared. His back appeared a bit bowed, and his head hung at a downward angle. Eddy Pinafore looked like a beaten man, physically and spiritually.

"This is a pleasant surprise," he said. His tone sounded less than sincere. "What brings you here this time of the day? Aren't you supposed to be at work?"

"I don't report until two, new shift."

"Yeah, Tina said something about that last week. I'm sorry. I don't remember things like I used to," Eddy said, more than a bit embarrassed at his memory loss. "Would you like to go inside?

"No thanks, Eddy. I thought maybe we could talk here, just you and me."

Eddy's mental cloud seemed to lift with the words, "just you and me."

"Sure. Let me get you a chair."

Grabbing a folded lawn chair from the corner of the garage, he handed it to Ryan, who unfolded it and set it next to Eddy's chair. As Ryan sat down, he hoped that Eddy, a man of immense personal pride, would be receptive to his suggestion. Ryan looked around at Eddy's attempts at organization.

"How are things going?" Ryan asked, knowing full well the answer.

Shaking his head, the defeated man said, "Take a look for yourself, and the inside of the house isn't much different."

"Eddy, Tina told me things weren't working out like you thought. It's no one's fault. Nothing ever works out exactly as planned. That's why they call it a plan."

Eddy gave a faint chuckle at Ryan's attempt at humor.

"But Eddy, on the serious side, I've got an idea that might be the answer you're looking for."

At the possibility of any better way, Eddy took a swig of his beer and said, "I'm open to any suggestions. I think I bit off more than I can chew."

Ryan shifted his chair to face Eddy.

"Okay, here's my plan. I talked with some of the guys at the Drug Task Force, and they are all willing to help. We order one of those U-Pack shipping containers. The company will deliver one right in front of the house. My guys will come over and pack everything you're not taking to the Gardens. They told me it could be done in two days, max."

Eddy was thankful for Ryan's generous offer to help, though he thought it a bit overambitious.

"How can you possibly get all that done in two days?" Eddy questioned, though inwardly, he hoped they had not overestimated their ability.

"Eddy, most of the guys are ex-military. When I told them about your background, everyone wanted to help. There's no 'can't do' with these guys!" Ryan replied emphatically.

For the first time in weeks, Eddy's spirits began to rise. Maybe, just maybe, things would finally work out. But he was not without some skepticism.

"But Ryan, there's still the stuff to take to the Gardens and the logistics to make that work."

"They figured that out too, Eddy. You show us everything you want to take—clothes, furniture, pictures, whatever. You get Maddy ready one morning. Tina will come over and take you two out for breakfast. After that, she'll take you and Maddy to see our house. In the meantime, my guys will rent a couple of moving vans. We'll come over here, load everything up, and take it to your suite at the Gardens. Mom will be there to make sure we put everything right where you want it. After some time at my place, Tina will bring you and Maddy over here. It should be a seamless transition for Maddy considering her mental state, and what could be easier for you?"

The forlornness that had plagued him for weeks seemed to ebb. The creativity of the plan, and the thought of fellow veterans helping, began to elevate his spirits. That's when something Ryan had said gave him pause. *"Our house,"* what did he mean by, *"Our house?"*

"Did you say our house? What did you mean by 'our house'?" Eddy was confused by Ryan's use of the possessive.

He instantly realized his grammatical faux pas. "There's something else I wanted to talk to you about, Eddy—it's Tina."

Next to his wife, his daughter was the love of his life. Eddy sat more erect in his chair, his mind shifting to a defensive posture if needed.

"What about Tina?"

Though he had prepared for this moment over and over in his mind, the reality of the here and now had Ryan feeling a bit queasy and apprehensive. He looked Eddy straight in the eyes. There were certain traditions that Ryan had been raised to believe in, and no amount of social evolution was going to change that. There was still a question to be asked, not a decision to tell someone had already been made. With uncharacteristic bluntness, Ryan said, "Sir, Tina and I are in love, and we would like to get married."

The recent years had done nothing to brighten Eddy Pinafore's anticipation of the future. The reality of Maddy's disease, the care that she would need that he could no longer provide for by himself, memories of a twenty-five year marriage that could no longer be shared with the love of his life was certainly not the future he had anticipated. There was a new sense for the future with Ryan's words, one filled with hope, and wondrous anticipation, a future where dreams became a reality and reality brought love, where a union of two created one. For Eddy Pinafore, it was a ray of brightness in a world that had become numbed with the stark, unfair realities of life. Slowly a smile formed on his aged and battle-scarred face.

"Nothing would make me happier than to see you two together," he said. "I only wish Maddy..." his voice trailed off as the inevitable tears began to pool.

"I'd like to ask her as well, sir, if that's alright?" Ryan said.

Eddy nodded and stood to take Ryan into the house. Maddy was sitting on the couch. Her auburn hair was nicely combed. A light layer of facial makeup, eyeliner, and lipstick expertly applied by Maddy's visiting angel, Paula, added a certain attractiveness to a face that had long ago lost its natural beauty. Paula adjusted a blue knitted shawl across Maddy's lap.

"There you are, Maddy. Ready to greet the day!" smiled

Paula as she stepped back to admire her cosmetological creation.

Maddy said nothing. Through a seemingly perpetual smile and hazel eyes, which now focused on nothing in particular, Maddy muttered, "Yes, I am." Paula patted Maddy on the shoulder. She would return later that afternoon to provide Eddy with a few hours of relief.

"Thank you so much for how you care for her," said a much appreciative Eddy. "You've given her a sense of dignity that was impossible for me," referring to the awkwardness of tending to Maddy's hygiene needs.

Paula nodded as any verbal affirmation to the obvious was unnecessary.

"I'll see you in a few hours," said Paula, leaving Maddy to Eddy and Ryan.

Eddy and Ryan sat on either side of her. Eddy softly stroked Maddy's hair, drawn mystically to the beauty that used to be.

"Sweetheart, Ryan has something he'd like to talk to you about."

Maddy turned to the stranger sitting next to her. Ryan reached out and gently lifted Maddy's hand into his. Her frail fingers were twisted by arthritis. The back of her hand was marked by purple blotches of skin and raised blood vessels.

"Maddy, I want you to know how much I love your daughter. I can't imagine life without her or Missy. I, I mean we, would like to get married, with your blessing of course!"

Dementia had robbed Maddy of nearly every cognitive function she had. What small shred of understanding that remained seemed to miraculously elicit a small smile and a glint of awareness in her eyes. Ryan looked at Eddy.

"Do you think she heard me?" he asked.

Eddy had long given up trying to understand if Maddy heard anything said to her, much less understood it. He wanted to believe she did. He never gave up hope that somehow, even if dementia was winning the battle over her mind, her heart fought on, clinging to the tiniest vestige of comprehension.

"Tell her again, son. It couldn't hurt," Eddy replied. In his mind, he thought it was fruitless, but his heart could not let him accept that all hope was gone.

Ryan placed his other hand on top of Maddy's and repeated his message. Hearing his words again was the stimulus Maddy's brain needed. Beneath his hand, Ryan felt a minute almost imperceptible movement of her fingers tightening around his fingers. Maddy started to say something. Ryan leaned closer as she barely spoke above a whisper. When she was finished, Ryan looked back at Eddy.

"What?" Eddy asked, his face contorted with a quizzical grin.

"She said, be happy. Maybe it's wishful thinking on my part, but I think she understood."

Eddy knew exactly what that microscopic bit of optimism felt like. It was all he had left at the end of a day caring for a wife who was nothing more than a living statue. He speculated with every twitch of her body, every blink of her eye that she understood something of what was going on around her. It would have been easier to see her go, but that finality was even more torturous.

"I hope so, son. She and I used to talk about when this day would come. What would he look like? What kind of a man would he be? Loving, caring, strong enough to deal with her personality? You know, all those things. Maddy's heart would pound at the excitement of planning Tina's wedding, being a part of such a joyful occasion. Mostly, knowing her daughter was in the arms of a man who would truly love her put her heart at peace."

There it was again. Was it a random physiological tic? Some involuntary neurological reaction? Not to Ryan Callahan. In his heart of hearts, he knew Maddy understood exactly what was happening. Speaking gently, Ryan said, "Thank you."

Ryan sat back in his chair. "She looks tired. Maybe I should be going?"

Eddy felt strangely contented as if something mystical had taken place.

"Perhaps so," he replied. The peacefulness in his voice had replaced the all-too-common tone of resignation and defeatism.

IN THE ENSUING DAYS, Eddy, along with help from Tina, went through the house, making that final decision as to what possessions would go to the suite at Magnolia Gardens and what would go into storage. Eddy had given Ryan carte blanche to take anything he wanted from the garage. Tina made sure that, even over her father's occasional objection, a sufficient number of sentimental memorabilia would make the trip; family pictures, certain curios from significant events during their lives together, favorite pieces of furniture, and all items that would transfer a sense of familiarity to their new residence. When the last of the selection process was completed, Eddy and Tina sat on the couch in the living room. Eddy had prepared a pitcher of iced tea. Each sipped their beverage in silence.

"I think we did a pretty good job, Daddy, don't you?" smiled Tina, quite satisfied with her efforts.

Eddy glanced around the living room and kitchen area taking special note of the large yellow post-it notes on everything in sight. Everything had been marked with a red Sharpie, MG, or storage. His words caught Tina off guard. He sounded morose.

"Everything in this house played a part in our lives together. I can't shake the image of sitting in our suite and staring at a beautiful mosaic with me, you, your mother portraying our lives and realizing there are pieces of that mosaic missing. I know the logistics of downsizing, but how do you downsize your memories?"

He rubbed his chilled glass across his forehead, hoping to numb the mental anguish of his imagery. Tina's heart ached for her father. She struggled to find some words of consolation. Her throat started to crack.

"Daddy, please never think that moving there is forcing you to say this memory stays here, that memory goes to storage. You don't need some physical item to remind you of the love you and mom felt for each other. That will last for eternity."

There was no stopping the flood of tears as Tina hugged her dad and sobbed, "Daddy, I love you and mom so much!"

The next day right on schedule, Tina arrived to help get her mother up and dressed before the moving company delivered the sixteen-foot moving pod. She had planned to take her to the Gardens to acquaint her with the staff and the level of care she would need. Ryan's mom was watching Missy at Ryan's house, where the four women would spend the rest of the day. Her mother maneuvered her walker out the front door with Tina at her side, to Tina's car parked in the driveway. With Eddy's help, Tina was able to get Maddy in the passenger seat. Eddy looked at his wife and said,

"You have a good day with Tina, sweetheart. I'll see you later." A frail hand rose slowly and then waved.

Eddy did not have to wait long after Tina left before the moving pod arrived. Eddy had notified his neighbors of its arrival and the help that would follow, so there was plenty of parking available along the street. Eddy directed the driver where he wanted the pod dropped. The driver expertly moved his flatbed into position next to the curb. He exited his cab with a small console in hand. After double-checking his location, the driver pressed a button on the console. Slowly, the legs of a metal frame surrounding the pod lowered to ground level. Once set firmly in place, the driver circled the pod to check the location for any possible mistakes. Satisfied with the placement, the driver held the button on the console down. The hydraulics pushed the pod upward until it cleared the trailer bed by about a foot. The driver then got back in his cab and moved his trailer forward about ten yards. He returned with his console in hand. Pressing the down button, he lowered the pod on its metal frame to the ground.

"You're all set," he said. "Give the company a call when you're done packing."

Somewhat awed by the entire process, Eddy could only shake his head in disbelief. "Thank you" was all he said.

In preparation for the arrival of Ryan's friends, Eddy had a large ice cooler in the garage packed with a case of Heineken. He didn't expect the cold beverages to last too long, with temperatures projected to be in the low nineties. The first to arrive was Ryan and his partner Willie Root. In quick succession, a number of vehicles began parking on the opposite side of the street. There were twelve in all. Some brought dollies, and others had ratchet tie-downs, ropes, and blankets. Ryan introduced each one to his father-in-law to be. Marty Knight spoke for the group.

"Mr. Pinafore, Ryan told us you could use some help," smiled Knight.

"You might say that," replied an appreciative Eddy Pinafore.

Looking at Ryan, Knight asked, "What's the plan?"

Ryan explained the contents in the garage needed to be boxed and labeled Storage. Any item in the house marked Storage would go into the pod along with the boxes from the garage. Everything else would remain until the next day.

"If we can get all that done today, I've got a sixteen-foot rental van to take whatever is left to their new place at Magnolia Gardens tomorrow."

Never one to acknowledge even the slightest possibility of failure, Knight replied firmly, "There is no 'if,' Ryan."

With that said, Knight quickly ordered four men to handle the garage assignment. The rest followed Ryan and Eddy into the house.

"I think it best to handle the kitchen and living room furniture first, then the bedroom furniture, and lastly the small items," Knight said. His assertiveness was tempered with a tone of permission.

"Sounds okay by me," replied Eddy.

With nothing more than a nod, the remaining help began. Whenever Eddy was about to issue a caution, Knight beat him to the punch with reminders such as, "don't forget to wrap a blanket around that" or "Tape those glass doors shut," referring to their oak china cabinet. With the announcement from Ed Popkey that he, Ortega, and Hodgner had finished packing and loading the garage contents, Knight redirected the four to help the others. Much to his amazement, it took a little less than six hours to get everything loaded into the pod. Knight did his own assessment of the day's efforts and what was left for the next day. Having moved his own family four times during his career, Knight had a keen eye for the small details. He shared those details with Ryan and Eddy.

"Ryan, that sixteen-foot moving van should easily handle what's left to move tomorrow morning. Mr. Pinafore, after we load up the van, there's plenty of time for some of us to give the place a final cleanup, you know, wipe the walls down, vacuum the floors, even putty over the nail holes in the walls. The rest can go with the moving van to offload your stuff at the Gardens."

The relief Ryan's friends had provided Eddy was overwhelming. He couldn't imagine expecting more help, but nevertheless, the offer was there.

"What you've done is already more than I expected, Marty."

Before Eddy could say no, Knight interjected, "Good, then we'll take care of those details tomorrow."

"In that case, how about a beer break?" Eddy offered the contents of his ice chest long since cooled to perfection.

The cooling afternoon breeze coming off the ocean made the cement garage the perfect place for a dozen or so sweaty, dirty cops to relax. After a round of self-congratulatory remarks, the conversation soon turned to cop talk, which meant the drug raid on the pier and the ensuing capture of one Trevor Barrington. No one took greater pleasure in listening to that escapade than Eddy Pinafore. He would have paid anything to see Trevor Barrington's smugness evaporate with each click of the wrist cuffs put on by the arresting officer. The piercing eyes of Ed Popkey as he searched the ice chest for the non-existent last beer alerted Knight it was probably time for him and the rest to leave.

"Guys, I think we'd better hit the road. I want to get an early start tomorrow."

As each man stood to say goodbye, Eddy thanked them profusely for their help. To a man, they responded, "It was no problem, Sir."

Left alone in a partially furnished home, Eddy went from room to room, reliving for the last time, every memory, every anecdote he and Maddy had created. A profound sense of gratitude swept over him. The long-time non-practicing Catholic made the sign of the cross. The arrival of Tina in an empty car caught Eddy off guard.

"I wonder if something went wrong?" asked a cautious sounding Eddy greeting Tina at the front door.

She was beaming with delight at the surprise she was about to spring on her father.

"Daddy, there's been a slight change of plans. We're going to spend the night at Ryan's house. His mom and I decided it would be easier to keep mom there tonight, then all of us could leave for the Gardens in the afternoon. I need to get a change of clothes for mom. You do the same. What do ya think?"

Eddy Pinafore had been married long enough to know when a woman asked, "What do you think?" the answer is yes.

"That sounds wonderful, sweetheart," Eddy replied.

For Eddy Pinafore, it was an invitation to form one last memory with his wife, Maddy, his daughter, and newest family member, Ryan Callahan.

32

THE FINAL STOP

E ddy Pinafore finished setting the patio table for their early Friday evening dinner with Samantha Callahan. With the arrival of twin grandchildren nearly three months ago, Samantha had made a habit of sharing an early evening meal with Eddy and Maddy. It allowed her to keep Eddy and Maddy updated with information about their shared grandchildren, a boy named Michael Edward and a girl named Madeline Anne. The logistics of transporting two infants plus Missy and the endless assortment of diapers, carriers, etc., had limited Ryan and Tina's ability to see her parents for monthly visits, at best. Samantha took no offense with the decision to name the daughter after Maddy. Her reward would be the opportunity to see that precious little baby grow, something her namesake would never be able to enjoy.

"Oh, Sweetheart, please don't apologize. I understand completely, and your mom does too. You come when you can," said Eddy into his cell phone. Eddy had grown accustomed to speaking of Maddy the way she used to be. It was easier that way rather than speaking of her as if in the past tense.

Tina placed her cell phone on speaker and laid it on the bed.

Her guilt at putting off another visit to see her parents was soon assuaged by the sight of the twins on their backs, their hands, and legs stretching and contracting in some sort of spasmodic rhythm. The simultaneous eruption of twin discharges of their bodily functions created an odor that caused even Tina to gag momentarily.

"Stay on the line, Daddy, I've got a sudden mess to clean up," begged Tina, as she reached for multiple baby wipes. She muttered aloud, "My God, how much of this do you two have inside you?" as she discarded one baby wipe after another until the whiteness of the twins' bottoms reappeared. Tina could hear her father's laughter over the phone. No amount of Febreze Air Freshener would eliminate the foul odor in the bedroom, so Tina placed the twins in their stroller and exited the bedroom forthwith. Ryan had taken Missy to the store with him for a prolonged shopping spree hoping to give the twins a quiet time for sleep. Tina curled up on the couch with the babies in front of her in their stroller. Their eyelids fluttered as they fought off the need to sleep. As much as Tina enjoyed the children, their slumber could be interpreted as a blessing from God when their eyes finally closed. Whispering softly so she would not awaken them, Tina said, "At last, they're asleep," into her phone.

Eddy's laughter caused his slumbering wife to awaken from her short nap.

"What?" she muttered, her eyes trying to focus as her head turned abruptly from side to side. Her mental confusion was evident in the remark and the expression on her deeply lined face. He walked carefully over to his wife's supine body, carefully placing the phone in her hand, so she did not drop it.

"It's Tina calling," Eddy replied, hoping the sound of their daughter's name would ease any uneasiness Maddy was feeling.

"Here, she wants to talk to you," said Eddy, as he handed Maddy his phone. Her hand crippled by arthritis was barely able to hold on to it. The object her husband had handed her meant nothing to Maddy. She held it obediently to her ear but said nothing. Her countenance remained blank, empty of emotion.

"Hi, Mom. I just wanted to call and say Hi. The twins say Hi too," Tina said, smiling at her babies. "You know what, Mom? I think Michael has Daddy's eyes, and little Maddy certainly has your chin."

Her smile soon disappeared, replaced by the heartbreaking realization that she could never share with her mother the joy of the cuddling infants in her arms, the giggles as they were washed in lukewarm water at night, or when they first begin to crawl. All the joys of motherhood a daughter would normally share with her mother were lost in the knowledge that her mother was rapidly slipping away. Tina made no efforts to control the silent tears flowing down her cheeks.

Eddy smiled at his daughter's description of the grandchildren. Maddy said nothing. The phone began to slide slowly down her face, her arthritic hand no longer able to hold even its light weight. Eddy gently leaned over and took the phone from her.

"I'd better let you go, honey. You and the twins get some rest. We'll talk later. Maybe you'll be able to come over when the kids are a bit less labor-intensive."

Tina struggled. Guilt overwhelmed her. Her children needed her attention, but seeing her mother was a priority as well. Tina's heart felt like it was caught in a giant vice, slowly squeezing her life away. It became difficult for her to breathe, much less speak. All she could manage was a mournful, "Yes, Daddy."

The irony of the moment caused an unabated flow of tears. Her heart swelled with the joy of the two young lives that laid before her, yet it ached that her mother was slowly disappearing before her.

~

FOR EDDY PINAFORE, happiness at Magnolia Garden was predicated on one thing, ensuring that he was keeping proper care of his wife. In that, he was not disappointed. Samantha had arranged for a volunteer named Dorothy to help Maddy. Dorothy, a woman in her mid-fifties, dressed plainly, and was almost monastic in appearance. Her gray hair was closely cropped, and her only accoutrement was a plain gold cross she wore around her neck. Eddie appreciated her conscientiousness. Each morning, she was there to help bathe Maddy, get her dressed, and, most importantly, make Maddy presentable by fixing her hair and a gentle application of mascara, makeup, and lipstick. These were tasks totally outside of Eddy's skill set. Dorothy talked to Maddy as if they were best friends, even sisters. She shared every aspect of her daily activities with Maddy, engaging her in endless one-way conversations. It pleased Eddy that someone other than he was paying attention to Maddy and going about it in a caring manner.

Having put Maddy to bed for her afternoon nap, Dorothy returned to the living room to speak with Eddy.

"She's resting now, Eddy. I'll check back later before dinner."

"Thank you, Dorothy. In her own way, I know Maddy appreciates all you do for her," replied Eddy. No longer able to hear her voice or engage in any meaningful conversation, Eddy found some consolation in conversing with those who provided for Maddy's needs. Eddy recognized that he, too, had needs.

By nature, Dorothy was an intuitive person. In her interactions with Eddy, she found him to be quite cerebral. From the presence of a Bible on the end table next to the couch and a picture of the Savior Jesus on the bedroom wall, Dorothy had no doubt there was a belief in God within Eddy and Maddy. A person of great spirituality, Dorothy rarely attempted to proselytize her beliefs to others, but in this instance, she saw a value in sharing it with Eddy. She carefully studied him prior to uttering,

"May I sit with you for a moment?"

More than receptive to some adult conversation with someone he had grown to admire as well as respect, he bid her sit down.

There was an uncanny softness in Dorothy's voice that prompted Eddy to lean slightly forward to hear as she began to speak. She began simply and in a straightforward manner.

"Do you believe in God, Eddy?"

Eddy was taken aback by the question. Yes, he believed in God, though Maddy's suffering had certainly caused him to question the notion of a benevolent Supreme Being. He began to sound defensive, almost insulted that this person would dare enter into such a personal topic. Yet, as the thoughts ran through his mind, he softened, realizing that Dorothy saw a need and was trying to be kind to him. Cautiously, he answered with a question.

"Why?"

In his voice, the quasi-skepticism was a sign to Dorothy that her original intention to initiate the conversation was well suited.

"Eddy, did you ever think that believing in God is a two-way street?"

If Eddy was confused by Dorothy's original question, her second question left him flummoxed.

"I'm afraid you've lost me, Dorothy," replied Eddy.

Dorothy chucked. "Yes, theological constructs are not easily understood. Let me put it in its simplest form. If you believe in God, God believes in you, Eddy. Because God believes in you, Eddy, he appreciates so much all you have done for Maddy and the other residents here at the Gardens."

She spoke with the peaceful assurance of someone well-grounded in her faith and confident in her power to persuade. An appreciative God, now that's something Eddy Pinafore had never given much thought. He had always been taught to be grateful to God for all God had given him, and that concept had been challenging enough considering his own injuries, much less watching his wife succumb to dementia. Eddy had made his peace with this appreciative God, preferring to see his life as half-full rather than half-empty; the former would have doomed him to a life of despair. Perhaps not the peace a believer like Dorothy would have envisioned, but it was the best Eddy Pinafore could do.

Despite her affirmation, Eddy failed to see what she was talking about.

"I'm not sure I see the appreciation you're referring to, Dorothy?"

The sweetest of smiles formed on Dorothy's face.

"Oh, but you have Eddy. Every angelic smile that forms on Maddy's face, every twitch of her fingers when you hold her hand, that's God saying, Thank You."

Eddy slumped back in his chair. His body language suggested this was a theological construct beyond his capability to understand. His eyes darted around the room as if he expected to find an answer written on the air. In the farthest stretches of his imagination, he would have never considered God would speak to him. He never remembered praying to God and hearing, "Yes!" or "It's coming, just not now!" Eddy Pinafore looked into Dorothy's eyes, soft, gentle blue eyes peering over folded hands that supported her chin, eyes that seemed to offer an assurance to so many questions if only he would reach out.

"I'm afraid God thanking me is a little hard to wrap my head around, Dorothy."

Dorothy smiled. "It is for many people, Eddy. Think of it this way, if someone had shown you or Maddy or your daughter some sort of kindness, what would have been your reaction?"

"Isn't that a bit of a simplistic question?" he asked, now slightly annoyed with her efforts to avoid giving him a direct answer.

She was used to this type of skepticism. She answered with a smile and an even simpler answer.

"Not really. I'll bet you would have said thank you and then try to reciprocate in some fashion. God is no different."

The look on his face told Dorothy she had pushed the limits of Eddy's thought process, at least for the moment.

"Listen, Eddy, we can have this discussion later if you wish."

Analyzing his life through some sort of spiritual lens was well outside Eddy's comfort zone. He would need some time before pursuing that topic again. Desperate to escape this uncomfortable topic, he moved to a more mundane topic.

"Yes, perhaps so," he replied, unconvinced at his own words. "Dorothy, what's your last name in case I need the staff to contact you?"

"Dorothy is my last name," she replied.

"Well then, how about your first name. There might be more than one Dorothy working here."

She had a beguiling smile as she answered.

"Sister, and there's only one of us working here."

She was barely able to stifle a giggle with the enunciation of the last word.

≈

IN THE ENSUING WEEKS, Sister Dorothy's comments caused Eddy to think more deeply about his life, about Maddy, and Magnolia Gardens. He had always considered Magnolia Gardens their final stop, a place to live peacefully together until the end. He intended to seek out Sister Dorothy for a deeper discussion about this matter.

Eddy continued to busy himself as a sort of roving ambassador of goodwill. When he was not with Maddy, Eddy could be found roaming the facility's hallways and grounds, chit-chatting with staff and residents. How was their day going? What activities were they involved with that day? How did they like the special meal of the week on Fridays? Most of the time, their answers were innocent and innocuous. At other times, their answers pointed out the absurdity of regulatory agencies.

Eddy had spotted a new resident by the name of Ethel Caradine, a woman in her late eighties, sitting with Hilda Queensland, a staff member, on the veranda outside the dining room. Hilda monitored the dietary needs of new residents to ensure their health needs were being met. She took to her responsibilities like that of an IRS auditor. Bull-doggedly determined to see that every requirement was fulfilled to the letter of the law, she was going over the options for breakfast, lunch, and dinner. Eddy walked over to their table and introduced himself to Ethel, clearly annoying the very focused Queensland.

"Hi Ethel, my name is Eddy Pinafore. Judging by the Queen being here, you must be a new resident," he stated.

It delighted Eddy no end to see Queensland's pursed lips and clenched jaw at the sound of the nickname Eddy had pinned on her. Ethel blushed at the unexpected attention being paid her by a still handsome looking, if battle-scarred, Eddy Pinafore. Adjusting her hair will a coy brush of her hand, she responded, "Why, yes I am. My name is Ethel Caradine. I'm eighty-eight years young," she exclaimed with the enchantment of a proud and aged screen siren.

"It's my pleasure, Ethel. My wife, Maddy, and I are residents here as well. Tell me, what did you think of today's breakfast special, Eggs Benedict?"

Ethel adjusted her posture to more upright as if to make a proclamation.

"Eggs are one of my favorite things to have for breakfast, but I want my bacon with my breakfast. Two slices of crispy bacon make anything taste good." Ethel looked defiantly toward Queensland.

The only thing more comical to Eddy than Ethel's defiant stance of the presence of a pork product on her plate was the grimace forming of Hilda Queensland's face. He relished agitating the woman one more time. Looking at her, he said, "You'd think a woman eighty-eight years old could have two small measly pieces of bacon for breakfast, wouldn't you, Hilda?" His enjoyment in mocking the Queen was growing by the minute.

Clutching her notebook of dietary requirements and recommendations by the National Association of Assisted Living Facilities like a Bible in the hands of a Southern Baptist preacher delivering a fire and brimstone sermon, Hilda declared, "The NAALF has determined bacon to be a health hazard for a person of Ethel's age."

It was the closed-mindedness of adhering to some administrative regulation that frustrated Eddy Pinafore. Having spent a career working with the Veterans Administration, Eddy Pinafore was keenly aware of the bureaucratic stupidity of iron-clad regulations. He challenged Queensland's reliance on such a rule.

"Hilda, seriously, the health hazard facing Ethel is being eighty-eight, not two slices of Hormel's maple-soaked bacon with her breakfast. Why not let her have her bacon, you know, kind of like a reward for having lived so long!"

Ethel beamed with comic smugness. "Yes, I deserve it. I have lived a long time!"

Eddy eyed Hilda, challenging her to rebut his statement until finally, she acquiesced.

"I'll make arrangements with the kitchen staff right away. Ethel, we can talk later."

Eddy relished his self-appointed role of resident advocate, though he tried to find some good in everyone.

"Hilda is really a good person, Ethel. She is very dedicated to looking after our best interests, nutritionally speaking. She sometimes forgets how important little things like two pieces of greasy bacon are to people of our age."

Ethel was quick to correct him. "Crispy, not greasy, crispy!"

"Right, Ethel, I forgot," smiled Eddy. "Crispy."

That smile would not last long.

∽

Eddy's return to his suite was interrupted by a congenial greeting from Samantha Callahan.

"Eddy, it's a wonder day isn't it?"

There it was, that mysterious twinkle in her eyes that told Eddy she had more to say.

"Indeed, Samantha, it is."

"Eddy, there's something I'd like to share with you. Would you mind sitting with me on the veranda?"

"Certainly, lead the way," answered the always affable Eddy.

The two walked down the hallway to the double French doors leading to the veranda. Samantha and Eddy sat at the closest table which was under the shaded pergola and offered partial protection from the afternoon sun. As adept as Eddy Pinafore thought he was at reading people, he could not get a read on Samantha's state of mind. Was she preparing him for some catastrophic revelation? Perhaps, it was some news about her son, Ryan, and Eddy's daughter, Tina? Either way, Eddy sat pensively. Samantha began her disclosure.

"The day you came to see me about securing a place for you

and Maddy when the time came, I had just had a horribly upsetting conversation with a Arthur Ashcroft, remember?"

Much had transpired in the past year or so, and truthfully, Eddy Pinafore could not remember the incident in question.

"I'm afraid I don't, Samantha."

Samantha felt somewhat relieved. She could now paint the complete picture without partial recollections on Eddy's part interfering.

"Let me start from the beginning. Arthur Ashcroft, acting on behalf of Paris Barrington, was attempting to sway three of the member on the Board of Directors to sell him their interest in Magnolia Gardens. The three were Drake Calhoun, Dr. Mathew Singer, and Dr. Abrams. There was every possibility that the three would succumb to Ashcroft's offer. Each were facing disastrous financial and legal issues. "

Realizing the agonizing burden Samantha must have been under at the time, Eddy responded, "My God, Samantha, I had no idea that was going on!" He reached out and took hold of her hand. "My dear, what didn't you tell me? Maybe I could have helped."

The sense of caring and protection that Samantha felt for all the residents, much less the parents of her son-in-law, swelled within her.

"Eddy, you had so much on your plate worrying about Maddy's deteriorating mental and physical condition, I just could not add more for you to worry about. Anyway, I want you to know how it all ended."

Eddy sat in stunned silence that so much had transpired without him being aware. Samantha began to reveal her story.

"For starters, after a joint investigation involved the FBI and the Charleston PD in the business affairs of Paris Barrington and Arthur Ashcroft, the senior Barrington went bankrupted. He is looking at decades in federal prison. His son, Trevor, had his own issues with the DEA and FBI. He will be in prison for years as well. As for the three rats, Calhoun, Abrams, and Singer, they fared no better. Drake Calhoun was arrested by DEA agents for trafficking in opiates, using his medical clinics throughout the south as a front. The government seized all his assets. The SEC had a field day uncovering the insider trading allegations against Dr. Abrams. The possibility of life in a federal prison was more than the jerk could take. He was found in his car in his garage, a hose from the tail pipes to the car window. The coward! Dr. Mathew Singer's genius for Ponzi schemes earned him thirty years in Atlanta Federal Prison. "

Samantha sat back in her chair, relieved that the burden of secrecy had finally been lifted off her shoulders.

"Eddy, we are going to be safe. There'll be no sale of Magnolia Gardens!"

Throughout her narrative, Eddy began to remember bits and pieces. At the time had set aside his fears of any possible sale of the Gardens to focus on his wife. His own precious Maddy was safe, now and forever.

∼

HIS EYES OPENED and moved slowly across a dark ceiling. He reached over to the light on his nightstand and turned it on. His AM/FM radio clock read 5:30 am. *At least it's a little later than yesterday,* he thought. A month ago, advancing arthritis along with issues of incontinency had made it impossible for Maddy to remain in their suite with him. Her physical nearness had at least helped Eddy to fill the void of an unresponsive Maddy, whose dementia had completely engulfed her. She rarely responded to any auditory stimuli. It usually consisted of a fleeting eye movement or the briefest of a facial tic when she did. Her once radiant hazel eyes were now milky in color with hardly a trace of their former glow.

Eddy rose quietly from his bed, his mind momentarily

believing Maddy was still sleeping beside him. Sitting on the side of the bed, he reached for his prosthetic arm, which laid on a nightstand next to his bed along with his prosthetic leg. After thirty years as a double amputee, it had become second nature for Eddy Pinafore to slip on a heavy sock over his knee stub with one hand, then slide on his prosthetic leg and wrap around the Velcro strap. His prosthetic arm was a similar process. With those two tasks completed, he proceeded to the bathroom for his morning shower and shave. After wiping his face with a wet rag to remove trace amounts of shaving cream, Eddy stared into the mirror above the sink. Tired eyes stared back from their sunken sockets. His face was thinner. That charming Eddy Pinafore smile was gone, reduced to a forced impersonal grin when necessary. Years of watching dementia slowly taking every ounce of life from his loving Maddy led to this.

Eddy slipped on his tan dockers pants, which hung from a standing butler next to his bed. A yellow polo shirt was neatly folded over the top of the butler frame. He retrieved his wallet and watch from the tray. Sliding into his slippers, he made his way to the kitchen. Eddy had prided himself on being able to use his Mr. Coffee with one hand, fitting in the filter and measuring the prescribed number of scoops of coffee. But now, even that once satisfying task had taken on a sense of mundane routine. In fact, most of Eddy's life was now just that. A series of tedious activities providing little in the way of stimulation or having any sense of purpose. Even his roving visits around the facility checking on the residents had become more of a habit without any sense of fulfillment. The company of others offered little pleasure to Eddy, except for an occasional visit by his daughter, Tina, her husband Ryan, and his three grandchildren.

Most days, Eddy ate breakfast alone in his suite. Following breakfast, he would take one of several photo albums and head to Maddy's room in the skilled nursing unit. There he would sit by her bedside and narrate to her the background of every picture, reminiscing of the good times and the happiness of their lives together. His monologues invariably brought a smile to his face, but when he finished, only tears remained. Rather than going directly to Maddy's room that morning, Eddy had decided to take a stroll around the grounds of Magnolia Gardens. He brought his treasured family album with him to peruse when he got to a bench at the pond's edge. He paused at the edge of the veranda, looking out across the grounds. It was a God-created morning. The skies were never bluer. The sun warmed his face. The beauty of Magnolia Gardens over-whelmed Eddy as he marveled at God's creation. Robins made their way through the damp grass, harvesting an abundance of earthworms. Hummingbirds swarmed the Azaleas planted along the edge of the veranda, feasting on the delicious nectar hidden within their blossoms. The path to the pond was lined with Butterfly Bush intermingled with numerous Bird of Paradise flowers. Each was an additional source of sweet nectar as well as a haven for the brightly colored Swallowtail and Emperor Butterflies. To his surprise, Eddy's heart swelled with the sound of an avian symphony of love emanating from the cooing Mourning Doves and Pigeons nested in the higher branches of the many Magnolia trees on the property.

He took a seat on the bench he and Maddy had so often occupied. The still waters of the pond glistened with the rising sun. Several flocks of young ducklings led by their mothers paraded across the pond in single file. As he watched the procession, Eddy wondered what happened to the Peregrine falcons that normally would have feasted on such careless movement uncharacteristic of the usually protective mother ducks. Perhaps, he thought, this was one more day of living for the often preyed on delicacy of the Peregrine falcons. He smiled to himself. At that moment, he felt engulfed by a strange sense of spiritual calmness, perhaps brought on by Sister Dorothy's words. Maybe God was pleased? He had brought Maddy to a place where she could receive the care she needed, and Eddy truly enjoyed looking after the other residents in his role as an informal advocate. He reached into his shirt pocket and pulled out a small pair of reading glasses. After adjusting them so he could both read and look over the rim for any sudden movement or noise that would garner his attention, he opened the photo album. From the moment his eyes fell on their wedding picture centered on the first page, Eddy's heart erupted with a resurgence of his love for Maddy. With each succeeding page chronicling their lives and love together, Eddy Pinafore was never more in love with his precious Maddy than at that moment.

～

IT WAS A NECESSARY CALL, but one that had to be made. As the Executive Director of Magnolia Gardens, Samantha Callahan usually was the one to make such calls. But this time, she was emotionally unable to handle the task. She had requested Sister Dorothy to make it.

The phone rang several times before going to voice mail. Just as she started to speak, a voice answered.

"Hi Samantha," Tina said, looking at the Caller ID, which read Magnolia Gardens. "Sorry I didn't pick up right away, but the twins needed a change." She was immediately alarmed as receiving a call from Samantha was unusual. There was a pause, and then the voice on the line gently said, "I'm sorry, Tina, this is Sister Dorothy. I'm calling for Samantha." Her sense of alarm was beginning to build.

"Oh, Sister Dorothy, I'm sorry. Usually, I only get calls from my dad or Samantha."

Sister Dorothy composed herself for the news she was about to deliver and that no one wanted to speak.

"Yes, I understand. Tina, Samantha asked me to make this call."

Suddenly fear gripped Tina's heart. No amount of softness and caring in Sister Dorothy's voice could abate the trembling that overtook her. She sank down on the couch. Her heart literally skipped the rhythmic pumping of blood to her brain. Her throat constricted to the point she thought she was going to choke. She managed to hold back a flood of tears long enough to ask, "It's about my mom, isn't it?" Tina was certain dementia had finally taken her mother's life.

Sister Dorothy clinched the rosary in her right hand as she delivered the news to Tina.

"No, it's not about your mother, Tina. She is fine. It's about your father. The staff found him sitting on a bench down by the pond. He had his family photo album on his lap. By the time they got to him, it was too late. He had passed away. I am told his face had a look of peace."

The scream caused Sister Dorothy to pull the phone away from her ears. It continued, accompanied by heart-wrenching sobs of torment. At that moment, Sister Dorothy bowed her head and prayed.

"Dear Father in Heaven, Eddy Pinafore, a loving father and devoted husband, has entered into your eternal presence. Please welcome him as his journey has ended."

ACKNOWLEDGMENTS

Always to my loving wife, Ginny, for her patience and critical eye to my writing, without which I would accomplish nothing. To Frank Eastland and his staff at Publish Authority for their continual support and encouragement to stretch my imagination and trust in the creative process. To my friend, Rob Gordon, for his much-needed advice to write so the reader understands what the writer means.

ABOUT THE AUTHOR

Michael J Sullivan is the author of the acclaimed *Forgotten Flowers* series of novels, among other works. The remarkable reception to his series inspired him to create the Forgotten Flowers Program, a non-profit organization established to help facilitate youth and adults to regularly visit the elderly ("forgotten flowers") in their homes and assisted living facilities. Michael and his wife Ginny live in Sonora, California.

FIND OUT MORE about Michael at
www.MichaelJSullivanBooks.com.

LISTEN TO "Michelle's Song" written by Michael J. Sullivan to inspire giving compassion and care to those with special needs, whether they are children born with them or the elderly who develop them through the aging process ("Forgotten Flowers") at bit.ly/3xZZibc

facebook.com/Michael.J.Sullivan.Author
twitter.com/MichaelJSulliv8
instagram.com/michael.j.sullivan.author

PUBLISHER'S NOTE

The Journey's End Is book #3 in Michael J. Sullivan's *Forgotten Flowers* trilogy.

If you would like to fully understand the origins of the story or the significance of the lives of Daniel, Jane, Tina, Eddy, and the others as they progress through the series, you can order *Forgotten Flowers* (book #1), *The Journey Home* (book #2), and *The Journey's End* (#3) at your favorite local bookstore or online wherever books are sold.

THANK YOU FOR READING

Publish Authority

If you enjoyed *The Journey's End*, we invite you to share your thoughts and reactions online and with family and friends.

CPSIA information can be obtained
at www.ICGtesting.com
Printed in the USA
FSHW020157120621
82194FS